THE RIGHT TO BEAR ARMS

AFTER THE RIOTS BEGIN

MICHAEL E. FOSTER

PROLOGUE

The riots in America started, just as they did in the European countries, when the people demanded more and more entitlements and continued to elect officials who would vote for more of the same. Then, they bit the hand that was feeding them when the government spending came to a halt due to overwhelming deficits and the sudden collapse of the Euro and dollar.

Initially, most people believed that the longstanding racial problems were the main sparks that ignited the flames of violence. This was a natural assumption, since both the rapid growth of minority populations and the influx of illegal aliens over the decades had further crowded the larger cities and strained government resources to the breaking point. This, along with the narrowing gap in the percentages of blacks, whites, Hispanics, and Asians, further aggravated racial tensions, as the different groups struggled for political control and blamed each other for the deteriorating economic conditions and crime.

Although racial tensions might have been the source of the sparks that ignited the initial rioting, it soon became obvious that the severe economic conditions in the country helped fuel the flames of violence that quickly spread throughout the nation. After all, this wasn't the first time inner-city violence had erupted in this country in response to some perceived injustice. But before, the riots had always been isolated to the downtown areas and usually subsided after a few days. This time, it was different. This time, the rioters and looters were not just bored minority youths angered by some courtroom TV drama looking to let out some pent-up frustration or grab a free big-screen TV.

This time, men and women of all ages and races who were left homeless or jobless by the depression, who felt abandoned by society and were now hungry, joined in the rioting and looting, which further escalated the violence. These people, who blamed the government for the sad state of affairs in this country, ironically were the same people who elected the tax-and-spend government of recent decades that they blamed for the problems.

Millions of people who had not lost jobs, businesses, homes, and their life savings in the previous recession before the election now lost them in the depression that followed the stock market crash and subsequent new tax hikes that came in the year after voters went to the polls. The resultant widespread unemployment and depressed economy that followed soon led to even more government spending in hopes of propping up the failed economy, just as government leaders had tried to do before. That increased the already burgeoning national debt even more, to the point that the dollar became unstable on the world market.

The end result was that the dollar became so severely devalued that it was no longer accepted as the international currency, which soon led to double-digit inflation. Naturally, this all had the greatest effect on the larger urban areas, where there was a greater concentration of poverty and an ever-growing population of those dependent on the government for almost every need.

At first, as the increasing inflation began to drain the buying power from the monthly government checks and food stamp allotments, nonviolent protests sprang up. Later, as the city dwellers began to run out of money, gas, and food sooner and sooner each month, they took to the streets in greater numbers, demanding an increase in government spending to offset the effects of inflation.

When the government was ultimately forced to cut spending on these programs altogether because of pressure from China and the other holders of our national debt, the millions of people all across the nation who were dependent on the government for all their needs suddenly found themselves cut off from their only source of sustenance.

Soon their frustration and hunger turned into hopelessness and anger. So after the riots started, they all joined in. Once the supermarkets and stores were stripped bare, the rioters found themselves, again, without any source of food or supplies. With nowhere else to turn, they started spilling over into the suburbs and areas surrounding the cities.

Although there was no question that the nation's economic problems were the major cause of the riots, there was a difference of opinion, based on political party lines, as to the cause of the woes and the underlying factors that allowed the violence to escalate. This drove a deeper wedge between those who blamed the government for spending and taxing too much and those who felt that the government should have done more to provide for the needs of the people.

The philosophical and idealistic differences between these two groups were so far apart, and their feelings against each other so strong, that they could not even discuss the situation without it deteriorating into name-calling, finger-pointing, and shouting matches. And, to add to the problem even more, politicians were more willing than ever to use these touchy issues to advance their political agendas. Rather than attempt to arrive at a reasonable compromise, they continued to vehemently argue with each other on the public airwaves whenever the opportunity presented itself. The same arguments that had been raging between the two major parties in Congress in every election and that were displayed on every cable news network and nightly news programs for the past several decades continued as the riots raged on. Once again, Nero was fiddling as Rome burned to the ground.

Now there was no longer public discourse—there was rage. And it was no longer just seen on TV. It was happening on the streets of every major city. Most of the Democratic members in Congress were still blaming the economic conditions on the lack of government spending and the lack of revenue and continued to push for higher taxes. Instead of cutting the ever-increasing federal budget, they continued to print money and try to spend their way out of the recession and the subsequent depression.

Democratic President Williams won reelection, as predicted, but the Democrats also kept the Senate and, unexpectedly, won back the House over the Republicans, who ran on a platform to cut spending in an attempt to bring the deficit down. This, of course, meant cuts in all the entitlement programs, which, to say the least, was not very popular. The first act of the newly elected Democratic Congress was to raise taxes for everyone making over $150,000. This became the dividing line for those who paid the bulk of the taxes that paid for everyone else's benefits.

In order to alleviate their fear of potential violence from the opposition party members, their second act was to pass the sweeping Handgun and Assault Weapons Ban, which essentially outlawed the sale of any new handguns or semiautomatic weapons to anyone except law enforcement, the military, and federal agents. Then, to appease their supporters, they converted the Health Care Reform Bill of 2010 into the National Health Care Act of 2013, which would complete the takeover of health care by the federal government over the next ten years. The insurance companies and hospitals were being forced into a one-payer system, and everyone was required to pay into the system through payroll taxes, which dramatically increased and expanded the Medicare deduction for everyone who received a paycheck. The last bold measure passed by the administration and newly elected Democratic Congress was to increase the amount and remove the cap on the Social Security payroll deductions.

And since both sides were against continuing to fund the enormous costs of the highly unpopular Middle East wars, it was easy for them to convince the president to pull all the troops out. As predicted by some, the sudden troop withdrawal left a power vacuum that was quickly filled by radical Islamic factions in Iraq, Iran, Afghanistan, and the other war-torn countries in the Middle East. The violence and war spread throughout the surrounding Islamic countries in the Middle East and North Africa, including direct attacks on Israel by a coalition of these countries.

While the Israelis were struggling to hold off the United Islamic Brotherhood Coalition, President Williams and the Democratic Congress refused to send troops or military aid to help them. They based their decision on the fact that Iran now had nuclear weapons and reportedly had dozens of sleeper cells of terrorists strategically placed throughout the United States, awaiting orders to attack targets all across the country. They argued that sending American military aid to assist Israel might prompt Iran to use the bomb or unleash its terrorists if it felt that the balance of power in the region had shifted in the wrong direction.

As expected, the oil supply to the United States from the Middle East continued to decline. Without any new drilling being allowed on federal lands for the past several years by the same Democratic administration, the supply became critically low, causing prices to skyrocket. Gas lines formed around the country that made those of the 1970s look small by comparison.

Despite the growing deficit, the message by the losing Tea Party and conservative Republican candidates in the last election, calling for government cutbacks in Medicare, Social Security, and other entitlement programs, did not resonate well with the majority of the American public, who were also the ones receiving the benefits and checks from the government. The hardworking, taxpaying, God-fearing majority of the twentieth century had become the even harder-working, taxpaying, God-forsaken minority of the twenty-first century.

All that allowed liberals to once again be elected to office by the dependent majority, resulting in even more government spending. With the exponentially growing debt and the impending default on the loans held by China, Germany, and other countries, the dollar was significantly devalued over and over, causing out-of-control inflation in the US. Inflation led to the higher gas, fuel, and food prices, which, along with the increased tax rate, caused even higher unemployment, which ultimately brought on the stock market crash and resulting economic crisis that followed.

Every left-wing radical group took advantage of the situation to advance its socialistic cause. Animal rights activists, tree-hugging environmentalists still trying to save the world from global warming, gay rights activist, civil rights activists, and all the rest took to the airwaves and the streets to push their prospective agendas. Self-appointed leaders of the rioters and special interest groups announced to the world, on every major news outlet that would turn a camera their way, that "we are the anointed ones chosen to lead the people from bondage" and that "all the oppressed people of the country should now band together to take what is, rightfully, theirs."

The Occupiers of Wall Street of the past became the marchers and protesters who carried banners through the city streets that read Share the Wealth or Die and Down with Capitalism. Then they joined the rioters when the gravy train derailed. And all the others who depended on government checks for rent, food, and even cell phones jumped on the new bandwagon.

As the situation continued to deteriorate, all that came out of Washington was the same political rhetoric that leaders had been putting out for decades. No results, just finger-pointing and talk. It was the same old game of kicking the can down the road that had gone on way too long and led to this. The problem was that what needed to be done was so unpopular with the majority of voters, who benefited from the government jobs and entitlements, that no one who proposed the harsh changes necessary to fix the problem could ever hope to get elected to office. So it was more of the same. The band played on as the Titanic sank.

Whatever the root cause of the economic conditions, the philosophical division between the two groups deteriorated so much that it was no longer a struggle between the haves and the have-nots over just food and necessities. The country was truly divided in half between those who just wanted the government to leave them alone and those who wanted the government to take care of them from the crib to the grave. It was no longer just a battle over taxes and government checks. It had become a battle over the direction of the country. Would the country continue to move toward a European socialist nanny state, devoid of religion and personal responsibility, or back to a country based on morals, individual work ethic, and family values?

With the majority of the troops just returning from the Middle East, still war-torn and weary, and with most state governments as broke as the federal government, the governors were slow to call out their National Guard troops. And, because the rioters were among those who had elected him, Democratic President Henry Williams was hesitant to call on the governors to do so. At first, before the National Guard could be mobilized in significant numbers in the different states, the rioters and the opportunistic troublemakers were, essentially, unopposed in many cities. Most police departments across the nation were already running on downsized forces because of cutbacks in overtime due to payroll restraints and were further spread thin to the breaking point due to ever-increasing crime rates. Most just didn't have the resources, or numbers, or will to effectively deal with the increasing violence.

During that short time of indecision by local and state leaders, tens of thousands of innocent people were injured or killed and their homes and businesses looted and destroyed. So, with their neighborhoods in flames and fearing for their safety, masses of people fled the cities in the wake of the violence and flooded out into the surrounding suburbs and countryside, like refuges from a war-torn country.

The law-abiding citizens who chose to stay for whatever reason—be it total denial that such a thing could happen here in the good ole US of A, or from a false sense of hope that the police or National Guard would ride in and save the day, or because they were simply unprepared—found themselves trapped within the cities and suburbs.

Most Americans had become fat, lazy, complacent, and lulled into a false sense of security that all would continue to be well, the power would stay on, the grocery store shelves would magically be restocked, and water would continue to come out of the tap. Or, if God forbid, a tornado or hurricane hit and the power was out for a few days or weeks, the government would bring in the needed food, water, and supplies to take care of them until it was fixed. That had been the way it was, and that was the mind-set that permeated the country. But they learned the hard way that the cavalry wasn't coming.

Those who tried to protect themselves found themselves overwhelmed and unprepared for what followed. Even those with guns were outnumbered, for the rioters were many, while they were few. And they were outgunned because many of the rioters had handguns, assault weapons, TEC-9s, and so on bought on the black market.

The few isolated pockets of those who were lucky enough to survive the initial wave of violence soon found themselves without electricity, as the fires burned utility poles and transformers blew and substations were destroyed. Then they had to face the reality that they did not have enough ammo, food, or water to hold out for very long.

As the uprising grew across the nation, even those who lived farther outside these cities were becoming fearful, as the violence continued to spread ever closer to their neighborhoods and towns. In the areas that were not yet directly affected, many people were unable to travel to work because of crowded highways and interstates leading out of the cities. They also could not check on loved ones because of downed phone lines and cell tower disruptions and power outages.

In the remote rural areas far outside the cities, people watched the news in total disbelief of what was happening and worried about their friends and families who lived in and around the cities. The whole nation sat transfixed in front of their TVs, wondering how far the violence would spread and how long it would go on. They were lulled by a false sense of security, waiting for someone else to do something. They were like those standing on a beach about to be hit by a tsunami—they see the water going out, but they don't see what's about to come crashing back until it's too late.

While the rioters were beginning to spread out from the cities, all of the pissed-off rednecks, white trash losers, and jobless good ole boys who had blamed the rioters and their lot for the economic conditions grabbed their daddies' pistols and deer rifles and loaded up their jacked-up, Big Foot-wannabe four-by-four trucks, with their rebel flags flying in the back, and headed into the cities to deliver some frontier justice. And in the cities, every pants-dragging, low-riding, music-thumping, rim-spinning, wannabe gang banger loaded up his TEC-9 and other pieces and headed into the fracas to hand out some street justice.

As the violence grew and spilled out from the larger cities, it presented a grand opportunity for radical and extremist groups on both sides of the political spectrum to attack each other in public with violence instead of words, with the KKK, white supremacists, and the people's militia supporters on one side, and the National Civil Rights Coalition, Black Panthers, and Islamic Nationalist Party supporters leading the fight on the other. Every other hate monger and lowlife who needed little or no excuse to steal or kill also joined in the nationwide bedlam, which further added to the violence. So, unlike the riots of the past, these were increasing day by day, and the taxpaying, hardworking, law-abiding citizens were caught in the crossfire.

CHAPTER 1
THE RIOTS

Thursday, April 10, 2014.
Southcrest, Mississippi.

The riots were entering their second week. They began in Los Angeles, with gangs and discontented inner-city youths taking to the streets, throwing rocks and bottles, looting stores and businesses, attacking innocent citizens, and overturning cars. They continued to escalate, and after a few days parts of the whole city were in flames. Several days later, the violence began to spread like a rampant virus, causing similar riots to erupt in New York, Philadelphia, Chicago, Detroit, Atlanta, Memphis, and almost every other major city throughout the country.

Like most of their neighbors in Southcrest, Mississippi, just a few miles across the Mississippi state line to the south of Memphis, Dr. Mark Edwards and his wife, Lisa, felt far removed from the violence in the city when the riots began. But as the violence continued to spread, creeping closer to them day by day, the situation was changing. Now it was beginning to threaten them and their neighbors.

After they put the boys to bed, Mark and Lisa sat down to watch the TV news reports, which were showing round-the-clock coverage of the violence. Some networks were having temporary technical difficulties or were offline altogether from power outages. Seeing so many stations out at one time was something neither of them could ever remember happening in their lifetimes.

One of the stations that was still on showed graphic pictures of the violence from different cities around the country. One horrifying scene of the riots after another flashed across the screen, showing innocent citizens being pulled from their cars and beaten, shot, stabbed, and robbed. Businesses and homes were being looted and burned, and the occupants were either shot or dragged into the streets and beaten.

Mark was one of those who knew this day was coming, sooner or later. He was not a true prepper, in the sense that he and Lisa didn't talk about bugging out or expecting the world to end, but they did have plans to get out of town to the farm if needed. Prepping had become more popular over the years and was now all over the Internet and TV. For most, it wasn't from a fear that the magnetic poles were going to shift or that a comet was going to hit the earth, but they did see the country heading for hard times.

Economists and talking heads on the cable news channels who followed the rising value of gold and silver, the increasing inflation, and the devaluation of the dollar had predicted the economic collapse for years. Mark and a few other like-minded people had occasionally discussed the national debt, the building economic storm, and this eventual scenario. It was a frequent topic of conversation at church, at work, and a few of the coffee shops and cafés where the locals gathered. And it was also a frequent topic around their dinner table and down at the farm for the past couple of years. Mark and Lisa had discussed the idea of prepping with Lisa's parents and some of her family members, who also knew this day was likely to come and were prepared for such.

Mark remembered how they laughed when he introduced the term *prepping* to them and explained some of the language, such as bug-out bags, and described how the farm, which was located almost an hour outside the big city, was the perfect retreat with its garden, farm animals, and well water. He had also mentioned how prepping had become a popular trend among urbanites since 9/11 and Katrina, even more so with the recent economic problems. Although the term was new to Lisa's parents, they had always lived self-sufficient lives and prepared for the worst and found it funny that some city folks were just now figuring it out.

Although Mark's parents were both gone and their farm sold off long ago to make way for a new subdivision, Lisa's family farm had become their refuge from the hustle and bustle of the city and their subdivision. Both Lisa and Mark were comfortable in their four-bedroom, two-car garage home in the subdivision. Like everyone else, they were spoiled by all the conveniences and comforts of a modern home, located conveniently close to twenty-four-hour grocery stores and shopping malls in the big city across the state line. But unlike most people of this day and age, both Lisa and Mark had grown up on a farm, and to them subdivision life just couldn't compare with the wide-open spaces of the country, where neighbors, although farther away, were almost like family. No traffic, no crime, no Fed Ex jets landing in the middle of the night; just the peaceful, quiet simple life of country living. It was ironic to Mark that, while he could not wait to get off the farm in the past, he couldn't wait to get back now. But the changes in the health care laws and Mark's contract to cover surgery at the hospital kept them where they were.

Despite their preparations and planning for this day, it all still seemed like a bad dream to Mark, Lisa, their families, and close friends—a nightmare that they hoped would soon be over. But instead it continued. It was all that was on every network and station that was still on the air. Mark found himself engrossed by it all, as if watching a hurricane or other natural disaster that is devastating on the one hand but you just can't turn away on the other. But now he could hear and see it all closing in; only it was real and getting closer by the day.

His thoughts were suddenly interrupted by a news flash that broke onto the screen. "There are reports that there has been an explosion near the White House. We repeat: There has been an explosion near the White House."

Stunned by this news, Mark walked slowly over to in front of the TV and stared at it in horror as the message continued. "Reports indicate that the president has been injured. At this time, we do not know the exact cause of the explosion or the extent of the president's injuries. All we know is that a sudden explosion involving the president's car occurred at approximately 9:05 EST outside the White House, just as the president was returning from a meeting. Please stay tuned for more information. We will have more details for you momentarily."

Mark turned slowly to Lisa and stared at her for a moment without saying a word. Lisa put down her tea and broke the silence first. "What does it mean?"

"I'm not sure, but it looks like someone is trying to kill the president. They have lost their minds," Mark said in disgust.

"Who would do such a thing?" Lisa asked anxiously.

"I'm not exactly sure, but this has gotten way out of control much faster than I thought it would. It looks like what we have all been worried about is finally happening," Mark said in frustration.

Just then, another report flashed on the screen. "Our station is confirming the report. The president has been injured by an explosion involving his car just outside the gates of the White House. The president has been injured and is being flown to Bethesda, Maryland. Our sources indicate that he is alive, but his exact condition is not known at this time. Information on the cause of the explosion is not yet available. Stay tuned for further information."

"Now is it time to get out of here and go to the farm?" Lisa asked.

"I don't know, Lisa. I thought they would have called out the National Guard by now," Mark said in disgust.

Although Lisa had brought up the idea of getting out of town to the farm several times in the past few days, she decided now was a good time to suggest it again. "Did you know they closed the county schools today, and more of our neighbors are leaving? Can't we please leave now and go to my parents' farm until this is over?" Lisa asked, almost in tears.

"Lisa, we've been over this already. You know I have patients in the hospital, and I'm on call this weekend. I can't just leave. I could lose my job," Mark explained with his arms stretched out, showing frustration with the whole situation.

"All I know is that I couldn't even go to the grocery store today. It was broken into last night. I'm scared," she said with tears welling up in her eyes.

"I'm worried, too, but several of the city hospitals have closed, and the ones that are still open, like ours, are overflowing with patients. I mean, it's been a madhouse lately. We've got patients lined up in the ER, in the hallways, and everywhere else we can put them. They have nurses working double and even triple shifts just trying to take care of all of them. And to make matters worse, for the past day or so, some of them and a lot of the other employees have not been showing up for work. And today, even some of the doctors have started calling in sick, or just not show-ing up, which just makes it even harder on the rest of us. You wouldn't want me to run out on them at a time like this, would you? Besides, if I leave without approval, it would be in violation of my contract, and Mr. Cox would probably have me kicked off the staff. You wouldn't want that, would you?" Mark asked hop-ing she would reconsider.

Lisa hesitated for a moment. "Well, I guess not. I don't want you to lose your job. I'm just worried about the boys," she said defensively.

Mark was well aware that the violence was closing in on them, and he thought it best that Lisa and the boys leave before things got any worse. And, as much as he wanted to go with them, he did not feel he had any choice. Even though Mark worked for the hospital and no longer owned his own practice, he did not think it would be morally or ethically right to leave his patients. Besides, there was also the overriding threat of being fired for leaving without the approval of the hospital administrator. Mr. Cox was a no-nonsense kind of guy who wielded a lot of power and was known to fire employees for even the most minor infrac-tions, particularly unexcused absences.

Mark knew the day might come when he would have to make this decision. Although he and Lisa had discussed the need to get out of town, he let her assume he would leave with them if the time did come. He knew she would not agree with his plan to let them go while he stayed behind. So his plan was to make a judgment call when the time came for his family to get out of town, and then he would leave when he felt he could.

The problem in the decision making was that there were too many variables that he could not predict or control. Leaving too early could mean losing his job because he would be in conflict with his contract. Leaving too late could jeopardize his safety, plus he might not make it to the farm to be with his wife and kids, which was what mattered most to him. But he knew it was time to let them go, before the roads became too crowded for them to travel safely.

There was also the issue of what the government would expect or demand of him. Although his contract was with the hospital, he knew there would be a great need for surgeons, especially general surgeons, who could handle trauma. The legions of new nurse practitioners whom the government flooded into the medical marketplace to offset the shortage of doctors caused by the new health care laws could do physicals and treat various medical problems, but they were not trained to handle surgery.

Despite the government's best efforts to shortcut the process or bypass the surgeons in private practice with substitutes in order to control them, the problem remained: No one else could do what surgeons do—there were no substitutes, no replacements, no one to fill in, or even try. No one else who could, or would, invade the sanctity of the human body, cut into another human being and rearrange, remove, bypass, or repair their insides. With the stakes so high and the chance of failure so great, with their life in your hands and no one else's, only a surgeon would dare. There comes a time when delay means death, where indecision leads to failure, and quitting is not an option. No matter how long one has been without sleep, or how exhausted, or how frustrated, there is no one else to pass the responsibility to, no one else to blame, no other option but to suck it up and give it all you have when someone's life is on the line.

Others can make excuses and call in sick, or play dumb, or pretend they don't know what to do, or when to do it. But a surgeon just doesn't have that option when someone is bleeding to death, or a patient's intestines are blocked or perforated, and peritonitis or gangrene is setting in. For all the above reasons, the volume of knowledge one has to know is immense, the years of training long and demanding, in order to be a board-certified surgeon.

The biggest fear the powers that be in Washington had concerning doctors was that they would finally figure out how powerful they could be if they would just band together and refuse to work for or be controlled by anyone and stop taking payment from any third party other than the patient. So even though the government made every effort to turn the medical profession into just another civil service job by replacing as many doctors as it could with physician assistants and nurse practitioners in order to help control costs and access to care, the best it could manage up to that point was to force them into employment with the hospitals. By controlling payments to hospitals, and therefore payments to the surgeons, the government could assert some control over them.

While surgery still paid relatively well compared with most jobs, it wasn't a career choice people just woke up one day and decided they wanted to pursue; it was something they were driven to do. It required a lifetime of study, of being up late at night and up early in the morning with little time off, not to mention the stress of the constant fear of lawsuits whenever something went wrong, despite one's best effort. But despite it all, it was what Mark had always wanted to do and worked so hard to become, and he did not want to give up, now, not yet. Leaving his duties without an excused absence could cost him his privileges and perhaps his license. Now the time had come for Mark to make a difficult decision.

"Hey, I'm worried about the boys, too. And I'm just as worried about you," Mark said. "Why don't you take the boys to the farm, like we talked about. I'm afraid if you don't leave now, it's going to be real hard to get out of here. It looks like the roads are getting more crowded each day. I'll just stay here and take my call this weekend. Then, if things settle down a bit, maybe I can come down there for a few days next weekend," Mark offered, hoping to calm Lisa down.

Seeing that he hadn't won her over yet, he continued. "Look, if it gets bad enough here, they'll have to close the hospital, then I'll be able to leave, right? So let's pack tonight, and I'll help you load the car. The roads will probably be crowded, but if you don't have to stop, you should still be able to get to the farm in an hour or so," Mark explained to Lisa as she nodded in agreement.

The farm was about forty-five minutes down Interstate 55, or about an hour taking the highway. It was located just a little over an hour directly south of Memphis. The farm was on a county road in the rolling hills, about five miles to the east of Batesville. Everyone living north, south, east, or west of Batesville had to go through town to access the interstate. This, they would find out later, was a good thing.

"I still don't want to leave you here, but I will feel better knowing the boys are safe," Lisa said reluctantly.

"Look, don't worry about me. As long as you and the boys are safe, I can get out of here if I need to," Mark said, trying to comfort her as he gave her another hug and a kiss on the cheek before they both went to pack and carry out their plan.

Even though they didn't get to bed until late, neither could go to sleep right away. As they lay awake in bed, the uncertainties about the next few days and weeks weighed heavily on them, while the distant sirens from the city screamed in the night. Lisa had an uneasy feeling about leaving Mark behind. When she closed her eyes, scenes of her past played over and over in her mind like an old home movie. She remembered Mark when she first met him back in college, with his handsome face, friendly smile, gentle manners, muscular build, and dark wavy hair. Even now, at forty, Mark was as handsome as ever, and he kept himself in good shape by working out at the gym and practicing Krav Maga regularly. Besides his good looks and brains, he also had a sharp wit and an air of confidence, but he was not conceited or stuck on himself. He always treated people of all walks of life well and with respect, especially those close to him.

Lisa remembered how, as she came to know him more and more, his sense of humor and passion for life made him even more irresistible to her. And, after many long, quiet walks and long conversations, they discovered that they shared many common dreams about life, marriage, and having a family. She remembered how they quickly fell in love and got married just after college and started a family while he was still in medical school. She thought back on those difficult years, during Mark's surgery residency, when she had the three boys to care for because Mark was on call much of the time. But having the boys to contend with kept her so busy that the years seemed to pass by quickly. She thought of how happy and fulfilling her life with Mark and the boys had been since moving into their new home in Southcrest. And she appreciated the fact that, although Mark's profession was demanding, he always made an effort to spend as much time with them as possible, unlike many of the other doctors they knew. But now, the nearby violence was threatening all of it. It was moving ever closer toward them, like a hungry beast devouring those in its path.

As Mark lie there listening to the distant sirens, he too worried about what lie ahead for them and reflected on his past. Many painful memories still haunted him. The tragic accidental death of his father when Mark was just a young boy on the farm. How his mother struggled all those years to raise him and his brothers, and then her untimely death when he was still in college. And he could not forget the shame of poverty he endured during his childhood, and how he was often ridiculed at school and rejected by those who were better off and thought they were better than others. Because of this, Mark was sensitive to the plight of those who were downtrodden and picked on, whether they were poor, mentally slow, overweight, funny looking, or just different. Having learned how to defend himself against bullies early in life, he was quick to take up for those who were less fortunate or picked on for whatever reason, even to the point of fighting to protect them if needed.

His ability to fight came naturally, and by the time he was in junior high, he was not afraid to take on bullies much bigger or older than him, and he could even hold his own against two or three at a time. He did not always come out on top, but everyone at school and around town knew he would not back down. Those who did take him on did not usually want to go at it with him again. Despite his natural fighting skills, he didn't like fighting for the sake of fighting; it was street justice, at best. He always tried to be fair and allow the aggressors an honorable exit. But if they wanted to go at it, he was their man.

Another benefit to growing up poor on a farm was that it forced him to learn how to work a garden, slaughter a hog, and clean a chicken, as well as how to hunt, fish, and handle a gun and knife. It was either that or go hungry, and Mark did not like to miss many meals.

The respect he earned with his fighting skills early on and later as middle linebacker on the football field eventually gained him acceptance to the in crowd at school and around town. And it didn't hurt to have been one of the smartest kids in class. By his senior year, he was voted class president and most likely to succeed. Even now, those early years of struggle were a source of pride to him. Over the years, he often boasted to others of his experiences while growing up on the farm. How he and his two brothers had to pull water from a well with a bucket and rope in the early morning hours, when it was so cold that the water would turn his hands numb. He remembered going to the bathroom in an outhouse in the dead of winter and shivering so hard he could hardly hit the mark. And then there were the memories of all the flies, mosquitoes, and typical rancid smells of a farm, and having to get up at the crack of dawn to feed and water the animals every single day of the year, rain or shine. He thought about how he worked in the garden and in the fields in the suffocating heat and humidity of the Mississippi summers. And having to cook supper and clean the house in the evenings to help his mother, and, afterward, doing homework until late at night while his mother worked the evening shift at the factory to pay the bills. His brothers now lived in California, and he hadn't seen either of them in many years, although he spoke with them on occasion on the phone. Such are the ways of brothers with dark secrets and without parents to keep them close.

But those difficult years filled with hard work and struggles to put food on the table did not make him bitter or cause him to make excuses for himself when things didn't go his way. Instead, they were the source of a strong desire to be successful in life. A will to make a better life for himself and his family. It gave him the raw determination and self-discipline that sustained him during college, medical school, and his residency. He figured out early in life that it wasn't enough to have brains or talent; it was determination and hard work that made someone the best at something, be it sports, music, or work. He saw many smart kids sitting on the tailgate of their pickup trucks after school, drinking beer and chasing skirts instead of practicing ball or doing their homework. They soon ended up in trouble, divorced, as drunkards, or in jail, not from a lack of smarts or ability but just an absence of will to do anything meaningful. But not Mark. He was determined to make a better life for himself and get off that godforsaken farm.

However, there were a few things from his past that he kept to himself, things he had done, things that had to be done. Things he was not proud of, things others would not understand unless they had been in a similar situation. That part of him was still there, buried deep within the recesses of his memories and his past. He always hoped that part of him would never have to surface again and the story would never have to be told to anyone else.

He could have chosen a different path in life, the path of a warrior, service in the military as a fighter pilot or an army Ranger or maybe a navy SEAL. It would have been easy for him to do, but he chose the path of medicine, surgery, healing the sick, helping others in need—whether it was in the office or on rounds at the hospital, handing money to a stranger in need, changing a flat tire for an elderly woman on the side of the road, or giving a lift to a hitchhiker.

Lisa was always telling him he might get hurt helping strangers like that, but Mark would tell her that by doing so, he was helping Jesus. Besides, he was not afraid, but not because he was too trusting, naive, or unaware of danger. It was just that his instincts were sharp, his reflexes quick, and he had the ability to remain calm and think in the face of danger. He knew this because he had been tested in the past, not in a simple school-yard fight or tragic accident but in an incident that he was forced to be a part of because he walked into the wrong place at the wrong time. He had to fight off a much bigger adult to protect a friend from abuse. It happened long before child abuse was exposed or reported. The details of the death of a prominent citizen remained a mystery in his small hometown, but Mark knew the details. This was one of the things he kept to himself, not out of guilt but out of necessity. Not to protect himself, but to protect someone else.

Even while he, Lisa, and the boys endured the many years of medical school and surgery residency with little money or time together, he felt fortunate to have the chance to go to college and to become a surgeon. He had been optimistic that the hard work and sacrifice would be worth it in the long run. But then, after only a few years in private practice, before he even had all his student loans paid off, Congress passed the Health Care Reform Act, eventually forcing him and most other doctors out of private practice.

It was a hard blow not just financially, but also because it placed so many mandated restrictions on the practice of medicine that it took away the financial incentives and independence that being a doctor once brought and which he had worked so hard and so many years to achieve. But he did not quit or become bitter. Instead, he went to work for Community Hospital in Southcrest, Mississippi. A decision he did not totally regret, especially now, since the doctors who were still in private practice hadn't received any payments from Medicare or Medicaid for several months.

But now, with the country suffering from the postcrash depression and hyperinflation setting in, the future looked bleak for everyone. With the onset of the riots and spreading violence, not only did he have to worry about providing for his family, but he also had concerns for their safety. Although he was apprehensive about letting them travel without him, he thought it was better for them to leave now, before things got any worse, rather than wait until he could go with them—whenever that may be. He knew the roads leading out of the city were getting more crowded every day and soon the traffic jams and stalled cars would block their way, as well. Whatever might happen in the weeks or months to come, his main goal was to see that his family was safe. Nothing was more important to him than them. Lisa was the love of his life. Her beauty caught his eye, with her blond hair and baby blue eyes and Playboy Bunny figure, but it was her heart that kept him. And his three boys meant the world to him. But what kind of world would they inherit was the question. With what was going on in America, the answer was not certain.

Even with all these thoughts spinning around in Mark's and Lisa's heads, the darkness of the night and exhaustion of the day's activities won out, and sleep finally came.

CHAPTER 2
HIJACKED

Friday, April 11.

Early the next morning, Mark showered and dressed for work as usual then went upstairs to say good-bye to his boys. They looked so peaceful and innocent as they lay asleep in their beds that he hated to wake them. However, Steve, the oldest at fourteen, was already awake, and he rolled over and sat up in bed. He had heard his mother in his room packing cloths during the night and sensed something was going on.

"Dad, are we going somewhere?" Steve asked.

"Yes, son, you boys and your mother are going to see Grandma and Grandpa at the farm for a few days," Mark answered quietly as he sat down on the side of Steve's bed.

"Aren't you going?" Steve asked.

"No. I have to work this weekend," Mark said.

"Why?"

"Well, I'm on call for surgery this weekend, I have to cover the emergency room, and I have patients in the hospital whom I have to take care of. I can't just leave them."

"What if the riots spread down here? I saw on the Internet that they are heading this way. How will you get to the farm? Or, what if you get hurt from all the fighting?" Steve asked, looking sadly at his father.

"Steve, sometimes we have to do things we don't want to do. There are policeman and firemen out there getting hurt trying to protect us. Somebody has to help take care of them if they get hurt, now don't they?" Mark said reassuringly.

"I guess so, Dad, but I don't want you to stay here," Steve said as he hugged Mark tightly.

Mark remembered back to when he was a young boy and how the pain of his father's death took years to get over. For days after his father's accident, he and his mother and many others from their church prayed for his recovery. But the injuries were severe and complications set in, and he died within a few days. At that time, Mark, still immature in his beliefs, felt that God had ignored his prayers and abandoned him. After that, he turned his energy toward learning all he could about science, the laws of nature, and the human body, so that he could do all that was humanly possible to defy death himself rather than rely on God, who didn't seem to be listening.

But after only a few years in the medical profession, one thing became obvious: Despite all the available medical knowledge and technology, eventually everyone gets sick and dies of one thing or another. Young, old, rich, and poor—everyone dies at an appointed time. Mark had since matured and began to read and study the Bible again, so with greater insight, he came to realize that trials make us stronger, that God's ways are not our ways, and that sometimes gifts and blessings come wrapped in problems and even tragedy. Now, Mark prayed with the knowledge that it is God's will that will be done, not his own. He gained knowledge from Proverbs 22:3: "A wise man foresees the difficulties ahead and prepares for them; the simpleton goes blindly on and suffers the consequences." Mark was prepared for whatever would happen in the future, good or bad, big or small. Whether it be by nature or man, he had worked it out in his mind and prepared his life to deal with whatever life threw at him. He had shared his ideas of emergency preparedness with his wife and kids—plans of escape from the house in case of fire, going into a hallway closet during a tornado, firearm safety, and a three-week supply of food and water on hand just in case.

"Son, I'm going to do all I can to stay safe. Listen. You're the oldest and I need you to look after your mother and your brothers for me until I get there. Okay?" Mark instructed him as he placed a hand on Steve's shoulder.

"Yes, sir," Steve said proudly, like a soldier with his first command. Although Steve was fairly big for his age and had a reputation as a heavy hitter in Little League, he was at that awkward age of uncertainty, just before a boy becomes a man, and this directive from his father made him feel proud and more important than ever.

Mark checked Daniel and Jeffrey again before he went back downstairs to help Lisa finish loading the car. "Honey, please be careful. Don't stop unless you have to, and stay on the main road if you can. Here, take your pistol with you and keep it handy, just in case," Mark said as he held out the carry case for the .380 SIG with two six-round clips.

"Okay, but I'm sure I won't. We're just going straight to the farm," Lisa said as she shrugged her shoulders.

"Well, just be careful, and call or text me when you get there, all right?" Mark pleaded. Then he gave Lisa a kiss and a hug, said good-bye, and turned and left for work before the tears in his eyes showed on his face.

Lisa looked at the gun case and started to take the .380 out and put it in her purse, but she decided instead to put the case in the back of the Suburban with the rest of the bags. Even though she had grown up around guns on the farm, had shot many times before with Mark, and knew she could handle it confidently on her own, she was still not comfortable with the idea of carrying a weapon with the intention of using it. She just didn't know if she could actually shoot someone if it came down to it.

On the way to Community Hospital, Mark saw more evidence of the violence in the city. Billows of smoke filled the horizon to the north, and for the first time, he heard gunshots ringing out in the distance on his side of the state line. The riots were getting closer day by day.

As he turned onto Goodman Road near the hospital, he noticed how heavy the flow of traffic was heading south on Interstate 55. It was much heavier than he had anticipated, and suddenly he felt uneasy about Lisa and the boys traveling by themselves. He tried to reassure himself that they would be safe as long as they were heading away from the city.

The hospital was only ten years old, having been built just a few years before passage of the Health Care Reform Act. With its magnolia tree-lined drive and tall white entry columns out front, it looked much like a Southern plantation. There was a small pasture off to one side and a wooded area behind it, which made the setting appear more rural than it actually was, since the whole area was surrounded by subdivisions and shopping malls. It was similar to many of the suburban hospitals built before the Health Care Reform Act. It served a mostly middle-class population of blue- and white-collar workers who had jobs and insurance, as well as a moderate amount of indigent patients with no health coverage. Originally built with fifty beds then expanding to two hundred within a few years, the hospital was fully staffed for all surgical, medical, rehabilitation, and outpatient services. Only Level I trauma and neurosurgery patients went to the medical center in downtown Memphis. With the hospital fairly close to home and the surgery caseload mostly elective in the beginning, Mark felt it was a good place to work and still be able to have time for a family and a somewhat normal life.

But over the years, the emergency room visits and caseload continued to grow. When the State Board of Health forced the hospitals to take on trauma, the nature of private surgery practices in the state changed. Most general surgeons in the state were forced to contract with the hospitals where they practiced to take trauma call. All but he and two other surgeons resigned and went with the bigger hospitals in Memphis, where there were more surgeons on call and therefore fewer call nights per month. This left Mark with every third night and every third weekend call. Not unmanageable, but certainly not what he wanted.

As he pulled into the hospital parking lot, he noticed there were even fewer employee and doctors' cars than the day before. He parked his red Explorer among the BMWs, Benzes, Audis, and new electric cars. Mark liked driving his SUV, with its V-8 engine and four-wheel drive, and he just couldn't bring himself to get rid of it. He didn't care for the so-called luxury cars and the whining motors of the new electric cars. So as long as it kept running and the service stations kept selling gasoline, he would keep driving his old Explorer.

When he arrived on the surgical floor, the charge nurse, Mrs. Richards, met him at the desk. "Dr. Edwards, Dr. Williams has called in sick this morning and canceled his cases, and he wants you to see his patients today," she said with a concerned look on her face.

"Called in sick! What's wrong?" Mark questioned sternly. He didn't mean to be rude or short, but with all that was going on, that did not sit well with him at all.

"He didn't say, Dr. Edwards. All I know is that he called early this morning and said he wasn't sure he would be here next week, either. I'm supposed to give you his list of patients," she offered as she handed him the list.

"It's okay, never mind," he apologized, knowing she was only the messenger. Mark looked at the list for a minute then realized that there were almost as many patients on Dr. Williams's list as there were on his own. Mark shook his head in disbelief, knowing that it would be almost impossible to keep up with all these new patients, along with his own, plus his morning surgery schedule, the afternoon surgery clinic, and the ER call for trauma and surgery for the weekend.

"One other thing. Mr. Cox has called a special meeting for the doctors and department directors for noon today. He said it was mandatory," Nurse Richards explained quickly, then turned and walked away so she wouldn't have to deal with his response to that bit of news.

Mark dropped his head and looked at his watch. It was almost 7:00 a.m. He had to be in the operating room for his first case in less than an hour. He had twelve people on the ward and four in the intensive care unit to see before starting his surgical cases for the morning, and then he had clinic to follow in the afternoon. And, on top of all that, he had to be at a meeting during his lunch hour. At some point during the day, he also had to make follow-up phone calls to patients concerning lab and X-ray reports, dictate the surgical cases, finish the charts on all the clinic patients he saw during the day, write letters to the referring doctors, write orders on any new patients, and answer a few dozen or so phone calls. And, to top all of it off, he had to handle any surgical emergencies that came in through the ER. For a moment, he just stood there shaking his head and mumbling a few choice words. After a few minutes, he brushed it all off and gritted his teeth, then he went to grab a cup of coffee before starting his rounds.

About forty-five miles away to the south, on Interstate 55, Lisa was making her way through the heavy traffic toward Batesville while the boys were watching their favorite movie. The traffic heading south was congested for many miles out of town, while hardly any traffic was heading north into Memphis. Lisa was feeling more at ease now that they were farther out and the traffic was thinning some. Daniel, the youngest at four, let it be known that he had to go to the bathroom right away.

Remembering what Mark had told her, she was reluctant to stop. "Can't you hold it for just a little longer? We'll be at Granny's in about thirty minutes," Lisa offered.

"No, I gotta go real bad. It's coming out," Daniel said, holding himself.

"All right, there's a gas station at the next exit. Just hold on." Lisa turned off the interstate exit and pulled into the parking lot next to the restrooms. People were coming and going into and out of the store, and as far as she could tell, everything looked safe. "You boys stay in the car and keep the doors locked. We'll be right back," Lisa said. Steve and Jeffrey waited in the car, while she took Daniel by the hand and led him into the women's bathroom.

After a few minutes, Lisa brought Daniel back to the car and helped him back into his seat. Just as she started to close the door, she felt a strong grip on her arm. She quickly turned and saw a gun being put to Daniel's neck. Then she heard a voice say, "Don't scream or I'll shoot the boy." Lisa was too terrified to move or scream. "Get in the car and drive," the man said as he slid in next to Daniel.

Lisa didn't have time to think, so she did what she was told and got in behind the wheel and started the car. That's when she got her first look at the man. In her mirror was a darkly tanned man in his late twenties, with a scraggly beard, a weathered face, and old, dirty clothes. His eyes were cold and mean, like those of an animal, dark and piercing. "Go that way," he said, motioning to the road with his gun. "Hurry!"

Lisa was sick with fear. She could only guess what he wanted. She started to ask him, but Steve spoke first. "What does he want, Mom?" The man said nothing.

"I don't know, son." Lisa looked back at him and started to ask, but he cut her off.

"Shut up! Everybody shut up!" he snapped. "Go that way," he said, pointing to a side road with his gun.

Lisa tried to think. What should she do? How should she handle the situation? But things were happening too fast. The .380 was in the case in the back. No way to get to it in time to use it. There wasn't time for her to think. She was afraid that if she tried anything, he would hurt the kids. As she drove, it became more obvious what he wanted. She could see in the mirror that the man kept staring at her in a way that was more than obvious to any woman. It hadn't gone unnoticed to her that this man wanted her. The kids would just be in his way. He would want to get rid of them. But she was determined not to let that happen.

Just then, Lisa felt a sudden jerk on the wheel and a strong pull that almost made her run off the road. She fought to maintain control, and as she slowed she realized that they had blown a tire.

"What are you doing?" the man demanded.

"We have a flat and I'm pulling over," Lisa shot back with a scowl.

"Not here. Keep going. There. Pull in there." He pointed to a gravel drive that led to an old abandoned farmhouse that was overgrown with weeds and surrounded by trees. "Stop here." The man looked around. "Yeah, this will do," he said as he got out of the car. "Turn it off. Give me the keys." Lisa complied, not knowing what else to do. "Stay here and don't get out." The man took the keys and went back to look at the tire. It was flat. He opened the back gate and dug out the jack and spare tire from under all the luggage, baseball bats and gloves and started changing the flat as quickly as he could, occasionally looking up at them to make sure they stayed put.

Lisa's mind started to click. *He must want the car to get away. I've got to do something now.* She checked the mirror. He had put the gun in his pocket. She had a plan. As soon as she was sure he had finished changing the tire, she would be ready. "Boys, listen. I'm going to get out of the car. When you hear me scream, get out of the car and run back to the road. Keep running and don't stop, no matter what."

Steve looked at her in disbelief. "What are you going to do?"

"Just do what I say, and don't ask any questions. Do you hear me?" she asked sharply. Jeffrey looked confused and worried, and Daniel started to cry. "Steve, get Daniel and Jeffrey and take them to the road, as fast as you can, and keep running as far as you can. Try to stop a car on the road if you see one. If he comes after you, hide your brothers. Do you understand?" Lisa checked the mirror again. The man was through changing the tire and was starting to put the tools in the back of the car. She looked directly at Steve. "Do you understand?" she repeated sternly just before she started out of the car.

"Yes, ma'am," Steve said with a worried look on his face, remembering what his father had told him as he watched his mother get out of the car.

Lisa slipped out of the car and approached the man as quietly as she could.

"Hey, get back in the car," he said as he looked up. Just as he started to reach in his pocket, she attacked. He wasn't expecting a fight. She grabbed him and lunged her full weight on top of him. They both fell to the ground with her scratching, clawing, and screaming like a mother tiger trying to protect her young from another predator. He tried to push her away, but she wrapped herself tightly around him with both her arms and legs and bit him on the neck as hard as she could. *I done screwed with a crazy bitch. The others didn't fight near as much as this,* he thought to himself. He tried to hit her with his fists, but she was too close against him, so he pulled at her hair. He tried to reach for his gun as they rolled on the ground in the dirt and grass behind the car, but all he could do was scream as he felt a searing pain in his neck when she sank her teeth deep into his flesh.

As she struggled and hung on to the man on the ground, Lisa heard the car doors open and the boys run by. Daniel and Jeffrey were crying and sobbing as Steve yelled and pulled them when they went by. "Run, Daniel! Run! Come on, Jeffrey! Mommy said run!"

Lisa bit and scratched and clawed with all her strength and the last ounce of her energy. After another minute or two, the man was able to push her away far enough to land several hard licks against her head and face that almost stunned her, but she hung on. The pain didn't matter to her anymore, because all she wanted was to buy time for her boys.

The man fumbled in his coat pocket and finally found what he wanted. *I'm going to kill this bitch and then get some of her while she dies, and maybe afterward too,* he thought to himself. She was fighting so hard that he struggled to get the gun out and not shoot himself in the process.

He struggled to get on top of her, and she was too exhausted to get him off. She tried to bite his hand, but he hit her again. She wanted to hang on, but there was no fight left in her. The world was spinning. She knew he was going to kill her, so she closed her eyes and hung on and prayed that the boys had time to get away. Suddenly, she felt something, a dull heavy thud that shook both of them, then again and again. Blood splattered. "Run, boys! Run!" she whispered to herself as she waited for the pain.

It wasn't as she thought it would be. She felt the blood run down her face and then his full weight on her, but something wasn't right. She waited for the pain, but it never came. She expected him to tear at her clothes, but he never did. For some strange reason, he wasn't moving at all. Lisa lay still for a moment then thought to herself, *Maybe the stupid bastard shot himself.* Then she pushed the man off her. As she wiped the blood from her eyes and looked up, she saw Steve standing over them, holding his aluminum baseball bat over his head with a wild look in his eyes. He hit the man again and called him names, using words Lisa had never heard him use. "My God, Steve! I thought he… Never mind." She stopped herself short after realizing what had happened. "Where are your brothers?" she asked as she looked around.

Steve, breathing heavily, pointed and said, "Running down the road, like you said."

Still shaken and scared, Lisa stood up, brushed herself off, and wiped more of the blood from her face. The gun had fallen from the man's hand. He wasn't moving, and she wasn't sure if he was still breathing. She picked the gun up and turned to Steve. "Go get your brothers. I'll bring the car out to the road and pick you up." Steve did what he was told and took off. Lisa looked the man over and still did not see him moving or breathing. She nudged him with her toe. Then she searched him and found the keys and her cell phone and picked up the gun from the ground next to him. He still did not move. She thought he was dead but wasn't sure. She wanted him dead, but she did not want to let Steve think he was the one who had killed him. Lisa went to the back of the car, dug out the gun case, took out the .380, loaded a clip, chambered a round, and pointed it at the man on the ground. Then she thought, *Evidence,* so she put on the safety, put the .380 in her pocket, and then put the man's gun in her other pocket and thought to herself, *Never again.* This situation had removed any doubt about using a gun to protect her family and herself in the future. Life is funny like that. It makes you do things and think things you never thought you would. And it would have been real easy for her to shoot the man at that moment to make sure he was dead. But instead Lisa started the car, put it in gear, and quickly backed it up. As she drove back toward the road, the car bumped on her side once, then again. Now, she was sure the man would not move again, and she would try to take that burden on herself. She started to call 911 but thought about having to explain it all, how much time it might take to clear it up, and how much it would disrupt their lives. Lawyers, police, and prosecutors with a bunch of questions were not part of her plan. Getting to the farm in one piece was. Anyway, with all the crap going on, it might be awhile before anyone found him—or cared about what happened to him.

The boys were walking together toward her as she pulled over to pick them up. Steve helped his brothers into the back of the car and then got into the front seat. She stared at him for a moment, and he stared at her. What struck her the most was how calm he was after what just happened. She knew how unnerved and upset she was feeling, so she wondered if maybe he was in shock or in denial. It didn't seem natural to her that her little boy was not hysterical, or at least tearful, over such a tragic event. Now he looked different to her. For the first time, she noticed he wasn't her little boy anymore. He was a young man.

"You want me to call Dad or somebody?" Steve asked.

"No, I think we better wait till we get to the farm, then we can talk it over and decide what to do. We need to get there, now, before anything else happens." She reached in her pocket and pulled out the dead man's pistol, a .38 special, and handed it to Steve. "You know how to use that, don't you?" she asked.

"Yes, ma'am. Dad taught me," he said, as he took the pistol, flipped open the cylinder and checked to make sure it was loaded. He closed the cylinder, put the gun in his back pocket, and smiled a little smile to himself, knowing he had done what his dad had told him to do and what had to be done.

They looked at each other, but neither said a word as she drove back to the interstate. She was hoping that Steve didn't think he had killed the man. She was hoping that running him over with the car would give him a reason to think otherwise. What she didn't know was that all good ball players know it's a home run as soon as the bat hits the ball. They can feel it in their hands. Steve knew that feeling, and he knew as soon as he struck his target that it was a solid hit. He felt the crush of the man's skull in his hands and saw the man drop. He never moved again. The second and third strikes were partly due to adrenaline, partly out of fear, and partly just for good measure so that animal wouldn't hurt his mother, or brothers, or anyone else again.

It's what a man has to do in a situation like that. Not all men can or will do what needs to be done when the time comes. Some freeze, some run, some curl up in the fetal position and cry in fear. Steve reacted without thinking. His instincts and reflexes took over. He did what needed to be done and would do it again, if needed, to protect his family. It has been said that out of every one hundred good men, ten can fight; and out of those, one is a warrior. It's what warriors do. It's not something you can teach. It comes naturally to only a few. Like the gladiators of old, only the ones with the right reflexes and instincts survive to fight another day. It's genetic. Like father, like son.

CHAPTER 3
TRAUMA IN THE ER

Community Hospital.
Southcrest, Mississippi.

Mark left the OR after his second case of the morning and went directly to the conference room, just in time for the noon meeting. Most of the seats were empty. He sat down next to Tom Stanley, the only other general surgeon at Community Hospital besides himself and Dr. Williams, who had already skipped town. They nodded to each other and said hello as Mr. Cox began speaking.

"As you can see, many staff members are, conveniently, calling in sick, and we are severely understaffed. I don't have to remind all of you that you are under contract with this hospital to provide coverage. I understand some could not be here because they live near areas affected by the riots, but for those of you who are not, I expect you to show up. I don't want to have to make threats, but if anyone else calls in sick or doesn't show up as scheduled, I have the authority to fire you as per your contracts. That's coming down from the board. If you call in sick, you better be on your deathbed." A few chuckles could be heard in the room, but mostly everyone just looked at each other and shrugged their shoulders.

Mark skipped lunch to finish rounds before the afternoon clinic. The ER was starting to fill with trauma victims. Thankfully, most of the injuries were minor fractures, superficial cuts, and other nonlethal injuries that the ER docs and the orthopedic surgeon could handle. Clinic was unusually light that afternoon, so Mark checked with the front desk to make sure he had seen everyone who needed to be seen. The secretary was gone, and only one nurse was there. "Mrs. Adams, where is everyone?" Mark asked.

"Haven't you heard the news today? The riots are spreading this way. Most of the appointments have been canceled, and people are leaving town. As you can see, most of the nurses have left, too. As a matter of fact, I'm outta here after today. I don't care what they say—this job isn't worth getting killed over," she said defiantly.

Just then, the ER paged him, stat. "We have a gunshot wound to the abdomen here. It's a five-year-old, and it looks bad!" the voice on the other end exclaimed.

"Why in God's name did the ambulances bring them here? We're not a Level I trauma center, and we certainly don't do pediatric trauma. That's for Children's Hospital. We've been sending gunshot victims downtown for years," he shouted over the phone.

"Look, Dr. Edwards, they are not taking any more patients. Don't you know? They had to close down. Their power just went out, and the police said they are pulling back from the area and can't protect them anymore," Dr. Lewis explained over the phone from the ER.

"Well, send them to Children's Hospital, or to Jackson, or somewhere where they are equipped for that kind of trauma. We are not equipped for that here," Mark argued in frustration.

"I'm sorry, Dr. Edwards. I don't like it any better than you do, but the few ambulances that are still running won't go up into Memphis anymore. We are on our own," Dr. Lewis explained.

Mark was pretty pissed about the whole situation already, and this was the last thing he needed right then. He hadn't routinely performed major Level I trauma surgery since his residency ten years ago at the medical center, and he didn't want to start again, especially on a pediatric patient. Even The Med, which was a designated Level I trauma center, sent injured kids to Children's Hospital. When he entered the ER, he was taken aback by how many people were there. All the rooms were full, and people were lined up along the walls and down the hallways, a significant increase from the day before. Patients with fractures, lacerations, burns, contusions, and various assorted other injuries, along with the usual mix of chest pain, pneumonia, and other medical maladies, lined the hallways. Despite the crowded conditions and turmoil, Mark couldn't help but notice the patients in trauma beds two and three. They were both covered with bloody sheets that were pulled up over their heads. The little girl in bed four was bloody, as well, but alive.

"What the hell happened?" Mark asked as he instinctively surveyed her injuries. *A single entrance wound to the left upper abdomen, no exit wound. Respirations twenty-four and nonlabored, breath sounds equal and clear. Pulse 150 and thready, blood pressure 60/30. Moving all four extremities. Primary neuro exam seemed intact. Small-caliber bullet in left upper quadrant on her X-ray, lungs inflated, no pneumothorax. No time for a secondary survey or a one-shot IVP to check the kidney.* Mark was surprised how quickly it was all coming back to him.

The nurse explained, as best she could, while she assisted him. "They got caught up in a crossfire at the shopping center today. Bunch of punks from Memphis, raiding and looting. That's her mother and father over there." She motioned to beds two and three as she spoke.

Mark looked up and suddenly felt a surge of anger. "Senseless," he muttered, to himself. "Well, if we are going to help her, we need to get her to the OR as soon as possible. Give her a unit of O neg blood and type and cross her for four units, get a folly in her and check her urine for blood, give her two grams of Ancef and five hundred milligrams of Flagyl in her IV, and pour the fluid to her," he said as he inserted a second large-bore IV in her other arm. "Someone call anesthesia and tell them what's going on. Let's go!" he shouted as he pushed the stretcher out of the room and down the hall toward the OR holding area, where he was met by the OR supervisor.

"Where are you going?" she asked sharply.

"Well, I was hoping you were going to tell me which OR we are going in," Mark replied back.

"I'm sorry, but I only have two crews here, and they are both busy with orthopedic fractures, and besides, I don't have a room equipped for pediatric trauma cases," she said defiantly.

"Don't have a crew? Where the hell is everybody? This little girl has been shot and is going to die if we don't do something now. I don't care if the rooms are equipped or not, I'm going to use one of them," he said as he pushed the stretcher by her. To his surprise, she stepped out of the way, grabbed the stretcher, went with them down the hall, and started barking orders to the nursing staff to get room four ready and to pull a scrub tech from each of the other rooms. He smiled at her and nodded his head in favor of her decision. "Thanks," he said.

Luckily, Dr. Morel, one of the anesthesiologists, had just finished a case and was still there. With a little prodding from Mark, he reluctantly agreed to help. Together, they moved her to the OR table and began to work, frantically, to stabilize her blood pressure with intravenous fluids and O negative blood transfusions. Dr. Morel quickly placed her under a rapid-sequence general anesthetic while the nurse prepped her abdomen with antiseptics and sterile drapes. Mark did a quick scrub at the sink then gowned and gloved, all within a few minutes. He was relieved to see Paul Black scrubbing in. He was, without a doubt, the best surgical assistant at the hospital. As Mark stood at the patient's side waiting to make the skin incision, his heart pounded away as he thought about what he needed to do and the possibility of the young child dying on the OR table. "Lights on. Cautery on forty, cut on thirty. Suction on high. Laps up. Knife. Everybody ready?" Mark asked as he was about to make an incision.

"Wait! We haven't done our time out yet," the OR nurse said as she hurried to keep up. "You can't start until we have identified the patient and the surgery site and confirmed that the operative consent form and the procedure match," the nurse said frantically as she searched the papers and her computer for a consent form.

"This is the patient with a bullet hole in her abdomen right there. There is no signed consent form because both of her parents are dead, and I think this qualifies as an emergency, so we can skip the time out," Mark barked as he reached for the knife.

"But I can't allow that. We have to have a time out or I can lose my job," she blurted back as she continued to fumble through her papers. Mark went ahead and made an incision despite the continued protests and threats from the nurse, who, he suspected, was going to write him up and turn him in to the administrator. Just then, the OR nurse supervisor walked back into the room with more blood from the blood bank and overheard the end of the conversation. "Miss Smith, it's okay," she said. "We can sort out the paperwork later."

Nurse Smith continued to argue. "But you told us to never, ever, let them start a case without a time out and a consent because the hospital can get sued, and…"

The OR nurse supervisor cut her off. "Miss Smith, *you* need to take a timeout. I think in this case we can make an exception."

After Mark made the incision and entered the abdominal cavity, a large amount of blood poured from the abdomen and down onto the floor. "More suction. Laps. Bookwalter retractor. Looks like we're going to need more blood in here," Mark demanded.

"All we have up and sterile are these retractors and the ones in the robotics set," the nurse replied.

"For the love of…" He cut himself off. "If we don't find the source of this bleeding, we'll lose her," Mark said as he and Paul struggled to control the bleeding. He held pressure on the area that was bleeding until anesthesia could catch up on the blood transfusions. Using what they had available, he took one more look into the left upper quadrant as the blood welled back up again. "There it is!" Mark saw it. A bullet hole in the left renal vein, and the bottom of the spleen was fractured beyond repair. With Paul's help, he was able to pack off the spleen and then clamp off the vein with a vascular clamp and repair it with a 5-0 proline. After he finished the repair, they quickly removed the spleen. Mark hung his head for a moment. "Well, that was fun," he muttered. Then the grizzly picture of the girl's parents, covered with the bloody sheets in the ER, came back in his mind. The little girl would live, but now she was alone. Mark quickly finished closing the incision, applied a dressing, and helped move her to the recovery room. Then he sat down at the desk in the recovery room, dictated the operative report, describing the case in detail for the hospital record, and then entered his orders and notes into the computer.

After the case, Paul and Mark talked for a few minutes in the lounge over a cup of coffee before the next call from the ER came. Paul was six years younger than Mark but slightly shorter with thinning brown hair. He had spent a few years in Afghanistan as an army medic at the turn of the century and liked to keep himself in good shape by running and lifting weights. Paul liked the military life and was an avid gun collector and had joined one of the local militia groups. He liked trauma, blood and guts, and a good firefight about as much as anything. "That was all right, Dr. Edwards," Paul said. "Just like the good ole days in the army."

"Maybe for you, but I can do without all the blood and guts stuff myself. I got over that, and all the chest pounding, ass slapping, and late nights that go with it years ago," Mark said as he laughed and took another sip of his coffee.

"I can tell you this—it's going to get worse before it gets better," Paul said seriously. "There are a lot of people out there who are really pissed off at the government and all the freeloaders. They have been living off our tax dollars for years and years. That's why we're in this mess. Some people think it's a good time to straighten things out again."

"I know you like your guns and all that, but what is all this fighting going to accomplish?" Mark asked.

"Maybe nothing, but people have a right to protect themselves and their property. The government keeps taking away more and more of our rights and more and more of our money. And what do they do with it? They keep giving themselves pay raises and giving our money away to those who don't work so they can keep getting voted back into office. Working folks who pay all the taxes are now a minority, so we can't vote them out or change the rules. Politicians can't get elected if they are for cutting taxes or benefits to anyone, because everyone says they want the government to cut spending, but just not their benefits. It's not just food stamps and welfare checks. It's disability, Social Security, Medicare, Medicaid, Aid to Dependent Children, rent subsidies, cell phones, school lunches, after-school care, preschool care, free day care and health care for all, and the list goes on and on. I'm not against helping those who truly need help, but too many people have found a way to live off the government tit and just don't want to work. Why should they? It's too damn easy not to if you are willing to play sick, or disabled, or crazy, or the role of a victim, or whatever. It's a viscous downward spiral with no way out. It has to all fall apart so we can put it back the way it should be. It's not about race, or women's rights, or any of that. It's about the government getting their hand out of our pockets and out of our personal business so we can make a living and live in peace and enjoy freedom," Paul lectured on from his soap box. Mark knew he could get him started by talking about taxes and the government.

"So what are you for, a revolution?" Mark asked, knowing it would keep him going.

"I just know there are a lot of people out there who are ready for a fight if this keeps on," Paul said.

Mark thought for a minute and then said, "I guess you are right. If these riots keep on, somebody has to stop them. If the government doesn't, then people will take matters into their own hands."

"I'm not just talking about the riots. I'm talking about taking our country back. People have taken all they can. You can't even piss on a tree without breaking some law. Now they have banned handguns and semiautomatic rifles. If you don't already have one, you can't get one legally. They are talking about taking them away altogether. All I know is you can push people to a certain point before they snap, and taking away their guns is going too far. I know a lot of folks who say they will go down fighting before they let that happen," Paul said with his fists clinched.

"Hey, I'm just jerking your chain just to get you riled up 'cause it's so easy to do. I'm with you. Do you think I like being told when, where, and how to practice surgery? And now they are saying that the president might enact part of the National Defense Preparedness Act. If they do that, the secretary of health and human services can force doctors and any other health care worker to work for the government, as they deem necessary. Essentially, you or I would be forced into conscription against our will or risk going to federal prison as an enemy combatant without so much as a phone call or hearing.

"Since we are on the subject, I heard the riots are starting to spread this way," Mark continued. "If it gets too bad around here, what in the world are we going to do with all these sick patients? I guess at some point, if it gets bad enough, we won't have a choice—we'll have to leave. If that happens, I'm heading down to the farm. Where will you go?"

"I don't really have anywhere to go, just yet," Paul said. "We don't really have any family around here. My wife's folks live in

Charlotte, and mine live in a condo in Florida—not really your ideal retreat locations."

Mark looked at Paul and made a pact with him. "If we have to get out of here, we can go to the farm together. Or if we get separated, then we need to meet up down there. Agreed?" Mark had known Paul for only a couple of years, but he felt that he was someone he could trust. And with his medical and military experience, he might come in handy in a tight situation. He looked at Paul, waiting for an answer, and thought for a moment he had said something wrong.

"Are you serious?" Paul asked. "I mean, if you really mean it, then it's a deal," Paul said hesitantly.

"Sure, I mean it," Mark said as he took another sip of coffee. "My wife's family has a big farm just about an hour or so from here. They have well water and everything we would need to hold out for a while except enough able-bodied men and women to hold down the fort, if needed. You know, I've been thinking about this for a while. But I didn't think it would be this soon. And I hate to admit it, but now that I know how you and others feel, there is a part of me that has sort of quietly been hoping for this, as well. I know that sounds crazy, but I would actually like to start a clinic in Batesville and practice medicine the way it used to be. Now, it looks like it's hitting the fan for real, and if this place goes down, I'm outta here and heading for the farm and may not come back. I was going to leave on my own, but if you are with me, we need to have a plan to get out of here when the time comes."

Paul stood and started pacing the floor in excitement. "Man, I can't wait to tell Martha. She will be so relieved to know we have a place to go. Look, I haven't really told a lot of other people at the hospital, but I am sort of an end-of-the-world-as-we-know-it kind of person. I've been prepping for some time and have enough beans, bullets, and bandages stored up for my wife and me to last about a year. But the only thing we don't have is a place to go if we have to bug out. One of my friends has a small place out in the country, but they just don't have enough room for everyone, and they live too far away to get to on short notice. And, I just didn't know anyone around here that well to ask."

"If this is the end of the world as we know it, trust me, you would not be imposing. I know you are not afraid of hard work, and besides, the way I got it figured, you probably can handle a gun better than most," Mark said. He finished telling Paul about the farm and then drew a map to it, just in case.

Evening rounds took much longer than usual, and he had several new ER patients to see, as well. Luckily, most had minor injuries and needed only stitches or a cast or two. Only one needed to be admitted, and none required surgery. When Mark went to get in his car to go home, he could hear gunshots and see the orange glow of fire from burning buildings just to the north. It was much closer than before, but luckily he lived a few miles south of the hospital. For now, he figured he was still safe. He headed along his usual route and noticed there was very little traffic. It was about nine o'clock when he pulled into his driveway. The afternoon was so hectic at the hospital that he just now had time to call Lisa. He knew they were safe at the farm, because he had received a text message from her earlier in the day. "Mark, made it to the farm, let me know how you are doing. Be careful. Love you." His brief response was, "Glad you are safe, things are crazy here, talk to you later."

Mark took a quick shower, grabbed a sandwich, sat in his favorite chair, picked up his phone, and called Lisa. She answered quickly. She was expecting his call. "Hello, Lisa. I got your message. I'm glad you and the boys are okay." Mark was glad to hear her voice and had no idea of what happened to them on the way.

"Hi, Mark. How are things there?" Lisa asked, not wanting to tell Mark about her ordeal right then. She wanted to wait and tell him in person, because she was afraid of breaking down.

"Okay, I guess—just wore out," he said, not wanting to worry her.

"I've been watching the news. It's getting worse there, isn't it?"

"Well, there was a little more confusion today. Dr. Williams called in sick, and I have to cover for him now. It's really busy right now." Mark didn't tell her about the riots getting closer and all the ensuing trauma, because she would just worry even more.

"Do you think you are going to be able to get off next week?" she asked.

"I don't know. It's kind of crazy right now. Maybe this will settle down soon and Dr. Williams will come back next week. If so, I can come down then," he answered.

"I hope so, Mark. Promise me one thing. If it gets really bad there, you will get out. Don't wait. The boys and I need you," she said as she broke down in tears.

"Lisa, don't worry about me." Mark sensed something was wrong. "Lisa, what's the matter?"

Lisa couldn't hold back the tears any longer. She broke down and told him the whole story, the part where she fought with the man, about Steve and the bat, about the gun, everything—even the part where she drove over the man.

Mark listened almost in shock as she finished the story. "I am so thankful you are all okay." Although he was relieved to know they were safe, he felt shaken and angry at himself for not having gone with them. "Lisa, I feel like it's my fault. I shouldn't have let you go without me."

"It's all right, dear. We know you had to stay," Lisa offered.

"Do the police know?" Mark asked, wondering if there would be any other problems for her.

"No. I was afraid to call them. I didn't want to have to explain it all. I'm afraid they might question the part about running over him with the car when he was already out. I just want to forget about it all."

"That's okay. Maybe it's just as well they not know. If he's dead, it doesn't matter anymore—he won't ever hurt anyone else. Just between you and me, I think you should keep the gun, but don't tell anyone," Mark suggested.

"I had to tell my parents about it. They could look at me and tell something happened. But I didn't tell them about the bat, and I told them that I ran over him accidentally. I just don't want Steve to get in any trouble later if something comes up. So he and I agreed that would remain between us. He knows that I was going to tell you but no one else. I'm still hoping he thinks the car actually killed him and he only wounded the man with the bat. I don't want him to carry that with him the rest of his life," Lisa explained. "We're safe now, but I'm worried about you. Promise me you will come down here as soon as you can," she pleaded.

"I will, Lisa."

"Good night, dear. I love you. Please be careful."

"Good night, Lisa. I love you. I am so proud of you and Steve for being so brave," Mark said as he hung up the phone and wiped the tears from his face. Now he felt even worse for not having gone with them and vowed to himself not to make that mistake again. Now his oldest son would have to carry the burden of what he did for the rest of his life, just as he had. Coincidence, fate, providence—call it what you want, but Mark knew his son's reaction was just instinct. He did what needed to be done, when it needed to be done. He had seen that trait in his son. The quick reflexes, the calmness in the face of a storm, the ability to think in the midst of danger that most people don't have. Little things that happened over the years, like him diving into the deep end of the pool when he was twelve and pulling the little kid from the bottom before the lifeguard or anyone else knew what was happening. Like putting out the fire his little brothers started with sparklers in the backyard with the water hose before it could spread farther. The fact that he was the one his brothers and friends ran to when there was trouble. And now this, all of which let Mark know he was different from most.

He turned on the news to check out the riots. Only one of the local stations was still on the air. Scenes of rioters overturning cars, looting stores, and setting fires in the cities continued to dominate the news. The sight of the National Guard arriving on the scene in Memphis was of some comfort to him. Perhaps now they would be able to get control of the situation.

New reports were coming in about the condition of the president. The latest indicated that he was in very serious condition but was expected to live. However, how long he would be in the hospital was not known. Mark went to bed hoping to himself that tomorrow would be a better day. He got only about five hours of interrupted sleep, thanks to half a dozen phone calls that night from the ER.

CHAPTER 4
MORE TRAUMA

Saturday, April 12.

Mark was awakened by the phone ringing on his nightstand beside his bed—again. As he reached for the phone, he noticed that it was 4:00 a.m. He shook the cobwebs from his head as he brought the receiver to his ear. "Dr. Edwards! Dr. Edwards! We have another gunshot victim in the ER. It looks bad! Real bad. Blood pressure is barely readable." Mark held the phone in silence for a moment, trying to gather his thoughts. "Dr. Edwards, this is Dr. Lewis. Are you there?" he heard on the other end.

"Yes, I'm here, just trying to wake up. What are his vital signs?"

"Blood pressure is only about seventy. We've got some blood hanging, but there's not much available."

"Where is he shot?" Mark asked while trying to get himself out of bed. Getting called in the middle of the night was something Mark always dreaded. It always made him wonder why he became a surgeon in the first place.

"In the chest, on the left side. I can still see the bullet on the X-ray, behind the heart," answered Dr. Lewis on the phone as he held the X-ray up to the light. "I tried to get him sent somewhere else, but the ambulances are still refusing to go into Memphis. What do you want me to do?"

Mark thought for another moment as he tried to pull his thoughts together. "Put in a thirty-six French chest tube on the left side and try to keep him alive. I'll be there in fifteen to twenty minutes. Make sure anesthesia and the OR crew are notified in case we have to open his chest."

When Mark entered the ER, he noticed Dr. Lewis doing external chest compressions on the patient in bed one. Dr. Lewis turned, looked at him, and shook his head as he continued CPR. Mark stepped to the head of the bed and tried to find a pulse. There was none. "What happened?" Mark asked as he pulled out his stethoscope and listened to the patient's chest.

"I don't know. I put the chest tube in and got about seven hundred cc's of blood out. That looks like it has slowed down. Then he just went out on us. We can't find a pulse or a pressure. So we started CPR just a few minutes ago," Dr. Lewis said between chest compressions.

Mark asked Dr. Lewis to stop CPR for a moment so he could listen to the heart. All he heard was low, muffled heart sounds. He studied the monitor, which still showed a heart rhythm, and noticed that the neck veins were severely distended. Something wasn't adding up. Then it hit him. "Tamponade!" he shouted. "Let me have a sixty cc syringe and a twenty-one-gauge spinal needle and some betadine prep." He carefully felt for the ziphoid process, chose his spot, and then inserted the needle deep into the chest into the pericardial sac around the heart until he drew back a large amount of dark blood. He continued to draw off blood for another minute or so, and then the patient's pulse returned. "Let's get him to the OR. We need to open his chest. Is anesthesia here?"

Mrs. Evans, one of the OR nurses next to the bed, answered. "Sorry, Dr. Edwards. He lives across town and said he could not make it. The OR is ready, but I'm the only nurse here, and Paul is the only OR tech here."

"What about one of the other anesthesiologists?"

Mrs. Simmons, the nurse supervisor, spoke up. "Dr. Smith is already tied up in a case out east, and Dr. Wheeler won't answer his phone or his pager."

Just then, Mrs. Evans shouted, "Dr. Edwards, his pressure is back down to seventy."

Mark drew some more blood from the pericardial sac and watched the monitor closely. "Then someone here will have to give the anesthesia." Mark looked at Dr. Lewis and pointed his way. "You can do it."

Dr. Lewis stepped back and held up both hands in front of him. "Not me. I'm not an anesthesiologist. I've got all I can handle right here."

"Look, I'm not a chest surgeon, either, but he's got a hole in his heart, and if we don't do something quick, he's going to die. I can get him under, and then all you have to do is push blood and give oxygen. You can do it. You have to do it. We have no other choice." Mark looked him straight in the eyes, waiting for an answer.

"Look, I'm sorry, but I can't do that. I could lose my license or something," Dr. Lewis argued.

"Are you worried about getting sued or something? For goodness' sake, a man is dying here, and you're worried about getting sued." Mark was furious now. "What about you, Mrs. Simmons, or one of the other nurses?"

Mrs. Simmons backed away defensively and shook her head with her lips drawn tight. "No way. I'm not going to do it either, and I won't ask any of the nurses to do it. They think he was one of the rioters who shot the little girl and killed her parents yesterday. As far as I'm concerned, he got what he deserved."

Mark looked sternly at her and said, "I don't remember him having a trial yet. Hell, let's just get a rope and hang him right here in the ER. I don't give a shit if he is one of them or not, we've got a job to do here." Deep down inside, he couldn't help but think about what happened to Lisa and the boys. It did make him think about the young man lying in front of him, and what he might have done to the little girl's parents or maybe other people. It would have been real easy not to help him. But Mark did not want to be the judge and jury, much less the executioner.

Just then, Mrs. Evans shouted, "We've lost his pressure. He's going out again."

Mark checked the monitor and tried draining more blood out of the pericardial sac. Suddenly, the heart rhythm changed to ventricular tachycardia and then to ventricular fibrillation. "He's arrested, folks. Start CPR." Within a few minutes, the patient was intubated and ventilated with 100 percent oxygen, given intravenous epinephrine, sodium bicarb, and calcium chloride, then shocked with the defibrillator several times without success. Mark refused to give up. "I'm going to open his chest. Get the chest set."

Mrs. Simmons looked in amazement. "Here in the ER? Are you kidding? We don't have a chest set down here!" she shouted.

"Dr. Edwards, he's gone. There's nothing else we can do." Dr. Lewis shook his head, put down the paddles, and walked away.

Mark looked at the monitor. All he could see was a straight line. He checked for vital signs. There was none. He stood next to the bed for a minute. "Any family?"

"Don't know. There's no one here," Mrs. Simmons said sharply then walked away, still mad about Dr. Edwards's earlier comments.

Later that morning on rounds, Mark ran into Dr. Stanley on the first floor. They took a few minutes in the break room to discuss the situation at the hospital over some coffee.

"Rough night, Mark?" Dr. Stanley asked as he stirred his coffee. "I heard about that. No anesthesia. That's a big problem."

"I feel like a resident again, with all this trauma and having to get up in the middle of the night. I hope this settles down soon, or we are all going to be in deep trouble. Everyone is leaving or calling in sick. Hell, half the staff is gone. You're not going to bail out on me, are you?" Mark prodded as he sipped his coffee.

"Well, I don't plan to, but if the bullets start flying, I may head south, too. I have a place out in the sticks in Marshall County. It's just a fishing cabin on a little fishing lake, but if things get worse here, I can ride it out there. The way it's going, I'm not sure how much longer I'll be able to get here from where I live out east. I've been going farther and farther out of my way to avoid trouble. It already takes me an hour and a half. Besides, no one is having elective surgery. Most people are wanting to go home or get out of town themselves." Dr. Stanley looked down at his watch and reached into his pocket for his keys. "I hate to do this to you, but if you're going to be here, then I'm not going to come back in this weekend. I've gotten as many of my patients out as I could in the last day or so. So if you don't mind, I'll give you my list and see you Monday, I hope. Thanks," Dr. Stanley said as he turned and walked down the hall toward the elevators.

"Sure, Tom, be careful. See you Monday. I hope," Mark said partly under his breath as he studied the list, not knowing it would be the last time they would speak. Mark really wasn't upset with

Dr. Stanley. They had been working together for several years and had gotten to know each other well. Dr. Stanley was generally a good guy and always took care of things for Mark when he was on call. And after all, this was Mark's weekend on call. So now Mark had the surgery service all to himself. He thought that as long as the orthopedic surgeons didn't run out on him, he might just make it through this weekend. Mark studied the rounding list again. Only a few patients in the ICU and only ten on the floor. Not too bad, he thought. As he made his rounds, he was able to discharge a few of the patients in the care of their families who were ready to get out of town.

Unfortunately, a few patients were still too sick to send home, such as those in the ICU and a couple of postoperative patients in the ICU step-down, including Tammy, the little girl who was shot and whose parents were killed yesterday. After several phone calls, the social worker had found an aunt near Chicago, but she was very noncommittal about coming to get Tammy. Despite several more phone calls, the social worker was unable to locate any other family members.

Mark saw Tammy last on rounds. After checking her chart and looking her over, Dr. Edwards was pleased with her recovery. Her incision was healing well, she had no significant fever, and she was able to tolerate a clear-liquid diet. Despite how well she was doing physically, mentally she was depressed and had obviously been crying. "How's my little patient this morning?" Mark asked, trying to be cheerful.

She attempted a smile. "Do you know where my mommy and daddy are?" she asked with a tear-streaked face.

Mark sat down on the side of her bed, placed a hand on her shoulder, brushed away her long brown hair and studied her soft brown eyes and little round face. He swallowed hard to clear the lump in his throat and took a slow, deep breath to keep his emotions in check. "Tammy, do you remember what happened yesterday?"

She stared across the room at the nurse and hesitated. "We were going down the road, and these guys, they started shooting at us."

"Do you remember what happened to your mother and father?"

"I think so. They got hurt real bad. They were bleeding." She stopped, closed her eyes, and started crying.

Mark held her and let her cry. "I know, honey. I know." On many occasions, he stood quietly and bit his lip while being cursed by patients, families, and professors. He had watched people die over the years, some young, some old, and always tried to offer words of comfort to them and their families when the end was near. He had remained steadfast when all the odds were against him while trying, desperately, to repair the broken and torn bodies of his patients as they took their last breaths. He dealt bravely with the cancers that savaged the human body and sat by the bed of patients suffering from all the pain and misery it caused. But none of that had bothered him as much as the sight of this scared, heartbroken, innocent little girl, all alone in the world, already hurting from the pain of surgery, and now with no mother or father or anyone to hold or comfort her. No one to love her and no one for her to love. The nurse who had entered the room with Dr. Edwards gave an approving look then left the room quietly in tears as Mark continued to hold the little girl.

All of a sudden, the lights flickered for a moment or two, and then the entire hospital went dark. For that same brief moment, everyone in the hospital stood still and silent, looking into the darkened hallways and listening, intently, as the dull roar of the diesel engines of the emergency generators engaged. To every-one's relief, the auxiliary power switched on, but at first only the emergency exit signs lit up, which gave off an eerie red glow at the end of each hallway. Afterward, the usual noise and commo-tion of the hospital slowly resumed, as everyone jokingly con-vinced each other that there was no apparent threat of immedi-ate danger.

Although the auxiliary power seemed to be working, Mark decided to make another trip through the ICU to check on the patients. As he entered through the double doors into the unit, he stood still momentarily and quickly surveyed the scene. He was relieved to hear the steady clicking and sighing of the venti-lators, but the place was unusually quiet, with only two nurses on duty instead of the usual eight. He could tell they were both too busy and too tired for conversation. However, each offered a few choice words that pretty much summed up the situation.

Nurse Cindy, a pretty young thin redhead just a few years out of nursing school, approached Mark and stood next to him. She had always had an eye for Mark and flirted with him whenever the opportunity presented itself, which was whenever he came into the unit while she was there. She knew he was happily married and off-limits, but she did not let that stop her. For a long time, she thought about telling him how she felt, but she was afraid that he might reject her for good; so, she was content to flirt. Mark had always attributed her teasing to her youth and figured she probably acted the same way toward everyone else, so he never took her seriously. But at that moment, she was too upset with the situation to be her usual playful self. "Dr. Edwards, if these ventilators go off, we're going to be in big trouble here. There is no way that just the two of us can handle all this by ourselves."

"Don't worry. The generators have enough fuel to run on their own for about three days. Surely, they'll get the power back on before that," Mark offered as a bit of encouragement. He could tell by their clothes, hair, lack of makeup, and stressed-out expressions that they had already been there a long time.

"I've already worked a double shift, and my replacement hasn't shown up yet," Cindy complained bitterly.

"If someone doesn't relieve you soon, you ought to call the nurse administrator," Mark suggested.

"Well, I already have, and she said there just isn't anyone else who can come in. If they think I'm going to stay all night again, they're crazy," Cindy said, almost in tears as she threw a chart on the front desk and watched as it slid off onto the floor.

"This is getting pretty serious. They are short-staffed all over the hospital, and I don't know what we're going to do. As soon as I finish here, I'll head over to the administrator's office to find out about the electricity. I'll be sure to talk to him about the nursing situation," Mark offered as he bent down to pick the chart up off the floor.

Mark handed the chart back to Cindy and gave her a reassuring pat on the shoulder and then went about his rounds checking on the patients. Fortunately, they all appeared to be stable. It still bothered him that the family of Mrs. Green, in bed two, insisted on placing her on life support, despite her terminal condition. Mark tried to explain the hopelessness of the situation to them. Unfortunately, he did not have a chance to discuss all of this with Mrs. Green before she underwent emergency surgery to stop the massive bleeding caused by her stomach cancer. Also, her family was not emotionally prepared to let her go and continued to hang on to the false hope of a cure. Jeff Veazey, in bed three, was a different story, though.

He was only thirty-nine years old with two small children and a young wife pulling for his recovery. He, too, had undergone emergency surgery for bleeding from his stomach, but his was due to a benign ulcer, and with time he should fully recover to live a full and productive life. Mark was determined to make sure that he did. After writing a few notes and orders, Mark left the ICU and headed for Mr. Cox's office.

The administration offices were located in a part of the hospital that was conveniently tucked away from all the sickness and commotion. Of course, no expense was spared when it was remodeled. With its marble-lined floor and walls and stained hardwood doors, furniture, cabinets, and bookshelves, it rivaled any corporate office in its decorations and finish. Mr. Cox, the administrator, was a heavy, short, balding, middle-aged man with a bad heart condition, and the crisis was taking its toll on him. He was already popping nitroglycerin tablets more frequently than usual and taking antacids like candy. He was on the phone at his desk with the higher-ups from Central Hospital Management as he had been most of the morning, discussing their options on how to best deal with the crisis. They were being bombarded with too many problems on too many different fronts. The central hospital was now closed, and the satellite hospitals in the suburbs all faced a critical lack of personnel, along with a severe shortage of food, medicine, and other critical supplies. And now, to make matters even worse, the electrical power was out at both satellite hospitals in East Memphis and at Southcrest.

Transformers were blown all over town, some shot out, some burned in the fires, and some due to the resulting overload on the remaining circuits. The power company was just as short on help and parts as the hospitals were, and with only a few brave linesmen still on duty, it could not assure anyone if and when the repairs would be made. The president of Central Hospital Management was conveniently going out of town on a trip and could not offer any help other than his demands that they all hang in there as long as possible, causing Mr. Cox even more aggravation, which added stress to his already enlarged heart.

When Mark entered the office, he could tell Mr. Cox wasn't doing very well. His face appeared unusually pale and sweaty, and his anger and frustration were obvious as he slammed down the phone. "Stupid bastards. What do they expect me to do? No nurses, no supplies, even the damn doctors are leaving," he shouted, intending for Mark to hear him. "What do you want, Dr. Edwards?" he demanded, trying to intimidate Mark into leaving.

One of the things that bothered Mark, as well as most of the other doctors at the hospital and across the country, was that while the salary of the doctors and nurses was steadily decreasing, the pay of the top administrators was steadily increasing. The doctors and nurses who actually took care of the patients lost the political battle years ago because they didn't have as strong a lobby as the hospitals. Mark was not a union supporter, but he knew, like most physicians, that the government blocked their ability to use collective bargaining years ago because the powers that be in Washington figured out if doctors went on strike or walked off the job, even for a couple of weeks, it would bring the country to its knees. But most doctors continued to work, despite the decreasing salaries, not because they didn't have any other options—after all, they were the best and brightest—but because they looked at their profession as a calling. The laying on of hands, healing the sick, relieving pain and suffering was something they were born to do. It was a most noble cause they fulfilled for the sake of their families and friends and society as a whole. It was not something they wanted someone less talented or less capable to do.

The thinking was the same among those who knew the difference between a good surgeon and a mediocre one. Who would want the pilot of a commercial flight to be the guy who graduated in the bottom of the class? Who would want a surgeon who barely made it through school to take the knife to your loved one? So Mark, like most of the others, took it in stride and had never let the business degree majors or the lawyers, who like Mr. Cox looked at everything from the perspective of dollars, numbers, and ledger sheets, bother him.

Unfortunately, by law the lawyers and MBAs made the rules and controlled the almighty dollar, but they did not and could not do what the doctors and nurses did. They didn't have the knowledge, the temperament, the nerve, or the stomach to do what needed to be done. Mark knew that many of them, as well as many in the public sector, considered surgeons to be arrogant. But if they were as diligent in their work, as dedicated to their profession, and as demanding on themselves as surgeons were, if they were as demanding of others that they do their job correctly, on time, and with the best of their ability, they would be judged as arrogant, as well. So, Mark thought, if surgeons were perceived as arrogant, then so be it, for anything less was not acceptable.

For all of those reasons, Mark was not intimidated by Mr. Cox— or anyone else, for that matter—and didn't hesitate to answer him. "Well, I think you just answered some of my questions. What's the story with the power?" Mark asked calmly.

"Hell, I don't know. The power company said there are transformers out all over town. They don't know when it will be back on." Mr. Cox stood and slowly walked to the window and stared out at the horizon toward the billows of smoke rising up in the north. "I don't know what we're going to do. We're on emergency power right now, but it can last only a few days unless we get more diesel fuel trucked in, and that looks doubtful. We don't have enough nurses, doctors, or supplies, and Central says they can't help. Any bright ideas, Dr. Edwards?" he asked sarcastically.

Mark went over and stood beside him and placed a hand on his shoulder and looked him over carefully. "You okay? You don't look well."

"Who me? Hell, I feel just wonderful," Mr. Cox scoffed as he turned and went back to his desk and sat down. "There's a damn riot heading our way, and God only knows how long it will be before it gets here. Mr. Clark says I've got to keep this place running as long as possible while he runs off out of town for a meeting," he muttered as he hung his head and put his face in his hands. "The National Guard was finally called out in Memphis. I don't know what took the governor so long to make that decision. It may be our only hope."

"Are you okay, Mr. Cox? Maybe you need to go to the ER and get checked out," Mark said, more interested in his condition than in what he was saying. He watched Mr. Cox take a deep breath and try to swallow another nitroglycerin tablet while clutching his chest.

"I'll be okay if you'll get back to work. You've got enough to worry about without bothering me. All of you are just going to have to do the best you can with what you've got. I've done all I can do about it," Mr. Cox growled.

The ER paged Mark again, just as Mr. Cox motioned for him to leave. Mark nodded to him and decided to take his invitation and left the office. Since no one was at the desk in the reception area,

Mark picked up the phone and called the ER. "Great! Another knife and gun club member. Be there in a minute," Mark grumbled loud enough for Mr. Cox to hear as he left for the ER.

"You better not run off like those other sorry scumbags. It's just you and a handful of others and a few nurses left, you know," Mr. Cox shouted out his office door as Mark left the administrative suite.

CHAPTER 5
THE COALITION

Saturday, April 12, 12:00
Noon. Washington, DC.

The most recent reports indicated that the president was not recovering as quickly as expected, and it would be many weeks or even longer before he would be able to return to his official duties. Vice President Carla Whitman called an emergency Cabinet meeting for noon in the West Wing of the White House. There had been little progress in finding out who was responsible for the attack, but intelligence reports indicated that the explosion was caused by a handheld missile launcher, and there was some evidence to suggest that the Islamic Nationalist Party was involved. Those in question were being vigorously investigated, and security had been beefed up in the White House and surrounding area.

Vice President Whitman was advised by several of her security advisers and senior Cabinet members to abandon the White

House for the White Sulphur Springs bunker at the Greenbrier Resort in West Virginia until the responsible parties were apprehended and the violence subsided. The bunker was a vast underground office complex built into the side of a hill, adjoining the hotel, by the order of President Eisenhower. It was built as a safe haven for the president and the Cabinet to hole up in if the capital was ever overrun or destroyed. Vice President Whitman appreciated the advice, but she insisted on staying in the White House as long as possible. She felt that abandoning the White House at this time would send out the wrong signal to the people that the federal government was weakened and vulnerable, so she was determined to stay.

As she sat in the study, looking over the latest news and intelligence reports, her thoughts kept drifting away. So many things had happened recently that they almost overwhelmed her at times, and she couldn't seem to focus her thoughts on the matters at hand. When she had agreed to take the nomination for vice president, she understood that having a woman on the ticket was mostly a political ploy to increase the female voter turnout and help get President Williams reelected. And it wasn't lost on the Washington insiders that having a good looking middle aged woman on the ticket would help increase the undecided male vote and their chances of getting elected. Not that she wasn't qualified, but she was well aware that she lacked experience in military and foreign matters. But now she was thrust into the position of acting commander in chief and was threatened with the most serious internal crisis that the country had faced in over half a century. Personally, she had mixed feelings about the whole situation and wasn't sure what to do about it. She had always been concerned about the underclass and acknowledged that these people had a right to speak out and protest. She even felt that the raids on the stores for food were somewhat under-standable in the face of the severe depression and their hunger. But the rioting and looting led to killing and fighting that was spreading throughout the country. That needed to stop.

Many of her advisers and members of the Senate and the House were calling for her to declare martial law and to bring in the military to put a stop to the fighting in the cities. The thought of using the military against the rioters caused her great anguish, for there would surely be many more deaths, and those who supported the rioters would harshly criticize her. However, the idea of letting the violence spread any farther bothered her just as much, because innocent people were being killed as the cities and surrounding areas were being destroyed. She was being advised by some that the uprising could be stopped if strong action were taken now, but there were just as many who were strongly opposed to using military force on their own peo-ple. Deep down, she wasn't sure she could bear the burden of deploying troops. But it was an agonizing decision that needed to be made, and the sooner, the better. Delaying it longer would make suppressing the revolt without greater bloodshed much more difficult.

Most high-level Cabinet members and White House staff mem-bers were at the meeting, including the chief of staff, secretary of defense, secretary of state, national security adviser, chiefs of the CIA and FBI, speaker of the House, and Senate majority leader. They were gathered around a long, dark, beautifully engraved wooden table. Various other deputy chiefs and high-level assis-tants were seated behind them. Vice President Whitman, presid-ing at the head of the table, was the only woman seated directly at the table. "Let's get down to business, gentlemen. First, let's hear about the status of the riots from our intelligence sources."

Mr. Clinton, the national security adviser, spoke first. "It doesn't look good. Based on the most recent reports from field officers around the country, it would appear that the riots are spreading rather quickly and seem to be growing each day. It's hard to get an actual count, but our best estimates based on satellite photos and computer calculations project in excess of twenty million people involved in the violence in over fifty major cities in almost every state, with few exceptions. In the states in which the National Guard have been called out, less than half reported for duty initially, and many left soon after to guard their own homes and families. The field commanders have been working under the orders to fire only when fired upon, but most of them were refusing to fire on their own people. The police have been able to control the violence in some of the smaller cities, but unfortunately in the larger cities they have been able to do very little."

"Thank you, Mr. Clinton. Secretary of Defense Hueling, how is our security situation here?"

"Madam Vice President, we have secured the immediate area around the White House and expect to keep expanding our zone of control until we have control of the entire area around the Capitol. At this point, most of the movement of the rioters has been toward the outer city and into the surrounding areas. That's good for us right here, but at the same time, it just means that someone else out there is going to be in harm's way. I see no immediate threat to us, however, at this time."

"May I interrupt, Madam Vice President?"

"Go ahead, Senator Clark, we are always honored to hear from our distinguished Senate majority leader."

Senator Clark was a tall lean distinguished looking gentleman from Massachusetts. He was a strong willed, outspoken supporter of all things liberal: women's rights, gay rights, abortion on demand, amnesty for illegal immigrants, affirmative action and every entitlement program on the books. "If you recall from our meeting just two days ago, Representative Wheeler, the honorable speaker of the House, and I advised against using any force. I would like to go on record with that and would like to suggest again, in no uncertain terms, that using force against the rioters may have disastrous consequences."

"So you don't have any problem with the military protecting us, but you just don't agree with them using force to protect the other citizens, is that right?" she asked rhetorically.

Senator Clark rose slowly to speak. "I don't have a problem with protecting the nation's capitol, but I do not feel that we should use military force against our own people, unless there is a direct threat to the government. We no longer feel that this situation can just be called riots. There are nearly twenty million people up in arms in this country. That, my folks, is not just a riot, but also a revolt bordering on a revolution.

"They feel that this country has turned its back on them, and if these people turn on us, my friends, we have had it," he argued.

"What do you suggest then, Senator Clark?" she asked.

"I think our only reasonable course is to give them what they want."

Vice President Whitman looked sternly at him. "We are all aware that their leaders have recently made some outrageous demands in front of the cameras, but we don't really know what they want."

"I have received direct communications from Jahbul Muhammad, the leader of the American Liberation Organization, which is by far the largest group, and he has been deemed the spokesman for most of the others. They have some specific demands that they haven't detailed yet. But they have made it obvious that they want to meet and discuss them. Although it's probably dangerous, I am willing to meet with them to see if we can negotiate a peaceful end to this violence," Senator Clark offered.

"Perhaps we were too harsh and quick with our entitlement cuts," House Speaker Wheeler interjected. Representative Wheeler from Illinois was a younger looking version of Senator Clark with the same liberal leanings and high political aspirations of his own. "We thought it was in the best interest of the country at the time, but perhaps we misjudged the consequences. Maybe we should meet with some of their leaders and find out if there is a peaceful solution to this. Besides, what other choice do we have other than waiting for this to end on its own or using military force against our own people, which I must admit, I'm strongly against?"

Henry Sage, the Senate minority leader from South Carolina, was a robust cigar smoking old school Republican. Even though rules prohibiting smoking indoors were put in place years ago, he continued to smoke when and where he wanted. At six foot four and over three hundred pounds, he was an intimidating figure. When he spoke it was in a deep southern drawl that he tended to accentuate for affect. He was someone to be reckoned with when he got mad, and all of this most certainly had him very upset. He was a staunch conservative, a strong supporter of states' rights and the right of the people to bear arms. To him, these rioters were nothing more than criminals and hoodlums. He felt that this whole mess was the end result of the entitlement programs that had bred an underclass that was so used to being taken care of by the government that it had become socialistic, demanding, helpless, void of any personal responsibility, and lacking the motivation to work. From his perspective, there were jobs and opportunities out there for anyone willing to work hard or get an education, but most of these people refused to stay in school and out of trouble or do manual labor. Those who would work wanted such high wages and benefits that most businesses could not afford to hire them. They found it easier to steal, deal drugs, sell guns on the black market, or just live off the government. To him, the crisis seemed to be much more than just about food and government entitlements. It was a conflict over the direction of the country—whether it would remain a free and capitalistic society, based on individual responsibility, founded on the principles of biblical morals and truths, or if it would become a socialistic society, based on man's own false sense of truth, devoid of religion or individual responsibility.

Senator Sage looked down over his glasses at the group and started to speak. "We must resolve this crisis without any concessions, even if it takes force to do so. Whatever their demands are, I'm sure they will include money and more handouts. In case you haven't heard, our country is broke. We cannot buy our way out of this one. After all, entitlements and uncontrolled government spending are what got us into this mess in the first place. If we don't return to and hold on to the principles of our Founding Fathers, then I fear that we will become a failed socialistic society, like all the others. There is no other way out of this."

"With all due respect, Senator Sage, I do not think we have the right or authority to call in the military against our own people. And if we do, they will surely turn on us," Senator Clark argued.

"I respect your opinion, Senator Clark, but since the president is still unable to fulfill his duties at the present time, I am the acting commander in chief, and according to the Constitution I have the authority to use the full force of the military, if need be." Vice President Whitman looked to the national security adviser and secretary of defense for their approval. They both quietly nodded in agreement.

"Senator, I will give you twenty-four hours to meet with the leaders of this so-called revolt and report back to us. I will listen to their demands on only one condition—that they can guarantee a quick and peaceful end to the violence. We will have a staff meeting at nine o'clock in the morning, then a full Cabinet meeting again at noon tomorrow, then we will hear from you on their proposals. I want to be kept fully informed of all significant events, understand?" Everyone nodded as she stood and left the room for a press conference, followed by her advisers.

Senator Sage remained behind with Mr. Wheeler and Senator Clark to further discuss their differences. Senator Sage lit a cigar and watched as the smoke lifted. "Well, our vice president is looking more presidential than you figured, gentlemen. If she calls out the military, I think we can expect to put an end to this rather quickly. You guys are playing with fire, trying to negotiate with that bunch of terrorists."

Mr. Wheeler disagreed. "She is unsure, or she would have already made her decision. I think she knows we are right. Our best bet is to meet with some of the leaders of the revolt. If we can come up with a compromise, I think we can resolve this peacefully. Otherwise, my friends, I think we are headed for serious trouble. If we use force against them, they could very well turn on us. Besides, I don't think we have the right to use military force against our own people. What do you think, Senator Clark?"

"I totally agree. We do not have the right to use the military against our own people. They are revolting for a reason. They feel oppressed by our capitalistic society, which they feel is run by big corporations and rich politicians. They are poor and desperate and see no other way out. We should meet with them and arrive at some type of compromise. That's our only reasonable option."

Senator Sage took another big puff on his cigar and intentionally blew smoke toward both of them. Then he took it from his mouth and pointed it at both of them. "Gentlemen, the country is divided and, apparently, we are too. These people are just a bunch of criminals. They do not have the right to riot, kill, or take the property of other citizens by force. Their leaders are a bunch of power-hungry socialists who are trying to use the situation to take control of the country. We have every right to use force, and I'm going to back the vice president when she makes that decision. And, I hope it is soon. You two have your meetings, but count me out," he said as he turned and walked out of the room.

Representative Wheeler and Senator Clark looked around the room to make sure they were alone. They both spoke in lowered voices, just in case. "I thought you said the vice president would go along with the meetings and concessions without any hesitation?"

Senator Clark smiled widely and patted Wheeler on the back. "It doesn't matter. With the president out of the way, there is only one person between you and the White House. If she doesn't go along with the concessions and calls out the military, we can turn this against her and call for her impeachment. With her out of the way, guess who becomes commander in chief? If the revolt spreads any further, I don't think we will have any trouble getting enough votes in Congress. They are just as ready as we are to see an end to this. Besides, she appears to be scared and unsure. If we can stall her for just a few more days, it will be even more difficult for her to call in the military, and I think she will have to go along with the concessions. Then, when the new elections come around, you will be the most likely person to win the confidence of both sides for helping bring this to a peaceful end. Let's arrange those meetings and get this started while the heat is on and we've got them on the run."

"I hope you're right. If this doesn't go down like we've planned, I'm going to take a lot of heat from my side of the aisle in the House. You know, we also run the risk of this whole thing backfiring on us," Wheeler said with a worried look.

"Look! How can this backfire? Unless you lose your nerve. They are either going to have to call in the military or give in. Either way, we come out on top as long as we play along with their leaders and show them we are on their side. Now, let's set up those meetings and get on with this." Senator Clark heard someone coming and motioned toward the door.

A member of the Secret Service entered the room and looked around. He was wearing the typical dark suit, sunglasses, and earpiece that distinguished him as an agent. "Everything okay, Senator?" he politely asked. "If you're finished, we're going to lock up."

"Fine, fine. We were just leaving, my good man. Don't want any more accidents around here, do we?" Senator Clark said and winked at Wheeler as he walked out past the agent.

Later that night, at approximately ten o'clock, a large group of The Coalition was gathered at the Grand Hotel Lobby in Washington, DC, just outside the zone controlled by the military. The convoy of armored personnel carriers that accompanied the senator's limousine pulled up to the front of the hotel. The hotel appeared mostly intact structurally, but the outside walls were riddled with bullet holes and most of the windows were broken out, leaving a grim reminder of the violence that had taken place just a few days earlier. Several heavily bearded men dressed in Islamic Nationalist uniforms and armed with automatic weapons were stationed outside the main entrance. Speaker Wheeler couldn't help but notice as he got out of the car with the senator how well armed and disciplined they looked. Despite his earlier conversations with Senator Clark about The Coalition and his assurances that they would be safe, he still felt uneasy. Senator Clark was not worried and thought it best to ask his army escort to remain outside to prevent any confrontation. The members of the small group were searched before they were escorted through the front door into the main lobby area. Speaker Wheeler thought it more than strange that cameras were set up around the table, and as they approached the table the equipment and bright lights were turned on them.

"Sit down, gentleman. Don't be alarmed by the cameras. We do not plan to give this to the news networks unless the demands of this Coalition are not met." Jahbul Mohammed introduced the other leaders at the table. "I'm sure you all know Reverend Jesse Bryant and his associates of the National Civil Rights Coalition." Several men nodded their heads as he spoke. "To my left is Mr. Andrew Smith of the New Socialist Party. And, of course, all of you have seen Mr. Abdul Hakeem of the National Islamic Party on the news." Speaker Wheeler was a little shaken to see Abdul at the meeting, because he was a suspected terrorist from the Middle East and the FBI was investigating his group for several bombings across the country.

Senator Clark introduced Speaker Wheeler and his aides then started the discussion. "First, I would like to say that Vice President Whitman has approved our meeting with you. She has authorized us to negotiate a possible agreement with you if you can guarantee an end to the violence. We are to take your proposals to her tomorrow, at noon. I feel I must warn you that she is considering using the US military to stop the violence."

Jahbul spoke first. "I have been elected by this Coalition to speak for all our people. We are over twenty-five million strong, and millions more believe in and support our cause. Our people have been oppressed for too long. They are tired of the false promises of this government. We will no longer be bound by the chains of the greedy capitalists of this nation. We have chosen a new path for our people. Our demands are simple. First, the wealth of this nation must be distributed evenly among all the people. All commerce must be regulated to stop the greed and repression of the corporations that have ruled this nation. Second, the government must make restitution for all past discrimination, for there can never be peace until we all have our fair share of this country. And third, we demand that new elections be held for president and all of Congress, so that we can replace those who brought this to bear on our people."

Speaker Wheeler slowly turned to Senator Clark in disbelief and waited a moment, expecting some display of outrage or surprise from him, but none was shown. He had expected some serious and possibly farfetched demands, but nothing this outrageous.

"We will deliver your demands to the vice president tomorrow and let you know something as soon as possible. Let me make sure I have this straight." Senator Clark showed no emotion as he read the demands back to them. "You want the entire wealth and land of the country divided among all the people and new elections for the presidency and all of Congress. Is that correct?"

"Yes, that is it," Jahbul declared.

"The only criteria the vice president placed on us was that you would guarantee an end to the violence if these demands were met. Can I assure her of that?" Senator Clark asked.

"The only guarantee we can make is that if our demands are not met, there will be more violence and bloodshed," Jahbul Mohammed declared defiantly in front of the cameras as cheers erupted by the armed men in the room.

Speaker Wheeler felt sick to his stomach and his hands were trembling, but he calmed himself as best he could, not wanting to show his fear in the presence of such poor company. He knew Vice President Whitman and the majority of the House and Senate would not go along with such outrageous demands. *Hell, a few concessions were one thing,* he thought, *but these people want to restructure the country into a socialistic society.* With over twenty-five million people on their side to dispense terror on the rest of the country, they appeared intent on following through with their threats. How could he even pretend to back such outrageous demands, especially when only a few months ago he was one of the strongest supporters of continuing the entitlements? It made him wonder if he had gotten in too deep.

The Coalition members sat quietly as the senator and Speaker Wheeler and the others were escorted from the hotel. As soon as they were gone, Jahbul Mohammed spoke to the others and to the cameras. "Our people are poised for a great battle. We shall not be denied. Our Coalition is strong and we shall prevail, for we have been ordained by Allah in a holy war." The room erupted again in cheers and battle cries as they waved their weapons in the air.

The drive back to the Capitol was quiet. Senator Clark studied his notes and said very little during the trip. Speaker Wheeler decided it would be best to not say anything until he had time to think everything through. What disturbed him most about the meeting was the presence of Abdul Hakeem, because of his possible connection to the recent attack on the president. It all seemed like too much of a coincidence to him. Although he had agreed to vote for the concessions in return for Senator Clark's support for his bid for the presidency, no mention was made of any involvement in the bombing at the White House. Although he disliked the idea of impeaching Whitman, he wanted to be president bad enough to go along with the plan. But terrorism was a game he wanted no part of.

Sunday, April 13, 12:00 Noon. Washington, DC.

The conference room was full of anticipation of the arrival of Senator Clark. Vice President Whitman was already seated at the head of the table and waiting impatiently. Speaker Wheeler was trying to look relaxed, but the anxiety showed on his face. Just then, Vice President Whitman spoke up. "Speaker Wheeler, since you were present at the meeting last night, would you please fill us in on the concessions that were proposed by The Coalition?"

As much as he disliked her for being selected as vice president instead of him, he was sorry he had agreed to go along with Senator Clark. He knew there was no way the people in that room would ever agree to such outlandish demands, so he had decided before the meeting to keep quiet. Just as he was about to offer an excuse, Senator Clark and his aides filed into the room carrying armloads of documents and files.

"Sorry we're late, but we had a lot of homework to do," the senator said as he set the documents in front of him on the center of the table. Then he instructed his aides to pass out copies of several documents, including the list of demands from The Coalition, to each Cabinet member. As they studied the information, it was apparent from the looks, gestures, and expressions that showed on their faces that almost everyone in the room was shocked and dismayed.

"This has got to be a joke, right?" Senator Sage said with a loud laugh. "They're crazy! If they think they are going to get away with this, they are out of their minds. Why, we ought to run the whole lot of 'em out of the country!"

"Just a minute, Senator. I think we all share some of your sentiments, but let's hear this out before we make any final decisions," Vice President Whitman said, trying to contain her obvious disbelief and frustration. "Senator Clark, since you are here now and seem to have taken this matter so seriously, would you please explain all this to us?"

"Thank you, Madam Vice President. Let's first turn our attention to the list of concessions that The Coalition has asked for."

"Just who the hell is this Coalition you refer to, Senator Clark? I don't think we're familiar with this group," Senator Sage interjected.

"Yes you are. Look on page two. The groups that make up The Coalition are listed. Separately, they are very familiar to us, but now they have come together for a common purpose and call themselves The Coalition."

"Yeah, to take over the damn country! Where did you find these nuts? We're not really going to take this seriously, are we?" Senator Sage asked, shaking his head in disgust as he studied the pages.

"Let's hear this out, gentlemen, if you don't mind. Now, go ahead, Senator," the vice president said.

"I must admit these demands seem unreasonable, but they don't give us any choice. They claim to have over twenty-five million people on their side, and several million more in the country who are sympathetic to their cause. They are frustrated and hopeless and therefore feel they have little to lose. They have already taken over most of the cities and are threatening further violence if we don't comply. At this point, if we want to stop the bloodshed, we don't really have any good options. Surely, we do not want another civil war in this country. They are not proposing a takeover of the country. They just want their fair share. A few laws would have to be rewritten and new elections would have to be held. Other than that, the Constitution and basic government structure would remain the same. The most difficult part would be deciding how to divide up the land and wealth of the country fairly among everyone. With the total assets of this country and the land, there is enough for everyone to be very well off. The rich would have to contribute their fair share. Then no one would have to be poor anymore, but also no one very rich. Everything would be shared equally. We can embark on a new society based on economic and social equality for all, or we can shed the blood of our fellow countrymen. Ladies and gentlemen, the decision is ours."

"Hell, this is socialism. I say let's send in the damn army, right now," Senator Sage demanded as he hit the table with his fist. "I can assure you that my side of the Senate will not stand for this, and I'm certain our side of the House will not either."

Senator Clark could sense an attitude change in the speaker, even from last night after the meeting, so rather than risk letting him commit to either side of the argument, he interrupted. "I think, if you research the Constitution, as I have, you will see that it does not make any provisions for the federal government, including our president, to use the military against our own people. Only the states have that authority by using the National Guard. As a matter of fact, it was tried back before the Civil War, and impeachment proceedings were started against President Jackson for attempting to do so. So, actually, we do not have the right, or Constitutional authority, to do so."

"Impeachment my ass! Who's going to impeach Vice President Whitman if she uses the military to stop the rioting and killing, for God's sake? This is an outrage! You know the National Guard cannot control this revolt, or whatever you want to call it. They just don't have the manpower, or discipline, to stand up to them. The army does, and I say we should use them, the sooner, the better," a red-faced Senator Sage said while pounding the desk.

"I would. And I think I can safely say that most of my colleagues would vote to impeach, as well. You and your conservative friends are to blame for this. If you hadn't opposed the spending bills needed to keep the economy going, there wouldn't have been any riots to start with. Now that the people have risen up against you, you want to use our own military against them. I can tell you this—they will not stand for this, impeachment or not. This country is divided between those who think like you and those who agree with us. The only way to resolve this without further bloodshed is by concessions. How can you justify letting the rich get richer while the poor get poorer, and then threaten them with force from their own government when they rise up against you? My friends, if we do not compromise with them, I'm afraid we will be at the brink of another civil war. The blood will be on your hands, not mine."

Senator Sage rose slowly from his chair and walked over to Senator Clark. He towered over him as he spoke. "Mister, don't threaten me with civil war. One thing is for certain—the liberals and all their excessive spending bankrupted this country, and if you think the American people are going to give up their land or their right to bear arms to you or anyone else, you are sadly mistaken. If their refusal to go along with that causes another civil war, then so be it. Neither you nor I have the right to decide that for them. That is for the people of this nation to decide."

"Gentlemen, gentlemen. Please, sit down. Now, let's see if we can work this out peacefully. Senator Clark, let's delay our decision at least until tomorrow, until we've had time to discuss this further. Let The Coalition know we are considering their proposals and will try to let them know something soon. Let's meet again in the morning at eleven a.m. and try to work this out." Although Vice President Whitman saw both sides of the argument, she decided to delay the decision until she had time to think things through.

Sunday, April 13, 4:00 p.m.

A black limousine surrounded by several armored cars slowly pulled up to the Grand Hotel main entrance and parked. Senator Clark got out of the car by himself and went inside without being searched or stopped by the guards. Jahbul Mohammed met him in the lobby and escorted him to a back office on the first floor. Abdul Hakeem was seated at a small round table in the dark room, which was dimly lit by a small lantern on the table. Several videocassette tapes were stacked on the table under the lamp. Jahbul ordered two of his men to guard the door from the outside, and then he shut the door. He pulled a bottle of cheap whiskey and two glasses out of a cabinet and joined them at the table. He let them pour themselves drinks while he watched and as they sat and talked.

Senator Clark started the conversation. "Gentlemen, I presented your demands at the Cabinet meeting. Senator Sage spouted off his right-wing crap, as usual, but Vice President Whitman did listen and is considering the situation. She called another meeting for in the morning. I think she will go along with us."

"What makes you think she will agree? Did she say anything to make you think that?" Abdul asked while taking another drink.

"What choice does she have? I have threatened to start impeachment proceedings if she calls in the military, and with Wheeler on our side she is unlikely to risk it. I'm not sure we would have the votes to actually do it, but we can at least stall her decision. Your people have shaken up the country, and everyone is scared of further violence. She is scared and indecisive, too. I think she will go for some of the concessions rather than risk any further violence. Our main problem will be getting all of this through Congress. There are a lot of staunch conservatives there who are not going to go along with this, unless the people are ready for a compromise," Senator Clark explained.

"The people are weak and afraid. They are spoiled, and there is no fight left in them. They watched while we burned the cities, and they did nothing. We have shown them that our people are not afraid to fight. If they refuse to compromise, our people will spread fear and terror even farther throughout the country, and then they will be ready to give us what we want. If they don't, we will rain terror on them until they do," Jahbul said. His eyes were wild with excitement, and he waved his hands and arms about as he spoke. Abdul, however, remained quiet and calm with his eyes fixed and his face expressionless. He was cool and calculating. Speeches were not his game, terrorism was. Although his voice might not be heard, his message would be delivered and seen and heard by many, just the same.

Senator Clark felt a little nervous with these latest rounds of threats, but he was used to their ranting and ravings. "Well, gentlemen, you do what you have to do. Just remember our little deal—I help you get your demands pushed through Congress, and when the new elections are held, your people support me. Right?"

"Our people will know who helped them. We will not forget."

Senator Clark took that as a yes. With their support and that of most of the liberals in the closely divided Senate and House, he felt assured of the nomination. The senator left quietly past the guards and took the tapes with him out to his limousine. As they drove off, he gave them to his aides and instructed them to get the tapes to the major news networks as quickly as possible. On the ride back to the Capitol, he thought about how he would explain this to Speaker Wheeler when the time came. After all, the poor sap went along with the plan only because he was led to believe that The Coalition would back him if he ran for president.

CHAPTER 6
THE FARM

Sunday, April 13.
That same afternoon.

Just outside Batesville, Mississippi, Lisa and the boys were settling in comfortably on the farm after arriving two days ago. She enjoyed seeing so many old friends and neighbors at church that morning with her parents and the boys. She was still somewhat shaken by what had happened to them on the drive down to the farm, so it was a good opportunity for her to ask God to forgive her for what she had done—even though she knew she didn't really have a choice in the matter, at least up to the point where she ran over the man. That was the part she felt she needed a little help from above in order to put it behind her. If God could forgive her, then she might find it easier to forgive herself.

When they first arrived, Lisa had to tell her parents what had happened, first because it was obvious to them from the look of her face that something bad had happened, and second because she simply had to get it off her chest. So she recounted the details up to the part where Steve hit the man with the bat and where she drove over him while he was out on the ground. Instead, she told them that she hit the man with the bat and might have accidentally run over him as she backed up to turn around. This allowed her to get that much off her chest and get in a good cry while not divulging too much about it. One reason for her concern was that she wasn't sure what kind of trouble she could be in. She wanted to protect herself from any blame, if there was any. It didn't seem reasonable to her that she could be held liable for her actions, but in the crazy world they lived in, where things seemed to be bassackwards, she couldn't be sure. It wouldn't be the first time an innocent victim of a violent crime ended up being charged for using too much force while protecting herself.

The farm, located about five miles outside of town just off the highway, had been in the Brown family for over one hundred years. Lisa's father grew up there and took over the place after he got out of the army when his father, Great-Grandpa Brown, passed away. Great-Grandma Brown continued to live with them until she passed years later. Great-Grandpa Brown homesteaded the place in the early part of the nineteen hundreds, when people still traveled by horses, wagons, and trains. With the help of his sons, he cleared the land and built the old barn and sheds out of the cedar trees, cut right from the farm and the sawmill down the road. The old, two-story farmhouse, built in 1905, was still in fairly good shape overall, but the outside needed painting and a few minor repairs to get it back in order. Although they had added a bathroom downstairs by the master bedroom and one upstairs for the three bedrooms to share, the old outhouse behind the house was still there.

Originally, the farm was 120 acres, but with a lot of hard work and a second job at the nearby sawmill, Great-Grandpa Brown slowly bought up two of his neighbors' farms. They had decided they were through with the farm life and left for the lure of the big city and better-paying jobs. Farmland was cheap then, and even with the depressed housing market and economic problems facing the country, it was still worth ten times more than what he paid for it.

With its rolling hills, many ponds and creeks, and cedar tree-lined fences surrounded by woods, the farm was picturesque, peaceful, and quiet. And with over 250 acres to roam and explore, the boys were having a blast. Despite the circumstances, the boys were glad to be out of school and filled their days with fishing, running the open fields, and exploring all the wonderful treasures that nature had to offer.

Lisa felt safe back on the farm in her old upstairs room and was enjoying the company of her parents. She had always loved the farm and country living, and she often dreamed and talked with Mark about having a farm of their own or moving back to this farm someday. She thought that even after all that had happened, she would be content, if only Mark could be with them.

Lisa's mother, Grandma Brown, as the boys liked to call her, was a pleasant lady with a ready smile, somewhat plump, but even at sixty-five, she was still agile enough to get around fairly well. Grandma knew that the situation in the cities was tragic. However, she was glad that her family was getting back together, even if it might be for only a short time. She was excited about having her house filled with the sights and sounds of little children again, for it brought back many pleasant memories of the past when her children were still at home.

Lisa, who was the youngest of the three, was a happy child. She was always fond of the farm and all its animals. Her chores while she lived there included tending to the barnyard animals. Although it was hard work, she enjoyed the animals so much that she had names for most of them, so her friends nicknamed her Ellie Mae. This was one of the things that she and Mark had in common. Both grew up on a farm and knew what hard work and morning and afternoon chores were. Summertime for their city friends meant nothing to do, swimming pools, and hanging out at the mall. For her and Mark and others like them, who grew up on a working farm, it meant even more work in the Mississippi summer heat: hauling hay, working the garden, mending fences, feeding the cows, shelling peas, and pulling corn. Anyone who had not hauled hay or pulled corn in July in Mississippi did not really know what hot was. Being in a hayloft or a corn crib, with the temperature in the high nineties and 90 percent humidity and no breeze, was like working in a sauna, only you didn't get to step out of it into the air-conditioning. It was all day long, day after day and week after week, of dust in your face, sweat dripping into your eyes, itchy hay down your shirt and, hopefully, a nice shade tree at lunch and at the end of the day.

When Lisa wasn't outside doing chores she was in the kitchen with her mother, helping her with the cooking, baking, and canning and listening to her stories about the good ole days. Her mother would reminisce about Great-Grandma and Grandpa and how life was when she was young. Back then, they didn't have all the newfangled electric appliances and window-unit air conditioners. Everything was done by hand with tools. They actually lived off the land and ate what they raised in the garden and on the farm. Grandpa and Grandma Brown learned the old ways from helping Great-Grandpa and Grandma, and Lisa learned from them.

Grandpa Brown was a lean man in his late sixties, nearly bald on top and always wore jeans or overalls. He was set in his ways and had a rough exterior worn by years of hard work in the sun but deep down inside was a soft as a kitten. He always went on about the history of this country and how farming was the way life for over two hundred years. For most people, life was rural and agricultural, where families lived together, worked together, learned from each other, and passed down knowledge from generation to generation. People rarely traveled far from home, and going to town for supplies meant saddling up a horse or hitching a mule or two to a wagon and at least a half day of travel over a dusty or muddy road. That's why most old towns or communities had a general store, a post office, a train station, a barbershop, and other needed services, because the people could travel only about five or ten miles and back home in half a day and rarely went to the big city.

He always talked about how the Industrial Revolution brought city jobs, machines to replace horses, and cars to replace wagons, allowing people to travel farther and faster. As the cities grew larger and more crowded, the farms got fewer, and the farms that remained grew larger and more mechanized. That meant there were fewer jobs on the farm, so the next generation moved away to the cities for better jobs. This gave way to a generation of plenty after the Great Depression and the world wars. Jobs were good and families lived apart but could travel back and forth to visit. But the cities ushered in an underclass of drug pushers, thieves, prostitutes, and others who learned how to live off the government, and the elected officials learned how to buy their votes with more government handouts. This led to the present situation, in which the country was divided between those who worked and took care of themselves and those who depended on checks that were doled out by the government. The majority had now become the minority.

Mark and Lisa always listened to his stories and talked about their messages often as they traveled along the back roads and highways, where they noticed the little towns and communities scattered about every five or ten miles. Most of the old stores and gas stations were abandoned or boarded up, left only as a reminder of a time gone by when they were the local hubs of farming communities. Nowadays, they were just a place people passed by in their fast cars on the way to the shopping malls or the nearest Walmart.

In the past, Grandma took great pride in her farm, family, and home. The daily chores outside helping with the animals and her housework filled her days. But after the kids grew up and moved away to start their own lives, things just weren't the same. Over the past few years, she tried to keep herself busy with her volunteer work at the church, her housework, and cooking for herself and Grandpa Brown. So she was enjoying having her children and grandchildren back home for a while to help fill the hours.

Grandpa Brown, who was sixty-seven now, was supposed to avoid heavy work after his coronary bypass surgery three years ago. So he no longer grew any crops and had sold off his animals, except for a couple of pigs, a few chickens, some turkeys, and a few cows and horses. Even though he was supposed to slow down, there was still a lot of work that had to be done. He tried to keep the place up as best he could, but he was frustrated by it all. Because, despite his best efforts, he just couldn't manage the place as he once had. He was slowly realizing that just the upkeep on the farm, with the barn and house repairs, the constant fence mending, the never-ending battle of cutting the pastures and the yard, often required a lot more energy and sometimes more money than he had to spare. It made him sad to see the farm slowly deteriorating from the way it used to be. But despite this, he just couldn't bring himself to sell the farm. It was too much a part of him. It was all he knew.

In his younger days, he kept the farm picture-perfect, but now, as he took his daily walks around the spread, he could see many things that needed repair, and it bothered him.

But he also remembered better days in the past when he cut hay in the pastures and stacked it neatly in the barn for the winter, and how he took great care of the cows and calves and other animals so that they would always have a ready supply of eggs and milk and meat. He even missed having a family garden, even though weeding it and harvesting the fruits and vegetables that Grandma canned for the winter every year was hard work. Even the fruit trees and pecan trees that used to bear delicious bounty every year needed pruning and no longer produced as they once had.

His morning walks took him by the old barn out back and by the little sheds that were filled with old horse-drawn equipment and tools from a different era. Two old wagons, a carriage, a plow, a harrow, a planter, a hay cutter, and a rake filled the back of the barn, like old skeletons from the past. A time when his father worked the fields from sunup till sundown with horses and mules instead of tractors, when sharecropper families lived and worked on the farm, side by side with the owner, when families still lived together and when neighbors were friends and helped each other.

The sheds were also full of many things used back when most of the work on a farm was done by hand: a butter churn, a scrub board, an old wood-burning cookstove, wash tubs, cast-iron pots, an old iron, and many other tools once used to make life easier before electrical appliances took their place. He often thought about selling all of it to the antique collectors who came around offering money so they could put it in their stores. Even though they were willing to pay cash and he knew he would probably never use any of it, he just couldn't bring himself to let it go. For it all reminded him of his mother as she stood by the wood cook-stove tending her meals, or cooking up a large kettle of lard to make soap, or singing hymns as she washed clothes in a tub with a scrub board. These things weren't just old antiques to him— they were part of his past. Little did he know that they would all be used again.

He thought about his children, Lisa and her two brothers. Lisa's older brother, Andy, who was killed in Afghanistan several years ago, had been very athletic all through school and enjoyed helping his father on the farm. He had size, quickness, and agility on the football field and probably could have played for almost any college and maybe even gone pro, but he chose to join the army after graduation and serve his country, like his dad. Grandpa Brown thought that of his three children, Andy would have been the one to come back after the war and take over the farm. That would have given him peace, knowing it would continue in the family as it had for two generations. Then there was Glen, the oldest, who was now forty-five. He was known as a lady's man in college but had lost his hair and gained a lot of weight over the past several years. As a child, he had always been rather lazy when it came to the farm chores and hated any type of hard physical labor. However, he excelled in school, so he went to college on academic scholarships, became a lawyer, and was working for a large corporation in Little Rock.

His thoughts were interrupted by the distinct clapping sound of a car crossing the old wooden bridge over the creek on the front drive. It was Glen and his wife, Sarah, and their two children arriving from Little Rock, as expected. When the violence started there, he and all the corporate executives conveniently took off for a so-called emergency out-of-town board meeting, leaving the midlevel managers and workers there to fend for themselves. As they got out of the car, they were obviously tired and relieved to finally be there. They rubbed their eyes and stretched as they gathered some of their bags and headed into the house. Before they could get inside, Steve, Daniel, and Jeffrey rushed out with excitement to meet them. They were glad to see their cousins and have someone else to play with on the farm. Grandma was overjoyed to see all of them and gave everyone a big hug and kiss as they came by her on the front porch.

Unfortunately, their two teenage kids, Tim and Rhonda, did not share everyone's excitement. They rolled their eyes, shrugged off the hugs, and went inside without saying much to anyone. Sarah tried to make excuses for their rudeness, but the kids ignored her and everyone else. Grandma figured they were just tired from the trip and welcomed them all inside. Sarah and Lisa followed while the boys and the men unloaded the car.

Grandpa hadn't seen Glen in several years and couldn't help but notice how much weight he had gained. "I'm so glad to see you," he said to Glen. "You look tired. How was your trip?"

"Terrible. The traffic coming out of Little Rock was backed up for miles. We heard on the radio that Memphis was just as bad, if not worse, so we went through Helena. We were lucky the National Guard was there to keep the bridge open. It was the only place we saw them the whole way over here," he explained as he let out a heavy sigh of relief. "You don't know how glad I am to be here. Batesville looked nice and quiet, and I sure hope it stays that way."

"Were you close to the rioting?" Grandpa asked, wanting to hear more about what they had seen in Little Rock.

"We weren't right in the middle of it, but it got pretty damn close. Too close for me. When we left, the riots were spreading to some nearby neighborhoods, and that's when we decided to get the hell out. I can tell you this—it was scary. We're not going back until all this crap clears up," Glen stated emphatically.

"Well, it's been fairly quiet down around here, mostly. I don't know if you heard about your sister's ordeal, or not. Come on in. I'll tell you all about it." Grandpa and the boys finished helping him unload the car and went inside to catch up on all the recent events.

The women had gone to the kitchen to talk and help Grandma finish getting supper ready. Earlier, Grandma had put a big roast smothered in potatoes, carrots, and onions in the oven, and it was just about ready. "If you girls will set the table, I'll take the roast out of the oven and start the biscuits." As Grandma was trying to organize things, Rhonda, who was sixteen and too thin by Grandma's standards, turned her nose up at the site of the roast.

"Oh, my God. What is that?" she asked.

"It's a roast, dear," Grandma explained. "You've never had a roast?"

"No, gross. I'm not going to eat that," Rhonda complained. "Don't you have any pizza or something?"

Grandma looked at her sternly and started to suggest that she try it before being so critical, but Sarah interrupted. "Now, Rhonda, if you don't like it, you know you don't have to eat it. I'm sure we can find something you like." Sarah and Rhonda didn't realize it, but they had just broken one of Grandma's household rules: If you don't eat what is fixed for you, you don't eat. However, she was willing to overlook it this time, since Rhonda and Sarah weren't familiar with the rules yet. She made a mental note to herself that if they were going to be here very long, she would have to fill them in on a few things.

Just then, a commotion could be heard in the upstairs hallway. Tim, who had just turned fifteen, was arguing with his father about having to stay in the same room with his younger cousins. "Why does Rhonda get a room to herself when I have to stay in the room with those three?"

"Because she is the only girl. She can't stay with the boys, now can she?" Glen offered, trying to satisfy him.

"Well, I'm not going to stay in there with them," Tim whined.

Grandpa overheard all the bickering and offered a compromise to the situation. "If you don't want to stay with the other boys, there is a small room up in the attic you can stay in, but there's not much furniture up there. You're welcome to stay up there, if you like. The only other place we have is out in the barn," Grandpa said with a sly grin.

Tim stood silent for a moment, contemplated the situation, and then said, "I'll stay in the attic." He picked up his bags and started climbing the stairs, mumbling something under his breath as he went. Grandpa thought the whole situation was kind of amusing and gave out a big laugh, which irritated Tim even more. Glen just shook his head and walked away.

After a while, Grandma called everyone to the table for supper. The adults all sat at the big table, while the boys sat at the breakfast table—except for Tim, who complained and refused to sit at the table with his younger cousins. Grandma heard the commotion, so she spoke up and said loud enough for all to hear. "If you don't eat supper there will be no snacking later.

If anyone is hungry, eat up now, or you may have to go to bed hungry." Tim didn't know it, but that was another household rule: Everyone comes to the table for supper. Tim was starving, so reluctantly he sat with the other boys.

It took some coaxing to get Rhonda to come down for supper. But when she found out that she would be sitting with the adults at the big table, she decided to join them just to further aggravate her brother who was now sitting with his cousins at the small table. Grandpa still found all of it quite amusing, but Grandma was somewhat troubled by how these two grandchildren were turning out. To her, they seemed spoiled, unhappy, and undisciplined. She wanted to say something but felt it would be best to wait until they all had time to settle in first.

After everyone was seated, Grandpa offered a blessing, which caught Rhonda by surprise. She had to be reminded to bow her head. "Let's all pray. Our heavenly Father, we are so thankful that you have brought these loved ones home safe to us. We ask you to be with Mark and watch over him, be with those that are sick and in need. Thank you for this food and our many blessings. Amen."

Sarah was impressed by the prayer and turned to Glen and said, "That was nice. Maybe we should start eating supper together, too." Glen was embarrassed. Her comment let his parents know that not only did they not say the blessing at the table, but they also never ate together as a family. Family meals had always been a tradition in their family when he was growing up. It had been a time to share their ideas and problems with the entire family. It was a time-honored tradition that gave them all a feeling of belonging and togetherness. Over the years, Glen and his family had just gotten so busy coming and going and doing their own thing back home in Little Rock that they just couldn't seem to find the time. Glen remembered how it used to be and how he missed it.

The table was spread with bowls of peas and corn, plates of biscuits, pitchers of tea and milk, and a large platter of roast. On the counter cooling off were two pecan pies. It looked like a feast, and it was. Everyone enjoyed the meal, except Lisa. Although she cooked for her family at home, to her, her mother's food was the best. But she could not enjoy it. No matter how hard she tried not to think about it, the empty chair at the table kept reminding her that Mark was not there. She hadn't heard from him since Friday night, and it troubled her greatly. She decided that she would not wait for him to call. She would call him. She ate what she could, even with the knot in the pit of her stomach.

After supper, Lisa and Sarah helped Grandma clean the kitchen and wash the dishes. Although Sarah didn't cook or clean much at home, she rather enjoyed helping in the kitchen. She was used to her comfortable role as a successful lawyer's wife and liked playing the part. Her designer clothes, hairdo and nails were the best money could buy. She rarely did housework which she gladly left to her maid, and spent most of her time at the mall or the country club. But strangely she found that it felt good to do something useful for a change. She had asked Rhonda to help, but Rhonda just rolled her eyes and said "Mom" as she left the room.

Grandpa and the boys went outside to shut the chicken house door for the night and to check on the other animals. Steve liked helping his grandfather and followed him around wherever he went. Often, his brothers would follow him, as well. Glen went into the bathroom after supper to avoid having to help out and was in there for almost an hour. As far as everyone knew, Tim was upstairs pouting in his little attic room.

After the kitchen was cleaned and all the animals were taken care of, everyone gathered in the living room to visit for a while. Grandpa retired to his favorite chair to smoke his pipe and read the paper. Grandma sat in her chair, knitting and talking with Lisa, Glen, and Sarah, while the boys watched television. After a while, Jeffrey fell asleep on the floor, so Lisa took the boys to their room and helped them to bed. Steve was still worried about his father and asked, "Mom, is Dad going to be okay?" Lisa tried to reassure him and the others, as well as herself. "Your dad is strong and smart. I'm sure he will find his way back to us. Now, good night, boys." She kissed them all good night and reminded them to pray for their father, then turned out the light.

As Steve lay in bed, thoughts and questions raced around in his mind. What was his dad going through? Was he safe? He thought about the trip down to the farm, the strange man, and the baseball bat. He knew what he did was necessary, and at first it didn't bother him. But now, after reflecting on it, he realized that he took another man's life and he wasn't sure how, or what, he was supposed to feel. He thought about the way his cousin Tim had acted toward them, and what he would give to see him get a good whipping.

CHAPTER 7
GETTING PREPARED

Monday, April 14.

Lisa had expected to hear from Mark and was tired of worrying, so she decided not to wait any longer and went to her room to give him another call. First, she tried to call him at home but got only a computerized message that stated the lines were temporarily down. Then she tried his cell phone. No answer. Next, she tried the hospital several times. It rang, but no one answered. She tried his answering service, but the lines were dead. Thoughts and questions raced through her mind. Was he hurt? Did something happen at the hospital? An idea came to her. Maybe she could find out something from someone else who worked at the hospital and still had a working phone. She thought hard but couldn't remember anyone or a number to call. Why hadn't Mark called? It was ten o'clock, She wondered where he was and if he was okay. Lisa hung her head and cried.

Back in the living room, the ten o'clock news came on from a station out of Grenada. All of the stations out of Memphis were off the air. The top news story on the cable channels continued to be the riots. Earlier, it seemed that things had calmed down a bit from the previous days, but they had picked back up again during the day as the recorded message from The Coalition was played over and over on almost every station across the country that was still on the air. Grandpa Brown and Glen stared at the set in disbelief as their leader, Jahbul Mohammed, dressed in his robe and sandals and surrounded by his supporters, announced their demands. He declared the start of a holy war against the devils of capitalism and threatened continued violence until the government met their demands. He promised all those who would follow and support their cause a share of the wealth and the land if they would rise up against the oppressors. The newscasters stated that there were reports of a significant increase in violence in many of the areas where the message had been played on the news. Memphis and Jackson were both mentioned, and both reported major outages of power and telephone services earlier in the day.

Grandma Brown heard what was on the news and went upstairs to check on Lisa. Lisa sat up and dried her eyes when she entered the room. "What's the matter, dear? You're worried about Mark, aren't you?" she asked.

"Yes. I've tried to call, but I can't get through. All the phones are out up there. No one answers."

"I know. I just heard about it on the news," she explained. "I'm sorry, dear." She let Lisa cry for a moment. "Let's go down to the living room and talk this over with everyone. We need to make some plans," Grandma offered. Lisa dried her eyes and went with her.

They watched the rest of the news together and listened carefully for any more reports about Memphis in particular. The only reports out of Memphis were about the explosions targeting electrical substations and telephone companies. No mention was made of any attacks on the hospitals.

Grandpa could tell Lisa had been crying. He intuitively knew what she was upset about. "He'll be all right, Lisa. He's a smart guy. He can take care of himself," he said as he went over to her and gave her a big hug. He turned to everyone and said, "It looks like this may be going on for a while. It may just be a matter of time before our power and phones go out too, so I think we need to be prepared for that."

"Dad, you don't really think it will get all the way out here, do you?" Glen asked.

"Maybe not, but the problem is that our power comes from the TVA out of Tennessee, and if the lines or substations get damaged or destroyed anywhere along the way, ours will go out too. That means the stores in town get their electricity out of Memphis, also. It's probably just a matter of time before we feel the effects out here. In the morning, we should go to town and get as many supplies as we can find and afford and start making plans, in case we lose our power. Does everyone agree?"

Glen answered, "I think that's overreacting a bit, don't you? I mean, surely this nonsense will end soon. You would think that they would call out the National Guard or the army or something."

Lisa wasn't sure what was going to happen, but she was worried it could get worse, as she and Mark had talked about before. "But, what if it doesn't end soon and things do get worse, what then?"

"Well, maybe, we are overreacting a little, but if this gets worse we might not be able to get supplies from town for the next few weeks, or longer. I think it would be a good idea to be prepared," Grandma offered.

Grandpa added, "It wouldn't hurt to plant a bigger garden to help feed all these mouths. And we might as well get some other supplies that we might need, such as some more ammo and kerosene for the lamps. And it wouldn't hurt to have the oil company come out and top off our gas and diesel tanks. And while we are at it, we might as well have the gas company come out and top off the propane tanks for the house and the shop."

Glen still argued that all of that wasn't necessary, mostly because he was worried that he might be asked to pay for some of it out of his own pocket. That was his real objection, but he didn't want to say so.

Lisa and Sarah both nodded in agreement and offered to help. The ladies got up and went to the kitchen to take inventory of their food supplies and make a list of other things they might need for the next few months. The list started out short but kept growing longer and longer: sugar, coffee, tea, salt, soap, canned goods, flour, beans, baking soda, yeast, cooking oil, canning jars, canned milk, tissue paper, and other kitchen and bathroom items.

Grandpa started his own list of things he might need for the farm. His list was almost as long: motor oil, kerosene, diesel fuel, gasoline, shotgun shells and extra bullets for his Ruger 10/22 and old Marlin .30-.30 rifles. Glen remained skeptical but agreed to help just to keep the peace with Sarah, who had already given him a stern look or two before she left the room.

The next morning after breakfast, Grandpa went out to feed the animals and do his morning chores. As usual, Steve was right there beside him, asking questions and helping when he could. When they finished and came back into the house, Grandpa noticed that Glen and both his kids were still in their rooms. It was almost nine o'clock. Grandma, Lisa, and Sarah were in the kitchen making a final check on their list before going into town.

Grandpa had Sarah check with Glen to see if he wanted to go into town with him. After much coercion, Glen got up, got dressed, and went out and climbed into the cab of the pickup with Grandpa, who had been patiently waiting for some time. It was a beautiful spring day, so they both rolled down their windows to let the wind blow in and admired the countryside as they drove into town. The highway, flanked on both sides with pastures and hayfields, gently winded into town through the rolling hills. The redbuds and wisteria were in full bloom, and a few dogwoods were starting to flower out as well, adding a splash of color and fragrance to the countryside as they drove along. Grandpa took the opportunity to poke a little fun at his son for sleeping in, something they never did on the farm. There were just too many chores and too much to do for that luxury. "I see you city folks like your beauty sleep," Grandpa said while trying to keep a straight face.

Glen kept staring out his window and answered, "I guess I was just tired from the trip over." He was not about to let on that he often slept in on the weekends, including Sundays, while at home. To him, this trip was just another vacation from the stress of his corporate job and the city. He was not there to work like he used to and had no intention of staying any longer than necessary.

Batesville was an old town founded before the Civil War. Its picturesque courthouse and town square had been used as a backdrop by many movie studios over the years to represent the typical southern town. Of its twelve thousand people, only a few had factory jobs. Most made their living from farming or other related services. Despite its racial and socioeconomic mix, the people had gotten along fairly well over the years. Even with all the trouble in the big cities, there had only been a few minor incidences that were easily taken care of by the local police.

Their first stop in town was the hardware store, where they bought a few extra gas cans, some motor oil, the last five boxes of twelve-gauge shotgun shells, and the last three boxes of .30-.30 bullets. Grandpa just laughed when the owner asked him if he was getting ready for a war. Their next stop was the co-op, where they selected an assortment of vegetable seeds and several bags of wheat and feed. The next stop was for fifty-pound bags of rice, flour, beans, salt, and sugar; bulk containers of toilet paper, feminine products, coffee, lard, and honey; and several cases of canning jars and lids, all of which garnered a few stares. Then they went to the gas station, where they filled all the cans with gas, diesel, and kerosene. Just before leaving town, Grandpa decided to stop by the Country Kitchen for some coffee and to catch up on the latest word around town. He parked out front in his usual spot and coaxed Glen through the front door. He spotted some of the regulars at the dead peckers table, as it was referred to by the locals, playing a game of rook and made his way over with Glen sheepishly following. After all the introductions were dispensed with, they helped themselves to the free coffee that was conveniently kept on the counter just for the regulars.

Old Man Simpson strained his neck to see what all Grandpa Brown had in the back of the truck. "Looks like you are getting ready for a long one there, Mr. Brown. You expecting a bad winter or something?" A few chuckles could be heard at the table next to theirs, where two younger men were sitting.

Grandpa Brown tried to ignore them and answered, "Not really. Just getting a few supplies, just in case."

"A few supplies? You got enough stuff in there to last half a year. You don't reckon the riots are going to get down here?" Mr. Simpson asked a little more seriously.

"Well, they might if they keep up the fighting in the cities. Even if they don't, I think it's likely that the power will go out. Unless they do something to stop them, those sons a bitches are going to ruin this country," Grandpa said.

The two young men at the next table overheard him, and one of them answered back, "What do you mean they are going to ruin this country? It's the pigheaded bigots like you who are going to ruin this country. People like you, and those greedy Republicans and those Tea Party folks in Washington, got us into this mess."

"How do you figure that, when it was all the worthless scumbags living off the government and the backs of us hardworking taxpaying citizens who got us into this mess?" Grandpa Brown shot back.

"Who you calling worthless, you old fart?" The man stood up from his chair and squared off at him.

Grandpa Brown, not being inclined to violence, decided to just ignore the man. Mr. Reynolds, however, was less inclined to let it go. "I guess you are, if you take their side, mister."

Glen didn't know what to do. He was too scared to get up and leave, but he surely didn't want any part of that argument. About that time, the young man stepped over toward their table and started cursing them like a drunken sailor on a three-day leave. Mr. Simpson took that opportunity to readjust the man's attitude a little and let him have some of it back. Without warning, the man took a swing at Mr. Simpson, hitting him upside his head. Mr. Simpson reeled back but caught himself on the way down and shook off the blow. Having been kicked and stomped by many a cow, it would take more than that to put Mr. Simpson down. Just as he straightened up, the second young man decided to join in the fracas and took a swing at him, as well.

Grandpa Brown figured that two on one was as good as turning the other cheek and let the second young man have one in the mouth, knocking him to his knees. A good swift kick to his privates ended his involvement in the discussion. It looked as if Mr. Simpson was holding his own with the first young man when the deputy sheriff entered the front door. The young man didn't see him come in and took another swing at Mr. Simpson. Just as he was about to take another, the deputy sheriff planted a solid lick on the back of his head with his nightstick. He fell beside his partner. After all the explaining and cleaning up was over, the young men were hauled off to jail to cool off for the night, even though Mr. Simpson and Grandpa Brown chose not to press charges.

The little scene at the Country Kitchen was the talk of the town the rest of the morning, and, unsurprisingly with the way gossip typically flew through the community, word of the fight got back to the house before Grandpa did. When Grandpa and Glen walked in, everyone gathered in the kitchen to hear the story firsthand. Steve, smiling ear to ear, wanted to hear every last detail. Grandpa Brown played it down and told everyone that they had a little disagreement with a couple of city boys in town, but Glen, still shook up by the whole incident, recounted the entire incident, blow by blow. Steve and his brothers listened to the story with wide-eyed amazement. They would have given anything to see it. They couldn't help but be proud of their grandpa. They figured he was the toughest guy around. Tim listened as well, but then he pretended to be unimpressed by it all and just walked away shaking his head.

CHAPTER 8
HOLDING
DOWN THE FORT

Monday, April 14. 10:00 a.m.

Dr. Mark Edwards sat in the surgery lounge after the latest trauma case. He was near exhaustion. Paul, the surgical scrub assistant, handed him a cup of coffee and sat next to him. "Here. You look like shit. One cream, one sugar."

"Thanks for noticing," Mark said as he sipped it slowly. "I don't know how much longer we can keep this up." He sat back in his chair and waited, knowing that would bring on a war story or two.

"This? This is nothing. I remember back in Afghanistan, when our unit went for days on end with hardly any sleep and very little to eat or drink. Every time we just about got caught up, they would bring in more wounded. It was during one of the worst battles of the war."

Mark had always enjoyed listening to Paul's war stories, but now it only made him realize how close their situation was to being a war story itself. He had essentially been working for three days now with only a few hours of sleep and couldn't remember his last hot meal. He had done no less than six trauma cases over the weekend. Or was it seven? He couldn't remember. Several others were brought in DOA to the ER, not counting the parents of the little girl, Tammy. They had been on auxiliary power since the electricity went out Saturday, and worst of all, the phones went out last night before he had a chance to call Lisa. Mark wanted to find Mr. Cox to see what was being done about the electricity and telephone services, but he had not seen him since their conversation in the administration office two days earlier.

Mark looked at his watch. It was a little after ten o'clock in the morning. As he sat and sipped his coffee, he stared through the window at the end of the hallway. It was the first time in the past couple of days that he had paid much attention to the outside world. The sun was shining brightly, birds were singing, and the trees and grass were starting to turn green after all the spring rains. It only served to remind him of Lisa and the boys and how he wished he could be with them or call them. But his cell phone was out of service along with all the other phones in the area. With such a beautiful and quiet day outside, it made it that much harder for him to believe or understand all the violence that he had seen over the past several days.

Paul Black turned on the TV and searched the channels until he found a station that was still on the air. He and the rest of the OR crew had been so busy over the past day or so that they had not paid much attention to the political events that were going on across the nation. As usual, the riots were the main news story. But now, they were reporting about the ongoing negotiations with The Coalition. Paul became angry as he listened to the news clips of Jahbul Mohammed's speeches. "Did you hear that crap? They are actually negotiating with this nut. Why do the stupid stations keep showing this crap, over and over, when all it does is fuel the fire even more?"

Paul's ranting and raving interrupted Mark's daydreaming. Curiosity pulled him away from the window. "What are you going on about in here?" Mark asked as he turned back to see what all the commotion was about.

"This Mohammed guy and something called The Coalition are demanding money and land and new elections. He even said something about a holy war if their demands are not met. It sounds like the violence has gotten worse since this Mohammed character started giving his speeches. Can you believe the vice president is actually negotiating with these nuts? She ought to send in the army and kick their butts right out of the country," Paul said.

"Now, wait just a minute. They did what? Who is this Coalition and this Mohammed fellow, and what do they want?" Mark asked.

"I'm not exactly sure what The Coalition is, but that Mohammed character is the same one who's been stirring up trouble for years," Paul answered.

"That Islamic nut that's been running around promising the downfall of America?" Marked asked.

"That's the guy. I guess he meant it all along, but no one took him seriously," Paul answered.

"Isn't he the one who took all that money from those terrorist nations years ago?" Mark questioned.

"Yep. Several billion dollars, I believe. Hell, he's probably got enough weapons for a small army of his own. He's nothing but an egotistical maniac. He's probably just trying to get more money and power for himself. He doesn't give a rat's ass about the poor people of this country. If he did, he would have given them all that money and they would all be rich." The more he thought about it, the angrier Paul became.

"I agree," Mark offered.

"He not only has weapons, but he probably has terrorists from all over the world behind him. I'm sure they would like nothing better than a civil war in this country so they can come in and cause as much chaos as possible." Paul was pacing the floor in the lounge. He was too worked up to sit still. "I'll bet this whole thing was started intentionally, just so he could come out with these proposals. I mean, it looked like people were just upset and hungry because of all the unemployment and the economy, but I wonder if these guys didn't just use that as an opportunity to start this so-called revolt. I know one thing—if they give in to them, every God-fearing capitalist in this country will be ready for a fight, including myself."

"Hey, calm down. I'm on your side, remember? Surely, they won't give in to them. If they thought that he was behind all of this, they would arrest him for treason or something," Mark suggested.

Paul was shaking his head in disagreement. "Nope. The liberal leaders of this country have been playing off people like him for years. He suits their purpose. By continuously proclaiming racial inequality and promoting class envy, he ensures their reelection. Without their continuous harping, people might forget that it's the mean-spirited conservatives in our country who are responsible for all their problems," Paul said sarcastically.

"I don't think it's that simple. I know a lot of the liberals believe in all that stuff, but surely none of them would back someone as radical as this Mohammed guy just to get elected. That's crazy. I agree that he is an egotistical maniac who probably only cares about power and that he has a lot of desperate people with little self-worth following him. I think that's the whole problem," Mark argued.

"I'm not saying that the people who are following him are after the same thing he is. They may really feel hopeless. And they may just see this whole mess as a way to get something for themselves. But he is using them to suit his own purpose. Someone has to be behind him and this Coalition, or they wouldn't negotiate with him in the first place. Personally, I think it's Senator Clark. He's the one who's been negotiating with Mohammed," Paul suggested.

"Come on. There is no question that Senator Clark is way out on the left wing, but what we just heard Mohammed and The Coalition propose is pure socialism. Not even Clark is that far left," Mark argued.

"Hey, I'm not the only one who feels this way. A lot of my buddies and many of their friends think the same thing. If this violence continues, I'll bet there will be hell to pay for Mohammed and The Coalition and anyone who stands with them," Paul stated firmly.

Mark could tell he was dead serious. He knew Paul was a friend with many militia members. Paul had mentioned them on a few occasions in confidence. From the conversations, Mark could tell that these people meant business and that there were many of them all across the country. Mark thought about the consequences of them rising up against the rioters and The Coalition. It would be the equivalent of a civil war.

Mark decided to let Paul cool off some, so he excused himself to make his rounds and check on the whereabouts of Mr. Cox.

Mark really wanted to talk to him about all that he and the nurses were having to cope with. Supplies were critically low, and the lack of personnel was critical. They were down to just a handful of nurses in the whole hospital, and most of the lab and radiology technicians had left. There hadn't been anyone in medical records or the cafeteria for days. Patients, their families, the nurses, and most of the hospital employees who were still around were being fed with the small amount of food remaining in the kitchen. Because the ones who stayed were not able to travel back and forth easily, few ventured out. The telephones and the computers were out and, to make matters worse, very few doctors were showing up for work, including Dr. Stanley. Mark was concerned that if something didn't change soon, they would soon be completely out of food, medications, and other critical supplies, not to mention nurses and doctors. He was hoping Mr. Cox was in his office and could offer him some hope or at least assure him that they could get food and medications for the patients.

As Mark passed the ICU, he dropped in to see how things were going there. He was discouraged to see only one nurse in the whole unit. It was Cindy, the pretty young redhead. Mark watched her for a moment before saying anything. She looked very tired, with no makeup on and her hair all a mess, as if she had slept on it. She moved very slowly and kept yawning and rubbing her face and eyes. Mark knew she had probably been there by herself for two or three days straight. Mark didn't want to bother her, but she spotted him standing behind the nurses desk and approached him.

"Dr. Edwards, am I glad to see you. There hasn't been anyone else in here, other than a few family members, for over twelve hours now. The phones went out, and I can't call anyone. I can't get any labs, or X-rays, or blood, or anything. I've had it." She tried to hold it in, but she buried her face in his shoulder and started crying. Mark felt very awkward, but he understood how she felt and let her cry. He also felt a little ashamed for feeling a tinge of passion as she pressed her firm young body against his. Any man would have felt the same way, but he quickly removed those thoughts from his mind and tried to console her.

"I know it's tough, Cindy. How long have you been here?" Mark asked.

"I've been here all weekend. None of the other nurses came in. I know they all have families. All of them, except me. I really don't have anyone. I brought my stuff up here. I feel safer here than in my apartment right now. I just don't know how much longer I can keep going. I'm tired, but there's no one else. I can't just leave these patients." She pulled away gently, smiled, dried her eyes, and apologized for crying on his shoulder.

"Hey, it's okay. I feel like crying myself sometimes. I don't know when all this is going to end. I sure hope it's soon. If it makes you feel any better, I have been in the OR just about all weekend myself. I haven't even seen any of the other surgeons, and I'm not sure, but I don't think any of them are coming back, either. By the way, who is covering for medicine?" Mark asked.

"Dr. Simmons was. I need to tell him a couple of things, but I haven't seen him since yesterday morning. Do you mind if I ask you?" Cindy quickly grabbed the chart and pointed out the rising fever and pulse of the patient in bed two. He had severe emphysema and was on a ventilator. His pulse oximeter showed declining oxygen saturation over the past few hours, as well.

Mark listened to the patient's chest with his stethoscope. The breath sounds in the right lower lung were diminished and coarse, and the chest sounded dull when he tapped on it. Since it appeared that Cindy was going to have to make some difficult decisions on her own, Mark wanted to give her some confidence, so he asked her to make the decision. "What do you think is wrong?"

Cindy hesitated then answered. "I think he may have pneumonia. He has fever, his oxygen is dropping, and the right lung sounds worse to me."

"I agree. Since you can't get an X-ray, you'll have to base your treatment on the physical findings. What do you want to do?"

"Start him on some antibiotics," she said hesitantly.

"What kind?"

"Something with broad coverage, since he has emphysema and is on the ventilator," she answered.

"What do you have?" Mark asked.

"I went to the pharmacy a little while ago and found several doses of this." She handed Mark one of the bottles and waited for his approval.

"Good choice. One gram every eight hours ought to do it." Mark saw her eyes light up and her step quicken.

"Thanks," she said with pride as she prepared a dose to give the patient.

While he was in the ICU, Mark checked on Jeff Veazey in bed three. He appeared much better. He was sitting up and tolerating a liquid diet. His wife was anxiously waiting to get him discharged so they could get their children to a safer place. "Mrs. Veazey, it's a little early for discharge. I would usually keep him another two or three days, but since things are so bad around here, I think all of you would be better off getting out of here. Maybe the nurse can round up a few pain pills and let you go. He'll need to get the stitches out in about a week, and just let him eat whatever he wants." He gave Cindy a nod as he finished his instructions and wrote the discharge orders by hand, since the computers weren't able to connect to the Internet and weren't working.

Before he left, Mark took Cindy to the side to speak to her again. "Look, you're in charge here until you hear from me or one of the other doctors. I trust you, so if you feel you need to make any changes, go ahead, I'll cover you. If anyone wants to make something out of it, tell them to take it up with me, okay?"

"Thanks, Dr. Edwards. I don't know how much longer I can hold on, but as long as I feel like I'm helping, I'll keep trying," Cindy said with renewed determination.

"Until we get some help, that's all we can do," Mark said in frustration as he left for the first floor to finish his rounds.

At first, the first floor seemed relatively quiet, but after a few minutes at the nursing station, Mark realized it was because there were not any nurses or aides on duty. He looked up and down the hallways for several minutes until he ran into the mother of one of his trauma patients. "Mrs. Kimbrough, have you seen any of the nurses lately?"

"Well, I think there was one here last night, but come to think of it, I haven't seen one lately," she answered.

"Thanks. I'll be around to check on your son, in a little while." Mark looked down at his watch. It was about ten forty-five in the morning. He went back to the front desk and pulled a few charts. As he pulled them from the rack one by one, he noted that there were no nurses' notes or orders on any of them since last night. A shudder went through him at the thought that there were no nurses or doctors other than him taking care of the patients on that floor. A sudden urge came over him, so he ran up the stairways to the second floor and was partially relieved to see a nurse at the desk. She too, looked tired and weary. Mark went up to her and spoke. "Am I glad to see you. Do you know what happened to the nurses on the first floor?"

"Yeah, the same thing that happened to my replacement and the others who were supposed to be here over the weekend and today—they're gone."

"You mean they just left?" Mark asked in amazement.

"That's exactly what I mean. What do you expect? She and the others had already been there for three shifts without any relief. I've been here since yesterday afternoon myself, and I'm leaving this afternoon. If someone else doesn't show up to replace me, that's too bad."

Mark gave her a strong look of disbelief. "How can you just leave your patients like that?"

"What do you mean? I'm not even supposed to be here right now. It's not my fault if the others didn't show up. Where are all the doctors? I haven't seen them, either. I've got a family to think about, you know. I'm leaving town before things get any worse." She turned sharply and walked down the hall before he could say anything else to her.

Mark stood there and thought about what she had said. He, too, had mixed feelings about being at the hospital. He felt a strong obligation to be there to take care of the patients. But at the same time, he realized that he should be with his family, as well. He missed Lisa and the boys very much. He had thoughts about leaving, just like the others, and heading south to the farm. As strong as those feelings were, though, he just couldn't walk out on the patients and leave them. He knew many would make it on their own, but many others would not, and he couldn't live with that. *Time to visit Mr. Cox,* he thought to himself as he took off toward the administrator's office.

There was no one in the reception area when he walked in, but that did not surprise Mark. Mr. Cox's door was closed, as usual. Mark walked over and stood next to his door and listened for a few moments. It was quiet inside. He knocked lightly on the door, but there was no answer. He knocked again a little harder. Again no answer. Mark listened again. It was still quiet. He looked around and then slowly turned the doorknob. It was unlocked. As he slowly pushed the door open, he saw Mr. Cox at his desk with his head down as if he was just taking a nap. At first, Mark thought he had probably been there all night working on the personnel and supply problems and was just asleep at his desk. But as he entered the room and stood next to him, it was apparent that Mr. Cox was not asleep. He didn't move or breath at all. He was dead.

Mark reached down and touched his hand. It was cold and stiff. He had been dead for a long time. Mark felt a sudden urge to call someone or do something, but then he quickly realized there was no way to call and no one to help. He thought about what to do with Mr. Cox's body. He couldn't just leave him there at his desk. Mark remembered that Mr. Cox was recently divorced and no longer had anything to do with his ex-wife, but he had mentioned some children. Unfortunately, they were in different parts of the country, and he had no idea where. Mark felt uneasy about it, but he looked in Mr. Cox's wallet to see if he could find a name or address. He could not find one.

Mark decided to go to the emergency room, hoping there would be someone down there willing to help him. As he walked down the hall, all he could think about was how terrible things were looking. As he entered the main area of the emergency room, he was struck at how quiet things were. Considering how busy it was over the weekend, the ER was certainly much quieter than he expected now.

The only nurse on duty was sleeping with her head on the desk. Mark woke her up. "What is going on here? How come it's so quiet?"

She slowly raised her head off the desk and squinted at him. "Dr. Edwards, I didn't know you were still here. What did you say?"

"Why is it so quiet in here?" he asked again.

"Well, Dr. Brandon didn't show up, so I locked the doors. Besides, there haven't been a whole lot of people trying to come in, anyway. I guess they are all getting the hell out of Dodge. As a matter of fact, as soon as my husband gets here, I'm outta here myself. If you're smart, you'll do the same. I've been hearing rumors that things are going to get even worse if the government turns down the demands of The Coalition, or whatever it's called."

Mark interrupted her. "Look! Mr. Cox is dead at his desk in his office, and I need some help."

"What do you mean, he's dead?" she asked in disbelief.

"He's dead. Just like I said. He probably had a heart attack. He looked like his heart was acting up, but he wouldn't see anybody about it. I need some help. We need to move his body to the morgue until we can notify his family and make other arrangements," Mark explained.

"Good luck. There's no one else around, as you can see," she joked with her arms stretched out.

"Where is the nurse supervisor? Is she around?" Mark asked in desperation.

"Are you kidding? Haven't seen or heard from her. I told you, there are very few people around. They're all gone or leaving town."

"Look, we can't just leave him there at the desk until someone else takes care of it," Mark said.

"If you want to move Mr. Cox, I guess you'll have to do it yourself. My husband will be here any minute now, and I don't want to miss him," she said defensively.

Mark saw that he was getting nowhere fast with her, so he decided to let it go and move on. On his way out of the emergency room, he checked the front doors. Sure enough, they were locked. He tried to open them, but they were dead bolted. He returned to the desk and politely asked the nurse for the keys, but she just looked at him, shrugged her shoulders, and laid her head back on the desk. Mark decided to take care of Mr. Cox himself then deal with the ER later.

Before leaving the ER, he found an empty stretcher and wheeled it down the hall to the administration wing into Mr. Cox's office. Next, he pushed it over to the dead body of Mr. Cox at the desk and locked the wheels. He lifted him up and tried to pivot him over to the stretcher. His lifeless body was heavy and stiff. Mark struggled to get him on the stretcher. Rigor mortis had already set in, and no matter how hard he tried, he couldn't get Mr. Cox's body to lie flat. After several more minutes of struggling, Mark finally got him to stay on the stretcher by laying him on his side. Mark covered him with a sheet and slowly wheeled the stretcher down the hall. Just as he rounded the corner to catch the elevators to the basement, the lights flickered twice then went out. Mark noticed how quiet it was. The generators had been running nonstop for two days. They were out of diesel. The lights never came back on.

"Great!" Mark said to himself. "That's just great!" He realized that there was no electricity in the entire hospital. None. No lights other than the emergency battery-powered lights that would run down soon. No anesthesia machines, no air ventilation, no elevators, and, of course, the most immediate problem, no ventilators. When their batteries ran down in a few hours, that would mean the death of the ICU patients, who were all on ventilators. One nurse could hand ventilate only one of them with an ambu bag for a little while before she wore down—much less handle all of them.

As he stood in the hallway holding on to the stretcher in front of the elevators, which were now useless, he felt an almost irresistible urge to just turn and walk away. But deep down inside, there was a part of him that wouldn't give up that easily. A part of him that had always kept him going after everyone else around him had given up. He grabbed Mr. Cox under the arms, pulled him off the stretcher, and slowly dragged the lifeless body into the stairwell, down the dimly lit stairs to the basement, down the long hallway, past the cafeteria, past the main supply room, and to the morgue. When he finally dragged the body through the door into the dark cold storage area, it suddenly occurred to him that, with the electricity off, it wasn't going to be cold much longer. But until he could think of something better, it would have to do.

By the time he disposed of the body, Mark was sweating profusely and exhausted from dragging the two hundred-plus pounds of dead weight the equivalent length of a football field. He was sleepy from being up most of the night, tired from working all weekend, hungry, and totally frustrated by all of the problems that faced him. He also worried about Lisa and the boys and how to let them know he was okay. Mark thought about going home for a little while, to take a shower and perhaps get a little sleep before coming back to help hold down the fort. But, since there were no nurses on duty on the first floor, he decided to go see what he could do for the patients first.

CHAPTER 9
THE SPREAD
OF VIOLENCE

Monday, April 14.

That same morning. Washington, DC.

Vice President Whitman, surrounded by her staff and Secret Service, entered the conference room and quickly took her place at the large conference table. Speaker Wheeler, Senator Sage, Senator Clark, and all of the other Cabinet members were in their usual places. She sat quietly for a moment and studied her notes then addressed the entire group. "Gentlemen, I have listened to the arguments on both sides of this situation and have thought long and hard. These are very difficult decisions. Unfortunately, there are no easy answers. I want to end the violence as much as anyone, but I feel that the demands of The Coalition are unrealistic."

With those words came a low rumble from those gathered in the room, some approving and others disapproving. Senator Clark, the most upset of all, grumbled and shook his head as the vice president continued. "I, too, am reluctant to use our military against our own people, but in order to ensure peace and the protection of our citizens, I have decided to declare martial law. This executive order has already been written up and signed by me. I will make this available to the news media after this meeting. I will be ordering the army to position themselves, defensively, between the rioters and the other citizens. They will be receiving their orders via the Pentagon, through the normal chain of command. Specifically, they will be told not to attack or use violence against either side, unless it is in self-defense. This is the quickest, fairest, and surest way to prevent the further spread of violence. At the same time, I am enacting the National Defense Authorization Act. And therefore, I am ordering all federal, state, county, and city employees to return to work, including all public utility workers, firemen, policemen, paramedics, EMS, hospital based nurses, doctors, and technicians. They are to immediately return to their jobs or report to the nearest available army position, as soon as possible, for assignments. We have a crisis of great proportions on our hands, and we need their services in order to take care of the injured and ensure police and fire protection. Anyone caught failing to report to duty within a reasonable time will be contacted, and, if they refuse, I will authorize the military to detain them. Now, does anyone have any major problems with this plan?"

Senator Clark was the first to speak up. "I share your desire to bring an end to this crisis as soon as possible, but I must insist that the military be kept out of this. There is the potential that their presence would anger the people even further and escalate the violence even more. Even if you instruct them to take a defensive position, there will still be much more bloodshed. I must again remind you that you do not have the constitutional authority to use the army in this manner. As I said before, if you order the troops in, myself and other members of Congress will move to stop them, by any means necessary, even if that includes impeachment proceedings against you. Nothing personal, you understand."

Senator Sage interrupted. "I agree with your decision, Madam Vice President. I only wish we had done it sooner. It's the only way to ensure the protection of the innocent citizens of this country. I would go even further and ask them to go into the cities, flush out the rioters, and bring them to justice, but I am willing to delay that for the time being. However, I do have a problem with trying to force private citizens into public service against their will. If they are willing to help, fine, put them to work. But if they refuse, we don't have the right to detain them against their will. And as far as Senator Clark's threats, he doesn't have the votes, or the guts, to stop you. I'll see to that."

"Thank you for your confidence, Senator Sage. I hope the other members of Congress agree with us. I understand your concern, Senator Clark, but what would you have us do? Let the violence go unchecked? Give in to The Coalition with the hope that they can quiet the protests? There's no guarantee they can," she said.

"Besides, what they are asking for is not ours to give. Only a constitutional amendment by the full Congress can do that, and I'm more than certain that won't happen. If you want to gather the votes and make the changes, go right ahead, and good luck," Senator Sage said sarcastically.

"Maybe I can't get the votes, but I will sure as hell try. Maybe The Coalition can't ensure an end to the violence, but they have promised more violence if you send in the troops. That we do know. These people are desperate. They have no hope for a future in this country as it is now. They feel powerless and sold out by the politicians, big business, and the well-to-do. They have very little to lose. All they have left are the promises of a new beginning in The Coalition. With them, they see a brighter future. As I have said before, the blood will be on your hands," Senator Clark explained.

"That's very touching, Senator, but like I said, what they are proposing is not ours to give. In my opinion, the members of The Coalition are guilty of treason and should be hunted down and brought to justice. They are using this situation to advance their own agenda and force their political goals on the rest of the country. If they want to change this country, they should vote their leaders into office and change the laws. Using violence, threats, and terrorism only leads to more of the same. I cannot believe you would back these criminals. It makes me wonder what you have to gain from all this," Senator Sage suggested.

"What do you mean by that? Are you suggesting that I am involved with these people, other than as a negotiator? I resent your accusations. I'm not going to listen to your insults any longer. You all have made the wrong decision. You will see," Senator Clark said angrily as he stood from his seat and left the room, followed by his aides.

"There's no reason to leave like this," Vice President Whitman said, trying to calm Senator Clark as he left the room. After he left, she stood quietly for a moment to gather herself. "Gentlemen, we have work to do. Let's get started, please."

Soon after the meeting, Vice President Whitman held a news conference to announce her decision to the nation and the details of the military involvement. She was careful to emphasize the defensive position that the army would assume and that troops were being sent in for peacekeeping purposes only. She tried to assure everyone that they would fight only if attacked, and as soon as the violence subsided, they would be withdrawn and replaced by local and state police and National Guard troops.

No sooner had the press conference ended than responses from the leaders of The Coalition were aired on television and radio stations across the country. For the most part, they claimed they were being denied any voice in the government and that their own army and their own government would attack the people who resisted. Jahbul Mohammed and Andrew Smith were shown standing in front of large crowds of people. They were shouting protests against Vice President Whitman, Senator Sage, and other leaders of the government. They declared "the revolt has started" and called on their supporters "to rise up against them." Jahbul Mohammed declared, "The blood of freedom shall flow," and he promised crowd members that they would be rewarded for their part in the holy war.

The violence seemed to spread like wildfire overnight. The Coalition and its millions of supporters unleashed decades of simmering racial and social hatred, and they avenged their own form of justice on the rest of the country. As the rioting and looting spread outside the cities, the sheer number of rioters and marauders intent on "taking what was rightfully theirs" overwhelmed and outgunned those who resisted them. Masses of armed rioters moved in waves into the areas around the cities. Homes and businesses in the suburbs were looted and burned. Churches and schools were ransacked and burned. Water towers, electric substations, and other public utilities were systematically damaged or destroyed, leaving whole suburbs and surrounding towns without power, water, telephone, or other services. Some of the damage appeared to be due to explosives and handheld rocket-propelled grenade launchers, a favored tool of the terrorists.

As the wave of violence spread, innocent people were forced to either fight back or flee in fear. People were forced to take sides in the conflict. There was no middle ground, even for the meek and politically indifferent, to whom the fighting seemed so useless and destructive. It was either fight with the rioters or fight against them, or flee into the surrounding countryside. It wasn't the first time in the country's history that people had taken up arms to settle their differences. Words would no longer suffice. Neighbors were pitted against neighbors and brothers against brothers.

During the night and into the next day, people who initially rode out the first wave of riots were forced to leave the suburbs and towns surrounding the cities in haste. With little time to prepare or plan, they loaded up what they could and headed for safety into the countryside. The streets and highways in and around the larger cities became so congested that traffic was almost at a standstill for miles, which made those stuck on the roads easy targets for the bands of rioters and thieves. In the first week, the roads and highways were merely crowded. The smart ones who foresaw the fall and were prepared for the shit to hit the fan got out of Dodge, and the lucky ones who instinctively left within the first few days after the onset of the riots, were able to escape the burning cities.

But the interstates and highways within and around the major cities were becoming jammed by those trying to flee to safety. Memphis was no exception. Cars and trucks with empty gas tanks littered all major highways and interstates, and the roadways were starting to overflow with families caught up in the logjam of those fleeing the violence. As more stalled vehicles blocked the major interstate routes and highways, even those who did have enough gas were hopelessly stuck with the rest. So they abandoned their vehicles and began walking, carrying their kids and what they could, most with little else but the clothes on their backs.

Many had brought more than they could carry: TVs, computers, family albums, hair dryers, piles of designer clothes, and other things they thought they could not part with. Soon, they discovered they could do without all of it. Some, at least, had the presence of mind to bring along some food and a few useful things, such as flashlights, with all the other stuff. A few outdoor types, who thought they were better prepared than everyone else, brought along their RVs and tents for what they thought would be a short stay at a state park or campground until things got back to normal. They would soon learn that most of this equipment was useless while stuck in the middle of a crowded parking lot on what used to be a highway.

Even fewer of those caught up in the logjam were actually prepared for the situation and grabbed their get-out-of-Dodge bags packed with food, water, camping gear, cash, and weapons and headed down the road. Those who had somewhere safe they could get to quickly fared better than the others. The rest who got out of town but had nowhere to go soon learned that they would have to keep moving, hiding, or protecting themselves from those needing, wanting, and willing to take what they had. In the long run, after all of the food was eaten, the water was gone, and the bullets were used up, those without a safe haven to go to suffered the same fate as the rest. The smart ones who were truly prepared had a safe place to go and left early enough to avoid the masses of refugees. The best prepared left in vehicles that could run off the road around the stalled cars or ram through them, if needed, and carried enough bullets, food, water, gas, and cash to get them where they needed to go. Unfortunately, those who were well prepared were few and far between, because most were not ready for a natural or a man-made disaster. They had nowhere to go, no real plans how to get there, and no significant long-term provisions to sustain them when they got there.

Those with family or friends out in the country still faced the difficult task of getting there. Even the lucky ones who were able to get to the highways and country roads soon learned that they were unprepared for what was ahead. For what used to be taken for granted, such as food and shelter, was often not available along the way, and whatever wasn't stolen or destroyed was kept for use by those who had it. Almost all the motels and hotels in or near the cities were shut down or abandoned. Only those farthest out from the violence were still open, and most of them were filled beyond capacity and short on supplies.

The majority of those fleeing the cities had only enough fuel or battery charge to last a day or two at the most. Even fewer had enough gasoline or batteries to get where they were going, which for many was unknown. The gas stations and battery recharge centers, like the motels and hotels, were prime targets for thieves and highway robbers.

The elderly, the sick, and families with small children, especially those with babies, faced the greatest challenges. It was difficult enough traveling with danger around each turn, but in some places finding baby formula, medical supplies, or enough food to feed their children was almost impossible. Those who were injured or became ill along the way were even more unfortunate, because few, if any, doctors' offices or clinics were open. Only the most heavily guarded inner-city hospitals or those far removed from the violence were still open. Even those were performing only the most basic services for the most seriously injured, because supplies were short and personnel were minimal.

Pharmacies and drugstores were hit hard and ransacked early on by the rioters, along with the grocery stores and supermarkets, which left those with a crucial need for medications in serious trouble.

The few public servants who remained behind in the aftermath of the violence put their own lives at risk, for despite the detailed plans for intervention by the army, the violence spread before the military had time to respond. It takes time to make plans to move armies, and armies take time to mobilize. Not days, but weeks.

CHAPTER 10
MOBILIZATION

Thursday, April 17.

Just three days ago, the executive order was handed down from the secretary of defense to the joint chiefs of staff. It went down the chain of command from the Pentagon to the commanders of the army bases all across the country. It went by telephone to those areas that still had such services and by radio to those that didn't. The orders were clear. All active and reserve members of the US Army and National Guard were to be mobilized into the specified cities, which for the most part included the largest of the metropolitan areas that were hardest hit by the rioting. They were to move in quickly and establish a buffer zone between the inner-city areas where the violence was concentrated and the surrounding suburbs and bedroom communities where the greatest number of citizens were in immediate danger from the further spread of rioting. They were to maintain a defensive position for peacekeeping purposes only and were not to use deadly force, unless they were attacked directly. Besides all of those duties, there were dead to bury, fires to put out, and sick and elderly left behind in the cities to care for.

Despite the orders for immediate mobilization, it took days for the base commanders to organize on such short notice. There were medical supplies, food, water, and other provisions to gather. Then there were logistic and transportation problems of immense proportions that had to be overcome in a few days that would have taken weeks under normal circumstances. And the widespread disruption of electrical power and communications across the country made it even more difficult for them to notify their troops for duty. There were not enough active-duty soldiers around the country to provide protection to all the cities to start with. Many of the army reserve soldiers who did receive the message failed to report for duty, which made the job even more daunting.

After a few days, the first troops started rolling into the cities as ordered, positioning themselves at the outer edge of the most violent-ridden areas. However, there were only a handful of cities that were that fortunate, since most of the troops were still gathering their men, women, and equipment or were en route to their destinations. The problem was, that with over 300 million people in the United States and only about one million active-duty soldiers of any stripe present in the United States at any time, the odds were not good. And with over 250 million people living in the cities, the army faced an impossible task. Of course, troops were sent to the most populous cities first: LA, New York, Chicago, etc., not leaving many to send to those that were down on the totem pole. And, with over fifty cities having more than one million citizens, cities like Memphis were out of luck for the first few days.

When the first troops arrived to set up their buffer zones, they were met with joyful cheers on one side and violent protests on the other. Citizens hoping for protection and an end to the violence were overjoyed to see the convoy of green transport trucks full of troops and armored vehicles roll into their cities and neighborhoods. It was the answer to their prayers. The cavalry had arrived. On the other side of the street, the rioters, murderers, and the like viewed the army as the enemy. The sight of the trucks rolling in struck almost as much terror in them as the rioters did in the innocent citizens. To the rioters, it signaled the possible end of their party.

In the areas where the US Army was able to set up a strong line of defense, the rioters were temporarily held back from advancing farther. However, it didn't take long for the cutthroats, robbers, and such to learn how to go around or through the barriers and roadblocks by pretending to be innocent victims escaping from the violence. Since there was no litmus test or possible way for the troops to tell the rioters from the victims, they poured through their buffer zones like a sieve. With death and ruin and fires burning behind them in the inner cities, they had no reason to stay in the rubble that they left behind. There were many good reasons to leave, though: little food, no water, nothing left to steal, and no one left to prey on, other than each other. So, with little left in the burned-out cities, the predators started leaving, just as their intended victims had done over the previous days, and they headed out into the surrounding areas, outside the buffer zones, to find new places and people to feed off of.

Citizens on the edge of the most violent-prone areas were initially ecstatic by the arrival of the army. For their mere presence had actually halted some of the violence in many areas and even stopped it in others. But in most cases, the violence stopped only in the areas immediately adjacent to the lines of troops, because there just weren't enough soldiers to go around the entire affected areas. In fact, farther out from the buffer zones, those intent on unlawful behavior practiced it unhindered. And, even though the presence of the army may have slowed or even stopped the wave of violence where the soldiers were stationed, it started again outside the cities, on the roads and highways leading into the small towns and suburbs. As the masses of people traveled out into the surrounding countryside to escape the death and destruction in the cities, those responsible for it followed.

It was quickly apparent that establishing and holding a defensive position against the rioters was going to be much harder than expected, leaving those behind to fend for themselves in the meanwhile.

Over the next several days, as the violence continued and spread farther into the surrounding countryside, other areas of the country were affected not only by the mass exodus of people who were straining their supplies and resources, but also because the goods and services that they depended on the cities for were interrupted. Things such as food processing plants, manufacturing plants, electric power plants, petroleum refineries, and telephone, cable, and online information services were either destroyed or cut off all across the nation by rioters hell-bent on inflicting damage to the nation and the terrorists who had been unleashed by The Coalition. Even some of those living in remote rural areas were now feeling the effects of the uprising with loss of electric power, interruption of telephone and cable services, and shortages of gasoline, heating fuel, natural gas, and water.

Even as far south as Batesville, people and cars littered the interstates and highways. Many had gone as far as they could before they needed to rest. Some ran out of gas or battery power, while others simply had nowhere to go. Many people and even families with small children had to camp in fields and in open spaces alongside the interstates and highways. Many were without even the most basic provisions and had to make do with what they had. Some were better prepared with campers, tents, and camping stoves. While some did without basic necessities, others stole or took what they needed or wanted from the other travelers or those who lived nearby. Those who lived on or near the most heavily traveled roads were overwhelmed by the continuous flow of travelers and were inundated by those seeking help or supplies or food. Some were forced to defend themselves and their property from travelers desperate enough to steal. Others were not as fortunate or prepared and were killed, tortured, raped, or run off. On the other hand, homeowners who were prepared to defend their property and family killed some of the travelers.

Even farther out on the smaller highways, the travelers, who were refugees in their own country, became stranded or stopped to rest for the night. The charitable nature of the country folks who lived in these outlying areas was greatly tested. For the most part, they did what they could for the refugees, in the way of providing food and allowing them to camp along the roads. But they, too, were often short on the same things the refugees needed, such as gasoline, food, and freshly charged batteries for their cars, cell phones, and gadgets. Some of the fortunate refugees were taken in by the more charitable people, but others were not so lucky and ended up wandering farther out into the countryside, hoping to find shelter and food instead of a fight.

At the farm, Grandpa and Grandma Brown had noticed an increase in traffic along the main road down front. They had even seen what looked like a young black family walking along the road a little while ago. Now, Grandpa watched them from the porch and noticed that they had stopped to rest. As he studied them, he noticed there were two little children with them who appeared very tired. His initial reaction was to run them off, but after watching them for a while, he realized they weren't looking for trouble. He decided to see if he could help, so he grabbed his shotgun and went down to the road to see what they wanted. Grandma and Lisa watched from the front window as Grandpa approached the man slowly. As he got closer to the strangers, they could see the man back away and turn to his wife and kids, who started running away.

As Grandpa approached him, the man started yelling, "Don't shoot. We aren't looking for any trouble, mister." The man started backing away, holding up his hands.

"Why would I shoot you if you haven't done anything?" Grandpa asked.

The man looked puzzled for a moment, then realized Grandpa meant it. "Because we are—" The man stopped before finishing his answer.

Grandpa thought for a moment then realized the man thought that he was going to shoot at them or run them off just because they were black. "Look, mister, I just came down here to see what you needed. I saw you had some small children with you, and we figured they had to be hungry and tired."

"You mean you came down to help us?" the man asked in disbelief.

"That's what I said," Grandpa offered.

"Why would you help us?" he asked, cautiously.

"You mean, why would I help a black man, or why would I help a stranger?" Grandpa said in jest.

"Both, I guess," the man answered back.

"Where you from, the city?" Grandpa asked as he watched the man's family running down the road.

"Memphis."

"That figures. Is everyone there as paranoid as you?" Grandpa kidded.

"I'm not paranoid. I'm just not used to folks I don't know being nice to me, especially a white man," he explained.

"Well, if you're going to hang around here, you're going to have to get over that. Folks out here don't judge a man according to his skin color, just his heart. It seems to me you have a good heart," Grandpa told him.

"Thank you, sir. I'm sorry. It's just that we've been through a lot, and the people in the city are not always nice. As a matter of fact, most of them are downright mean right now. We left there a few days ago to get away from all that and came down here to find my uncle's place," he explained.

"Your uncle's place? Where's that?" Grandpa asked.

"I'm not exactly sure. He died a few months ago, and I got a letter saying he was leaving the place to me, since he didn't have any children. I guess it's still going through probate or something, because I haven't heard anything else. I spent a lot of summers down here as a kid, but other than the letter, I haven't seen or heard from him in years. I'm pretty sure it's down this road."

All of a sudden, it struck Grandpa who he was. "You're not Mr. Thompson's nephew, are you?"

"Yes, sir, sure am. Did you know him?" he asked.

"Know him? Hell, son, he worked for me for years, before he got his own place."

"You mean you know where it is?" the man asked excitedly.

"Sure I do. Just a mile down the road. Right across from my east property line. My wife took food over there every Sunday after church, back when his wife was sick last year. Believe it or not, I remember you, son. Wondered whatever happened to you. Looks like you're all grown up now," Grandpa said as he playfully grabbed his shoulder and gave him a little squeeze. "Well, it's getting late. Probably ain't gonna be no food or lights down there. Ya'll might as well come up and stay the night. Better wait and take you there in the morning, so we can help ya'll get set up. By the way, the name's Brown," Grandpa said as he reached out his hand.

The man was so surprised and relieved that he almost started to cry, and then he shook Grandpa's hand really hard. "Thompson, Jerry Thompson. Thank you very much."

"Well, if y'all are going to come up to the house for some supper, you better go catch those kids and wife of yours," Grandpa joked. As Jerry turned and ran back and hollered for them to stop and come back, Grandpa chuckled to himself.

Grandma and Lisa watched everything from the window. At first Grandma thought the visitors were leaving, but then she saw the man gather up his wife and children and follow Grandpa up the drive. Grandma smiled and announced to the others, "Looks like we are going to have company for dinner tonight, folks."

Grandpa entered the front door and invited the travelers in. "Guess who I have here, folks. This is Jerry and Wanda Thompson and their two children, Doug and Cathy. They are from Memphis. Jerry is the nephew of ole Leroy Thompson. They came down here hoping to stay at his farm, but their car ran out of juice just up the road. They couldn't remember exactly where his place was. As far as I know, no one is staying there, and the old place is still in pretty good shape. I asked them to stay here with us tonight and have supper. Then in the morning, we can take them over there and help them get set up."

"Well, we're glad to have you, folks. I'm sure you're tired, and those two young ones of yours are probably starving. Ya'll come on in, and we'll put some food on the table," Grandma said proudly.

Just then, Wanda, the new visitor, started crying in relief. "I'm so grateful to you. I didn't know what we were going to do. We didn't know where else to go, or what else to do, other than come down here. We got caught up in the traffic. The kids are tired and hungry. Thank you so much," she said, sobbing on Grandma's shoulder.

"Now, now. Don't you worry, dear," Grandma said as she led them inside. "You're safe here. Now, let's get ya'll cleaned up for supper."

CHAPTER 11
IN THE
DARKNESS OF NIGHT

Thursday, April 17.

Within a few days of the announcement of the military intervention, the wave of violence escalated throughout the area, essentially cutting off the hospital from the rest of the world. Most of the remaining employees had left for good, and patients who were able to left on their own or were taken away by their families. Only a few nurses and doctors remained to care for a couple of dozen or so of the terminally ill, those too sick to move, and a few who just didn't have anywhere to go. Besides Dr. Mark Edwards, only Dr. John Osborne from the ER, Paul Black and his wife, Martha, Nurse Cindy from the ICU, and a few other nurses from various floors chose to hold out in the darkness of the hospital.

Although no direct attacks had been made against the hospital, on several occasions carloads of youths and truckloads of thugs drove through the parking lots, looted some of the cars at the outer edges of the parking lots, and randomly shot at the hospital. Since almost everyone else in the surrounding area had fled, no one had come to the emergency room for the past day or so. Anyone who was shot or beaten was left for dead, because those who were left were unwilling to take them to the hospital for fear of their own life. So those who remained in the hospital locked all the doors to the outside for their own protection.

Despite the apparent dangers around them, they all agreed to stay put, as long as the rioters left them alone and the patients needed them. Of those who remained, only Dr. Edwards had a safe place to go to away from the city. A couple of days ago, the others tried to convince Mark to leave and go be with his family. But, just as he decided to leave, the rioting closed in on them, and then it was too dangerous to go.

They all resigned themselves to the fact that they were stuck where they were until the National Guard or US Army came to their rescue, so they set up a makeshift camp in the cafeteria on the first floor. Just before the riots closed in around them, Sally Reynolds, one of the nurses, brought some oil lamps and candles and food to the hospital to help prepare meals for the patients. The others followed her lead and brought food, blankets, cookstoves, and other camping gear from their homes, not realizing at the time that it would be needed for themselves, as well.

Mark brought his backpack with him on his last trip home, along with some extra MREs and lanterns, not knowing then he would be going back home very soon. He also brought his Beretta 9mm pistol and extra clips up to his locker, even though he knew it was forbidden to bring firearms into the hospital. But at that point, he wasn't as concerned about the rules so much as just staying alive. There was also an AR-15 rifle with more ammo and MREs hidden in the spare tire compartment of his Explorer just outside the ER, where he hoped it would be safe for the time being.

After the ventilator batteries ran out and despite their best efforts, the few remaining patients in the ICU died, so they moved the surviving patients from other floors to the large ground-floor conference room next to the cafeteria. They formed a makeshift sick ward to make it easier to care for the patients and to avoid the stray bullets from outside. With the two dozen or so patients crammed into one room with nothing but sheets draped between the beds, the whole scenario resembled the charity wards of the old public hospitals of days gone by.

The group gathered in the cafeteria to discuss the situation and make plans for the next few days. Thus far, they had been able to work around most of the problems, such as the lack of supplies, electricity, telephones, and other utilities. But now, with the food running low and the water pressure quickly running out, they knew they were headed for trouble. They would need more food and water if they had to stay there much longer. Hunger was one thing, but water was essential. Mark knew they could go only about three or four days, at the most, without water before they would die.

Again, talk of being rescued by the National Guard or US Army circled the room. But, despite their hopes, everyone agreed that the water shortage was the most pressing problem, other than the ever-present danger from the rioters outside. Somehow, they would have to find a source of water soon. Despite the risk of injury outside and objections from his wife, Paul volunteered to

go out early in the morning and look for water. Mark appreciated his enthusiasm.

After the group agreed on a work schedule and divided up
the patient care and other duties, those who could went to bed
for the night. Dr. Edwards went to his makeshift bedroom in the
back of the small dining room off the back of the main cafeteria.
He could have slept in one of the call rooms, but he chose an
area farther away from the outside walls, just in case stray bullets
found their way into the hospital. His small room had no windows and only a small mattress on the floor. Dr. Osborne went
across the hall to the patient ward for his night on duty. Paul
stayed with his wife in the other small room off the dining room.
The nurses took turns sleeping across the hall in the chapel next
to the conference room. Their few flashlights, lamps, and lanterns were put to use by those on duty in the patient ward and
kitchen areas, where they were needed most, leaving the sleeping areas in darkness at night, except for a few flickering candles
to dress by.

Mark settled onto his sleeping bag on the makeshift bed on
the floor for the night. Despite being exhausted from the stress
and daily duties they all had to contend with in trying to care for
the sick, as well as themselves, under such meager conditions, he
couldn't fall off to sleep right away. His thoughts kept returning
to Lisa and the boys and his regrets for not going with them. His
sense of duty to care for the sick had interfered with his sense of
responsibility for his family one time too many. He kept telling
himself that if he had it to do over again, he would have gone
with them when he had the chance. Although he took some consolation in the fact that he was needed where he was and that if
he had left several people might have died, he still kept coming
to the conclusion that his family should have come first. Even

though he knew they were safe, he felt guilty for not being there when they needed him on the way to the farm.

He wondered how he and the others were going to get out of this situation. He chose not to leave before, but now he knew they might have to leave for their own safety. They were surrounded by violence, without any realistic hope of protection by the police or anyone anytime soon, as far as they knew. A city police officer did come by two days ago and said he or someone from the force would try to come back by and check on them, but no officers had been seen since. The few patients left were totally helpless, and if they were abruptly abandoned, they would surely die. Yet the food and water were running out fast, and unless some supplies could be found soon, they might all die anyway. Mark also recalled that after Hurricane Katrina, inner-city hospitals were left to fend for themselves without food, or water, or protection.

He also remembered that the medical staff at Charity Hospital in New Orleans was left to deal with the entire hospital and the critically ill patients, some of whom died in their care due to circumstances out of their control. And those same medical staff members were later blamed for not doing enough, even though they went way beyond the call of duty. It was later determined that they displayed courage and made a heroic effort to help everyone they could with little medicine, no power, no water, no food, and no communications internally or with the outside world. There was no outside help—no police force, no paramedics, and no firefighters—for a long time, and people died. Hard decisions had to made about whom they could save and whom they had to let go. Anyone who has been in a similar life-and-death situation knows that is the way it is: You save whom you can, and some die. Mark also understood that in those kinds of situations, it's natural for even public servants and National Guard troops to abandon their posts. They have family and homes and businesses to take care of as well, and for most those come first.

He thought about his options. He could sneak out at night with his pack and supplies and make his way to the farm. He was confident he could make it by taking the back roads and approaching the farm from the east, where there would be fewer people and less traffic. If he ran into trouble and couldn't make it all the way by car, he could hike there. He had everything he needed in his pack to survive almost any situation: a small tent, a WhisperLite stove with fuel, a three-day supply of MREs, a flashlight, a PUR water filter, waterproof matches, a magnesium strip, a one-liter water bottle, utensils, cooking pan, extra clothes, a raincoat, gloves, boots, and a first aid kit. With all that and the 9mm with ammo in his locker and the AR-15 with extra clips and a few extra MREs in his car, he would be fine on his own.

But leaving the others and the patients like that just wasn't something he could bring himself to do. So he decided to stay put and make the best of the situation and hope it would all end soon, or that the police or National Guard would come and bring supplies and protection. Or, if no help, or supplies, or water were forthcoming, then he could wait it out with the others until the very end and leave with them when there was no other option. His last thought before falling asleep was that maybe luck would be on their side and help would come in the morning.

Sometime in the middle of the night, Mark was awakened from a restless sleep by the sound of someone close by breathing in the darkness. Mark turned his head slowly and strained his eyes, but he could see nothing. He thought at first it was Dr. Osborne coming into the room for something he forgot, but he would have brought a lamp or flashlight with him. The sound of gentle breathing and the smell of perfume came closer and closer. Mark remained still as long as he could, hoping whoever it was would think he was sleeping and would go away. Just as he decided to say something, he felt a smooth hand touch his arm and a soft voice whisper his name.

"Dr. Edwards."

At first, he couldn't tell who it was, but from the sound of her voice he figured it was a nurse who needed his help in the ward or something, so he answered her.

"Yes. What is it?"

She knelt down next to him without answering. He could smell her perfume and feel her warm breath on his face. Mark was not exactly sure of her intentions at that moment, so he just kept still and quiet and waited for her to say something.

She reached down and gently touched his chest. "Dr. Edwards. I'm scared." It was Cindy.

Before Mark realized what she wanted or what to say or what to do, she was lying next to him. Her firm young breasts were pressed against his bare chest. Cindy was young and full of uninhibited passion. She wasn't sure how Mark would react, but she figured that with the situation they were all in, the usual rules did not apply anymore. After all, they were stuck there for who knows how long, and there was even some uncertainty if they would get out. And his wife was somewhere else and would never have to know. Cindy had thought about it for a long time and felt as if the opportunity had come. So despite the possibility of rejection, a chance she was willing to take, she kissed him and pressed herself against him even more, letting him know she wanted him.

At first, Mark was too surprised to react, but then his senses returned and he tried to fight the strong, natural human urges.

Her firm body felt good to him. Despite his best efforts not to, he found himself attracted to her, as any normal man would. It had been a while since he had been with his wife, and Cindy was openly offering herself to him. It was almost impossible for him to resist her. His mind told him to do one thing, but his body was telling him to do another. He could have easily excused his actions, and Mark knew he would probably regret what he was about to do.

"Cindy. I can't," Mark said as gently as he could. She hesitated for a moment but then she kissed him again, deep and long, and her hand found what she wanted. Mark almost gave in at that point, and for one brief moment, he felt a spark of passion that could have turned into a wildfire that night. He could tell by her kiss and touch that she was full of passion. It was more than a man could bear, more than a man should be expected to. But just as he was about to give in and enjoy the desire that was swelling up in him, a voice called out to him from somewhere deep inside his soul. And despite the overwhelming pleasure that he was about to find, a pleasure that would be difficult for any man to resist, he somehow found the strength to push her away. "Cindy, I'm sorry. I just can't."

Cindy hesitated momentarily. "Why not? It looks to me like you can," she said half-jokingly as she held him firmly.

"It's not that. I just can't. I'm married. I just can't do this," Mark said, hoping Cindy would understand.

"But she won't know," Cindy pleaded, finding it hard to suppress the fire that burned within her. Mark tried to push her away again, but she had waited for that moment too long to give up so easily. "You don't know how I feel about you. I wouldn't do this with just anybody. It's more than that. I felt it when we kissed, and I know you felt it too," Cindy said in desperation, hoping he would give in and not let principles stand in the way of her desire.

Mark touched her face gently. "I could easily fall for you. You're young and beautiful. And in a different place and time, this would have been wonderful. But if you and I were married to each other, would you want me to be doing this with someone else?" Mark asked sincerely.

Cindy slowly let go of him and sat up, realizing that Mark was right. She wanted Mark, but when she thought of them being married and him being with another woman, it made her realize that what she was doing wasn't right. Then she felt ashamed of herself for trying to seduce him. "I'm sorry," she said as she hung her head and cried tears of pain and shame.

"Don't be sorry. I'm very flattered that you care for me. If things were different, who knows, we might have been great together. I don't want you to hate me, but I have to get back to Lisa and my boys. I hope you understand," Mark explained as he sat up next to her.

"I don't hate you," she said as she dried her eyes. "I understand. You're right."

"Look. You better get back before the others start talking. You know how rumors can go around," Mark said jokingly.

Cindy laughed softly. "I don't care what those old hags think. Who are they to say anything? They have all been married and divorced several times. I guess it just goes with the territory."

"Well, you're different, and I don't want anyone to think bad of either of us. So sneak back off to bed and get some sleep. Morning is going to come awful early," Mark said.

"Okay," Cindy said as she pulled her robe back around herself and gave him a friendly good-night kiss on the cheek and quietly left the room.

Mark lay there in the still of the night thinking how close he came to crossing a line he swore he would never cross. Another kiss or one more minute of her warm, young body next to his might have taken him past the point of no return. It frightened him to think how easy it would have been to give in to her. At that point, he became even more determined to make it through all of this and be with Lisa and his boys.

Just as he was about to drift off to sleep, he heard someone coming through the doorway into the room again. He first thought it was Cindy and that she had changed her mind and was coming back for another try. He hoped he had the courage to resist her a second time. It was difficult enough before, but the thought of what it might have been like could drive a man to do things he wouldn't ordinarily do. Before he could decide what he would do or say to her, the soft voice of a child cried out in the darkness. It was Tammy. Mark sat up and searched the darkness for her with his eyes. "Tammy, what's the matter?"

"I'm scared," she sobbed. It had been only a short time since her parents were killed, and the memory of that terrible night still haunted her. The uncertainty of life without her parents overwhelmed her. She was searching for comfort and reassurance from someone who cared. Tammy tried to seek comfort from the nurses, but they seemed too busy to give her the kind of attention she needed. So she turned to the only person whom she felt really cared for her.

"It's okay," Mark said as he hugged her, sensing the pain in her little voice. It broke his heart to see a child suffer that way, and a tear rolled down his cheek as he held her and let her cry. After a little while, she quietly fell asleep in his arms. Mark didn't think it would look right to let her sleep in his room, so he picked her up and made his way through the hospital back to her room in the ward. On his way back, he ran into one of the nurses in the hallway.

"My, you're popular tonight," she said as she gave him a fake smile.

Mark rolled his eyes, shook his head, and kept walking without saying a word. *Great,* he thought to himself as he found his way back to his room. *I didn't do anything, but the rumors have already started. Let them think what they want.* He was too tired to fight it. As he passed Paul's room, he could see a figure in army fatigues in the faint candlelight. He appeared to be getting ready for battle. He had a field belt on with what looked to be a pistol on his right side, covered by a jacket, along with a flashlight, a couple of wrenches, and a pair of pliers sticking out of his pockets. Mark glanced at his watch. It was only 5:00 a.m. Paul saw Mark as he passed by and came to the door.

"You're up early. Have some late-night visitors?" Paul said with a wink.

"It's not what you think," Mark insisted.

"Well, you don't have to worry about me. I won't say anything," Paul kidded.

"Look, nothing happened. We talked and then…never mind. It doesn't matter. You're up early yourself," Mark said to change the subject.

"Yeah. Thought I better get out before daylight while things are quiet outside," Paul offered.

"Where are you going this time of day?" Mark asked.

"To the water tower just across the field. We need water, and I agreed to try and find some, so I figured I would go over and check it out. I thought it might be a little safer this time of day. Most of the bad guys should be sleeping, but just in case…" Paul said as he tapped the pistol on his side.

"What are you going to do?" Mark asked, wondering about the details of his plan.

"Well, there's no water because the electricity is off, which means the pumps aren't working, but there may still be water left in the tower. First I'm going to check the drain valves and hope I can get some out that way, but if I can't, I'm going to shoot a hole in the pipes and get what I can. If this works, we should be able to carry enough water over from time to time to make it for a little while. Maybe by then, all this will be over," Paul explained.

"That sounds like a good plan, but if you shoot a hole in the pipes, won't that waste what's left in there? We may need that later," Mark suggested.

Paul held up a couple of corks and a role of duct tape he had found in the kitchen and smiled. "Already thought of that, Doc."

Mark smiled back and patted Paul on the shoulder. "You're a regular Boy Scout, aren't you? Always prepared. Good luck, and be careful out there. I can still hear gunshots from time to time." Mark watched as Paul set out on his mission. He could only hope that Paul was right about this all being over in a few days.

Everything that people had become dependent on for their daily comfort, and even the very mechanisms of modern civilization itself, required electricity and computers and machines. Without electricity, there was no power to run the machines that took the place of manual labor to make, transport, package, and distribute goods and food. There were no computers to run the banks and stores and businesses they needed to buy food and goods. No power for lights, transportation, communications, heat, or air-conditioning for the homes and businesses. But worst of all, no pumps to provide water. Mark knew they could make it without the lights and air-conditioning, if needed. With their supplies miserably low and many medicines already gone, some of the weaker and terminally ill patients had already died. And even though they were in desperate need of a few things themselves, they could make do for a little longer.

But since the refrigerators weren't working, the food was spoiling and the supply was critically low, and it would only feed a few people for several days at the most. And with the dozen or so patients and the staff to feed, they were headed for trouble quickly, even if the violence outside managed to stay there. Without water, none of that would matter. The thought occurred to Mark that he should have gone with Paul, but by then he was long gone. Mark told himself that if Paul did manage to find some water, he would go with him the next time to help carry what he could. He went to his room to wait for Paul's return and, hopefully, get a little rest before his turn at duty in the sick ward at 7:00 a.m., which was just a little over two hours away.

Outside, all was quiet and peaceful at the moment. Paul slipped through the parking lot, pleased with his decision to carry out his mission in the early morning hours. The sun was just now starting to peak, ever so slightly, over the distant horizon to the east. There was still smoke rising from the smoldering fires, giving the sunrise a strange bluish hue. Paul crouched next to a car with broken windows at the southeastern corner of the parking lot. A large field of waist-tall sage lay between him and the water tower about one hundred yards away. Fifty yards to his left, a stand of hardwood trees and brush grew along the drainage ditch that ran behind the hospital, toward the interstate to the west. One last look reassured him that all was clear.

Just as he was about to step out into the field, he heard a vehicle round the corner from the other side of the hospital, coming from the main street and into the front parking lot area behind him. Paul stepped to the other side of the car next to him to stay hidden and then peered around the side to see who it was. By the speed and erratic movement of the pickup, Paul figured that whoever was behind the wheel must be either drunk or high or in a big hurry. As Paul watched the truck get closer, it became apparent that several armed men were sitting in the back, and they appeared to be looking for trouble. They drove around the hospital shooting out any windows still left partially intact from the other recent raids. When no return fire came, they stopped next to an abandoned car in the back of the employee parking lot. In the matter of a few moments, the men piled out of the back of the truck, broke out the windows, pried open the trunk and hood, took the spare tire, radio, and battery, and siphoned the gas. Paul sat as still as he could and watched the men do their work. They were as efficient at what they did as vultures were at picking meat off the bones of a dead carcass. To Paul, they were not much higher in the evolutionary chain. It would have been more than satisfying to sneak up on them and empty a couple of clips from his Glock .40 on them, but caution seemed to be the best course. After they finished stripping their prey clean, they quickly loaded up in the truck and took off.

To Paul's utter dismay and disbelief, they were coming directly toward him. He knew that if they came much closer, they might see him. If they were to pull up next to him, he would not have enough coverage to hold them off for very long, and his route of escape back to the hospital would be cut off. He looked around to see what his options were. The water tower in the clearing was definitely out. The woods by the ditch would be his best bet if needed, but for the moment he decided to stay put. The only problem with that plan was that the truckload of thugs was still coming right at him. A big, heavy-set bearded man with long, greasy brown hair stood just behind the cab. He pointed in

Paul's direction and shouted something at the others. Paul had been spotted.

Paul figured he had to move quickly or be trapped where he was. He was one against many, and they were armed to the hilt with rifles and pistols. The odds were definitely not in his favor if he stayed there. He made his move as the truck veered around a skeleton of a car at the other end of the parking lot row in which he was hiding. He sprinted across the field toward the woods as fast as he could, running in a zigzag pattern to make himself a more difficult target in case they opened fire on him. To his pleasant surprise, no shots were fired, but he did hear a lot of shouting and the truck speeding in his direction. The truck roared closer and closer as he ran for the trees. They were going to run him over. Just as he could hear the truck right behind him, he dived to the side and rolled back to his feet and continued toward the trees. The truck turned sharply and slid sideways, preparing to make another run at him. Paul calculated the distance to the woods against the speed of truck and knew he had a chance, maybe. Just as he crashed through the trees and brush, the truck skidded to a halt in the clearing behind him. Although they could no longer see him as he pushed deeper into the brush and slid down the side of the ditch, they cursed at him and opened fire in his general direction just the same.

Paul was out of breath, but the sound of bullets zinging just over his head inspired him to scurry down the ditch toward the back of the hospital. As he splashed through the water and mud, he could hear the men running through the trees and brush at a distance behind him, cursing vulgarities at him the whole way. The group consisted of a half dozen or so dope heads, pushers, thugs, and the like, none of whom was much into physical activity other than an occasional short run from a cop or a quick trick with a cheap whore. The ones who did make it to the ditch gave up the chase after they spotted Paul rounding a turn some distance from where they stood. So just for good measure, they cursed at him some more and shot several rounds in his direction.

Mark Edwards awoke to the sound of the gunfire close by outside. He brushed the cobwebs from his mind and stumbled up the stairs to the back side of the southwest wing, where the shots sounded the closest. He peered around the wall and out the window into the light of dawn rising over the woods behind the hospital. At first, he could not tell where the shots were coming from. He scanned the parking lots to the west and east but saw only the cars and trucks scattered about in the parking lots. After another moment or so, he spotted a truck loaded with armed men moving down the field next to the woods. They seemed to be looking for something or someone. Then it occurred to Mark: *They're looking for Paul.* At that moment, he saw Paul, covered with mud and wet from head to toe, dash from the ditch behind the woods and run full speed toward the loading dock in the back of the hospital, where he had left from earlier in the morning. The men in the truck spotted him at the same time and sped toward him with their guns aimed in his direction, ready to fire at him when they had a shot.

Fortunately, Paul had only a short distance to cover. He cleared the road and bolted through the door before they could get any shots off. Out of frustration they fired several rounds at random toward the back of the hospital as they sped past the back door just as the door slammed shut. Not quite ready to commit a direct assault on the building itself, mostly out of fear of the unknown enemy within, they drove away swearing to return later to finish the job.

Mark saw Paul, all out of breath dripping mud and water into a puddle on the otherwise clean tile floor in Central Supply, standing behind a metal cabinet with his gun drawn, watching and waiting for anyone to break through the door. Mark cautiously called out for Paul and then assured him that the truck full of men had driven off. He also said they promised to return. After Paul caught his breath and calmed down enough to talk, they decided that it would be best to tell the others about the incident and make plans just in case they did come back. Although they were both thankful that Paul was not seriously hurt, neither could celebrate for long, since they still had no water to show for all his efforts, except for the puddle on the floor under Paul's feet.

CHAPTER 12
THE BURNING

Thursday, April 17.
Later that day.

The rest of the group gathered around Paul in the cafeteria to hear his account of the attack. His story would have seemed too remarkable to believe had they had not all heard the gunshots outside earlier that morning and witnessed all the violence of the past couple of weeks. After he finished, Paul's wife, Martha, and the other nurses were visibly shaken and sat quietly for a moment as the reality of it soaked in. After some discussion, they all agreed that, despite the risks, someone would have to make another attempt at getting water. The only question remaining was, should they go out again right away, or wait until after dark? Paul and Mark agreed that it would probably be safer for them to go out after dark and make their way along the shadows of the moonlit trees at the edge of the woods. They all agreed that it was just a matter of time before the roughnecks came back for them, perhaps this time with some larger group even more determined to see what sort of treasures were behind the walls of the hospital.

Fortunately, they did have a few weapons with them. After the attack on Paul, Mark decided that the AR-15 and ammo and MREs were needed inside, rather than in the car. Besides Mark's 9mm pistol and AR-15, there was Paul's AR-15 and shotgun, along with several boxes of shells for each and his Glock .40 that he had brought to the hospital earlier in the week. Everyone knew firearms were forbidden in the hospital, but few objections were raised when the guns were brought inside. Under the circumstances, the most of them were glad they finally had some firepower on their side for a change. Next time, Paul and Mark would go out well armed while the others kept a close lookout and signaled them at the first sign of trouble.

The mobilization of the US Army by Vice President Whitman still offered some hope that order would once again be established in the area—hopefully before they starved from thirst or hunger or were attacked again. No details about the timing or intended destinations of the troop mobilizations were given on the radio, other than to mention that troops would be sent to the most populated and violent-prone areas of the country first, and that all active-duty and army reserve personnel were ordered to report immediately.

Needless to say, they all hoped and prayed that Memphis and its suburbs would be included in the mobilization areas, and that it would be sooner rather than later. Mark had known these people for a number of years and had surmised that most of them had not been faithful about religion in the past. He found it very odd that, like many of his sickest patients who thought they might die, they too all of a sudden found religion. Although most of them weren't regular churchgoers and seldom prayed on a regular basis before all this trouble started, it seemed that they had all done their fair share of it recently. And he had noticed Paul and his wife reading the Bible to Tammy on occasion.

After the meeting, Mark went back to the ward and helped out with the sick as much as he could. The air was heavy with the odors of feces, urine, and bile. The beds were covered with dirty and soiled linens. Bedpans and urinals were in desperate need of a good rinsing. The patients were scared and reeked of their own excrement and body odors. They were all in need of a good bath, but there wasn't enough water even to drink, much less wash with. There was also the odor coming from the decomposing bodies in ICU and upper floors of the hospital. They would have to dispose of them soon, but the problem was where and when. They couldn't stack them up outside like cordwood, but if they left the bodies inside, the smell would eventually overcome them, even with all the doors shut off to the upper floors.

Other things they had no means of doing also needed to be done, so Mark and the others tried to focus on what they could accomplish. There were drugs to be mixed, injections to be given, open wounds to be packed, and limbs to be wrapped. There were few, if any, sterile bandages, and the medications were running out, so they made do with what they had. Almost all the usual medications used for treating the more common illnesses were long gone. They were down to giving outdated and second- and third-line drugs and even using different combinations of medications to keep some of the sicker ones going.

Most everyone was downright miserable from not having air-conditioning, lights, refrigerators, running water, hot showers, and all those other little things that make life more comfortable. Mark, however, was getting along fairly well, as was Paul.

Paul's military training had prepared him for situations such as this, and Mark, having grown up with a lack of comforts in his youth, found it easier to adjust, as well. Mark had also been an avid outdoorsman and often camped with his boys and knew how to make do with few personal comforts. While the others were constantly complaining and bemoaning all the discomforts and inconveniences, Mark and Paul continued to maintain an upbeat attitude and at times even poked a little fun at the others for their lack of coping skills.

Dr. Osborne was becoming more and more irritable each passing day, to the point of being almost belligerent toward the others. He had grown up in a wealthy family, surrounded by comfort all his life, and he lived in an exclusive neighborhood just outside Memphis, surrounded by rich executives and lawyers and the like whose idea of roughing it was running out of chilled wine in the middle of a dinner party. Cindy was coping well, perhaps because she was young and Dr. Edwards was there and whenever he was present, she was fine. Like the other women, she found it rather repulsive not to be able to bathe or take better care of the other delicate things that women, by their very nature, have to deal with.

Little Tammy was already so distraught over the death of her parents that it was hard to tell if the uncomfortable surroundings and hunger were bothering her, or whether she was still simply overcome by grief. She had, however, seemed to perk up just a little whenever Mark was around or when Paul or Martha would read to her.

There were times, though, that all of them felt the immense stress and fear of the violence squeezing in tighter and tighter on them. And despite trying to keep an upbeat and positive attitude, even Mark and Paul were unsure how the next few days would turn out. They were essentially out of food and water, and if relief didn't come soon, they would all die of thirst or, for those who could, be forced to leave. And although to the best of their knowledge the army was being mobilized, they had no way of knowing if troops would arrive in time to fend off other possible attacks from the thugs.

Except for Mark's battery-powered emergency radio that they listened to, to keep up with what was happening in the country, they were essentially cut off from the rest of the world. Since the phones and other forms of communications were all down, there was no effective way to send out any messages for help—and probably no one nearby who could or would help anyway. So the idea of going for help was discussed. They decided that rather than try for the water tower, they would send two people for help, using one of their cars that was parked outside the ER door that hadn't been shot up or ransacked.

The problem was it seemed very risky, and there was also the question of whom to send and where to go, since they had not seen any police or emergency vehicles in several days—only angry bands of thugs and gun-wielding bandits. Just as they were finishing rounds in the sick ward that morning, the sound of revving motors and screeching tires accompanied by rounds of gunfire came closer and closer outside. It was a sound they had all heard many times over the past several days, but it was not something they would get used to.

Shots once again tore through the bullet-riddled walls and shattered windows of the first floor above them as they hunkered down on the ground floor beneath the level of the parking lots outside. They listened as the glass shattered and bullets ricocheted in the hallways just over their heads. As they waited for the attack to subside as the others before had, it became obvious that something was different this time. Instead of waning after a few seconds, the shots continued to ring out for several minutes, which to them seemed like hours.

Then suddenly the shooting stopped, and the sound of a car screeching to a sudden stop and doors slamming shut brought a sense of terror to them. Then it became deathly quiet. For a moment, no one moved a muscle as they listened for the next sound above. Paul instinctively went for his pistol and shotgun and handed Mark his rifle. Paul continued to listen as he moved quietly to the doorway of the cafeteria and looked out into the hallway. Just then, the sounds of a vehicle slamming into the front of the ER and doors and windows crashing in above them startled everyone. Paul looked at Mark and asked, "You coming?" Then without hesitation, he disappeared into the hallway, against the protests of the others.

"Yeah, sure," Mark said, as he shook his head then followed after him as far as the doorway. He didn't feel that he had any choice in the matter, since Paul had already left, and Mark wasn't about to let him go by himself. He watched as Paul ascended the stairway to the first floor. Mark followed to the bottom of the stairs and waited while Paul slowly opened the door to check out the hallway. Down below, all the others could do was wait quietly and listen to the sounds coming from the hospital above and wonder.

As far as Paul could figure, these guys had come for drugs or revenge or something along that order. And, in his opinion, any scumbag who would enter the sacred domain of a hospital, where the sick and injured go for care and the terminally ill go to die, was no different from a grave robber. They obviously had no conscience and were therefore capable of doing almost anything to anyone. His wife and the others were down below, and he was not about to let them come to any harm, so his best defense was to go on offense. Otherwise, they would all be trapped below, and the women and patients would have no way out.

Mark wasn't exactly sure what Paul was up to, but apparently his military training mode had kicked into gear, so following him seemed like the right thing to do. Paul scoured the hallways for signs of the intruders. Then all of a sudden, one of them rounded the corner right beside him. Paul took him down with a single shot to the head from his pistol, and the man fell hard to the floor with a thud. Two others came at him from the other end of the hallway, and before he had time to react, they fired several shots at him with AK-47s. Paul took cover as best he could, but there was not much cover against two semiautomatic weapons. Paul fired back with several rounds, but the men kept advancing, confident that they had their opponent outgunned. Their only mistake was that they hadn't seen Mark in the stairwell.

Mark started to run down the stairs and hide when he saw and heard the men coming his way, but that would have left Paul cornered. The men passed by the doorway so hell-bent on killing Paul that they didn't even see Mark. Mark sprang on them. He didn't have a clear shot because the supply shelving was in the way, so he moved around to the front to intercept them and shot at the first one almost point-blank, but the man jumped and the bullet only grazed his side. He winced but didn't fall immediately. His partner in crime turned to shoot back at Mark, but before he could, Mark stepped to the side and used the butt end of his rifle to hit him on his forehead, sending him reeling. The first man recovered and took a swing at Mark. Mark saw him out of the corner of his eye and stepped into his swing in order to grab his arm and throw him to the ground. His partner now came at Mark from the other side, but Mark straight-leg kicked him in the abdomen, then delivered a left-handed punch to the face, then a right hand fist to the spleen. The first man came back at Mark and took a roundhouse swing at his head, but Mark ducked down and into the punch and delivered a hard right fist to the heart, then a left to the chin and, finally, a kick to the groin. Before either could come to his feet, Paul had joined the fight. The second man reached for his weapon, but he wasn't quick enough. Paul shot him twice in the chest with his pistol and put his foot on his weapon. The man died quickly. The first man went for his gun, but by then Mark already had his rifle in his hands. Mark realized he didn't have time to turn it around and shoot him, so he hit him on the temple with the butt end of his rifle just as the man was about to shoot him. Then for good measure, he hit him again. The man went still.

Mark stared at the men on the floor. It had been a long time since he had been in a fight. A strange thought came over him. He had spent the better part of his life helping the sick and injured, and now here he was crushing a man's skull with the butt end of a rifle. And even stranger still, he wasn't even concerned about whether the guy lived or died. Killing them was like cutting someone open in surgery—a nasty job, not something anyone would ordinarily want to do, but something that had to be done nevertheless. Paul stood beside him, and they both stared at the men for a moment.

There wasn't much time to ponder the situation, because two more intruders came around the corner at the other end of the hallway and stopped about twenty-five to thirty feet away. Before the men realized what had happened, and before they could turn and lift their weapons, Paul and Mark both lifted theirs and shot first. The men lay on the floor and took their last breaths. Then there was silence.

There was no way for them to tell how many others were lurking about, but if these first few pathetic specimens were like the rest, there was going to be more killing before it was over. Paul and Mark stood over the dead men and listened for a few moments. It remained quiet. Mark helped himself to the TEC-9 on the floor, since it used the same ammo as the 9mm he was carrying on his side. Paul followed suit and picked up the other weapons. Then they both carefully went about checking out the rest of the hallways for other invaders, weapons, and ammo.

The others below heard the shooting and noise just above the stairwell, but none had the courage to venture out and see what was going on. Dr. Osborne stayed with them under the pretense that he would protect them in case the intruders got past Mark and Paul. Cindy and Martha knew why he stayed, but they were too scared to say or do anything, either. Then to everyone's surprise, the crashing and banging and shooting stopped. No one knew if the fight was over, or whether Paul and Mark were dead or what. They waited in silence hoping for some sign above that they were okay. To their relief, both Mark and Paul came back down the stairs unharmed and filled them in on what happened.

After the dust settled and everyone had time to gather their thoughts and nerve, it was decided that Paul and Martha would go for help in their car. Mark and the others covered them until they were out of the parking lot and out of sight. Then they were going to set a rotating watch for their own protection. Dr. Osborne and some of the other nurses wanted to go, but Mark and Paul were not sure they would actually get help or come back if they didn't find any. They were hoping that Paul and Martha would bring back the cavalry, but after they were gone only thirty minutes, they came tearing back into the parking lot, being chased by two carloads of thugs shooting at them out of their windows. Mark began shooting at the cars with his AR-15, which held them at bay until Paul and Martha made it inside. The cars turned and sped off the same way they came, not expecting armed resistance from inside the hospital. After watching for several minutes, Mark decided they weren't going to return anytime soon.

They had to decide their next move, for the situation was getting worse by the hour. Paul volunteered to serve as look-out while the doctors and nurses decided what to do with the patients. Some hard decisions had to be made. Without water, they would not be able to hold out much longer. Without some outside help, they might not make it at all. They finally decided to send two teams of two people per car who would head south, where there might be some help. They decided that on their way to look for help, they would stop by Mark's house to pick up water and food, since it was south of the hospital and hopefully had not been ransacked. All the others lived east of Memphis, and going that direction was out of the question.

Mark and Cindy would go in one car and Paul and Martha in the other, with the guys riding shotgun heavily armed. They would take the back roads and try to steer clear of the highways and Interstate 55. With some luck and a lot of ammo at their disposal, they might make it. Their first stop would be the police station or a firehouse, but if they couldn't find help, they would head to Mark's house, which was closer, and bring back some food and water from there. If they didn't find help this time, then on the next outing they would head to Batesville, where they would certainly find help.

Paul started loading the cars with the few supplies they needed for the trip and kept a watch for more trouble from the front of the hospital, while Mark and the others checked on the patients.

Cindy was in the cafeteria getting a dose of insulin from the last refrigerator with ice in it when she smelled smoke coming down from the back stairwell. Cindy ran to the door and saw smoke coming through the cracks between the door and its facing.

"Smoke!" she shouted to herself as she ran back to tell the others. When they went up the stairwell and opened the door, they saw something none of them were prepared for. Fire was raging in the back part of the hospital. From where they were, there was no way to know exactly where it was coming from or how serious it was. But it was clear there was a fire and it would spread and they might all be trapped. They didn't know that multiple fires had been intentionally started with gasoline, so they were spreading faster than expected. Without any water in the pipes, the sprinklers were mere ornaments, like the pictures on the wall. And without working fire alarms, no one else in the world would know that the hospital was burning until it was too late. And there wouldn't be anybody to help anyway. By the time Cindy and Mark found Paul, he too had smelled the smoke from the front of the hospital. They peered around the corners and down hallways, only to see that much of the building was already engulfed in flames.

The sorry bastards had returned to finish the job they started earlier and revenge their dead friends. Knowing those holed up in the hospital had weapons, and because they were cowards afraid to face them head-on, they snuck around back with the intention of burning them out. But, being the idiots they were, they didn't think about the fact that the fire would spread and destroy anything of value they were after, especially the drugs.

Mark raced to find Paul and Cindy. Together, they went to help Dr. Osborne and the other nurses, who had already started trying to get the patients out. The smoke in the sick ward was now thick and made breathing difficult. Unfortunately, most of the patients who remained were either bedridden from a crippling illness or otherwise too sick to get up on their own. A few who were able to walk, stumble, or crawl had already started for the front stairwell where Paul, Mark, and Cindy had just come from. But before any of them could get to the stairwell, the ceiling started to burn through and fall, raining fire on those below.

In heroic desperation, one of the nurses tried to drag someone out by herself, but the smoke overcame her, and she fell and was trapped by falling flames in a fiery grave, as if hell itself had come to claim an early prize. The others could only listen in horror as screams came from the room. Now all they could do was get themselves out. Mark dashed into his room and grabbed his backpack as the others scrambled for a few needed items, and the whole group fought the smoke up the stairwell out to fresh air on the outside. Just as they were coming out of the stairwell, Cindy realized that Tammy was not with them anymore. "Where's Tammy?" she shouted. No one knew.

"I thought she was following you up the stairs," Martha shouted back. They all looked up and down the smoke filled hallways as they made their way out of the building. No one wanted to leave without her, but the smoke was getting so thick that it was hard to see anything and even harder to breath.

"Maybe she is outside," Mark said, hoping his words would come true. "We've got to get out, or the smoke will kill us." Mark and Paul both knew that any further delay would mean Cindy and Martha and the others might not make it out, either. So they trudged on, hoping they would see her on the way out or on the outside. To their utter surprise, as they started out the front doorway, what was left of the band of murderers and thieves opened fire on them. They had set the fires and stood by outside waiting for the group's exit. It was incomprehensible to them that any human being could be that evil and callous, so it did not occur to them that such a trap had been set. All the exits had been set on fire except the one in front of them, and it appeared to be their only means of escape.

Martha, Dr. Osborne, and the other nurses were the first out the door and were hit by a spray of bullets that tore through their bodies, driving them back into the building and splattering blood and tissue on those behind them as they fell. The others fell back into the hallway, too, narrowly escaping the barrage of bullets and death themselves. Mark and Cindy had to pull Paul back away from certain death and hold him fast as he fought to pull his wife to safety. Paul had been hit in his side, as well, but it was only a flesh wound, and his screams were not for himself but for Martha. There was nothing else they could do. Martha was seriously wounded, but the others were dead. Their only chance was to find another way out. Mark carried Martha over his shoulder and Cindy pulled Paul along with them as they coughed and choked and stumbled back through the thick, blistering smoke.

On the back side of the hospital, in Central Supply, the back loading dock and door were concrete and steel. The gas had burned, but without much to ignite, the flames died. It was a way out. Mark stopped at the door and held Paul by the shoulders and looked him in the eyes. "You've got to get Martha and Cindy out of here. Take them to the ditch. It's our only chance."

Paul was still in shock from what just happened, but those words brought him back to the reality of their situation. Mark opened the door. Nothing happened. He looked out and saw no one. Apparently, the attackers hadn't planned on one of their fires going out. Mark pushed them out the door and hollered for them to run while he covered them. They ran for their lives, across the drive and open field and into the ditch. When they turned to watch for Mark to come behind them, he was not there.

Paul tended to Martha's wounds, while Cindy kept a lookout for any signs of the dirty bastards for what seemed like an eternity. As the building continued to burn, it filled with black smoke until billows of it rolled out of the burned-out shell that once was a place of healing but now had become a place of death. The fire melted glass and twisted steel beams, which created haunting sounds, like the screams of lost souls. It was almost more than Paul and Cindy could bear to listen to. Just as they had almost given up hope, out from the back of the building appeared an image of a man carrying a child. Cindy cried at the sight and asked herself, *Who else would have crawled through the rubble of a dark, smoke-filled building to the voice of a crying child?* It only made her infatuation with Mark even stronger.

"Idiot! You could have been killed!" Paul cried out. But he, too, would have done the same if he didn't have to take care of his wounded wife. After they were all safely down in the ditch undercover, Mark laid Tammy on the ground. She was unconscious but still breathing.

"She was laying on the floor just inside the hallway. I guess she tried to follow us out. She probably has some smoke injury to her lungs, but I don't know how bad it is," Mark said as he coughed hard and tried to catch his breath.

"What are we going to do?" Cindy asked as she caressed Tammy and tried to make her as comfortable as she could. Tammy was such a sweet and pretty child, and Cindy couldn't help but feel sorry for her for all that she had suffered recently. It broke her heart to know that she, too, might die. It seemed so unfair.

"I'll take care of her," Cindy cried with tears streaking down her own face, pulling Tammy into her arms and hugging her.

She wiped her face clean of the soot and dirt. "She's going to make it. I won't let her die."

Mark quickly checked out Martha's wounds. She had a through-and-through gunshot wound to the left lateral thigh that he packed with strips of Paul's T-shirt, as well as a wound to the right lower abdomen. "The leg is not that serious, but she may be gut shot. We need to get them somewhere safe. We don't have much time. I think we should try to make it to one of the cars and try to get to my house. It's our only chance," Mark said. He waited for a response before he pressed further. He hoped that Paul or Cindy would not break down or freeze up on him right then and there. After all, Paul had just watched his wife get shot in front of his very eyes, and he knew she could very well die. And Cindy saw the others get shot and burned in the fire, and there would be no funeral or time for grief. And they didn't know who else might be waiting on them to come out of hiding. He needed their help to get Martha and Tammy to safety. Moving them would be dangerous and difficult, but they couldn't stay there in the ditch.

Paul looked him straight in the eye. "We have to get to the cars. Those sum-bitches are still out there. Stay here with them. If I'm not back in a little while—" He didn't finish his sentence, and the look on his face showed that he was not in the mood for an argument. Paul mechanically checked the clips on his pistol and the AK-47 he was still carrying over his shoulder. Just before he climbed out of the ditch, he kissed his wife on the forehead and patted the little girl on the head and left without saying another word.

Cindy looked at Mark and asked, "Where is he going?"

Mark knew that Paul was either going to kill them all or be killed. In his state of mind, it probably didn't matter to him.

These men had killed his friends and shot his wife, yet they lived. Even with his own wounds that needed attention, he couldn't leave it that way. The only solution was to finish it. Mark stood guard over Cindy as she nursed her sick little patient and Martha, while Paul worked his way down the ditch and around to the front of the burning building.

Paul carefully made his way under the cover of the ditch. He peeked under a car by the ditch so he wouldn't be seen by anyone out front. He saw five of the remaining murderers sitting on the back of their pickup, passing around a bottle of cheap whiskey and laughing and pointing at the burning hospital. To them, the whole thing was just like a joke. It meant no more to them than a tailgate party after a Friday night football game. It didn't seem to matter to them that four of their own were dead and scores of innocent people were burned alive or buried in a grave of embers and hot melted steel. Pure entertainment.

They obviously had assumed that everyone inside had died in the fire. But they had assumed wrong, and it was the only advantage Paul needed. He sprang up from behind the burned-out shell of a car, not fifteen feet from them. "Hey, you sorry bastards, my wife was in there," he cursed at them to get their attention. Surprised, they all turned toward Paul with a look on their faces as if they had seen the devil himself. Just as they tried to turn their weapons on him, he emptied the thirty-round clip of the AK on them. And just for good measure, he put one round in each of their heads with his pistol. In the matter of a few seconds, it was over.

From the safety of the ditch, Mark and Cindy were not able to see what happened. All they could hear was a single burst of automatic weapon fire that lasted only a few seconds. Then five single shots in row, a few seconds apart. Then silence. After the shooting stopped, they waited nervously, hoping to see Paul come back around the building. After a while, Mark decided he couldn't wait any longer. He didn't know if Paul was dead or alive. He had to go see for himself. Cindy grabbed his arm and pleaded with him. "Please don't go. I need you." Then, realizing what she had said, she looked down at the girl and Martha. "We all need you."

Mark had no intention of getting himself killed, but just in case, he gave Cindy his pistol and his keys and told her to stay in the ditch until he came back for them. He told her if he wasn't back in a few minutes, she would have to take Tammy and try to make it to his car and to the farm. He told Cindy where to go and who to ask for. "If Paul is dead, I need to know. If he is hurt, then I have to help." Then he headed down the ditch in the same direction that he had seen Paul go. He went around to the front side of the parking lot so he could see what just happened. There were five men sprawled out on the ground and in the back of the truck. They weren't moving at all. Paul was sitting on the hood of the car next to the truck with his head bowed. As he walked up closer to get a better look, he could see that each of them had several bullet wounds and a single shot to the head. Paul was praying and asking for forgiveness for what he had done.

Mark left Paul to grieve for a moment and went over to check out his car. They were in luck. It seemed to be in pretty good shape, except for a bullet hole or two in a fender, but there was no gas leak or damage to the engine compartment. After he made sure the car was in one piece and would run, he went back to the ditch to check on Cindy and tell her what happened. After a while, Paul picked himself up and returned to the ditch. "You okay?" Mark asked Paul.

"I'm good," Paul answered. Then he helped Cindy and Mark gather up their things and carry Tammy and then Martha to the car, as gently as they could. They laid down one of the backseats so Martha could lie flat in the back of the car with Tammy next to her. Then they gathered up the backpack, guns, and ammo. After everyone was settled in the car and the gear loaded, they headed out of the parking lot. Cindy rode in the backseat next to Tammy so she could look after her and Martha, while Paul rode shotgun with the AK-47, loaded with a thirty-round clip and several more next to him and the TEC-9 for backup. Mark had his AR-15 locked and loaded next to him, and both had their pistols on their sides. If anyone wanted any trouble, they would find it. Neither Mark nor Paul was in the mood for any more crap from anyone.

Mark knew that traveling would be slow and dangerous, with the crowded roads full of desperate people. Martha probably would not make it all the way to Batesville, even if they did. So he headed south toward his house, which was only a few miles from there. Hopefully, it was still there and they could make it in one piece. They had nowhere else to go. It was their only hope. Just then, Mark noticed a heavy thunderstorm rapidly approaching from the west, and just as he turned onto Goodman Road, the bottom dropped out. Heavy winds were bending trees along the road. Sheets of rain were driven sideways and came down so hard he could barely see the road ahead of him. Maybe this was the break they needed. No one would be out in this weather.

CHAPTER 13
SPRING PLANTING

Thursday, April 17.
That same day.

Spring was in full bloom at the farm. Buttercups had popped up in clusters over the hillsides, living reminders of where the cabins of settlers had stood years ago. Several varieties of pink and red azaleas bloomed in the front yard and along the driveway down by the road. Pink and white dogwood trees, in full bloom, welcomed the robins and blue jays returning from their winter homes. In the pastures, horses and cows grazed among wild onions, whose green stalks stood out against the background of brown field grass, still asleep from the cold days of winter that had now passed. All along the fence rows and in the woods, small green buds of newborn leaves dotted the limbs of hardwood trees, along with the occasional splash of purple from wisteria vines, redbud trees, and blooming wild plum trees, signaling the full arrival of spring.

That morning after breakfast, Grandpa and Grandma Brown, along with Glen and Steve, loaded up a few supplies and cut some firewood and then took the Thompsons down the road to their uncle's farm. The Browns helped them knock down the cobwebs and clean out the old woodstove, then they stacked half a cord of firewood and made sure the well water was good and that they had tools and a little food to last them until the garden would start producing. Grandpa even left them a few chickens and loaned them a mama cow for milk. Before leaving, he made sure Uncle Leroy's shotgun was oiled and working and left a box of shells on the mantle, just in case.

Jerry shook Grandpa's hand and thanked him. "I really appreciate all you have done. I don't know how or when we can repay you, but if there is anything you need, let me know."

"Same here, that's what neighbors are for. Your uncle was a big help to me over the years. It's the least I can do. We're just up the road if you need anything or get bored or just want to visit or anything."

Grandma hugged Wanda and rounded up Steve, who had already made friends with Doug and Cathy, from the backyard. They loaded up and headed back to the farm to get caught up with the daily chores.

After supper, Grandpa Brown sat on the porch with his pipe, surveying the scenery as the sun slowly set behind some dark clouds just across the Mississippi River in the distance to the west. The Edwards boys sat on the steps and listened to his stories. Tim continued to keep to himself upstairs rather than join the rest of them on the porch in the evenings. Glen decided to join them, since most of the stations had gone out a few days on the TV, so he had nothing better to do. Grandpa pointed out an occasional flash of lightning and roll of thunder indicating the approach of another springtime thunderstorm. After decades of watching nature play out its yearly cycles and noting the subtle changes of the seasons and weather patterns, he could almost always tell when a storm was approaching long before the rolling thunder proved him right. Earlier in the day, he and the boys had plowed an acre or so in the old garden spot so that it would get a good soaking by the approaching rain and settle enough to be harrowed and rowed after a few days of drying in preparation for planting of the early vegetables. With the house full again, and with many mouths to feed and the availability of supplies and goods in question for the next few months or perhaps longer, a good vegetable garden could mean the difference between hunger and plenty. Just one acre would provide more than enough beans, squash, peas, tomatoes, corn, turnips, peppers, okra, carrots, cabbage, potatoes, radishes, cucumbers, cauliflower, watermelons, and cantaloupes to keep them all well fed for the year, with plenty left over to can for the coming winter. The blackberry bushes along the fence rows, the peach, apple, plum, and pecan trees in the orchards, and the wild muscadine vines in the woods would provide the fruits and nuts and berries for desserts, jams, jellies, and cider. A hog or two killed in the fall, after the first frost, could be salted and cured in the old smokehouse to provide meat, and the fat could be used for cooking and, if needed, to make lye soap. The brood of chickens and new chicks would provide a steady source of meat and eggs. A good mother cow would be caught at weaning time and put up for daily milking to provide milk and cream for butter for the household. Grandpa knew that with some hard work and planning and just a little luck, they would have plenty for the entire year.

There would also be pastures to cut, hay to put up, fences to mend, and plenty of repairs to keep them all busy. He had done this his whole life, and as much as he hated all that had happened in the cities, he had a feeling of being needed again. His knowledge of the land and the seasons and the old ways made him feel useful. The others now looked to him to show them the ways of a time gone by, when people lived off the land and depended on themselves and their families and their neighbors to survive, not on malls or large superstores full of all kinds of food and wares packaged, processed, and delivered from the cities. Now, they were mere empty shells that stood as reminders of how spoiled and dependent people had become. People had trusted science and technology and the mechanisms of modern society to provide for all their wants and needs, never once considering the possibility that they might one day find themselves without.

Even if the supplies and goods were cut off for the rest of the year, they would be all right. There was a good team of horses in the pasture that could pull a plow if needed. And a good herd of cows and calves to use, as needed, for food and leather or to trade for other goods. The ponds were full of fish and the woods and fields were full of deer, rabbit, squirrel, dove and other game. A well would supply plenty of clean water and the old outhouse would serve its purpose, just fine. There was plenty of wood for the fireplace and old stove when the propane in the large tank ran out. They had plenty of lanterns, lamps and oil. Even if the problems around the country continued for the rest of the year, or even longer, they could survive.

As Grandpa stood looking at the approaching storm, he couldn't help but wonder how all those city folks would make it. No way to find, grow or gather the most basic of human needs; food, water and shelter. A deep feeling of foreboding came over him, as he thought about all those people heading out of the cities into the countryside, looking for a place to settle. They were far from Memphis, but maybe, not far enough, they would be coming, and he knew it. Maybe not in great numbers, but they would come. Some by themselves, expecting handouts, begging for food and water. Families with desperate fathers and mothers with children in dire need of rest and something to eat would come also. And some would come, just looking for trouble, wherever they could find it. They would come, and Grandpa would help those he could, it didn't matter if they were Black, White, Asian, Mexican or any others, as long as they were willing to work and showed a little appreciation, and the food held out. Freeloaders, troublemakers and thieves would have to be dealt with. He believed in helping and sharing, but his family had to come first. They were all depending on him to provide for them and keep them safe. Grandpa was not just an old has been, he was needed again. He felt important and more self-assured than he had in a long time.

In the kitchen, Grandma Brown, Lisa, Sarah, and even Rhonda were gathering the old canning jars and lids for a good cleaning. Along with the new ones, they would hold the fruits and vegetables that would get them through the winter months. It had been a long time since Grandma Brown had cooked and cared for such a crew, but she eagerly anticipated the new garden and all it would provide for them. She, too, remembered back to years gone by, when the women of the house would cook vegetables and fruits way into the middle of the night and then put them into the jars in the pressure cookers and seal them for storage, all the while, telling stories and sharing the latest talk of the day. Mothers, daughters, sisters, aunts, grandmothers, and even neighbors all working together for a common purpose. The sharing of work and history and tradition that once gave her a strong sense of belonging and purpose in life had been missing of late. Now it would be back again, at least for a while.

As bad as she felt about all the things that had happened and the people who were hurt, she couldn't help but feel that this was the way life should be. Family working, sharing, and living together with a sense of belonging and purpose, to be needed and wanted and loved by family and friends, to be part of a community that knows and helps one another. Not with families spread all about, seeing each other only once in a while, living in crowded suburbs and cities where neighbors seldom speak to one another and rarely help one another. A life spent constantly running around, hither and yon, all the time coming and going, eating and living on the run, filling their lives with things such as ball games and so on, the whole time missing out on the most important things in life; God, family, friends.

Back out on the porch, Grandpa was keeping a keen eye on the approaching storm. "Steve, you think you can go out and shut up the barn and chickens for the night?"

"Sure," Steve said proudly. He had taken a liking to the farm chores, and it made him feel grown up when Grandpa entrusted him with certain duties that were once his domain.

"Best get it done before the rain starts."

"Yes, sir," Steve said as he bolted off the porch and headed out for the barn.

Grandpa smiled as he watched the display of youthful enthusiasm that he once had many years ago. He turned to Glen as he relit his pipe. "Where's Tim been all day? Haven't seen him at all. He's missing out on all the work."

"Yeah. I don't think he cares for physical labor much," Glen offered as an excuse for the both of them.

"Bet he likes to eat, just the same," Grandpa offered as he blew smoke from the pipe.

"Well, yes. But I think, I mean, it seems like we've kinda gone overboard with this big garden and all that. What are the chances that we'll actually need all that stuff, anyway? Besides we, I mean, Tim doesn't care much for vegetables and such. He has mostly just kind of eaten out most of the time. You know, burgers, pizza, stuff like that," Glen said halfheartedly, not wanting to fully disclose his true disgust for hard work or his lack of appreciation for fresh fruits and vegetables himself. In fact, he had always despised the idea of hard physical labor and dirt and sweat. And he had become accustomed to living on the go over the years, eating out almost every night. Food, to him, consisted of cheeseburgers, fries, pizza, beer, and chili dogs. He shuffled his feet slightly, feeling somewhat guilty since he hadn't helped out much earlier during the day, either.

"Maybe so, but if we do need it and aren't prepared, then it will be too little, too late. We have to be ready. There's no other way. And like I said, if anyone wants to eat, they have to work," Grandpa stated, in a matter-of-fact way that let Glen know that the rules applied to everyone, including him.

Just then, Tim came barging out of the house, slamming doors behind him. It was obvious that he was sore about something. "Someone's been messing with my stuff. Which one of you little twerps have been in my room?" Tim stared at Daniel and Jeffrey, who sat motionless, too afraid to say anything or move. "It had to be one of you little shitheads," Tim cursed.

Glen started to stop him, but Tim turned to him and began to whine, as he had learned to do over the years in order to get his way. "But Dad, someone got into my stuff today and messed it all up. Now I can't find the batteries for my games. There's no TV, no computer, no nothing, I don't have anything to do around this stupid place."

Daniel looked up timidly, not sure whether to say anything or not. "Steve took your batteries. I saw him." He started to continue with his explanation, but he hesitated, as a four-year-old often does when he is trying to tell a story, and Tim was too charged up to wait for the rest.

"Where is that shithead? I'll teach him to mess with my stuff." Tim was beaded up with sweat, and the veins were popping out on his forehead. Glen started to say something else, but before he could, Grandpa raised his hand and pointed a finger toward the barn, with his pipe in his hand. Before anyone had time to say another word, Tim lit off for the barn.

Glen started to get up to go after him, but Grandpa motioned for him to sit down. "They need to work this out between them."

"Yeah, but Tim is a lot bigger than Steve and I don't want anyone to get hurt. Besides, I don't believe in fighting," Glen said, trying to sound noble when he was actually kind of glad that Tim had the opportunity to straighten out Steve.

"Maybe so, but the sooner they get this out of their system, the better," Grandpa said as he drew on his pipe and blew a perfect smoke ring into the air. Daniel and Jeffrey both watched the ring float off into space, oblivious to the problem at hand.

Steve had locked the back door of the barn and checked the stalls and was heading toward the front door when Tim barged in, almost knocking him over. It was obvious to Steve that he was pissed about something. "You got my batteries, didn't you?" Tim said, digging a finger into Steve's chest.

Steve was caught off guard. "Well, yes. But I—"

Tim didn't wait for the rest of the answer before he pushed Steve down onto the dirt floor. "You don't touch my stuff. You hear me, you little thief?"

Steve was not sure what to say, since Grandpa had told him to gather up all the batteries earlier in the day to use in the flashlights, including those from the kitchen drawer Tim had helped himself to without asking the day before. Tim was a good six inches taller and twenty pounds heavier than Steve, so needless to say, Steve was not looking for a fight. "I was just doing what I was told, that's all," he said as he slowly got up and dusted himself off.

"Yeah, right. Someone told you to steal the batteries out of my game. So now you're a liar and a thief," Tim said sarcastically as he gave Steve another hard shove.

"Look, you jerk, all I was doing was—"

Tim was so outraged by Steve talking back to him that he didn't even let him finish his answer before he tried to push Steve down again. Only this time, Steve stepped quickly to the side and slapped his hands away. That made Tim mad. Ready to show him who was boss, he lunged at Steve to get him in a headlock, but Steve grabbed Tim's arm and body slung him over his back and onto the ground.

"That's it! You're dead now," Tim snorted as he jumped up and started swinging for Steve's face and head.

Steve covered up for a few licks and realized Tim was out to hurt him. Steve stepped back, blocking some of the punches, and tried to make Tim back off. "Look, I don't want to fight you. It's just some dumb old batteries. What's wrong with you?"

Tim mistook that as a sign of fear on Steve's part and decided to go for it. He grabbed Steve around the waist and took him to the ground and worked his way over on top of him, intending to straddle his chest to face punch him. Steve had all he was going to take. He had turned the other cheek, and it was time to fight. Steve caught Tim off balance and rolled him off to the side. As they struggled on the ground for position, Steve elbowed Tim in the nose, drawing blood. Tim cried out and cursed words that Steve had never heard before and started kicking at him with reckless abandon. A few of the kicks caught Steve hard and knocked the wind out of him for a few seconds. Tim then landed a couple of punches to the back of Steve's head, but neither did damage. Now, Steve was fighting mad himself and tore into Tim with all he had. Tim was unprepared for the fury that ensued. Steve landed a punch to the mouth, another to the nose, and one to the gut before Tim could react. Steve pounded him hard, again and again, as Tim fell to the ground. Steve stood over him cursing a few choice words of his own, daring Tim to get up, until he felt a strong hand on his shoulder. "That's enough. I think you two understand each other now," Grandpa said as he pulled them apart, giving Steve a half smile that no one else saw.

They all stood silently over Tim as he lay on the ground curled up in the fetal position, crying like a baby. His mouth and nose were bloody, and both eyes were swollen and bruised. Steve was out of breath, dirty, and ruffled himself, but otherwise he was no worse for the wear. Glen pretended to be surprised that the boys were fighting but was really taken back by the fact that a boy a year younger and much smaller had just whooped up on his son. Trying to sound indignant, Glen began to chastise both boys for fighting, but Grandpa cut him off and let out the fact that they had been watching most of it from just outside the door. Glen realized that he was letting his shame for his boy getting beat up by a smaller boy show, and he quickly changed his attitude to one of consolation. "You boys had a fair fight, and now you need to make up, so shake hands."

Tim continued to cry so vigorously that his father was now embarrassed by the whole scene and finally told him, "Grow up. You started the fight, you big sissy, so quit your crying and get up." Tim looked up and stopped his crying almost immediately, surprised because his father had never really spoken to him so directly. He started to whimper again, but Glen stopped him. "Get up and act like a man. You got whipped fair and square, so shake yourself off and get in the house and get cleaned up. And don't you go in there crying to your mother, either." Tim got up slowly, wiping the tears and blood from his face and reluctantly shook Steve's hand. Then, defeated, he lumbered off to the house. It was a long walk. Glen looked somberly at Steve and then Grandpa. "We'll both be out to help you in the morning." Then he turned and followed Tim to the house.

Grandpa patted Steve on the shoulder and gave him a wink and a smile. "Well, I guess things will be a little different around here now. You know, your mother's going to have a fit when she hears about this," he said with a laugh as they walked to the house.

The women were all in the kitchen when the boys came in to lick their wounds, first Tim and then Steve. Lisa was beside herself when she first saw the boys, and even though she was not happy with the situation, she calmed down after hearing the first part of the story. Sarah, however, became hysterical almost immediately and began ranting and raving before they could finish their story. Glen tried to ignore her as he attempted to explain what happened. He helped Tim clean the blood from his face, but the longer it went on the louder she became, until Glen finally had all he could take. To everyone's surprise, he turned and grabbed her firmly by both shoulders and loudly stated, "Give it a rest, woman It was just a fight. Tim started it, and he got what he deserved, okay? Now, if you'll be quiet, I'll finish telling everyone what happened."

Sarah was so stunned by Glen's actions that all she could do was stare silently at him with her eyes and mouth wide open as he turned back to the sink to finish cleaning Tim's injuries. At first, his actions made her mad. But as she watched his confident movements and listened to Glen telling the story, she detected a marked difference in his personality. For all the years that they had been married, Sarah could remember only a rare display of any firmness with her, and Glen's lack of discipline with the kids was always a sore spot between them. Despite his aggressive behavior toward her, Sarah could not help but admire this new-found intestinal fortitude in her previously passive man.

After all the dust settled, the only thing Lisa could think to say to Steve was, "What will your father say when he hears about this?" And with that, she started crying, not because of the fight but because of Mark. They had not heard from him in days and had no way to know where he was, or how he was, or when he would get to come home to the farm. When Daniel and Jeffrey saw their mommy crying, they started crying. They cried for having to leave their home so abruptly and for having to leave school and their friends before the year was over, and for all the other people who had been hurt. But mostly, they cried for their daddy. They wanted to know when he would come home.

Steve tried not to cry. He was supposed to be a man now. He held it in as best he could, but tears rolled silently down his cheeks as he bit his lip. He wanted to be with his daddy again so much. Despite knowing that what he did to the stranger was necessary, and that he would do again if needed, he had to tell his dad. He would understand and be able to tell him it was okay. That he did what needed to be done. The feeling a child has for a missing parent or a parent has for a missing child is so strong, it is like a visceral pain coming from deep inside. A nagging, aching pain that hurts without relief, like a cancer growing in your belly that gnaws at you all the time, day and night. One that you would cut out if you could get to it. And even though your body is starving, you cannot eat. And, regardless of how tired you are, you cannot sleep. The kind of consuming and unrelenting longing and mental anguish that causes even the strongest of men to fall to their knees and cry out to heaven for relief. But relief for Steve would come only when his father was with them again.

CHAPTER 14
MORTALLY WOUNDED

Thursday, April 17.

The trip to Mark's house was slow going with the heavy wind and rain. Water was standing on the road in many places, and the ditches filled quickly. They could see very little due to the heavy rain, but with every flash of lightning they could make out signs of recent violence: storefronts with broken windows, overturned cars, smoldering fires being put out by the heavy rain. The farther they drove south toward Mark's house, things didn't seem quite as bad, but there were still many broken-down cars along the side of the road and occasionally in the middle of the road. Shattered windshields and the belongings of recent inhabitants scattered the roadside, along with what looked like an occasional body lying in the grass off to the side of the road. As they turned off the main road and drove along to his street, they even caught glimpses of tents and campers on the side streets, with shadows of people huddled around lanterns and candlelight, trying to ride out the storm from the past week and the rainstorm that was thrashing them now. They made it to the entrance to his subdivision without further incident, thanks to the storm, which washed the roads clean of troublemakers.

As Mark pulled up to the entrance gate of his subdivision, he was suddenly stopped by two armed men dressed in fatigues and rain ponchos, who appeared from the cover of a tent just behind the brick wall. With an M1A pointed at them from one side and an AR-10 from the other, Mark was caught off guard and forced to stop dead in his tracks before he could react. After Mark stopped the car, even with the windows still up and the rain pouring down, he could hear the men shout for them to show their hands and not move a muscle.

The man on Mark's side pointed his gun at Mark's face through the glass and motioned for him to roll down his window.

"Who are you, and what do you want?" the man asked.

"I'm Dr. Mark Edwards. I live here!" Mark shouted into the rain, as it poured through the open window into his face.

"Who is it?" the man from the other side of the car shouted, his rifle pointed at Paul's head.

"He says he is Dr. Mark Edwards."

The man from the other side of the car slowly came around to their side, with his gun still pointed at the car. "Dr. Edwards, is that you?"

"Yes, sir," Mark said as he strained to see who the man was through the rain.

"Damn it, boy! I didn't think we would see you anytime soon. We thought you got the hell out of Dodge with your wife and kids last week," the man said as he dropped the tip of his rifle. He looked at his partner at the gate and said, "Hey, put your rifle down. Don't you know your neighbor when you see him?"

"I'm sorry, Dr. Edwards, we've had some trouble around here, and I guess we're all a little nervous."

"Mr. Henry, is that you?" Mark asked.

"Yep, the one and only," he joked, trying to lighten the mood.

Mark was so relieved that it was his neighbors holding him at gunpoint that he didn't mind the rain in his car or his face. He figured if they were guarding the front entrance, the area was still somewhat safe, and he was glad he was not about to be robbed or shot two hundred feet from his front door.

But as Mr. Henry came closer to pat Mark on the shoulder and welcome him back, he saw Paul with his hand on his pistol, as well as all the weapons in the front seats and the woman in the back of the car covered in blood. He knew they had run into some serious trouble and immediately backed away and pointed his rifle at Paul again. "You guys okay?"

"No, sir, we have a sick girl and a wounded woman in here. That's his wife," Mark offered as he nodded toward Paul. "They are from the hospital," Mark said, hoping everyone would relax a little and not start shooting the place up. "She's been shot and we need to get her inside, right now."

"Hey, I don't want to tell you your business, Doc, but it looks like you need to get her to the hospital," Mr. Henry offered as he stepped aside to make way, sensing the urgency of the situation.

"We just came from the hospital. It's not there anymore. They burned it down," Mark blurted out as he rolled up is window and drove past them toward his house. As he pulled into the drive, he looked in his mirror and saw Mr. Henry coming toward them. Mr. Henry helped them carry Tammy and Martha into the house and then went to get his wife to come help. Mark never really got to know the Henrys all that well, but Lisa talked of them often, about how they were always helping out when Mark was on call at the hospital. He knew only a little bit about them but remembered that Mr. Henry was a retired US Army colonel who had been in Vietnam in the early seventies and his wife, Mary, was a teacher at the local elementary school.

Mark had them put Tammy in Daniel's room, where they could keep an eye on her, and then they put Martha on the couch, so they could check her wounds better. Mark had Cindy check both of their vital signs and try to make them as comfortable as possible. Mark checked Tammy over while they finished cleaning Martha's wounds. As he examined her closely for the first time, he noticed that she had carbonaceous sputum and rapid respirations with wheezing and retractions with each breath, all signs of smoke inhalation injury.

Mark knew that smoke was highly toxic to the airway and lung tissue, which causes the lungs to fill with fluid, making it harder for the oxygen to diffuse from the lungs to the blood. And he knew that smoke also causes the airway to restrict, resulting in a buildup of carbon dioxide. The most immediate danger was that of low blood oxygen or hypoxemia. In order to treat her, he needed to administer high-flow oxygen and bronchodilators right away, or she might not make it through the day. But he knew that the most important treatment in severe smoke inhalation injury, besides oxygen, was maintaining the airway with an endotrachial tube and a ventilator, if necessary. Without the ability to look into her airway with a bronchoscope, or get a chest X-ray or arterial blood gases, he was unable to tell how severe her airway injury was. And without a hospital and all the technology he was used to, it was like practicing medicine one hundred years ago. He felt that he could do very little to help her.

Martha's blood pressure was low and her pulse weak and rapid, and she was semiconscious, pale, and sweaty, indicating she was going into shock from the bleeding. He examined the left thigh wound more closely and saw that it was through and through without any signs of nerve, vessel, or bone injury. He knew the bleeding with an injury like that was not usually immediately life threatening and could usually be controlled with gauze packing and a pressure dressing. That, he could do. The risk of infection was high due to the injured tissue and bacterial contamination from the bullet wound, but it could usually be controlled with wound care and antibiotics. However, the abdomen wound was much more serious. The bleeding had all but stopped on the outside, but her abdomen was getting more distended, with guarding and rebound tenderness in all four quadrants, which were the signs of peritonitis and internal bleeding.

Mark knew she probably had an intestinal injury, along with the internal bleeding. From the position of the entrance wound in the right lower quadrant, it was most likely a right colon injury. The stool bacteria leaking out of the intestine would grow quickly in the injured tissue and blood in the abdominal cavity over the next twenty-four to forty-eight hours. The infection would subsequently cause peritonitis and eventually enter her bloodstream and cause shock and multiple organ failure before ending in a painful death in just a few days. If that was the case, she would need the bowel repaired or diverted and the abdomen irrigated with saline, or she would die of sepsis.

But he knew, as serious as that was, the most immediate danger from a penetrating abdominal injury, be it a knife or a bullet, was the bleeding. If a major artery or vein had been injured, she could die within a few minutes or a few hours. Even with moderate bleeding from many small vessels, she would die within a few hours or a day or two, at the most. It needed to be stopped as soon as possible, and the only way to stop it and repair the bowel was surgery. And without blood transfusions, her chances were not good. He needed to get her to an operating room right away, but as far as he knew, there was not one anywhere nearby. The ones in Memphis had probably suffered the same fate, and traveling into Memphis would most likely be suicidal anyway. Traveling anywhere at this time was dangerous, and to try to attempt a long, difficult trip to the nearest trauma center in Jackson or Tupelo, with so many unknowns, meant she would probably in all likelihood die.

Mark did what he could for both of them. He went to the back of his car and pulled out his emergency medical pack and brought it inside. He had kept it in his car at all times, just in case, and kept it stocked with the full range of emergency equipment and medications for everything from simple lacerations to full cardiac arrest; everything but a defibrillator. He had used it only a few times to sew up kids from the neighborhood to save them a trip to the ER. He found the IV catheters and inserted an eighteen-gauge needle into Martha's arm, hung a one-liter bag of ringers lactate, and ran it in at a steady rate to give her some fluids. Then he pulled out one of the medicine trays and found the antibiotics and gave her two grams of Ancef and five hundred milligrams of Flagyl. Then he gave her four milligrams of morphine and advised Cindy to watch her. If she became restless from the pain, she was to give her another dose as needed, as long as her pressure was over seventy systolic. If it went below that, she was to turn up her fluids until it came back up.

Then he started an IV on Tammy and ran the fluids at a much slower rate, to adjust for her small size. Then he gave her one milligram of morphine and 0.25 milligrams of terbutaline subcutaneously, and he advised Cindy to repeat the dose every thirty minutes if her wheezing continued. He also explained that there were only two bags of IV fluids in his kit, one for Martha and one for Tammy. So, when Martha's bag was down to only two hundred cc's, she should switch the bags in order to give Martha more volume, since she needed it to keep her pressure up. That would not be acceptable in any hospital, but in this situation, it was all he could do to buy time until they could figure out what to do next.

Just as Mark finished helping Cindy stabilize Tammy and Martha, there was a knock on the door. Mr. Henry and his wife, Mary, came in carrying a tray of sandwiches and a pitcher of sweet tea, accompanied by two other neighbors from their cove. Mr. Henry was retired military but friendly and warm. He had broad square shoulders, crew cut greying hair, a square jaw and still seemed to be in command wherever he went. "This is Fred and Nancy Dickerson, from the end of the cove. This is Dr. Edwards, and I believe this is Paul, and over there is Cindy. That is Paul's wife on the couch—she is the one who is hurt— and there was a little girl somewhere," Mr. Henry said, looking around the room.

"Yes, little Tammy has been through a lot. She is in the first bedroom there," Mark said and pointed. "Paul works with me in surgery at the hospital, and his wife is a nurse there—well, used to be. There's not really a hospital there anymore. Cindy was an ICU nurse there, too. Anyway, guys, thanks for your help and the food. It's been awhile since we've eaten."

"No problem, what are neighbors for? We are kind of glad to see some friendly faces around here for a change. Everyone pretty much took off when things got bad around here last week. It's just us and a few others left in the neighborhood," Mr. Henry explained, as everyone shook hands and shared introductions and the newcomers began to stuff down the sandwiches.

Mark went on to explain what happened at the hospital, and about how Martha was shot as they tried to escape, how Tammy was hurt, and how Paul had finished them off. He told them about Lisa and the kids leaving for the farm last week, before things got too bad, and how he was going to go down there when the time was right. Now, it looked as if the time was right for him, but he had Martha and Tammy to look after, and he didn't think they would make the trip with their injuries. The most pressing thing was the need to evaluate the extent of their injuries and to tend to them, regroup, gather supplies, and make plans before taking off. So, for the time being, they needed to hole up there at Mark's house.

Mr. Henry was impressed by how Paul took the bad guys out on his own and told him how glad he was that they had someone else with military experience on their side. He went on to explain how the group had sort of put him in charge and how they had banded together to defend the neighborhood after everyone else had left. He explained that there was only the four of them and two other families left in the neighborhood that they knew of. Besides themselves, there was Jerry and Heather Watson with their two kids, Sally, who was sixteen, and Billy, who was fourteen. The other family was Robert and Terri Jones and their two children, Curtis, fifteen, and Andrew, thirteen. He told them how most fled when they heard that the rioters had crossed the state line, and the rest left in a hurry when the first bullets started flying in their area.

He went on to explain that they were the last holdouts and were having to stand guard twenty-four/seven to keep the riffraff out. They were all stuck there for the same reason. When the violence started, they were hopeful it would resolve soon. And when it didn't, they all thought the National Guard would be called out. And when it wasn't, they were stuck with no place to go. So they banded together and were trying to weather the storm.

Mark hated to cut the stories and introductions short, but he knew something had to be done for Tammy and Cindy right away, so he explained to the group the urgency of the situation. Then he gathered up Paul and Cindy and explained the seriousness of the injuries and what needed to be done to help Martha and Tammy. Paul was visibly upset and willing to do whatever was needed to help his wife. They discussed all their options, including making a run into Memphis, but all agreed that was out of the question.

The second option was to head south in hopes of finding a hospital somewhere that was open and could care for their wounds and injuries. But since their own hospital was the only one in north Mississippi that took care of any Level II trauma, it was very unlikely they would be successful. They would, in all likelihood, not have a general surgeon available who could treat either of them, and since Mark would not have privileges at any of the other hospitals, he would certainly not be allowed to treat them either. No hospital would allow that under the current system. Even under normal circumstances, it would take at least three months to get through all the red tape in order to get privileges. And with all the turmoil going on now, it would be impossible.

Trying to make it all the way to Jackson or Tupelo, which were the only other trauma centers in the area and which were both over three hours away, was a dangerous gamble at best. And that would be true only if they were open, if there were surgeons available, and if they could get there in time—or at all. That was a lot of ifs. Besides, there was no guarantee either would make the trip, and they would all most likely end up stuck in traffic, robbed, or shot themselves.

The farm was the third option. It was only about an hour away, but with the situation being what it was, it could take hours or a day or who knows how long. Besides, there were no medical supplies there, either. The local hospital at Batesville did have operating rooms, but it did not have a full-time general surgeon who did trauma cases, so that would not help their situation.

None of the options looked good. It was a hopeless situation. If they stayed put, either or both would most likely die. If they tried to get them somewhere else, the same would occur. Cindy was not trained or inclined to make such life-altering decisions, so she got up and shrugged her shoulders and said she would do whatever they decided. Then she left the room to go take care of her patients. Mark shook his head and walked around the kitchen trying to think of any other way. Paul buried his face in his hands and prayed to God for some help, an answer, a glimmer of hope—anything—for his wife and for Tammy.

Mr. Henry started to speak but stopped himself, shook his head, and mumbled something under his breath. Mark noticed his hesitation, so he asked him, "What is it? Do you have an idea? Come on, we need some help here—anything."

It took some more prodding, but Mark finally got him to say it out loud. "Well, I'm just an old retired army man, but in Vietnam, we couldn't always get the injured to the hospital, so you had to bring the hospital to them."

"I'm sorry, but I don't follow you."

"MASH units. Field hospitals. We used to carry the wounded to tents near the battle zones. They would operate right there. They didn't have all the conveniences that the big hospital had, but they saved lives."

Mark thought for a minute then asked, "You mean right here, in the house?"

"Well, do you have a better idea? Tammy needs a doctor, and you're a doctor. Martha needs surgery, and you're a surgeon. All we need are some medical supplies. If we could find—"

Mark cut him off. "Look, I'd be lucky to be able to help them in a hospital, but right here is crazy."

Mr. Henry looked sternly at Mark. "Look, son, desperate measures mean desperate acts. I saw guys who were gut shot, arms and legs blown off. Some of them made it, some didn't. We have to try. Doing nothing is not an option. You said so yourself."

"But I can't do that kind of surgery outside a trauma hospital operating room without anesthesia and help."

"I'll help you. We did all right the last two weeks on our own. You have to try. I can't just watch her die," Paul pleaded.

"We might not be able to get everything you're used to, but back in 'Nam, they dropped ether and operated on plywood operating tables held up by sawhorses in tents with muddy floors and flies everywhere. We had to make do with what we had. In the military, they teach you to improvise, son. So what do we absolutely need for you to operate right here?"

Mark remained unconvinced. "I don't know. I've never…I mean there's just no way. What if she doesn't make it? We will at least need some kind of anesthesia, more IV fluids, surgical instruments, lights, and sterile drapes. I have some sutures in my bag, but I don't know where we would get the rest."

"Wait a minute!" Paul exclaimed. "The surgery center. Across the street from the hospital. It was still pretty much intact. I mean, it looked okay to me. It has everything we need. What if we make a run up there, do the surgery, and get back here as quickly as possible? It may be risky, but I'm willing to try it if you are, Doc."

Cindy overhead what Paul said and volunteered to help, as well. Mr. Henry then seconded the motion and offered to escort them to the center and act as security. He explained that he had given the neighbors a crash course on weapons and a sort of abbreviated boot camp for dummies, so they could hold down the fort while he was gone. Then Mr. Dickerson volunteered to go as well, and the wives offered to watch after Tammy while they were gone.

Everyone stopped and stared at Dr. Edwards. There was a moment of silence as they waited for an answer. Mark saw the hope in Paul's eyes and could not refuse to help. It was dangerous and risky, but it was the best plan they had. He knew it just might work. "Okay, let's do it. I guess if worse comes to worst, I can do a spinal on Martha and Cindy can help monitor her. If we're going to do this, we need to go now."

"Wait a second," Mr. Henry interrupted. "Let's think this through just a minute. By your own estimate, the surgery could take one to three hours. If things are as bad as you say up there, we may not get through without an interruption, if you know what I mean. Then we will all be stuck up there, trying to do surgery, while the bullets are flying. Not a good situation."

Mark looked at him, confused and irritated, because Mr. Henry was initially all fired up about taking Martha to surgery and trying save her. "Are you saying we shouldn't go now? I thought you just said the MASH units were close to the front lines?"

"I did, but we didn't take the OR to the battlefield. We took the wounded to the OR near the front lines, not on the front lines. I know you want to help her, Doc, but we can't risk it. Besides, if the riots continue much longer, others are going to get shot and wounded and need your services. We can't run up there over and over. It's too risky."

"It's a risk I'm willing to take, Mr. Henry. I can understand if you folks don't want to go. But we have to do something, or Martha will die. If we have to, we will go on our own," Mark answered back.

"You don't understand, Doc. It's not me I'm worried about. I don't want any of us to get hurt, but you, sir, are worth more than your weight in gold. You are too valuable an asset to lose. Society as we know it right now needs you as much as we need food, water, and bullets. We cannot risk losing you for her or anyone," Mr. Henry explained as calmly as he could.

"Hey, that's my wife in there who is dying, and if Dr. Edwards and I are willing to risk our lives, then that ought to be our decision," Paul interjected angrily.

"Yes, sir, I understand. I want to help her, too, and we will. But I want us to be able to help others, not just now, but in the future. It's part of the bigger picture. We need to cover all our bases, the things necessary to take care of our group—security, supplies, weapons, ammunition, food, transportation, communication, and medical care. Stop and think about it.

"There is another way to do this. We go get the equipment and bring it back and set it up here. That way, you can do her surgery in a safer location, and if someone else needs help, or we need to move out of here, we will be ready to go. That's what MASH stands for—it's a mobile army surgical hospital. And one other thing—all that fancy equipment will need electricity, and there is none there. But we do have a five-kilowatt generator here that should run everything you need. Look, guys, this ain't my first rodeo. You give us an hour or so, and with a little luck, we'll be back with your operating room and set it up right there in your garage."

Mark and Paul discussed it between themselves, then shook their heads and told Mr. Henry they weren't sure that was the best option. They were used to operating in an operating room, and there was one a few miles away. They still thought it might be best to get Martha there as soon as possible. Everything they would need would be there.

Just then there was another knock on the door. It was Robert Jones and his wife, Terri, helping their son Andrew into the house. "Dr. Edwards, sorry to bother you. I know ya'll have other problems to deal with, but my son here is real sick. He's been hurting really bad in his belly since last night, and now he can't keep anything down. He's been throwing up all morning, and now he's running a fever. We were gonna try to take him to the hospital, but now, we heard it isn't there anymore. We didn't know what else to do."

Mark could tell the boy was sick by his pale color and the pained look on his face every time he moved. "Here, let's take him into the other bedroom and let me check him. Cindy, if you don't mind, can you check his vitals while I get my bag?" When Mark entered the room, Cindy told him the boy's temperature was 101.5 and he had a rapid pulse. Mark determined he had point tenderness in the right lower quadrant, with rigidity, guarding, and rebound tenderness. Mark stood and looked down at his newest sick patient and mumbled to himself, "Great, what else can go wrong?" Then he went back to the kitchen, where everyone was waiting on him. "Folks, it looks like he has acute appendicitis. I can't be one hundred percent sure without a CT scan, but I'm almost certain. He needs his appendix out today."

Mark turned to Mr. Henry. "You're right, sir. I was in such a hurry to do something, even if it was wrong, that I didn't see the bigger picture. I'll give you a list of what I need, and we'll be ready here when you get back. Mark realized that helping Tammy and Martha wasn't the end of their troubles—it was just the beginning.

"Good. I'm glad you understand what we are up against here. If we are going to get through this situation, we are all going to have to work together. Everyone has a role to play. Paul, besides Mr. Dickerson, you are the only other person in our group with battle experience. I'll need your help if things get rough up there. Plus, if you are as good as the doc says you are, you'll know what he needs. While we're there, we'll grab as many extra supplies as we can—medicines, anything we think we can use. This may be our best last chance to get medical supplies for a long time. If any of you have a problem with it, look at it this way: We are not taking anything. We are relocating it to a safer area until things settle down, and then we can return it. Under the circumstances, I don't think they will miss it."

"Yes, sir, I'll be glad to go. I know exactly what we need," Paul said as he stood up and saluted the colonel out of respect. Paul wasn't afraid. He had been in battle situations before, and he knew if they couldn't get back safely with the medical supplies, his wife would probably die. And if she died, he didn't care to live without her. Getting the supplies was the most important thing he could do for her—for all of them.

"Saddle up, troops. Looks like we got a plan. Time's a wastin'," Mr. Henry barked. He was back in command mode. "Let's get rolling while the rain is still coming down and keeping the wolves at bay. Right now, it's our best friend. Mr. Dickerson, would you get a couple of the boys to bring up the truck and hook up my trailer so we can haul as much as possible and keep it dry, and so that no one else can see what we are hauling?"

"Yes, sir, right away," Mr. Dickerson said as he went out the door to round up the boys.

"Mr. Jones, I would think that since your son needs this as much as anyone, you would go with us. If you would, load up our weapons and get the other boys to stand guard. Tell them to be on the lookout for our quick return, so we don't get shot if we have to come in hot."

"Got it," Mr. Jones said as he took off to carry out his orders.

Mark was impressed how everyone responded to what Mr. Henry said. When everyone was loaded up, they headed back the same route that Paul and Mark had just taken a little less than two hours ago, with Paul driving Mark's Explorer in the lead car, Robert Jones riding shotgun and his son Curtis in the backseat, all fully armed and ready. Mr. Henry followed in the truck, with the trailer in tow and Mr. Dickerson riding shotgun.

After they left, Mark and Cindy went over what they needed to do for Tammy, Martha and Andrew when Paul and the others got back with the equipment and supplies. Cindy checked their vital signs again, and Mark made his rounds before settling down in the kitchen with Cindy and the other ladies from the subdivision. It was midafternoon, but they were already planning supper. Mrs. Henry sat down with Mark and Cindy to fill them in on everything that had happened around there since the riots and the mass exodus. Mark couldn't help but notice how Mrs. Henry looked a lot like Grandma Brown, so much so that she could pass as her sister.

Mary explained how her husband had not really been content since his retirement just two years ago and was having difficulty adjusting to it. As a lieutenant colonel, he was a battalion commander in charge of the welfare and duties of hundreds of men and women, everything from beans and bullets to Band-Aids was used to responsibility, making decisions, and giving orders. She told of the phone call he received from an army general just before the lines went down. She didn't know exactly what he told him, but he did say that they may need his services and might need to activate him again, and they would be in touch. The colonel would not say whether he would go or not if called, but he seemed proud that his services were needed, and deep down inside, despite all the chaos, he liked it. It's what he had done for thirty years.

She described how the four households in their cove had banded together for support and security and had pooled, inventoried, and shared all their resources and even cooked and ate all their meals together. Although not ideal, their cove was the only defensible area in the subdivision. The gate down front offered security, as did the six-foot-tall privacy fence that lined all the backyards . If the fence didn't stop intruders altogether, it would at least slow them down considerably and make it much more difficult for them to sneak up from the rear. Most of it was at the suggestion of the colonel, who sort of became the natural group leader they all turned to.

She explained how he had organized the men and the teens and trained them on weapons, sentry duty, patrols, and communication with the two-way radios to help protect them from the rioters or whoever was breaking into the houses in the neighborhood. They had held off several small groups of attackers who tried to overrun their cove. She said the attacks were becoming more frequent, and that Jerry and Sally Watson were watching the gate while Billy was patrolling. They were all armed, had radios, and stayed in contact at all times. Then she showed Mark her radio and described how to use it.

Mark now understood that Mr. Henry had a set of skills he didn't possess, a wealth of experience in managing a large number of men and women in peacetime and battle situations, and that was the situation they were in. From that moment on, he would be the colonel to Mark. He had earned his stripes.

Mrs. Dickerson added her take on the whole thing. She was a home health nurse and worked only about three days a week. She and the other mothers were not happy that their sons and daughters were carrying guns, but they had no choice. It was either shoot back or be shot, patrol and protect or be overrun. They weren't sure, but some of the other neighbors might not have been so lucky. Before their group banded together, some of the others who stayed behind in the neighborhood may have been killed or run off, but the men took care of it and wouldn't tell them exactly what happened.

After that, they were all more serious about the training and patrols, and no one questioned their necessity anymore. Since they really did not have anywhere else to go, it was their only option. She admitted that if it hadn't been for the colonel and Mary, they would have given up and hit the road like all the others and gone who knows where. All of them had families in other parts of the country, but they were all too far away to get to under the circumstances. The whole ordeal was wearing them down, and she wasn't sure how much longer they could hold out.

Mrs. Jones took her turn explaining her side of the story. They had gathered up the food, batteries, and anything useful from the houses in the cove, including his. Mary knew where the spare key was, so they let themselves into his house and cleaned out his refrigerator because they didn't think he was coming back anytime soon and figured the food would spoil, so they put it to use. Then they went through and took what they needed from the abandoned houses in the outer perimeter of the neighborhood that they couldn't protect before the looters could take it.

The biggest problem had been the lack of water, but they had started collecting rainwater in barrels and trash cans lined with bags. She told Mark and Cindy how much they appreciated them helping her son and that their return was a ray of hope. They had all become discouraged over the past few days, as the looters were coming out of the city in larger numbers into their area. The colonel said they could expect it to get worse, but there was safety in numbers. With Mark and his crew joining them, there were now seventeen people instead of just the twelve against the world.

Mark asked questions until he fully grasped their situation. He appreciated the colonel's experience even more and understood that, at some point, the wave of hungry and desperate people would head farther into the surrounding areas until they reached them there in the cove and then, eventually, the farm. He needed to consider his options a little more, but he was seeing the writing on the wall. They did need more warm bodies to defend where they were, and when the time came, they were going to need more warm bodies to defend the farm. And it might be sooner than later, but they had other pressing problems. He suggested to the ladies that they use his kitchen and any of his food supplies for supper. It looked as if it might be a long night.

CHAPTER 15
TEAM EFFORT

On the way to the surgery center, the rain had let up some, but the lightning was still flashing and the wind was still blowing hard enough to keep most people inside. As before, it was slow and difficult driving because of the stalled cars and the rain, But better raindrops than bullets any day of the week. It was the first time the colonel and the others had seen firsthand what Paul and Mark had experienced. They saw the evidence of violence as they neared the hospital, which was much closer to Memphis than any of them wanted to be. Overturned cars, broken windows, smoldering buildings, looted businesses, and what looked like an occasional dead body lined both sides and sometimes the middle of Goodman Road, which led to the interstate and hospital.

They saw only a few people out and about in the downpour, some obviously carrying guns and the spoils of their latest robbery or break-in. One gun battle played out in front of their eyes as they passed by. Under different circumstances, they would have tried to help, but it was over before they could do anything, as the lone defender armed with only a pistol while trying to protect his business was outmanned and outgunned by several armed intruders. Justice would have to wait for another day. Fortunately, no one challenged them as they drove on. Perhaps it was the rain, or maybe it was because it was their vehicles were loaded with several heavily armed men in camo fatigues holding their weapons in plain view. It was just enough of a deterrent to bluff all but the most determined Takers, as they were called by the group. Since before the riots started, there were two kinds of people, not based on race, or religion, or even political affiliation: those who took care of themselves and those who took from others, the Takers.

This is what it had come down to: those who respected the sanctity of human life, who helped out their neighbors, their town, their families and friends and gave and worked and just wanted to be left alone by the government, versus the Takers, who just wanted to take. They took from the government until there was nothing left to take, and then they set out to take from everyone else, including each other. They took anything and everything from anyone and everyone. They didn't just take what they needed. They took what they wanted. They took as much as they could, as often as they could, because they had grown up taking and felt it was their right to take. They did not respect human life or the right to own property that was earned with hard work. Any of them could have gotten an education. They could have gotten a job flipping burgers or mowing lawns and worked their way up in life as many others had done over the decades. But it was easier for them to take from the government, and when the government couldn't give any more, they took from everyone else.

The colonel couldn't believe what he was seeing. The country he had given his life to, the country that he fought and served for all those years, had come to this. It was not right. He would not stand for it. If he knew his former chain of command as he thought he did, they would not stand for it, either. It would have to change. Not right then and there, but some day.

As they slowly pulled into the surgery center parking lot, keeping an eye out for the signs of trouble, they slowed to a stop next to each other. They spotted the broken glass in the door leading into the main hallway. Paul told the colonel that the center was on the south side of the first floor and was separated from the main hallway by two heavy metal fire doors that required an access code to enter. Since the electricity was off, that would be a problem. Their military training kicked in. Everyone listened up as they discussed their plan. They would secure the perimeter first, then gain access and secure both floors of the building, then access and secure their target. And last but not least, they would load up the needed supplies and make a quick escape.

Paul and Mr. Jones drove around the perimeter of the parking lot but saw no signs of an active threat. They left Curtis, with his two-way radio on and the car running, to stand guard on the west side to keep a lookout for trouble. Mr. Dickerson stayed with the truck on the east side of the building to keep watch and drive the trailer up to the entrance when he got the all-clear. The colonel, followed by Paul and Mr. Jones, gained access through the broken door, cleared the main hallway, and checked all the doors, which were locked. They went up to the second floor and did the same. No signs of life. Then they tried to access the surgery center, but the doors were locked and, because of the dead bolts, were difficult to pry open. There were already three small-caliber bullet holes in the door, from when someone had tried to force their way in, and what appeared to be an exit bullet hole. They all looked at each other.

"That means someone was, or is, in there. Stand back," Paul ordered as he knocked on the door from the side, so he wouldn't get shot, and yelled for someone to open the door. He waited but got no answer. "Watch out, guys, I'm going to use the master key," Paul said as he lifted his rifle to shoot out the lock. It took about a half dozen shots to finally gain access. "That's one tough lock." They kicked in the door and began to clear the surgery center room by room. There was evidence that someone had been staying there: a Coleman stove, recently opened cans of food, dirty dishes, and clothes scattered about the lounge. Just then, the sound of a fire exit door slamming shut came from the back hallway that led outside. Then they heard Mr. Dickerson on the radio. "We have a runner! We have a runner! I've got him! I've got him!"

Paul ran out to help Mr. Dickerson, who was holding at gunpoint a young black man standing with his hands above his head. Paul checked him for weapons and found a .32-caliber carry pistol, with an empty clip, in one back pocket and his billfold in the other. The man began pleading with them. "Don't shoot! Please, don't shoot me! Take what you want. I was just staying here—"

The colonel came up and interrupted him. "Shut up! We're not going to shoot you, unless you don't stop yelling. Take his pistol and turn him loose. We don't need any prisoners."

"Yes, sir, Colonel," Paul said as he was checking his billfold. "Sir, you may want to take a look at this. I think he is a nurse. He has a nursing license from Mississippi in here, along with a carry permit from Tennessee."

"Gimme that." The colonel took the ID and checked it out. "What is your name, sir?"

"Jack Pounders," the man said hesitantly, not sure whether he was supposed to talk or not.

The colonel looked him over. "What is your address?"

"1221 East Parkway South."

"Is this you?" the colonel asked as he showed Jack his own ID and driver's license.

"Yes, sir."

"Are you a nurse?"

"Yes, sir."

"Well, dammit man, why didn't you say so, and why were you running?"

"I didn't want to get shot. They have been trying to get in here for several days, and then they shot some people today and burned the hospital. I thought you were going to—"

"Mr. Pounders, what made you think we were going to shoot you?"

"Well, all of you are white and wearing camo, and I'm black. I thought you were some of those, you know, supremacist dudes."

"Look, mister, I don't care what color you are," the colonel said as he turned to Paul. "Go get Mr. Jones." Paul spun and went inside to get Robert. "What in the world were you doing here?" the colonel asked, curious why anyone would be camping out in a surgery center.

"I had to get out of my apartment. It was too dangerous. I was working here the week things went bad, so I just started staying here. Then they shot my car up and siphoned all my gas, so I was sort of stuck here."

Paul and Mr. Jones walked up, and the colonel looked at Robert and smiled. "He thought we were going to shoot him because he is black."

Mr. Jones smiled and said, "Only if you shoot first."

"Paul, if he promises not to shoot us, give him his weapon back and turn him loose. We need to get going." The colonel turned around to head back to the task at hand.

"Wait! Turn me loose? I just told you, I don't have anywhere to go. I just moved here from Houston. I don't have any family here. Why can't you take me with you?"

The colonel thought about it for a minute, and then told Paul, "I don't know if we need another nurse. I think we have that covered right now, and we certainly don't need another mouth to feed. Let him go."

"Wait, I know it's none of my business, but what do you want in the surgery center? I know it's not just drugs. You guys aren't drug dealers. You called him colonel, and ya'll would have shot me if you were. Maybe I can help. I know where everything is in there."

The colonel thought about what he said. "We need the equipment for surgery. We have a surgeon and patients, but no equipment. Maybe you could save us some time."

"A surgeon? Surgery? What the hell? Where in the world did you find a surgeon in this mess? Dr. Edwards was the last surgeon around here, but he's gone now. He left the other day when the hospital started burning. I watched the whole thing from here. I would have helped, but I was out of bullets, and I—"

"That's okay, son. There was nothing you could do," the colonel interrupted.

"Wait a minute. You know Dr. Edwards?" Paul asked.

"Sure, I've worked with him many times since I've been here. I do most of his anesthesia."

Paul and the colonel looked at each other at the same time, and then back at Pounders. "I thought you said you were a nurse?" Paul questioned again, trying to get to the bottom of what he just said.

"I am. I'm a nurse anesthetist. A CRNA. A certified nurse anesthetist," Jack said, as if they weren't getting it.

"Holy crap! Why didn't you say that earlier? Get in there and help us get what we need. Mister, you're going with us, now. We can use your services. We need to get going. We have surgery to do," the colonel said as he hurried everyone inside to start loading up the truck and trailer.

They loaded up everything they thought they might need, and then some, until the back of the truck and trailer were full. They were all out of breath and dripping wet from the rain and the sweat and from loading the supplies so quickly. Then they loaded themselves up and headed back the same way they came. The rain had almost stopped when they pulled up to Mark's house. It had been an hour and a half since they left the cove.

Mark rushed outside and confronted them as they were getting out of their vehicles. "Where the hell have you guys been? It's been almost two hours. I don't know how much longer Martha can hang on. The IV fluids are out and her pressure is down."

"Sorry, Doc. It took a little longer than we planned, but we brought some help back with us." The colonel smiled as he looked toward the backseat of the car as Jack was getting out. "I think he can help you get this done quicker."

Mark was silent for a long moment as he gathered in what he was seeing. "Jack, what the…? Where in the world did you come from?"

"It's a long story, Doc. They tell me we have some surgery to do."

"Yes, glad you're here. I need some help. Paul's wife took a bullet to the abdomen. Right lower quadrant. Over three and a half hours ago. Some bleeding. No idea what her hematocrit is. Possible bowel injury. Pressure is low. Only two liters of fluid to give her. She did get antibiotics. No blood to give her. She needs to go first, ASAP. Then we have a thirteen-year-old male with a hot appendix that needs to go after that," Mark explained in rapid fire as they went to help unload the equipment and supplies.

"Where are we going to do this?" Jack asked, looking around to get his bearings straight.

"The garage. I cleaned it out as best as I could while waiting on you guys to get back. I guess we'll put the kitchen table in there. I hope you guys have everything we need."

Paul came up and asked what they needed first. "You're not going to believe this, but we brought an OR table, an anesthesia machine, oxygen, gooseneck lamps, pulse ox machine, defibrillator, crash cart, a bunch of saline and sterile water, sutures, drapes, lap packs, cautery machine, we emptied out the medicine room, a bookwalter retractor, and last but not least, several instrument trays, from hand trays all the way to general basic. Everything but the kitchen sink. What do you want first?"

"Wow, you did bring it all. I guess the OR table and the anesthesia machine first, then the cautery, a lap pack, drapes, sterile water, and something to prep the abdomen with. Cindy, get the ringers lactate, hang two more liters on Martha, and run them in. She needs the volume. Start another bag of fluid on Tammy and keep it at fifty cc's and check her O2 with the pulse ox. When they get the oxygen out, put her on nasal O2 and adjust it to get her sat over ninety-two percent, if you can. If not, let me know. Make sure the Jones boy gets a liter or two of fluid and some antibiotics." Mark tried to think of anything else they needed to do, but he decided that was it until they could start the surgery.

While Dr. Edwards and Nurse Cindy were discussing patient care issues, Paul and Jack were busy setting up the OR with the help of the other men. The colonel already had the generator set up behind the garage with extension cords running everywhere, so they could power up the equipment and lights. Everyone moved quickly, with as little conversation as needed, to get the job done. It looked like a NASCAR pit crew in action. After the garage was turned into an OR, and the power was up and the equipment on and tested, it was time to transfer Martha.

After he did his assessment, Jack helped Cindy bring Martha in on the stretcher that they brought back with the rest of the equipment. They carefully moved her to the OR table and began preparing her for surgery. While she was being intubated and put under anesthesia, Paul opened and set up the back table with the instruments and drapes. Cindy prepped her abdomen, and then Dr. Edwards and Paul draped her abdomen with the sterile sheets. Dr. Edwards then asked, "Paul, you okay working on your own wife?"

"Yeah, I guess. Don't really have much choice, do I?"

"Everybody ready? Lights. Cautery on thirty cut, forty coag. Suction."

Paul looked up from across the table. "Oh, crap. Suction. We have the suction tip and tubing and canisters, but no wall suction here. Sorry, we couldn't bring that with us."

"Come on, guys, we have to have suction. Any ideas?" Silence. "What about the crash cart? There is usually a portable suction machine on the crash cart. It's a state requirement for surgery centers." Mark waited as Cindy went to the cart and brought back the portable suction, plugged it in, and hooked it to the suction canisters, which took several minutes to do.

"I can't wait any longer. I'm going in. Knife. Laps up." Mark made a skin incision with the scalpel in the midline of the abdomen and entered the peritoneal cavity using the cautery to cut through the fat then the muscle fascia. A large amount of old and clotted blood poured out and ran onto the table, then to the floor, then onto their shoes. "More suction."

"I am sucking," Paul said, noticeably upset by the sight of that much blood in his wife's abdomen. "This stupid thing is not strong enough."

"Check the suction. We need more suction," Mark said as he took the suction from Paul to check it himself.

"I did. It's all the way up. That's it," Cindy offered in defense.

"Shit. More laps. That thing is a piece of crap. We'll need something better than that." Mark and Paul continued their exploration using laps to soak up the blood and scooped out the large clots of blood with their gloved hands. They concentrated their efforts to the right lower quadrant where the bullet entered. They found a through-and-through bullet wound to the cecum that went into the psoas muscle. There was only a small amount of fecal contamination in the abdomen causing early peritonitis. Mark clamped across the base of the cecum with a noncrushing bowel clamp to stop the leakage so they could concentrate on stopping the blood loss. Fortunately, the bullet just missed the common iliac vessels and the ureter. The only significant bleeding was from the mesenteric vessels, next to the right colon, which had mostly clotted off but was still bleeding some. Thankfully, the main branch of the right colic artery was intact, which spared the rest of the right colon from ischemia.

Mark, assisted by Paul, carefully but quickly clamped and ligated all the arteries and veins injured by the bullet. That left them with the injured colon to deal with. Mark discussed the options with Paul. A single injury, or tear, or perforation of the right colon can usually be oversewn with good success, but with a high-velocity wound from a bullet, the risk of post-op leak was a little higher. And with the presence of fecal contamination and peritonitis, it was even higher. With the blood vessel supply injury to the cecum, the risk was significant.

Under normal circumstances, Mark would repair or resect the damaged colon and place the patient on strong IV antibiotics and IV nutrition until it healed. If the patient developed any signs of a leak from the repair or anastomosis, he would get a CT scan and reoperate if needed. Or, if an abscess developed, he would have an interventional radiologist place a percutaneous drain in the area. But in the situation they were in, none of that was possible. So the safest course was to do a temporary diverting loop colostomy by bringing out the injured bowel and sewing it open to the skin. Better a skin bag than a toe tag. That would eliminate the risk of post-op leakage and peritonitis and allow Martha to be able to start on a diet much sooner.

Once the colostomy was finished, Mark inserted a finger into the bullet wound in the psoas muscle and could feel the bullet at his fingertip. He handed Paul a Kelly clamp. "Here, you do the honors."

Paul did the same and felt the bullet with the tip of his finger, then gently pulled it out with the clamp and held it up for all to see. By that time, everyone in the house had come into the room to see what was going on. Mark reached over to the back table and held out a metal pan. Paul dropped the bullet. It made a metallic clinking sound, and everyone laughed. Paul smiled at Mark through his mask. "Thanks, Doc. Just like on TV."

When they finished, they irrigated the abdomen with several liters of sterile saline to wash out the stool, blood, and bacteria to help prevent any further infection after surgery. Then they closed the abdominal wall muscle and fascia but left the skin and subcutaneous layer open to prevent a wound infection. The last step was maturing the colostomy to the skin. Mark looked up at

Paul and started to ask if he could dress the wound while he dictated the op report and wrote orders, but then he caught himself and realized that was not necessary. There was no computer to write orders on, no dictating machines, no medical records or transcription. There was no need for any of that because there were no rules or regulations where they were, no lawyers looking over their shoulders, no administrators trying to point out any errors in hindsight, no threat of a lawsuit if Martha had an unforeseen complication. All he had to do was tell Cindy what fluids and antibiotics and care he wanted her to have post-op. He was not used to that, but he liked it. That was the way it was long ago, when doctors and nurses and Catholic nuns ran hospitals, before the administrators with MBAs, lawyers, and politicians took over health care. It was just the patient, the doctor, and the nurses.

After they moved Martha to the master bedroom and settled her in, they turned their attention to their next patient, Andrew Jones, for an appendectomy. Again, Mark was ready to go talk to the family and give them a detailed account of the proposed surgery, informing them of all the potential risks, benefits, and options, as well as obtain a signed consent to help protect him from a lawsuit if something unforeseen happened. But as he went to give them the details, Mr. Jones cut him off. "Doc, I know you're supposed to do all that. I had surgery last year myself. But we know you are going to do the best you can, and we appreciate whatever you can do for Andrew. Just do what you can. We owe you." Mark was so moved by his sincerity that he almost got choked up. He just shook his hand then went back to the garage for the second surgery of the day.

Mark did the appendectomy through a two-inch incision in the right lower quadrant at McBurney's point, just above and medial to the anterior iliac crest. The appendix was severely inflamed with the onset of early gangrene, but thankfully it had not yet ruptured. It was routine, just like the hundreds of others he had done over the years, and took only about twenty minutes, skin to skin. After they closed and dressed the wound, they moved him back to the bedroom for recovery. Again, all Mark had to do was tell Cindy what he wanted, and she in turn told Mrs. Dickinson, who earlier had volunteered her services as a nurse.

CHAPTER 16
THE SICK AND SHUT IN

Mark went and checked on his patients after surgery. He was running on very little sleep, little food, and no rest for days now, and it all seemed to hit him at once. He wanted to go lie down and sleep, but he knew he had to keep going, although he felt as if he at least needed to sit down. He smelled coffee and went to the kitchen to check it out. The ladies were starting supper and had a large pot of coffee on. "Thanks for the coffee, ladies."

"You're welcome, Dr. Edwards. You just sit yourself down right here and have some coffee. We'll have supper ready in just a bit. We know you guys must be tired," Mrs. Henry said as she brought him some cream and sugar.

"I hope ya'll found everything you need."

"Sure did. You know, this isn't the first time I've been in here. Sorry, we helped ourselves to your fridge last week, but we didn't think you would be back anytime soon. If all that food spoiled after the power went out, it would have been a big mess. I don't think Lisa would have been too happy about that when she came home. You know, when you were on call, I would come over and visit with Lisa and help her with the boys."

"I know, she told me how much help you were," Mark offered as a belated thank-you.

"I kind of miss those boys of yours. I guess they remind me of my grandchildren. They are scattered all over the world, and I don't know when I will get to see them again, if ever," Mrs. Henry said, almost in tears. Mrs. Jones went over and gave her a hug and told her she would see them again someday.

After they cleaned up the garage and got it ready to go again, just in case, Jack and Paul found Mark sitting in the kitchen sipping a cup of coffee and talking to the ladies.

"How can you drink coffee this late in the day and still sleep at night?" Jack asked.

"It's easy. I just close my eyes," Mark said with a smile as he sipped his coffee. "Man, I haven't had a cup in days. The ladies were good enough to make a pot while they had the generator on. Better get one while you can. Don't know when the next cup will be."

"Who would have thought? Two weeks ago, if someone had said we were going to be doing surgery in a garage, I would have told them they were crazy." Paul laughed at his own words, and the others joined in.

"That was a new one on me, too. I hope we don't have to do that again. I played the drums in a garage band in high school, but I never thought I would be doing anesthesia in a garage," Jack said.

Mark had often wondered why medical personnel didn't claim post-traumatic stress disorder, like others in high-stress jobs. He figured it was due to a personality trait inherent in health care workers that allowed them to compartmentalize what they did at work and leave it there. Or maybe it was the humor. It was routine for all of them to joke and kid around during and after surgery. It was called OR humor. It was sometimes dark, sometimes off color, and sometimes just down and dirty. They could joke about anything—blood, guts, bad smells, feces, gangrene, and death. It relieved tension, kept them sane, and usually kept them from crying—but not always.

About that time, the colonel and Mr. Dickerson came in from shutting down the generator and tweaking the guard schedule with Mr. Watson and Mr. Jones and sat at the table with them. "Man, that smells good. Thanks, don't mind if I do." The colonel got up and fixed himself a cup and gave his wife a pat on the backside as he went by. Mrs. Henry just smiled to herself. "Supper smells good. What are we having?" The colonel asked as he sat back down.

"That's for us to know and you to find out, dear," she said back at him, just to pick on him a bit.

Jack watched them sip their coffee then got up poured a cup for himself. "Well, what's next on the agenda? I mean, where do we go from here?"

Everyone got quiet for a moment then the colonel spoke. "Not sure. We didn't really have time to get into the details of our situation here earlier today, but we're going to run out of bullets before we run out of bandages or beans, if you know what I mean. With this rain we'll have plenty of water for a while. The biggest problem is that we've had several recent break-ins and a few run-ins that ended in our favor. But they are getting more frequent and more violent. From what we saw today, I don't think we can stay here much longer. I think it's just a matter of time before our luck runs out and we get overrun. I don't think we have enough firepower or bullets, even with you guys here and what you brought. I've looked the place over. We just don't have a strong defensible position here. If they come at us from three sides, in any numbers, some of us, many of us, are going to…Well, you get the picture. If it wasn't for the fact that we are off the main road a bit and partly secluded by the brick wall along the front and the gate and drainage ditch along the east side and the privacy fences between the houses, we would probably have been run out of here already. It has sort of kept us out of the main flow of traffic and trouble so far. But as the city folks spread out, looking for food and whatever else they want, and the numbers grow, our luck will run out. We just don't have the numbers to hold off a large group. Up till now, we have been able to hold off a few here and there, and we have been lucky none of us have gotten shot or hurt. But if they hit us in any numbers, they can overrun us or burn us out of here. That I am sure of. When that will happen, we don't know, but it won't be too long from now. But when to leave and where we go from here is the problem. Traveling anywhere right now would be dangerous, to say the least. And another problem is that we have wounded, which will slow us down considerably."

Cindy came into the kitchen and sat with them for a minute. No one said anything. Mark sat quietly as well, then asked Cindy, "How's she looking?"

"Okay, I guess. Her pressure is still down. I'm still pouring the fluid to her."

Mark sat still, deep in thought and didn't say anything, then got up and left to check on Martha.

"Something we said?" the colonel asked, half-jokingly.

"No, he's just doing his doctor thing. What did I hear about us going somewhere?" Cindy asked as she decided coffee was a good idea, too.

The colonel gave her the *Reader's Digest* version of their situation. He debated whether or not to tell them but decided they had the right to know about the phone call he received from General Franks, the previous commanding officer of his old brigade.

"I didn't have time to tell you earlier, but I received a call from General Franks, my old commander. They are probably going to reactivate me and put me in charge of my old brigade, around three thousand soldiers, to help reestablish order in and around Memphis. General Franks was previously a colonel but was promoted to major general over the division to which the present brigade belongs. General Franks said it wasn't a request. This was all due to the vice president declaring martial law and mobilizing troops stateside to establish order in the cities. They said they would let me know when and where to report. But since the phones are out, I'm not sure when that will happen. I think it will be soon."

Mark came back into the room and sat without saying a word. Paul couldn't stand it any longer. "How's she doing, Doc?"

"Well, overall I'd say she is doing okay, but her pressure is still down. I think she needs a blood transfusion. I figure she lost about twelve hundred cc's of blood that we can account for, about half her blood volume. It may have been more. Her blood count is probably somewhere around twenty or so. Could be lower. Probably pumping Kool-Aid through her veins. She needs a transfusion. We have given her a lot of IV fluid to keep her pressure up. She may end up with pulmonary edema. Fluid on her lungs. Her O2 sats are already borderline. If she bleeds any more, I don't know if she will make it."

Paul went to Martha, sat beside her bed, held her hand, and tried to get a response from her. She did not respond. Paul prayed and cried. Cindy came in a few minutes later to hang another bag of fluid and sat beside Paul. "He will think of something. She is going to make it."

"Thanks, Cindy. We made an OR appear out of nowhere, but getting a blood transfusion…" Paul dropped his head into his hands and fought back the tears.

Mark and the colonel discussed their situation and what he told Cindy and the others about the phone call from the general. Then it occurred to Mark, if and when the army gets word to the colonel, he would have to leave them in the middle of the mess they were in. Then they would be stuck there, with critically sick patients to take care of, teenagers to rely on to help defend them from the dangers lurking outside the gate, and a limited supply of food, water, bullets, and medicine. He thought back on the past week or so and wondered if he should have just thrown in the towel and gone to the farm with Lisa and the boys. He missed them very much and wondered how they were doing. Were they safe? Was the violence headed their way? Was it already there? All he knew was that he needed to get to the farm. No, they all needed to get to the farm. They would need the extra hands to work the fields and to defend the farm. That was what they needed to do.

Cindy came back into the kitchen and interrupted his train of thought. "Dr. Edwards, Tammy's O2 sat is down. I have her on a forty percent mask. She is having more trouble breathing. Mrs. Dickerson is with her. Martha's O2 sat is down to ninety percent, and her pressure is still low after another liter of fluid. Her urine output is low. She's had over five liters of fluid today. I'm worried she…Paul is…I told him you would…I don't know what else to do…" She couldn't finish what she was trying to say.

Mark sat for a moment and said nothing. All eyes were on him in the kitchen. It was deathly quiet. Then he spoke slowly and directly. "Colonel, can we run the generator all night if we need to?"

"We can if we need to, but it's gonna draw unwanted attention, if you know what I mean," the colonel said.

"Jack, that anesthesia machine has a respirator on it, doesn't it?"

"Yeah, sure. What are we going to do with that?"

"Help Nurse Dickerson move Tammy into the OR. Then set up for a pediatric intubation. Set the vent for a tidal volume of two hundred, rate of twelve, and PEEP of five. Let me know when everything is ready."

"Cindy, look through the supplies they brought back today and see if they have some red top lab tubes. Probably will be in one of the boxes from the supply room. Paul, help her find them. If you find them, draw a tube of blood on Martha and everyone who's walking. Ask them if they know their blood type and write it down. Then find me."

"Okay, but what are we going to do with them?" Paul asked.

"We are going to transfuse Martha." Mark got up from the table and stood for a moment. "Colonel, we all need to get to the farm. The sooner the better. Let's figure out a way." Then he left the room and went to his study.

Everyone sat still for a minute to let what he just said sink in. They all looked at each other and shrugged their shoulders. "You heard him, guys. Let's get moving," Jack said as he got up to go help move Tammy.

Paul looked over at Cindy and asked, "Can he do that? I mean, no lab, no blood bank, no whatever it takes to do that." Cindy looked at Paul. "Come on. Let's go find those tubes and draw some blood." They left discussing blood types and transfusion reactions as they went to the garage.

"Can he do that?" Mrs. Henry asked.

"I don't know. He's kind of bossy, isn't he? I mean, he thinks he can tell us all what to do," Mrs. Jones suggested rather timidly. "Did you see how they all got up and did what he told them without so much as an explanation?"

The colonel smiled to himself. "Oh, I bet he can. And he's not bossy, Mrs. Jones. They do what he asks because they believe in him. And they follow him because he's their leader. That is something I do know a little about. And from what I've seen, he may not always be right, but when he is wrong, he will admit it. That, my good woman, takes character. And I do think we need to find a way to get all of you to this farm he keeps talking about. It's your best chance to make it through all of this."

Jack found Mark at his desk quietly, studying an old textbook on hematology and serology. "Doing a little light reading, I see. Got Tammy and the vent ready."

Mark went with him to the garage. He had Jack give her a sedative in her IV, and when she was relaxed, he looked into her larynx with the lighted laryngoscope. He was able to see her vocal cords and the upper part of the trachea between her cords when she took a breath. The swelling and redness was mild, definitely not as severe as he feared it might be. It was a good sign. He went on and inserted the endotracheal tube in her airway and had Jack place her on the ventilator on the settings he ordered to let her rest for the night. He knew that placing her on the ventilator, even for one or two days, would make a big difference in her oxygenation and recovery. He watched her for a few minutes on the ventilator. Her O2 sat was ninety-eight percent. He smiled at

Jack. "We can take turns keeping an eye on her tonight. I'll tell them to make more coffee."

Cindy and Paul found a box of the lab tubes and began drawing blood from everyone and marking down the known blood types. It took most of the evening, but when they were finished, they went to find Mark in his study. "Tammy looks better already," Cindy said with a wide grin. "How long will she need to be on the vent?"

"I hope just a day or two. Where are we on the blood drawing?"

"Got 'er done, Doc," Paul said, trying his best to sound like the Cable Guy.

"Very funny. Don't give up your day job. Let's see what you got." Mark studied the tubes and made notes on the ones with known blood types. "Very good. I'll be back with an answer in a little bit." An hour or so later, Mark reappeared in the kitchen and announced his findings. "Martha is type A. Two others have type A blood—Paul and Mrs. Jones."

Everyone in the kitchen wanted to know how he came up with that. Cindy and Jack knew a little bit about blood transfusions, so they wanted Mark to explain it to them. Everyone listened in as he explained it in detail. "Okay, you asked for it. First I set up a series of test slides, mixing a drop of the different known blood types with each of the unknown types then looking for them to clot. To increase the sensitivity of the cross-matching, I mixed a drop of serum with a drop of blood from each in a similar fashion, and by using the microscope I was able to determine microclumping and hemolysis, which is not apparent to the naked eye. By using this process, I was able to determine each of the blood types for everyone here."

Everyone stared at Mark as if they were interested, so he went on. "There are about thirty known blood group types, and over six hundred known antigens to deal with when it comes to transfusing blood, but the main four blood types that matter the most are O, A, B, and AB. In the US, O is the most common at a little over forty percent, then type A right at forty percent, then B at about twelve percent, and AB at about five percent. These blood types are based on the antigens attached to the red blood cell outer wall. But the plasma of a recipient contains antibodies to the other cell types. Even though O is known as the universal donor, that only applies to transfusing washed packed red blood cells. That means the plasma, white blood cells, and platelets have all been removed to be used for other purposes. But when transfusing whole blood, which is necessary in our case, since we do not have the ability to wash or separate the other components, then the antibodies in the plasma have to be considered, as well. So the best match for Martha, who has an A blood type, is actually another A donor."

Mark was about to give up, but they said they wanted him to continue. He couldn't tell if they were really interested or just bored. "The only other thing that we deal with in blood transfusion cross matching is the patient's Rh factor. You either have the antigen or you don't. Therefore, the negative or positive blood type, or in Martha's case, A positive or A negative. There is no way to test for that without specialized laboratory equipment, but the good news is that about eighty-five percent of Americans have Rh-positive blood. And unless someone has been transfused before, or is Rh negative and had an Rh-positive baby, the risk of reaction is minimal. Therefore we can transfuse Martha with someone else's A blood and the odds are she will do fine. Last but not least is the risk of blood-borne infections, hepatitis, HIV, and so on. The safest person to get a transfusion from is a close family member whom she has already been exposed to, which would be Paul. By my calculations, she would need at least fifteen hundred cc's of whole blood. That is the equivalent of transfusing three units of packed red cells. The usual amount of blood taken from a donor is five hundred cc's. Each unit will usually raise the hematocrit by two points. If her blood count is twenty, then three units would raise it to about twenty-six or so. If Paul can tolerate it, he should donate the first five hundred to one thousand cc's. Then, we can get the next five hundred from Mrs. Jones, if we need to."

By this time, he could tell he had totally lost everyone, except Cindy and Jack, who were now sold on the idea. "Okay, Dr. Frankenstein, how do we actually transfuse the blood from Paul to Martha without a blood bank?" Jack prodded so he could get the rest of the story.

"Elementary, my Dear Watson. Red cells are stable in normal saline, and to keep from having to use anticoagulants, all we have to do is slowly drain five hundred cc's of blood by gravity out of Paul's arm into a half-full liter bag of saline and then give this to Martha. We can repeat that with Paul for the second bag, and with each donor, as we need to. We will start the transfusion into Martha, slowly, for about fifteen minutes and then stop it for an hour to watch for evidence of a transfusion reaction. If she develops fever, tachycardia, dark urine, or flulike symptoms, we would not give the rest. A transfusion reaction is dangerous because it causes the blood to clump together, which blocks the kidneys and causes kidney failure, uses up the clotting factors, and causes severe bleeding. Other than that, nothing to worry about. Okay, class, any further questions?"

"When do we get started?" Paul stood up, anxious to help his wife start getting better.

"Right now is as good a time as any," Mark offered as he got up and left the room with Paul, Cindy, Jack, and Mrs. Dickerson to get started.

After they left the room, the colonel looked at the women in the kitchen and said, "I told you he could do it." Now they were believers, as well.

Everyone had supper in shifts, including those on watch. The rain was gone, and the skies were clearing up. Mark stepped outside to get some fresh air to help keep him alert. The stars were out bright that night, and the constellation of Orion was especially beautiful. It made him think of Lisa and the boys. They would occasionally go out with him at night to look through his telescope at Saturn and its rings, Jupiter and its Galilean moons, and all the constellations. He didn't know if they were really interested in astronomy, like him, or just humoring him. To him, all the stars were beautiful, but his favorites were Orion and the Pleiades. They reminded him how big the universe was and how great the creator was. That made him want to talk to God, and that made him fall to his knees and pray. He prayed for his family. He prayed for Martha and Tammy. He prayed for all of them. But most of all he prayed that he could be with his family again. The tears fell, but his spirit lifted. It made him even more determined.

Mark and the other medical team members also ate in shifts as the blood transfusions from Paul to Martha were completed. The only problem was that Paul insisted that they take all three bags from him only. He would not listen to any arguments from the rest. Martha needed it, and he was going to give it. End of story. Mark didn't force the issue. He knew once Paul made up his mind about something, that was it. So he advised Cindy to make sure to go slow, make sure he took in extra fluids and food, and make him rest overnight so he wouldn't pass out or go into shock. Paul didn't bat an eye.

Mark and Jack spent the rest of the night watching and checking on Tammy while she was on the ventilator. It looked as if she was making slow progress, and they were hopeful she wouldn't be on the ventilator too long. Apparently, her smoke inhalation injury was not that severe. On one of Mark's shifts, while he was alone in the garage and everyone else was asleep, Cindy went in to visit. Neither had bathed or slept more than an hour or so at a time for days. They had dodged bullets, watched friends die, lost their place of employment, and now were facing an uncertain future.

As Cindy came closer to Mark, she brushed against him. Sleep-deprived. Nerves frayed. Emotions on edge. Cerebral cortical functions depressed. Judgment impaired. Defenses down. They fell into each other's arms. She cried. The tears came. Delirious. Mark closed his eyes and slipped into a dream world. Lisa was holding him. He missed her so much. He longed for her touch. He held her. He kissed her. He caressed her. So soft. So warm. Hormones raged. Senses aroused. Crashing noises. Loud voices. Loud bangs. Mark opened his eyes. Something was wrong. Was it a dream? Or was he dreaming before? Bullets were flying. Glass was breaking.

He snapped back to reality. The windows had been shattered. There were bullet holes in the door. Cindy was still lost in her own dream world, so he pulled her to the floor with him to protect her. They hit the cold, hard floor. She came back to reality. Someone was shooting at them.

"Stay down." Mark waited a few seconds. The bullets stopped flying. He checked Tammy. She was okay. "Come on." Mark pulled Cindy from the floor to her feet and into the kitchen. The kitchen was empty. The women and the colonel had gone home earlier. Paul heard the noise, too, and got up slowly with the IV still in his arm. The room spun for a minute before he could get his legs under him.

Jack met them in the kitchen. "What the hell was that?"

"Someone is shooting at us," Mark said, trying to look out the window without getting himself shot in the process. It was dark and quiet, except for an occasional shout out front by the gate and the dull hum of the generator behind the garage. The shooting had stopped.

After a few minutes, Mr. Jones came to the door and let himself in. "Everybody okay?"

"I guess. What happened?" Mark asked, still trying to look out the window and the door.

"Had some visitors. Two carloads. They tried to run through the gate. We stopped the first one. All four are dead. Glass doesn't stop a .308. The second turned around and left but then drove back by, shooting up the place. They said they would be back." Mr. Jones stopped himself for a few seconds before finishing. "They said we would be sorry."

"Great, just what we need. Drive-bys, on top of everything else." Paul pulled the IV out of his arm. "Looks like you may need an extra pair of eyes out front." He went to get dressed, grabbed his newly acquired AK-47, and slipped out the door toward the gate to help out on watch.

"Should he be doing that, after giving all that blood?" Jack asked.

"You don't know him very well, do you? I wasn't going to try to stop him." Mark smiled, shrugged his shoulders, and went back to the garage to check on Tammy. She was resting well, despite the noise and commotion. Then he went to check on Andrew. He was sitting up in bed, trying to look out the window. Mark assured him everything was okay and told him to get a little more sleep. Then he went to check on Martha. Her color was better, her heart rate was down, and she was starting to wake up. He checked her wounds and colostomy. They were healing without infection.

She opened her eyes. "What happened?"

Mark wasn't sure what to tell her and decided the truth would be best. "You got shot. I had to do a temporary colostomy."

"Where are we?"

"My house."

"How did we get here?"

"The hospital is gone. They burned it down. You rest now."

Cindy came in to check on Martha and was surprised to see her awake. "She's awake. I'll bet we'll have you up and eating in no time," she said, ignoring Mark and trying to pretend as if nothing had happened between them earlier. Mark gave her a nod and left quietly, not exactly sure what to say, if anything.

The colonel came into the kitchen to discuss the situation with Mark and the others. "I think it's here. From what I saw yesterday when we went into town, the wave is about to crest here. Next day or so, most likely. Doubt we can ride it out. Most likely, we will get overrun, or shot up, or both, before it's over. Even if we can ride it out for the next week or so, we will run out of food and ammunition. Our best option is to get out of here soon. The question is, where?"

"My vote is to head to Batesville, to the farm. I know I'm being selfish, because that is where my family is, but it has everything we need. The problem will be getting there with this mess all around us." Mark looked around to see everyone's reaction. There were smiles all around.

"Are you talking about all of us? All seventeen?" the colonel asked.

"Yes, sir. They aren't expecting us, but if I'm right, they will need us before it is over with. The way I figure it, they only have a few weapons and even fewer people to protect the place. If the wave of violence or even the refugees gets to them, they will get run out, as well. Besides, down there at the farm, there is water, the ability to grow food, plenty of firewood, and all the not-so-modern conveniences from the last century to get us through this—woodstoves, hand tools, oil lamps, lanterns. Some of you may end up in tents, or out in the shop or the loft of the barn, until things blow over. But we can stand together, protect each other, grow our own food, if needed. That's the best I can offer." Then Mark sat down and waited for an answer. He was somewhat confused because some of the women started crying.

Mr. Dickerson looked Mark directly in the eyes. "You were serious before? You would take all of us down there?"

Mark looked at everyone, a little puzzled. "You mean you want to go with me? I mean, it's going to be a rough trip. The living quarters may be a little rustic."

The colonel spoke up. "Dr. Edwards, you don't understand. It is our only hope. We have all talked this over. We were praying you would ask us. We know if we stay here, it's over. Mister, we are with you one hundred percent."

"Well, I guess we need to make plans then," Mark said as everyone hugged each other and slapped shoulders in celebration, except Cindy. She was not happy. She turned and quietly left the kitchen without saying a word. She would no longer have Mark to herself anymore. Mrs. Edwards would be at the farm.

CHAPTER 17
ON THE ROAD

Friday, April 18.

The colonel and Mark discussed what it would take to move the entire group to the farm. It was going to be a daunting task. Mark was glad to have the colonel there with all his experience in logistics to make a plan of action. Mark's role was clear. Get the patients ready for the trip as soon as possible. Martha was starting to look better, and barring any unforeseen complications, she would be ready in the next day or so. Tammy's condition was a little less certain. If he could get her off the vent and on oxygen by mask, or nasal cannula, then she would be able to travel. But whether that would be sooner or later was not something he could predict. But if he had to guess, it would be at least a day or two, but they did not have the luxury of time on their side.

The colonel wanted to hit the road by early morning. The earlier the better. The bad guys usually slept before sunrise and into early morning. That was the safest time to travel in hostile territory. They would take the back roads and stay off the main highways and as far away from the interstate as possible and come into the farm from the east. By his calculations, traveling at an average of forty miles per hour, if they didn't encounter trouble, didn't run into any obstructions, didn't break down, and didn't have to take a bladder break, it would take about two hours to get there. Not too far to go on a Sunday drive, but this would be no leisurely cruise.

The colonel had the troops start preparing for the trip. They gassed up the vehicles with the borrowed gas siphoned from the neighborhood mowers and cars left behind by the others. They gathered up as much food, water, lamps, oil, bullets, and other supplies that they could carry with them. Last but not least would be the OR, the generator, and the ventilator that Tammy was still connected to. No reason to leave it behind. It could come in handy again. The colonel would have the caravan armed, loaded, and ready to roll. After that, it would be up to Mark to make the call when they were ready to get out of Dodge.

Things were fairly quiet the rest of the day. Mark, Cindy, Jack, and Mrs. Dickerson spent the day taking care of their patients. Andrew had a bath in the tub with water heated on the stove and was up walking in the house and eating everything he could find. Martha was taking sips of liquids and keeping them down and was passing gas into her colostomy bag, evidence her intestines were starting to work again. Tammy was making slow but good progress on the vent. Mark had her on a T-piece trial. She was breathing on her own, and he was able to get her off the ventilator and on nasal oxygen much earlier than expected. The colonel knew time was of the essence, so he wasted no time in having the men load the OR equipment and spare medical supplies into the enclosed trailer behind his truck.

Just as they were finishing up, a commotion came from the kitchen. Curtis Jones knocked and came in without waiting for an answer. Mark went to the kitchen to see what was up. "Colonel, there is a Captain Ellis with the US Army out front at the gate. He says he is here to see you. And he's not alone." Everyone looked at each other for a moment without saying a word.

The colonel got up slowly. "Well, they certainly took their time." He walked out to the gate. There was an entire company of about 150 men in trucks, armored personnel carriers, and Humvees, some fitted with .50-caliber machine guns, and one two-ton truck fitted with a grader blade out front for clearing the road. He recognized Captain Ellis, who was previously a lieutenant in charge of one of his platoons from his old battalion. He was in his late thirties with jet black hair and a somewhat handsome but unfriendly face. "Captain Ellis. I see you're moving up in the world. What brings you to our neck of the woods?"

"Sir, I have orders here for you from the division commander, General Franks," Captain Ellis said while holding out a sealed envelope labeled with the colonel's name and address.

"Let's go inside, Captain." The colonel turned to walk back inside before opening the envelope.

Captain Ellis turned to one of his lieutenants. "Keep an eye out, and keep the motors running. We'll be back in a few minutes."

They invited Captain Ellis in for a cup of coffee at the kitchen table. The colonel opened the envelope and carefully read the letter in its entirety in silence then folded it up and placed it back in the envelope and into his pocket. He half smiled, but then he looked at Mark and said, "Looks like you guys are going to have to go to the farm without me. I've been promoted to full colonel. Gave me my own brigade to command. Must be hard up for help these days." Mary started crying and left the room. The colonel excused himself and went to check on his wife.

Mark took the opportunity to press the captain for information about conditions in Memphis and the surrounding areas, especially Batesville. The captain was not in the mood to talk, was told not to discuss the subject with any civilians, or was just being an ass. He got nothing. Thankfully, the colonel came back to the table to break the silence. "She's just a little upset. Said she would miss all of you. Not really excited about military base housing again. Believe it or not, she wants to go with you guys."

"She knows we have a potentially dangerous trip to make. I'm sure you have thought about that too," Mark said, a little surprised that was even on option. The colonel just smiled and turned back to the captain.

"Captain, what were your orders?"

"To find you, give you the letter, and await your orders, sir."

The colonel smiled again to himself. "Captain Ellis, have the men load up these good people and their supplies in their vehicles, have the medics take the wounded with them in the ambulance, and send one of your platoons to escort them where they need to go. Then have them report back to you for further orders. Any questions?"

"No, sir. I understand, sir. Right on it." Captain Ellis spun on his heels and headed out the door to gather the troops into action.

The colonel waited until Captain Ellis was out of the house before he said anything. "Everyone listen up. Do not say a word about the surgery, the patients, or that any of you are nurses or doctors. When you put the patients in the vehicles, if anyone asks any questions, say they just got out of the hospital last week and are still recovering. Do not let them see what is in the trailer, either. Let them escort you to the farm, thank them, and let them be on their way. Do not invite them into the house, or onto the farm. Take the radios with you, and I will check on you when I can. Doc, let's take a walk."

They both got up from the table and went into the garage, where they could talk in private. Mark waited until they were out of earshot before he said anything. "Okay, what's the deal with all the secrecy?"

"I think I know you well enough to trust you with what I'm about to tell you. If you repeat it to the wrong people, I will have to deny I told you, and then you will be on your own. I won't be able to help you after that. In fact, I could get in serious trouble myself, and so could you. Do I have your word?"

Mark squared his shoulders and answered, "Yes, sir."

"Okay, then. The president has declared martial law. Under the National Defense Authorization Act of 2012, the military can be used as a police force, but they also have the authority to take over everything from communications, electrical power, fuel sources, food supplies, farms, transportation, and business that they deem essential to the welfare of the country. All of this was done by executive order of the president. If you resist, they can treat you as an enemy combatant and hold you without a hearing or a trial indefinitely. They are calling for all police, fire, paramedic, and medical personnel, including doctors and nurses, to be conscripted into duty, wherever they are needed most. That would be you and your team."

Mark interrupted. "They can't do that. I don't have to work for them against my will."

The colonel looked at Mark. "Now, listen. Yes they can. And they will. And if you resist, they will haul you off. That's why I'm telling you this. They do not need to know that you are a surgeon right now. If they find out, they will come for you. There is a critical need for general surgeons, because of all the shooting and trauma. So I want you to get to the farm to see your family and make sure Mary is safe. They will probably find out sooner or later that you are a surgeon and that some are nurses, and when they do they will report it. It will go up through the chain of command. As the Mid-South regional brigade commander, I will be the one who has to authorize it and make that call. If someone reports it on up the chain to the general, then I won't be able to sweep it under the rug without potential consequences. And just know, if things get worse and this doesn't settle down soon, even the farm can be confiscated along with the weapons, ammunition, food, equipment, fuel, and so on. So keep things quiet, lay low, and don't advertise the fact that you are a surgeon or that you have a food supply. I'm telling you this because my wife is going with you, and I don't want her to be put in a bad situation. I like you and Lisa and the boys, and I have grown close to all these folks. Do what you have to do to keep everyone safe, but just know what's going on out there."

Mark stood there for a minute trying to take it all in. He found it hard to believe that the government would do that to its own citizens. "What about the Constitution, the Sixth Amendment's guarantee of a right to trial, the Bill of Rights, habeas corpus?"

"All out the window by the stroke of a pen by the president. The army has been ordered to restore order and given the authority to carry it out. We just don't know how this will play out. Our orders, for now, are to gain control of the larger cities first, which for us is Memphis, and to restore power, water, and other utilities, as well as reestablish police, fire, and medical services. Once that is done, we will then go out into the surrounding county seats, sheriff's departments, and so on until things get back to normal. That means it may be weeks, or even months, before we get down to Batesville. So I think you will have some time before you will be under the microscope down there. Could be sooner, could be later."

"Are you supposed to take sides?" Mark asked. "I mean, whom do you pick out of the crowd if both sides are shooting at each other? This thing could turn into a civil war. Hell, people may start shooting at you if they feel their constitutional rights are being taken away."

"Trust me, I have already thought about that. Our orders are to keep order and don't shoot unless shot at. There is no question the US Army has superior firepower, and if faced with a direct attack we can inflict massive casualties on the enemy. But if one hundred million people with guns turn on us right here in our own backyard, they would be able to take us out in due time. If the people had the will, they could cut off our supply lines, transportation, and communications, and get to our families and friends, and eventually our own men would drag the politicians and us officers out of power. It would not end well. There is one thing we know from history, and that is we do not win against guerilla warfare. It's difficult to fight a war when you don't know who your enemy is. They wear you down with attrition. The big brass knows this. They don't want that any more than I do. Shooting our own is not something we want to do. I will tell you in full confidence that if it comes to that, even if ordered to, most of us will not turn our guns on our own people. Before that would happen, we would turn them the other way."

"That's good to know. I will keep that in mind." Mark thought for a minute then asked the colonel, "Why don't you just come with us now?"

"Already thought it over. If I refuse to go with them, they will take me into custody, and then you and the others wouldn't get an escort to the farm. This is the best way, for now."

"Sorry, should have thought of that myself. You have my word that I will do my best to take care of Mary and the rest. I'm going to trust that you will do what you can for us on your end. Guess we better get out of here while we can. Thanks for all your help. We couldn't have done it without you," Mark said as he held out his hand.

"No, thank *you*, son. Take care of my Mary until I come to get her. I owe you one." The colonel shook his hand, and both left to help get the show on the road.

Mark and Paul talked briefly to get their story straight, and then each went to quietly talk to the others. Martha was told not to let on that she just had surgery yesterday, and they would pretend that Tammy was just having another asthma attack and just needed her meds. Then they helped the others finish loading the last few items in their vehicles. The colonel gave Mark his old M1A and told him to hold on to it until he saw him again. There was one stop they needed to make on the way. It was Paul's house. It was only a few minutes off the planned route but well worth it for them. Paul had a large supply of ammunition and a few more weapons to pick up that would most certainly come in handy down at the farm. Lieutenant Stern, the officer in charge of the platoon, was reluctant but agreed, especially when suggested to do so by the colonel. He was not happy about it and insisted that their weapons be stowed away for the trip. He didn't want any loose cannons if something were to happen. The colonel thought it was a good idea. Mark agreed and convinced everyone to comply with his request.

When Lieutenant Stern gave the order to his sergeant, he had the men load up, and they headed out of the subdivision. The two-ton truck with the grader blade led the way out of the subdivision, followed by one of the Humvees with a .50 cal. The four civilian vehicles followed in line between the other personnel carriers and Humvees. The Dickersons drove the colonel's truck and trailer, with Mary in the backseat. The Watsons drove their own truck, and the Joneses drove their own SUV. Cindy chose to ride in the ambulance with Tammy, Martha, and Paul. Mark drove his Explorer, with Jack riding shotgun.

Mark was excited to be finally going to the farm to be with his family. He missed his wife and the boys and could not wait to see them. As he drove along, he thought about what the group had been through over the past few days—the violence, the deaths, the hospital's destruction—as well as about his regret over what happened between him and Cindy. He did not intend to let her get that close to him. He admitted to himself that he had feelings for her, that he liked her, but he convinced himself it was only passion and sexual chemistry, not love. He loved his wife. He had promised himself years ago there would never be another woman. He knew he had let things go too far this time, but it was the situation, the moment. He had been lonely, tired, weak, and tempted. Mark understood human nature, how the mind works, what makes people do what they do. People who say they would never do such a thing were either deceiving themselves or everyone else. Everyone is subject to sins of the flesh. That's why priests molest children, preachers have affairs with the church secretary, and great men and women do stupid things that other people look at and pretend they would never do.

He understood that everyone is subject to the desires for food, sex, drugs, and alcohol. It is built into the human brain. The parts that are the centers of desire, satisfied by being full, stimulated by drugs of pleasure, alcohol and love are run by chemicals, hormones, serotonin, dopamine, and endorphins. It is only sheer will that comes from the cerebral cortex that allows us to override and suppress those urges and impulses. Otherwise, we would be no different from primates such as gorillas, among which the biggest and baddest silverback male takes whom he wants, where he wants, and when he wants. But it takes more than forethought and constant determination to be able to suppress the brain pleasure centers that drive us to desire those things. We also have to intentionally avoid the things that make us weak and surround ourselves with those we love and who love us. If it hadn't been for the bullets in that garage, something else might have happened that night—something he would have regretted the rest of his life. He understood that it's not just a matter of staying away from temptation, but as the Good Book says, running away from it.

He knew that he needed to stay as far away from Cindy as possible, because he was only human. It wasn't the first time a pretty young woman had made herself available to him. But he had learned to stay as far away as possible. He desired the touch of a firm young woman as much as any man, but he also had thought through the consequences, the damage to his boys, the pain it would cause Lisa. And most of all, he did not want to suffer the guilt it would cause him. Like most young men, he had done things earlier in life that he was not proud of. They caused him to feel guilty for doing wrong in the eyes of man, but even more so, before the eyes of God.

Although Mark was determined not to let things get to that point again, they were going to be stuck at the farm together for God knew how long and would probably be in close quarters or at least in regular contact with each other on a daily basis. Not a good situation when trying to stay away from someone. He worried that despite his best efforts, at some point Lisa may see that there was something between them. Women can sense those things. And he could not predict what Cindy would do or how she would react. Would she continue to press the issue? Would she be able to move on and let it all go? Not likely. Women are not made that way. But he did not think that telling Lisa about what happened would serve any good purpose. Not yet. Some things a man needs to carry to his grave.

Then he started thinking about all the things they would need to do at the farm when he got there. Caring for Martha and Tammy. Making sure they had enough food and shelter for all the new mouths to feed. He worried about the response from Lisa and her family when sixteen more people show up on their doorstep unannounced. He felt justified in bringing them along. He certainly couldn't just turn them away. Some of these people were close neighbors and family friends. There were wounded among them, and they were trapped in a subdivision in the path of a violent uprising and facing constant danger. They were certain to be run out or killed. He had to help them get out.

And those on the farm were most likely unaware of and unprepared for what was heading their way. They had enough water and wood and the ability to grow food, but they wouldn't have enough firepower or warm bodies to defend themselves. If Mark had any say, that was all about to change. It was a lot to think about on the drive to the farm.

Cindy chose to ride in the ambulance with Tammy, whom she had come to care for. The thought of Tammy not having any family had touched her deeply. They had become close, and she wanted what was best for her. She had made up her mind that she would take care of her as if she her own until other family could be found. As she rode along in the ambulance, she talked to the medic and found out they were taking patients to the hospital at the Naval Air Station in Millington, Tennessee, just north of Memphis. Things were still functional on the base, behind the gated fences and armed guards.

She thought about what happened with Mark over the past week and especially about being in his arms earlier that morning in the garage. She couldn't stand the thought of being near him and not being with him. She knew how she felt about him. It was not just a strong sexual attraction or a crush on a successful doctor by another young nurse hoping to move into a big house and drive a BMW. She truly loved him. But she knew he would never leave his wife. Being around him, pretending not to care, trying to act as if there was nothing between them, and having to see him with Lisa was just more than she could bear. She could not live like that. She knew what she had to do. It was going to be a long ride to the farm.

CHAPTER 18
ARMED AND READY

Friday, April 18. Later that day.

Things were going much better for Lisa and everyone at the farm. Tim and Steve had come to an understanding, and some of the adults who needed to were starting to act like adults again. The garden was being planted with purple hull peas, sweet corn, lima beans, tomatoes, carrots, peppers, okra, eggplants, potatoes, radishes, cauliflower, cucumbers, cabbage, watermelon, cantaloupe, and squash—all with heirloom seeds, so they could gather the seeds and replant next year, and the next, if needed. The fruit trees still needed to be trimmed, and the blackberry bushes needed to be cut back to new cane. The gas and diesel tanks were full, the storage closets and pantry were well stocked with extra bags of salt, sugar, rice, beans, and coffee, and the canning jars had new lids.

Grandpa Brown had the horse harness out oiling it up, and Grandma Brown had her old hand-crank washing machine and wringer out. The old woodstove was cleaned and the stove-pipes checked for leaks. Glen and Tim were helping Grandpa and Steve with the daily farm chores, but firewood still needed to be cut and stacked for the stove and fireplace, the fences needed mending, and hay would need to be put up. Lisa and Sarah helped Grandma out in the kitchen and around the house and took turns watching after the boys. Even Rhonda had started coming out of her room and joining the others for supper, now that Grandma Brown was enforcing the no-snacks-between-meals rule again. Hunger has a way of persuading people.

Beyond all the folks who had moved into the house over the past week, the normal peace and quiet that they were used to was interrupted only by an occasional car or a few people passing by down front. Besides the increase in traffic along the road, they had only a few travelers stop by to ask for directions or food. Grandpa told the women to feed them as long as they were asking and moving on. He was starting to get a sense that more travelers were coming their way.

A neighbor or two had stopped by to check on them and tell them the latest news from town. Traffic had picked up on the interstate and highway, and every hotel and motel in town was full. Even the RV parks and state parks in every direction were all overflowing with travelers. It reminded Grandpa of Katrina. When the hurricane came through New Orleans, the same thing happened then. Even the churches were full of people with no jobs, no food, and nowhere to go for months. He figured if New Orleans had a population of only about a half million and that many people had come all the way up here, then with a population of about 650,000 in Memphis, which is much closer, things were probably going to get much worse before they get better.

But the question was, how much worse. They were about to find out.

The first sign of real trouble came in the form of a group of four riders on crotch rockets that stopped at the end of the drive. Grandpa heard them before he saw them. They stopped, looked around, pointed here and there a few times, and appeared to be talking about something. After a minute or so, they went on down the road. Grandpa wasn't sure, but it appeared one or two of them were carrying pistols in the waistbands of their pants. It appeared as if they were looking for trouble, but after seeing the long, winding drive with a wooden bridge that crossed a big, deep ditch and led up a hill to a house, shop, and barn that were barely visible from the road, they decided to move on. Grandpa watched and listened, and just as he was sure that they we're gone, it occurred to him which way they were headed. "The Thompsons," he said out loud.

He went into the house to the gun cabinet and got out his Marlin .30-.30 lever-action rifle and Remington 870 pump-action twelve-gauge shotgun. He made sure both were loaded and grabbed an extra box of shells for both. He found Glen and handed him the shotgun and shells. "Be careful, it's loaded. You do remember how to shoot that thing, don't you?" Grandpa said half-jokingly but in a hurry.

Glen just smiled back. "Where are we going? It's almost time for lunch."

"I'm not sure, but there may be trouble brewing. I just saw some motorcycle riders who looked like trouble to me. Probably nothing, but I'm going to check on the Thompsons. You going with me or not?" By then, the women in the kitchen had heard the commotion and came into the living room wanting to know what was going on. Grandpa reluctantly repeated the story as he was heading out the door with Glen. "One of you call the sheriff's department and tell them we may have trouble out here."

Lisa stopped them. "I'll call. Take Steve with you, in case you run into trouble. He can go for help." Lisa gave Steve a look that let him know she really meant for him to watch their backs. He was more than willing to go.

Grandpa hesitated for a moment but then said, "Well, come on if you're going. Time's a wasting." They loaded into the truck and drove down the drive, sending up a dust cloud along the way. He slowed the truck before he rounded the last bend right before getting to the Thompsons' drive, so as not to be seen or heard, until he could see if the motorcycles were there. He came to a sudden stop. He saw the back of one bike just past the bushes along the front drive. He put the truck in reverse and backed up along the side of the road, where he couldn't be seen from the house. He thought for a minute. "Steve, stay with the truck. If you hear me holler for you, bring the truck up to the house. You do know how to drive, don't you?"

"Yes, sir. You showed me last summer, when we were hauling hay."

Grandpa cocked his head to the side. "Oh, yeah, right. Glen, you know your way around. Go down that way, through the trees, and come up to the back of the house. I'll go down the front, along the bushes. If they start something, we'll have 'em in a crossfire. Steve, if the shootin' starts, go get help. Ya'll got it?"

"Yes, sir," Steve said, knowing he had no intention of leaving them but not about to argue with his grandpa. He watched them both head out to carry out their plan. Once they were both out of sight, he snuck down the bushes behind Grandpa but far enough back not to be seen. He wedged up between the bushes so he could see the house. Two of the bikers were standing at the end of the drive, as if they were waiting on something, while the other two were sneaking up the drive to the house. From where he was, he could not see his Uncle Glen yet, but he could hear him thrashing through the woods. One of the bikers with a Fu Manchu beard and tattoos had made it to the house and was looking in the windows, while the other was watching out. He looked in several windows then held up four fingers and pointed in the kitchen window and made motions as if he was eating. The Thompsons were just sitting down for lunch.

The biker who was watching out had a ponytail and was shirtless, except for a leather vest with some type of insignia on the back that Steve couldn't read. He got on a radio and talked to someone, then walked back toward the end of the drive to join the others. Ponytail joined the other two at the end of the drive, just out of sight of the house and Steve. Steve knew his grandpa was heading right for the men, so he decided to catch up to him and warn him. Just then, he heard someone shout out. "Hey, what are you doing here?" It was Grandpa, facing the three men with his rifle pointed at them. Ponytail was about to go for a gun, but Grandpa pointed his rifle right at him. "I wouldn't do that, if I were you."

Fu Manchu heard the shouting and was sneaking up behind the others and Grandpa with his pistol drawn. Grandpa didn't see him coming and was too busy with the three to notice. Glen was still thrashing around the woods and didn't have a clue anything was going down. Steve had to make a decision. He saw that his grandpa had the others disarmed, so Steve came up behind Fu Manchu just as he was about to surprise Grandpa and pulled the .38 special pistol out from his belt and pointed it at the back of Fu Manchu's head. "Don't move, shithead." Steve had learned a new word from Tim and had been waiting to use it. The man turned his head slowly and saw a fourteen-year-old boy holding a pistol on him. He didn't think the boy would shoot, so he started to turn his gun on him, but Steve was quicker and shot a round into the ground right next to Fu Manchu's foot. "Drop it, or I'll shoot you."

Fu Manchu was enraged. "You little bastard, I'm going to kick your ass." He lunged at Steve, thinking he could take him, but he miscalculated. Before Fu Manchu could grab him, Steve took a couple of steps back out of his reach and shot the man in the leg. Fu Manchu felt the searing pain in his leg when the bullet hit the bone. Then he dropped his pistol, grabbed his leg, and fell to the ground. Steve stood over him, ready to shoot again. By then, Grandpa had disarmed and left the others to come help Steve. Just then, the front door swung open and Mr. Thompson came out on the porch with a shotgun in hand, ready to shoot.

"Mr. Brown, what in the hell is going on out here?"

"Caught these guys hanging out around your house. Didn't look like they were here for a friendly visit," Grandpa said while holding his gun on Fu Manchu, who was writhing around on the ground, cursing everyone in sight. He looked at Steve. "Did you have to shoot him? Now what are we going to do with him?"

Glen finally made his way to them, all out of breath from the walk. "He was going to shoot you. Steve stopped him. I saw it all from over there," he said, pointing to the trees. Grandpa looked over at Steve, looked at Fu Manchu, sized up the situation, and realized what almost happened. Steve smiled at him, picked up the man's gun, and looked at it. A Glock .40 cal. He decided it would make a nice addition to his collection.

Just then, they heard more bikes coming from the west, and from the sound of their motors, they had just passed the farm and were heading toward them. The other three bikers ran toward them on the road, shouting and waving their arms, trying to stop them from riding into an ambush. Mr. Thompson, Grandpa, Glen, and Steve all realized, at the same time, what was happening. More bikers were coming, Ponytail must have radioed for them to come in for the kill after they found easy prey.

"Take cover, guys. Spread out," Grandpa said. He headed for cover behind the car under the carport, Glen ran for the nearest cover behind the woodshed, Mr. Thompson went back in the house to protect his family, and Steve ran for the ditch by the bushes near the road. He wanted to see what was coming. About fifteen to twenty bikers riding choppers and crotch rockets were heading right at them. Ponytail and the others stopped the rest of the bikers at the curve, right where the truck was parked, and started shouting something at them. Big Al, their leader, a huge, bald, bearded man riding the lead chopper, wearing leather chaps and a vest and covered in tattoos, had everyone stop and get off their bikes right in the middle of the road. At his command, they pulled out their pistols, TEC-9s, and sawed-off shotguns and spread out as they approached Grandpa and the Thompsons' house.

Steve jumped up and ran back toward Grandpa and the others to warn them what was coming. He crossed the yard toward the back of the woodshed in a dead run. "They're coming! They're coming! Guns! Guns!" Just about the time he rounded the corner, the bullets started flying in his direction. Steve and Glen hit the ground behind the shed as bullets tore through the old, dry wood walls, which offered little protection. There were so many bullets tearing through the walls, neither had a chance to shoot back. Steve started crawling on his belly toward the trees behind the woodshed, while Glen stayed behind the shed on his belly with his hands over his head, trying to protect himself from all the wood splinters and bullets flying about. Because of the bushes and the shed between him and the bikers, the bikers could not see Steve crawling toward the woods. Steve made his way behind the house all the way to the barn and climbed into the loft. He had a clear view of the end of the drive, where the burly bald biker was leading the rest toward the house. Steve pulled out both pistols and started shooting as fast as he could until they were both empty. The barrage of bullets flying at them sent all of the bikers back toward the road for cover.

Just then, a dull rumbling came from the east and grew louder by the minute. For a minute or two, no one moved. Everyone looked around to see what was happening. The rumbling got louder and louder. The ground started shaking, a slight trembling at first, then more and more intense. All eyes and ears were turned to where the noise was coming from. All of a sudden, the bikers started shouting to each other and ran for their bikes. They jumped on, fired them up, and scurried off as fast as they could, leaving their wounded comrade in arms alone on the ground in the drive, bleeding and cursing the day they were born. The way they scrambled out of there made Grandpa think that maybe the sheriff had finally shown up.

Steve could see farther down the road than the rest and saw what all the noise and rumbling was. About fifteen or so green trucks and Humvees, led by a huge truck with a grader blade flying the American flag, were coming down the road toward them. It looked like a US Army convoy. Steve climbed out of the barn and ran to his grandpa, shouting, "It's the army! It's the army!" Grandpa stopped him from running out into the road. He didn't know if the cavalry had just shown up in the nick of time to save the day, or if it was another group of crazies just pretending to be the army.

Then Steve saw what looked like his dad's red Explorer. He broke away from his grandpa, who tried to stop him again, and ran toward the road to get a better look. He saw his dad's vehicle moving along, between all the trucks, with his dad driving and another man riding in the passenger seat. "Dad! Dad! It's my dad!" he shouted as he ran toward the convoy waving his arms, not realizing he still had both guns in his hands. At almost the same time, the entire convoy came to a sudden stop. The .50 cal. mounted on the lead Humvee swung toward Steve and the gunner shouted at him. "Stop! Put down your weapons! Get on the ground, facedown." Steve froze in his tracks. A .50 cal pointed at someone has a way of being very convincing.

Lieutenant Stern saw a young man running and shouting at the convoy, waving guns in the air with a bleeding wounded unarmed man on the ground behind him, and came to the wrong conclusion. He ordered his men to disarm and arrest the young man with the pistols and for the medics to tend to the wounded man on the gravel drive. His men quickly jumped into action and before Mark knew what was happening. Before Grandpa could stop them, they surrounded Steve and ordered him to put down his weapons. Glen stayed put behind the shed, and Mr. Thompson watched the whole scenario play out through his living room window.

Mark got out of his car and walked up closer to the man on the ground. His first instinct was to help the wounded man, to stop the bleeding, but he had to stop himself and Paul from intervening so they would not give away their secret. Mark grabbed Paul's arm and gave him a look to remind him that they were just civilians trying to get home. Paul stopped, got the message, and stood down. Then he saw Grandpa Brown surrounded by several soldiers, who were holding him at gunpoint and ordering him to put down his weapon. Mark couldn't quite wrap his head around what was going on. He finally got a better look at the young man being taken into custody and realized it was his oldest son, Steve. "Lieutenant. That's my son!"

Lieutenant Stern had his men help the young man up, and Steve ran to his dad and embraced him. They cried in each other's arms. By now, everyone had come out of the vehicles, including all the Southcrest residents and Cindy, who chose to stay back by the ambulance and watch from a distance. It took several minutes for the lieutenant, Mark, Grandpa, and Mr. Thompson, who had finally come out of the house, to straighten out who was whom and who did what. Lieutenant Stern ordered his men to take the wounded biker into custody and tend to his wounds. He then realized that the swarm of bikers who left in such a hurry were all involved and needed to be rounded up.

Just then, Lisa and Rhonda drove up to see what all the commotion was about and to see if everyone was all right. They were relieved to see the US Army trucks at the scene, but worried something terrible had happened. Rhonda came along largely because she craved some excitement. To her, even a little danger was better than boredom. But as they started to get out of the truck, several of the soldiers pointed their weapons at them and told them to stop and put their hands up. Mark saw Lisa drive up and ran to her and embraced her with a big hug and kiss, and they cried in each other's arms. Cindy could only watch in silence as they embraced. She knew she had lost him. It hurt her very much, so she hid her face and cried out of sight of everyone. While everyone else greeted each other, Mark explained some of what happened over the past week to Lisa and told her not to say anything to the soldiers about his profession and asked her to discreetly go tell her dad to do the same.

Lieutenant Stern was in a hurry to check on the whereabouts of the other bikers to make sure they were not an immediate threat, so he sent a sergeant along with two squads to make sure they were gone from the area. He was anxious to get back to Captain Ellis for further orders, so he asked Mark, "Where do you want me to take you? We need to get on back, sir."

Mark thought about it for a minute. His first thought was to have them escort them up the road to the farm, but then he changed his mind. "Right here is good. Thank you for your help, Lieutenant." Then Mark shook his hand and looked around at the others. "Okay, folks, we're home. Y'all can pull in here, and we can let these good men be on their way." Everyone looked a little puzzled but did what Mark had told them before they left home: be quiet and follow his lead. Mr. Thompson was not in on the ruse, so he started to speak up and ask a question, but Grandpa elbowed him in the ribs and lipped for him to keep quiet, so he went along with it.

Lieutenant Stern looked around the place, tilted his head to one side, and wrinkled his brows. "You sure this is where you wanted to go? I mean, it's a nice place and all, but all of you...? I'm sorry, I guess I just expected a bigger...I mean, good luck, folks. I'll let the colonel know you guys made it here in one piece." He made a note of the address then had his men return the weapons, ammo, and supplies to Mark and the others and waited until the sergeant came back with the other two squads. They reported that the bikers were nowhere to be seen. Then he loaded up his men and headed back toward the east.

Mark looked around and took inventory of the cars, trucks, trailer, and people. That's when he noticed that Tammy and Cindy were missing. Jack had anticipated that Mark would miss them sooner or later, so Jack went up to him and whispered,

"Cindy told the soldiers she was a nurse and decided to go with them to the Naval Air Station in Millington. She told them about Tammy's parents and that she knew her aunt, so they took her with her, too. Lieutenant Stern questioned her about you and the others, but she just told them you were just hospital workers, maintenance, lab techs, and such."

Mark felt tightness in his chest and a lump in his throat. He did not expect Cindy to leave without saying good-bye and was surprised how much it hurt. It was then that he realized that he cared for her more than he had been willing to admit. He looked over at Lisa, who was still beaming, smiling, and happy that he was back with her. Then he realized why Cindy left. He swallowed hard and made an effort to keep his feelings to himself. He walked back over to Lisa and gave her another hug. Despite all that had happened, he knew he had made the right choice and was glad to be back with his wife and family.

All of the Southcrest people who remained started looking around, not sure what to make of the place. Mark could sense a certain air of disappointment on their faces. After all, the place they were standing in front of was nothing like what they had heard. In front of them was a small, single-story, three-bedroom house with a carport, a woodshed off to the side by the drive, and an outhouse and a small barn out back, with a momma cow and calf and a few chickens running around. They were expecting a big, two-story white farmhouse with a wraparound porch on top of a hill, hidden from view down a long, winding white limestone drive, a big garden out back, a big shop and sheds full of tools, a big barn with a barnyard full of animals, ponds, fruit trees, blackberries, tractors, and plow horses, and 250 acres to run on.

Mark decided to let everyone know they were not yet at the farm. He turned and whispered to Lisa. She whispered back, and then he announced, "Everyone, this is Mr. Thompson and his family, and this is his uncle's farm. I guess, his farm now. They are our neighbors. Looks like they had a little trouble today. If you would all give me a minute, we'll head down the road to the farm." He could see the relief on all the former Southcrest residents' faces, but also the confusion on the face of Lisa and the others.

Grandpa wasn't sure if he was still supposed to be playing along, so he quietly turned to Mark. "What was that all about? And who are all these people?"

Mark smiled and answered him for everyone to hear. "It's a long story, Grandpa Brown. All these people were either our neighbors in Southcrest or were from the hospital, and they are all now my friends. They came down here to stay with us and help protect us for a while. At least until all this blows over. I would have asked before we just dropped in, but we sort of had to leave in a hurry. The bullets were flying up there when we left. I figured the same would happen down here sooner or later, so I brought some help back. Looks like to me we will need them sooner rather than later."

Grandpa looked over the crowd and saw all the men and teen-age boys armed with rifles and pistols. He thought about what they had just been through, and then it hit him. If the cavalry hadn't shown up when it did, they would probably all be dead. If those characters or others like them come back, they were going to need a lot more firepower, and the Good Lord just provided it. The women would need more help feeding all of them, which means they would need a bigger garden, so all the extra hands were actually a blessing in disguise.

He wasn't sure what to make of the woman with the IV bag hanging on a pole. She looked as if she was wounded or just had surgery. And he still wasn't sure what all the secrecy was about, but he figured he would find out soon enough. The one thing he was sure of was that he was glad to have some more warm bodies on his side. "You know, Mark, I always said you were smarter than you look. Glen, you and Steve stay here for a bit. Help them clean things up and stay until things quiet down, then bring the Thompsons up to the house, and we'll talk and sort out our sleeping arrangements. Well, y'all don't just stand there looking at me. We got some things we need to do before those bikers come back."

Mark smiled at Lisa, relieved that none of them was seriously hurt and everything was working out. He had hoped that they would all be welcomed and was glad that Grandpa understood. Mark was so happy to be back with his family and couldn't wait to see his other two boys and all the rest. He couldn't believe what Steve had been through over the past week. Steve was no longer his little boy. He had grown up almost overnight into a brave young man. Mark was very proud of what Steve had done.

But Mark also knew their troubles weren't over. Especially based on what just happened, more trouble would likely be coming. They needed to get ready—set up guard posts; schedule guard duty; inventory their supplies, weapons, and ammo; and work out communications, farm work schedules, meal times, kitchen duties, division of labor, and even a chain of command. He had learned a lot from the colonel; now he needed to put it to good use. In all, there were twenty-eight mouths to feed, including the Thompsons. That meant there was a lot to do, and probably not much time to do it, before trouble came knocking again.

Just as everyone was loading up to head up the road to the farm, Mark noticed the motorcycle still sitting on the road just past the entrance of the drive. Then it hit him. The injured biker. It was his bike. "Anyone here know how to ride a motorcycle?" Mark asked as he looked around to see if there were any takers.

Jack came up to Mark. "I do. I had one before moving down here, and I've been riding one all my life."

Marked pointed at the bike and laughed. "Looks like you are riding one again."

"Seriously?" Jack answered.

"Think so. I don't think he'll be back for it anytime soon. Might as well bring it up to the house. It might come in handy."

Grandpa came over to intervene. "Shouldn't we let the sheriff take care of that?"

Lisa stepped into the conversation. "I called. They are not coming. Said they were up to their hind ends with complaints— fights, break-ins, and other problems from the flood of people coming out of the Memphis area. I called back when I heard the gunshots. They got ugly with me. Said they are covered up. Some of the deputies haven't shown up lately. Can't get the EMTs to respond. Didn't know when someone would be out. They are dealing with all the calls the best they can."

Grandpa looked down and kicked the dirt. "Well, folks, looks like we are on our own. Guess we better get on up to the farm and figure this out." Mark helped gather up the rest of the troops, and they all headed up the road to the farm.

CHAPTER 19
ON THEIR OWN

Friday, April 18.
Later that evening.

It took only about ten minutes to get everyone loaded up and down the road to the farm. Mark watched the relief and smiles on everyone's faces as they got out of their vehicles at the farm and took in the sight. He could tell they were glad to finally be there and weren't disappointed in what they saw. The large, white two-story farmhouse sitting on top of the hill overlooking a long, winding drive was just as they expected. The flowers, azaleas, and dogwood trees were in full bloom around the yard and house. Cows and calves spotted the green grass in the rolling pastures, which were lined with cedar trees along the fencerows. The barnyard was full of farm animals of every type, including goats, pigs, sheep, and chickens, which roamed about the huge, two-story barn with a loft. The large garden area was freshly plowed and planted. Several outbuildings, such as a woodshed, pump house, outhouse, smokehouse, toolsheds, and a large shop for the tractors and equipment, surrounded the house and barn. An old windmill stood tall in the middle of it all, just like in a postcard picture.

Grandma Brown, Sarah, and Tim came out of the house to see what was going on. They were all surprised at the sight of all the people, most of whom they didn't know. Grandpa went and explained the situation to them. Grandma looked overwhelmed but tried to be a gracious host, as usual. Sarah didn't know what to say, and Tim just shrugged his shoulders but was glad to see other teenagers in the group.

Once everyone was out of the their cars and gathered around, Mark suggested that everyone use the bathroom, get a drink of water, and stretch their legs for a few minutes before unloading. Daniel and Jeffrey spotted their dad and ran to him and gave him big hugs and kisses. Lisa, Mark, and the boys had a quick family reunion in the living room while the others were settling in. Mark took a few minutes to explain some more of what he had been through to Lisa, who wanted to know all the details. He could give her only bits and pieces right then, but he smiled and promised her all the details later. Grandma and Sarah did what they were best at—they went to the kitchen to make iced tea and put together some snacks for their new guests.

Mark waited until Steve and Glen got back from the Thompsons' before conferring with the entire Brown family in the kitchen about how to proceed. The whole family discussed the situation they were in and seemed to understand what they were up against. After what happened at the Thompsons', they all saw the need for more warm bodies in case they needed to defend themselves, but what to do with all of these folks was beyond them. They knew things were going to get bad after the riots, but they never dreamed the troubles would spread all the way out to where they lived. They also understood things might get even worse. They all agreed they wanted to be prepared so they could stay safe and be able to feed everyone, but they were leaving all the planning to Mark. He seemed to have an ability to get people to do what needed to get done.

Mark told the Browns it was their farm, so they ultimately had to decide what the rules were, and they all got first choice in what they would be in charge of. And each would get the final say in that person's chosen area if any disagreements were to arise. To keep the peace and prevent arguments from deteriorating into chaos, any significant disagreements or breeches of rules or misbehavior that could not be settled among the parties involved would ultimately be decided by Grandpa Brown. The structure of the chain of command would be like the military. There was only one commander in chief: Grandpa Brown.

Grandpa knew how to run a farm and agreed to oversee the crops, pastures, and garden, but trying to figure out how to feed and house everyone and plan all that was necessary to keep them safe from attack was just too much for him to take on at his age. Glen was a lawyer, used to following the letter of law, so he volunteered to be in charge of managing the supply inventory and the farm rules that they would all set up. Sarah and Grandma Brown offered to be in charge of the kitchen duties and food preparation but wanted nothing to do with the rest. Lisa agreed to be in charge of overseeing the care of the animals. After they all talked it over, they unanimously agreed to let Mark be in charge of the overall organizational process and allocation of resources and people, however he saw fit. It was all too much for them. And, of course, Mark would also be responsible for everyone's health and well-being.

Mark didn't necessarily want to be in charge of all those people, but he did bring all the folks down to the farm, and he was the only member of the family who knew what needed to be done to keep them safe. He had gone over in his mind the different scenarios that they might face, the different skills and the needs of the people there, and what they needed to do to organize everything. So, like it or not, he was in charge. But Mark also knew that one of the most important jobs of a leader was not just telling people what to do, but getting them to want to do it for their own good and for the good of the group.

Mark invited everyone inside to the living room, which opened into the kitchen, allowing all twenty-eight of them to gather together. Grandpa Brown sat in his chair near the fireplace while Grandma Brown, Sarah, and Lisa served everyone tea and snacks. Every seat was taken in the living room and at the kitchen counter and table and on the living room floor. Everyone was present—family and Southcrest folks alike. Mark spent a few minutes thinking over what to say to everyone. All the guests and even the family members anticipated what he would say.

Mark stood and introduced the Browns. "Everyone, this is Mr. and Mrs. Brown. This farm is their home. Other than their children and grandchildren, we are all guests of theirs. Because I brought all of you together for the purpose of surviving, they have put me in charge of the planning and logistics for the group here at the farm. All of you know what has happened in the cities, and you saw or heard what happened just down the road. The Southcrest residents encountered similar situations over the past two weeks for themselves, and Paul, Jack, Martha, and myself have seen it all, and then some.

"Thanks to the colonel and his men, we are safe, for the moment. We want to keep it that way. So we will have to guard and defend ourselves against intruders. That means guard duty and guns. Anyone who has a problem with that might as well leave now. And I think everyone would agree we all like to eat. In order to do that, we all have to share what we have and work together in the garden and on the farm. There will be rules for everyone to follow in order to keep the peace. And to make sure things get done when they need to get done, and that we don't waste critical supplies and resources necessary for our survival, everyone will have to go along with the rules that we all agree on.

"Grandpa Brown—and I'm sure he checks with Grandma Brown about things—gets the final say on any disagreements that arise. If someone becomes a problem for the group, Grandpa Brown has the final say on who stays and who goes. It's his place. This is not a democracy where we all get to vote. That's the way it has to be. Small groups that try to rule by voting on everything or by making a group decision on every issue waste huge amounts of time, and it almost always deteriorates into arguments and chaos. Anyone who doesn't agree to that, leave now or forever hold your peace. So does everyone agree?"

Mark waited for a response. Everyone looked around and nodded their heads in agreement. No one left. So he continued. "Besides following the rules, everyone will have responsibilities and jobs to do. Notice, I said *jobs,* and *everyone.* Every man, woman, and child. That will include everything from laundry and latrine duties, to farm chores and guard duty. We will also need to take an inventory of all our supplies, weapons, ammunition, food—everything. Everything we all brought with us goes in the pile, the food goes in the pantry, the bullets and weapons go into the stockpile, as do the radios and batteries, as well. Personal items can remain just that.

"The next order of business will be the most immediate, and that is sleeping arrangements. Some of you will be working different shifts so we can double up in beds, just like the military. Once that is done, then we need to post guards and a guard duty schedule. Our safety is the most pressing issue. Then, the next order of business will be work duties and schedules, which will be posted in the kitchen after discussing these with you individually. If someone likes a different job better, they can swap if both parties agree, but once it is on the board it is your job, no excuses. You don't work, you don't eat. Everyone okay with the rules?"

Again, Mark looked around the room, and everyone nodded in agreement. "All right, everyone hang around to decide on sleeping arrangements, and then we will work on the schedules. Young men out on the porch with Paul, women to the kitchen with Grandma Brown, men stay here with Grandpa Brown, and the young ladies go with my wife, Lisa. Once you have figured out your chores and schedule, then you may take your personal belongings to your sleeping quarters. Remember, there will be others sharing the same space, so unless you want everyone to use your toothbrush or hairbrush, keep it in your bag or drawer, or put your name on it.

"Supper will be at six every evening, and breakfast at eight in the morning. Those going to work will eat first and then go relieve the others. Meals will be nutritional and portions gauged to your ideal body weight and work-duty calorie requirements. Folks hauling hay will need more calories than someone feeding chickens or sitting on guard duty. Sorry, folks, it has to be that way until the garden starts coming in. All right, folks, we have work to do."

Everyone talked among themselves for a few minutes, while Mark, the Thompsons, and Grandma Brown discussed sleeping arrangements for everyone. Mark first went to Jerry Thompson to find out what his intentions were. "Jerry, we invited you over because we think it would be best for all of us to work together. The east side of our property line ends right in front of your property. There is a gate and a dirt field road across from your drive that is hidden by grass and weeds but is still usable. It comes right up the fence to the barnyard, in the east pasture. With the four-wheelers, it gives us direct access to each other without having to go down the main road, if needed. With the two-way radios, we can have direct contact, as well. If you are willing to put up some folks in your spare bedroom, you can watch from the east and we can watch from the west and know when trouble is coming. If someone starts something at one place, the others can come in from behind to flank them. Working together, I think we will all be better off than you doing your thing and us doing ours."

Mark left the idea out there for Jerry to think over before pressing him, but before he could ask, Jerry erupted with, "Thank God, I was hoping you would ask. I don't know what we would do if those bikers came back or, God forbid, something worse comes down the road. We would be glad to have some company, especially if they brought some more guns. Hell, you can put people in two bedrooms. The kids can sleep on the floor in our room on a mattress. The wife won't mind. She's scared to death that they will come back. I think we will both sleep better with some other folks there. The more, the merrier."

Mark laughed and slapped Jerry on the back. "We definitely want them armed. And we want you to help with the work schedule and guard schedule, and in return, we will share our food and supplies. No need to duplicate effort." Mark could see the relief on his face.

"Man, I didn't really know what we were going to do for food, after what y'all gave us ran out. I mean, I never had a garden before. And milking the cow and the chicken thing, they might be better off up here with the others, too. If you want, we can come up here for the meals, or someone can bring it down there, or whatever. We'll work and do whatever you guys need. Really, I don't think we can make it on our own."

"Good, it's settled." Mark shook his hand and asked them to join the others to work out guard duty, farm chores, and work schedules. Having two more bedrooms made the job of sleeping arrangements much easier to deal with. Things would be crowded, and they would all have to learn to adjust and share resources and space, but they would all have a dry roof over their heads, hot meals, and a bed to sleep in, at least for the time being.

After the work duties and schedules were decided, they were posted in the kitchen on the bulletin board for all to see. The next order of business was to take inventory of all the supplies. Glen started working on it as soon as the meeting was over. He was in his element. He interviewed all the previous Southcrest residents to see what they brought with them. It was stacking up to be quite a list and would take a day or two to sort out. Then they would have to decide on the rationing of the food and perishable supplies. The problem was, they didn't know whether it would need to last for three weeks, three months, or three years. That was the big unknown.

But the most pressing issue they faced was their safety. If the bikers came back for blood, or others like them, they needed to be ready. They had enough weapons and ammunition and men to hold off a small army, as long as they were ready and had a plan. If the group was too large or too heavily armed, chances were some of them would get hurt, but how many and how bad was the question. But, they had no other choice. The army was miles away in Memphis trying to regain control of the city, and the sheriff's department was already swamped and unavailable. In essence, they were on their own.

Mark and Paul sat down with Mr. Dickerson, who seemed the most confident with a rifle among the old Southcrest crew. They found out he had served two tours of duty in Vietnam and had been a marine sergeant when he was a young man and even though his hair was grey he still looked the part. He knew a thing or two about guard duty, patrols, and fighting. Among the three of them, they came up with a workable plan of defense. They decided to dig a bunker just behind the tree line next to the field road at the east property line, across from the Thompsons' house, where they could watch the Thompsons' house and that end of the main road and farm. Someone looking for trouble at the Thompsons' house would not expect a lookout hidden across the road. A second post would be dug at the west end of the property that would overlook the main road and driveway to the house. In order for someone to access the farm directly from the south, east, or west without coming down the main road would require a long hike across other farms and open fields, and unless someone was familiar with the area, that would not be very likely.

Both guard posts would be manned at all times, and communication would be maintained by radio with the head of watch, who would be carrying their radio at the house at night or while working on the farm during the day. The guards on duty would rotate every four hours, seven days a week, until they felt safe again. All the men and the teenage boys would have to take turns on guard duty. With two guards per shift, and six shifts per day, that would be a total of twelve daily guard shifts, just for watch, not to mention all the other farm work. There were only eleven men and teenage boys to carry the load, which meant that someone would have to take two shifts a day. Now Grandpa and Glen fully understood why, and were grateful, that Mark brought more people back with him from Southcrest.

The guards were instructed to watch and observe and report any suspicious activity to the head watch at the house. A log would be kept of suspicious activity, including a description of the people and vehicles, including tag numbers. They were not to approach or intercept, unless directly threatened or attacked, or ordered to do so by the head watch. Either Mark, Paul, Mr. Dickerson, or Grandpa would be on head watch duty at all times. All of the men, teens, and women were trained on how to handle, load, unload, and fire the AR-15s and the .22 rifles safely. The four head watchmen were to also carry a pistol on their side at all times when out of the house. Lisa never left the house without her .380, either.

Glen refused to take responsibility for having to decide whether the guards were to shoot or retreat if it came down to it. He said he would not be willing to shoot at someone himself or to give that order to someone else unless shot at first. He felt that was too much legal liability for him to assume, so he relegated his role to guard duty only; the lawyer in him finally came out. Paul and Mr. Dickerson did not have a problem making those decisions, because of their military training and experience that had taught them that sometimes it's best to shoot first and ask questions later. Mark and Grandpa Brown had no problem with it, if it came down to keeping them safe.

Each guard would carry a radio with them at all times while on duty, along with an AR-15 loaded with a twenty-round magazine and three spares, a raincoat or a poncho, binoculars, water, and a snack in a backpack. While on a four-hour guard duty, they were to report in every thirty minutes to help them stay awake and alert. Steve and Tim wanted to carry a pistol while on duty, along with the rifle. Although Glen didn't like the idea, Tim decided that if Steve could do it, he could, as well. Grandpa and Mark didn't have a problem with it. They had instructed them on gun safety and felt they were both responsible enough to carry while on the farm. Soon, all the teens were carrying the pistols on guard duty.

The next couple of days were relatively quiet. Everyone had unpacked and settled into sleep and mealtime routines, farm duties, and getting used to being around so many people all the time. The women settled into their duties preparing the meals, sorting out the laundry, watching the younger children, and doing their farm chores. Grandma and some of the other ladies made plans to can as much of the garden vegetables as possible and fully stock the root cellar, just in case things went on for a while.

Besides guard duty, the men stayed busy enlarging and replanting the garden and pruning the blackberry bushes and the fruit trees. Since there were more mouths to feed, Grandpa decided to let the bull run with the cows again, in order to increase the herd. That meant some of the fences would need mending. He also planned to put up more hay for the animals. The other men made plans to cut more firewood for the stoves, in case it was needed.

Glen spent most of his time taking inventory of all the supplies—food, ammunition, weapons, fuel, medical supplies and equipment, canning jars, candles, lanterns, lamp oil, radios, batteries, paper products, and anything and everything that they would need, use, or run out of. Including what they already had at the farm and what the old Southcrest residents, Mark, and Paul brought with them, they had five twelve-gauge shotguns with forty boxes of shells, two AR-15s with over six thousand rounds, a .308 rifle with a 12x scope and the colonel's M1A with one thousand rounds, four .22 rifles with about five thousand rounds, Mr. Dickerson's M1 Garand with one thousand rounds and his .45 pistol with five hundred rounds, two Glock .40s with about five hundred rounds, Mark's 9mm pistol with five hundred rounds, Steve's newly acquired .38 special and Lisa's .380 pistol with one hundred rounds, six AK-47s and the TEC-9s and pistols they took from the dead intruders at the hospital and at Southcrest.

The food supplies were stacking up, as well. They had over one thousand MREs, five hundred pounds of rice, five hundred pounds of dried beans, three hundred pounds of flour, salt, and sugar, fifty pounds of coffee, four cases of toilet paper, and shelves of canned goods in the pantry. Before, when Grandpa and the others made plans and went to town for supplies, they did not plan on having twenty-eight mouths to feed. While the food supplies would get them through the next few months, they would definitely need the garden and animals to make it through the year into next spring. After a meeting with the Southcrest residents, everyone agreed they needed to get to town to buy more bulk food and a few toiletries and paper products before things got any worse and the power went off in Batesville. They pooled their money, and Grandpa, Mr. Dickerson, and two of the teens would make a run to town Monday morning.

Mark stayed busy doing his assigned chores, guard duty, and keeping the peace whenever a conflict arose over delineation of duties and schedule conflicts, which naturally occur when there are that many people in one place. When he wasn't taking care of his assigned duties, he stayed busy going over his medical supplies and setting up a clinic and OR in the garage with the occasional help of Paul and Jack. He decided that his MASH unit might be needed again. Between what he brought in his emergency kit and what was in the trailer from the surgery center, he had enough supplies and medicines to take care of a small army, exactly what they had at the farm.

Martha was recovering well from the surgery, getting stronger every day and trying to get used to the colostomy. Her wound was healing well and closing in nicely. Her appetite had picked up and her fever had gone. Mark took her IV out and advised her to stay on the antibiotic tablets for another two or three days. The thing she liked best was being able to take a bath and clean up. That could be said for everyone, especially the women and girls. Warm meals and hot and cold running water and a toilet that flushed were welcomed relief to all the Southcrest folks. They were those things no one really appreciates until they have to do without. Even with the crowded sleeping arrangements and the busy schedule, it beat what they had been through over the past two weeks.

On Sunday morning, the Browns and the Edwardses decided to make it to church, while the others stayed behind to hold down the fort. Their cell phones seemed to be working down at the farm, so they would be able to call if a problem came up for either group. Mark borrowed one of Grandpa's old suit coats for church and to help conceal his 9mm that he didn't want to be without but didn't want to flaunt in public. They went in two vehicles, with a loaded shotgun and a .22 rifle in each car.

The Baptist church was on the same county road the farm was on, about halfway to town. On the way to the church, they saw an occasional refugee walking down the road. A few loners and some in pairs and even families with children were camping on the side of the road, anywhere they could find to pitch a tent or park their campers near a source of water. The trip to church was otherwise quiet, but when they pulled in they noticed less than half the usual number of cars in the parking lot. There were a couple of dozen cars and trucks with different county tags and some from out of state mixed in with the regulars. Some were pulling trailers and some were packed as if they were moving.

It all reminded Grandpa of Hurricane Katrina when about twenty families showed up at the church and stayed for over two months. They were run out of their homes by an act of God, but this time they were run out by the acts of men. Then, families who were displaced by the storm packed every campground, rest stop, state park, and roadside stop all the way past Memphis. This time, it was even worse. This time, the only places left to absorb the refugees from all the big cities were the small towns and the countryside.

Inside, it was the same with only about half the usual number of church members, but there were about one hundred or more new faces scattered about the church. They occupied all the classrooms as makeshift bedrooms. Clothes and personal possessions were strewn all about, giving the place that lived-in look. During the service, the preacher asked several times for help for all the families and refugees: food, water, clothes, jobs, and places for them to stay. The church was overwhelmed with requests and was having to turn people away, as were the other churches in the area. After the service was over, Grandpa spotted one of the sheriff's deputies in the crowd and went over to pick his brain and fill him in on what happened at the farm the other day with the bikers. It seemed as if everyone had the same idea. Several men were crowded around him, talking about what was going on in the county.

The deputy told them he had resigned the other day and was at home taking care of his family. Things had been escalating over the past week. They were getting too many calls, and some of the deputies and dispatchers weren't showing up. So he was having to take double shifts and had been shot at in his car twice, so he quit. He said the job just didn't pay enough for him to put up with all that. Grandpa was able to find out that there had been reports of several break-ins and attacks by a motorcycle gang over the past several days. He told the others about the episode at the farm and the army platoon that took the wounded biker in. He wanted to get word to the sheriff, but they had not been able to get a message to him and no one responded to the 911 calls.

The deputy told everyone that things would probably get much worse before they got better and they better be ready to take care of themselves. The Batesville police and the sheriff's office were swamped with all the folks, fights, break-ins, and run-ins. The National Guard was mobilizing to Jackson and Memphis, along with the army, to get things under control there first. It would probably be a while before they got to Batesville.

Mark and the rest caught up with Grandpa and asked what he had found out. Grandpa told everyone the news: Essentially, they were on their own. On the way back to the farm, they noticed that some of the refugees had made it down the road almost to the farm. Now it looked as if more trouble was heading their way. They all knew if it was like that here, things in town were probably much worse. They had already taken in eighteen new people at the farm in the past few days, and Grandpa felt that they could not afford to feed any more without the risk of running out themselves. He decided it was probably time to shut the gate and tell the others what was heading their way.

CHAPTER 20
REFUGEES

Monday, April 21.

Grandpa and Mr. Dickerson decided if they were going to get more supplies, they better do it soon. From what was said at church, things were getting bad in town. They had noticed a small but steady increase in the number of people driving and walking down the road. Keeping the gate closed was keeping them off the farm up to that point. The men on guard duty were reporting that people were stopping at the end of the drive, looking at the closed gate, and then moving on. The gate, along with the long, winding drive lined on both sides by fences and the bridge over the creek, had been enough of a deterrent to keep people out.

The Thompsons also closed their gate, and it also was keeping folks out of their yard so far. The feeling among Grandpa and Mark and the others was sooner or later someone would climb the gates or try to break through. That would be the next issue to deal with. Mark, Grandpa, Paul, and Mr. Dickerson decided that if that were to happen, the guards would stay hidden and call for help, and several of the men would intercept the intruders and force them to leave at gunpoint. If a large group tried to break onto the property, then all the men would need to respond, armed and ready to fight them off. Otherwise, they risk being overrun.

The problem was, if that started occurring on a regular basis, it would start consuming much of their time, and the farm chores would not get done. If they posted more guards as a show of force, it would also keep too many of them from the farm chores and would wear everyone down quickly. That would be a problem they would have to work out. Mark offered an observation. "It might be worth the effort to find the sheriff today while you're in town to see how he thinks things are looking. We may not have enough people to defend this farm if enough people want what we have. So if we know of some good folks who are honest and trustworthy and well armed but need a place to hold up, it may be in our interest to take in a few more."

Grandpa cut him off. "A few more? Hell, we got more than we planned on now. No offense, Mr. Dickerson, y'all are welcome, but more mouths to feed is the last thing we need."

"If this goes on much longer, even honest folks are going to get hungry, and when people get hungry, they get desperate. If their kids get hungry, they will do almost anything to feed them. So we will need to be in a position to defend what we have, or be ready to give it up voluntarily or by force," Mark offered.

"Well, we have eleven armed men and, if needed, some of the women can shoot. I think we'll be just fine like we are. Now, I reckon we best get to town, so we can get on back and get some chores done," Grandpa said, trying to end the conversation.

Grandpa and Steve loaded up in one truck, and Mr. Dickerson and Tim loaded up in another. They checked their cell phones to see if they were still working. The signals were low and sporadic but working, so they set off for town.

On the way to town, they noticed a continued steady increase in the number of refugees along the roads the closer they got to town. Every church parking lot they saw resembled their own, with out-of-town cars and trucks loaded with possessions, as if they were moving cross-country. Tent cities were developing around any open area with access to fresh water. The Walmart parking lot looked like a camper and tent city. As they approached Batesville, traffic was almost at a standstill. Stalled cars along the road and some in the road obstructed the flow of traffic. Red traffic lights were flashing, but to no avail. People were honking their horns and shouting out of their windows at each other. Road rage was all the rage. The quick marts and gas stations that were still open were bottlenecked to a standstill. Impromptu signs stating Out of Gas, written with Magic Markers on cardboard, were taped to most pumps. Sporadic fights broke out over the last cans of beans and loaves of bread on the shelves.

The farther they drove into town, the worse things were. When they topped the last hill, just before the Interstate 55 overpass, they were shocked at what they saw. Thousands of cars, trucks, RVs, and vehicles of every kind packed the interstate in both directions. They were not moving. People were outside their vehicles, walking about almost aimlessly, like a stranded herd. Men, women, and children were walking down the road, like refugees from a war-torn nation from some third world country in the midst of a civil war. The roads in town were impassable. Tents and RVs and makeshift shelters were strewn about as far as the eye could see, like race week at Talladega. Several scattered plumes of smoke billowed around town. Grandpa listened and looked out his open truck window. There were no sirens, no cops, no ambulances to be seen or heard. The hospital parking lot on the hill overlooking the town was the same, a tent and camper city. From what he could tell, there was only chaos. He had seen enough. It was time to get back to the farm. They were, truly, on their own.

Mark and Paul sat in the kitchen and continued to discuss the situation after Grandpa left for town. "Paul, I hope I didn't make Grandpa mad, but I guess what I'm worried about is that the longer things go on, the more likely it is people will get more desperate and band together to take what they need. If the army or National Guard doesn't get down to Batesville soon, the folks from the cities will overrun the town and then everything around it, including this place. The sheer numbers will be overwhelming. They will soon run out of food and the grocery stores will not be able to get shipments in fast enough, because the trucking supply lines are cut off or at least severely interrupted. Gas stations will run dry, and people will be stranded. And if—make that, *when*—the power in town goes off, they will run out of water, and then all hell will break loose. Then all those folks will head for the hills in search of food and water."

"Hey, you're preaching to the choir, boss. I think you are right, but how many more can we take care of here? We don't really have any more sleeping quarters, and like Grandpa said, the food we have will run short if we take on too many more."

"Well, I don't really know. I guess we could put people in tents. It's a little rustic, but if it's that or nothing, they can make their choice. If we need to, we can build log cabins out back. There are enough trees to build a small town. As far as food, we have well water and enough land here to feed half the county, if we plant a big enough garden and have everyone work it. Putting stuff up for the winter will be the challenge. But we have a large root cellar and canning jars, we have beehives for honey, pigs that can have a new litter every four to six months, cows that will calf and make milk, rabbits that can have a litter every month or two, chickens that lay eggs and can hatch more chicks. And all of us can fish and hunt deer, squirrel, turkey, rabbits, and ducks in the river bottoms behind us, and we can smoke the meat to get us through the winter, just like they did one hundred years ago. Grandma and Grandpa know how to do all those things, and what they don't know we can look up in the Foxfire books in our library. Even if things get worse and the whole country goes to crap, it will run its course and, sooner or later, we will rebuild. The people who survive will be the ones who determine what kind of country this will be. That's why we have to protect ourselves. I want it to be our children and those who think like us. Those who want freedom, who are not afraid to work, and are charitable, to a point, toward those who are in need but are willing to help themselves. And most of all, honest and law-abiding on their own, people who don't need lawyers and politicians to tell them how to live, what to eat or drink, or what to say or do." Mark stopped himself and realized he sounded a lot like Paul when he got on his soapbox.

Paul said, "Amen. I know some folks like that. The Southcrest Militia that I was talking about at the hospital. They are not really a militia in the sense that they were looking for a fight, but they were preppers like me, and that's just what we called ourselves. It sounded good at the time. They are organized and probably communicating by short-wave radio right now. They have a ham radio station and are well armed and mobile. Most have RVs or tents and four-wheel-drive trucks and

SUVs. If we could get them a message, they might come down here to ride this out. Just like me, they have stockpiles of MREs that would last each of them a year, along with ammunition, generators, extra gas, diesel, and other supplies. But, at our last meeting, we still didn't have a set place to bug out to. One of the members had a small place outside town where we met and had target practice, but it was only about twenty acres. And it didn't have well water or enough land to live off of, like you are talking about. I can try to call them by cell phone, but if we can't get them by phone, we could try to contact them by radio to see if they are willing to bug out down here. What do you think?" Paul was starting to get excited about the prospects of having his buddies on their side.

"How many are we talking about?" Mark asked. The idea started to sound better the more he thought about it.

"Last meeting there were twenty of us. In all we had about thirty members. All fairly young men, some in their forties and a few in their fifties and sixties, but in good shape, and all can shoot. Many have military experience and they are engineers, firefighters, heat and air guys—men from all walks of life, some married, some with kids. Probably talking about fifty to sixty people in all. But like I said, they are self-sufficient for the most part. Just need water and a place to park."

Mark sat and thought it over for a minute. "We need to call them or get to a radio to see what their situation is, to see if they are settled somewhere or maybe ready to roll down here. I don't think we need to tell the others just yet, but sooner or later, the time will be right."

"Copy that, Captain," Paul joked in his best army radio voice.

Just then, the west-end bunker radio crackled. "Grandpa and them are back already. Opening the gate."

Mark looked at Paul. "That can't be good. They haven't even been gone thirty minutes."

Paul looked at his watch. "Twenty-five to be exact. Probably not good news."

"Nope. Probably not." Mark sat quietly with Paul at the kitchen table and waited for them to come in and report on what was going on in town.

Grandpa parked behind the house, got out of his truck, slammed the door, and cursed a few swear words on his way up the porch into the kitchen. He slammed the kitchen screen door, put his gun in the corner, made himself a cup of coffee, and then sat down with Mark and Paul. The others straggled in behind him. He took a long sip from his coffee and stared at his cup for a minute before he said anything. "What's that prepper term you told us about last Christmas? Oh yeah, the shit done hit the fan in town, and I'm afraid it won't be long before it hits us. There were more folks than you can shake a stick at in town. Tents, people everywhere. Fights breaking out. No gas. Probably not much food left, from what we saw. Hospital looked overrun. Looked like a few fires burning in town, and not a cop, or ambulance, or fire truck in sight. It pains me to admit it, son, but like I said, you are smarter than you look. We are going to need more folks out here."

Mark looked at Paul and held back a grin. "We were just talking about that. It turns out Paul knows a group of militia members that he was part of. They might need to and be willing to come down here. He can vouch for them."

Grandpa looked at Paul. "Tell me about these folks. They're not a bunch of troublemakers or hotheads, are they?"

"No, sir, they are just like me and you: teachers, accountants, engineers, heat and air guys, carpenters, some ex-military, and so on."

"How many are there?"

"Probably about fifty or sixty or so, if their families come along."

"Are they like you, you know, preppers?"

"Yes, sir. We were in a group called the Southcrest Militia. We were actually just preppers. We were not looking to overthrow the government or anything. They all have their own supplies, transportation, MREs, guns and ammo to last at least a year. Most have RVs or tents that they can stay in. Matter of fact, I would guess that's probably where most are staying now. But I don't know if they are still together or scattered all around. This is the sort of thing we were all ready for."

Grandpa sat back and sipped his coffee again. "Do you think you could give them a call?"

Paul smiled widely. "Yes, sir."

Grandpa waited a moment and then turned back to Paul. "Well, what are you waiting for? Make the call." Then Grandpa looked over at Mark and smiled. "If you say I told you so, I'm going to kick your ass."

Paul and Mark got up from the table and walked out back to see if Paul could reach one of his buddies on the phone. Mark slapped him on the shoulder. "You heard him, make the call."

"I am. I am. I'm just trying to think who to call." Paul checked his contacts list and chose a name and called. It rang several times. No answer. He chose another number and called it. Again, no answer. He tried one more number. It rang, and rang. On the fourth ring, someone answered. "This is Gunny."

"Gunny, this is Paul. How's it going?"

"Not so good, man. We're packing up and getting the hell out of here. Been staying at my place. There are too many folks here to keep at bay. No way to defend ourselves. Too close to town.

Power's still out. Water's out. Don't know where we're going yet. All I know is we need to go farther out. Where the hell are you, man? Last we heard, you were at the hospital. I'm sorry, I'm rambling, but it's been crazy around here. Anyway, glad you're okay. What's up?"

"Well, you remember that doctor I told you about? The one with the family farm, outside Batesville?"

"Yeah, Dr. Edwards, right?"

"Yep, that's right. Martha and I are down here with them. It's a long story. Actually, the reason I called is to see if you guys would consider coming down here."

"You mean me and Jen?"

"No, I mean all of you. The militia. Move down here until this is over."

"Are you kidding? There are fifty-two of us. Some are ready to get out of Dodge, right now. I better check before everyone splits. Don't really know where everyone is going. Sorry, I think I already said that. Okay, let me check with everyone. I'll call you right back."

Paul looked at Mark. "He said he would call right back. He sounds excited. I think he wants to come. Sounds like things are bad there."

"Wow, okay. I guess we just wait then," Mark said.

They both stood outside and looked up at the sky and the clouds that drifted by. It was an otherwise beautiful spring day. A slight breeze from the west made the trees sway in the wind. Everything was in full bloom, and the smell of honeysuckle hung sweetly in the air. From where they were on top of the hill where the house stood, they could see most of the farm, with its green pastures and rolling hills, crossed by cedar tree-lined fences and surrounded by woods on all sides. To the south, the very back of the farm dropped off as it joined with the river bottom and the dense hardwood forest.

Just as Paul and Mark got lost in their thoughts and the scenery of the farm, Paul's phone rang. "Hey."

"Well, I passed it by everyone. They took a vote, and they want to head down there— everybody— and the sooner, the better. We are ready to roll now. Just give me the word."

Paul looked at Mark and held his hand over the phone. "He says they are ready to roll, just need to give them the word."

Mark didn't hesitate. "Tell them to come on. Best to take the back way and come in from the east."

Paul put the phone back to his ear. "Come on down, take the back way, come in from the east to avoid all the highway and interstate traffic. I'll text you the address and you can check it on your map. When you get here, stop at the gate and we'll let you in. See you down here." Paul hung up the phone and fist-pumped the air. "They are on the way."

"Great, I hope they make it in one piece and we can hold out until they get here," Mark said as they turned and went into the kitchen to report to Grandpa. "Well, they said they are on their way. All fifty or so of them," Mark explained hesitantly, expecting Grandpa to balk at that many new people down at the farm.

"How many of them can shoot?"

Mark looked at Paul for an answer. "Actually, all of the men and even some of the women would rather shoot than cook or do laundry, so I would guess at least thirty."

Grandpa rubbed his chin in deep thought. "I hope that's enough."

"Enough? This morning, you said we didn't need more mouths to feed," Mark said, trying to prod more out of Grandpa.

"If you had seen what we saw this morning in town, you would feel the same way. If the power or water goes out in town, we're going to have a huge problem. Or, if that biker gang comes back looking for revenge, people are going to get hurt. I was hopeful that I could get to the sheriff and get some assurances for some help if needed. But now I know we are on our own. We can't depend on the police or military, so we are going to need more able-bodied men down here, and soon. We need our own militia. Tell me about this Gunny you keep talking about."

Paul's eyes lit up. "You guys are going to like Gunny. He's a smart ass, but a lot of fun. He comes across as a real hard ass too, but he really has a big heart. He is actually a retired marine gunnery sergeant. Tough as nails. The guy has seen more action than all of us put together. He is our leader. When he says jump, we say how high. He's just one of those guys everybody listens too, like the colonel, just louder. You'll see. If they get here, we'll have our militia." Paul smiled big as he was describing him.

CHAPTER 21
PRESIDENTIAL DIRECTIVES

Monday April 21.
Washington, DC.

Vice President Whitman met with her Cabinet again to get the latest information on the riots and the state of the country. Mr. Clinton, the national security adviser, reviewed the conditions in the larger cities hit hardest by the riots. "The good news is the riots have actually subsided in most of the larger cities. But the bad news is, those folks have now moved out into the surrounding areas. We are starting to see massive logjams and accumulations of refugees in the surrounding towns and smaller cities. The same problems are developing in those areas due to the sheer numbers of people: lack of food, water, and shelter, and a breakdown in law enforcement and civil unrest. We have seen more concentrated and directed attacks on infrastructure, including power plants, water systems, bridges, and cell towers. Our best information points to the National Islamic Party. They make up a big part of The Coalition, which gave us the ultimatums. It appears that they had multiple sleeper cells imbedded in our country since 9/11 and were waiting for this very situation before they struck. We also have confirmed reports of a marked increase in the attrition of police, firefighters, sheriff's deputies, and medical personnel all across the country. With all the trauma from the violence, it has become a critical situation. Many hospitals have closed, either from loss of power or water, direct attacks by the rioters, or the medical staff just failed to show. That's all I have at this time, Madam Vice President."

"Thank you, Mr. Clinton. Let's hear from Mr. Hueling, secretary of defense. What is the situation from your perspective?"

"First, I would concur with Mr. Clinton's assessment within the larger cities. The riots have calmed down there considerably, but not because of anything we did. Mostly due to the fact that people have moved out into the surrounding areas in search of food and water and richer target areas. But we are establishing buffer zones at the perimeters of our target cities, as you ordered. We are starting to make progress toward reestablishing infrastructure. In an ironic turn of events, we became so good at country rebuilding in the Middle East that we know how to do that efficiently here at home. We expect to have the power grid up and running, as well as water, within a few weeks in some of the major cities. We anticipate an influx back into the cities after that. How much and over what time period is anybody's guess." Mr. Hueling sat down, hoping that was all he was asked to report on. He knew the situation in the towns and areas surrounding the major cities was deteriorating rapidly. His troops were stretched to the max as it was, and he worried that more would be asked of him and his men.

"Thank you, Secretary Hueling. Both of you have reported deteriorating conditions in the towns and areas surrounding the cities. Would both of you get us up to speed on that? You first, Mr. Clinton."

"Yes. As I mentioned, we have numerous confirmed reports of massive population shifts from the cities to the surrounding areas. As you know, the major cities with populations over one million people or more contain about eighty percent of the total population of this country. A majority of them have evacuated into the areas surrounding those cities, at first to escape the violence, but now in search of food and water. The towns and small cities have taken the brunt of the shifts. You can imagine, many small towns within a one-hundred-mile radius of these cities have seen their population increase five- to tenfold in a week or so. There would not be enough food or water or accommodations for even a small portion of those under normal conditions. But with the continued attacks on infrastructure in those areas by the rioters—I mean terrorists, if I may call them that—the conditions are deteriorating quickly. Not to mention that the normal food supply lines from the farm to the processing plants to the warehouses to the grocery stores have all been delayed or disrupted. As I mentioned, the police, firefighters, and medical personnel in those affected areas have been overwhelmed and have either been run off or abandoned their posts in huge numbers, leaving the people essentially without protection or medical care. So far, little progress has been made regarding that in the areas that have been affected."

"Thank you, Mr. Clinton." Vice President Whitman was noticeably upset by the lack of progress in regards to resolving the lack of critical personnel. "Secretary Hueling, why have we not made progress in rounding up the critical police, fire, utility, and medical personnel, as I specifically mentioned in our meeting last week? Is there a problem with your people carrying out those directives?"

"No, Madam Vice President. We do not have a problem with the directive. We are working on it, but we just haven't made much progress in carrying it out. I agree we need their help. We don't have near enough doctors or nurses to manage this. Many of the hospitals have closed, and those that are open are only partially staffed. The same with police stations and fire stations. Up to this point, we have been overwhelmed with our efforts to quell the violence and repair the infrastructure. But the biggest problem is most of those people have fled the cities along with everyone else. As you can imagine, most are not at their listed known addresses or answering their phones. We just don't have any efficient means to contact or find them, unless they cross our checkpoints or we run into them. A few have actually turned themselves in, looking for food and water and shelter for their families. But basically, we just haven't caught up with the majority of them yet. We do have them in our database. When we have control of the situation in the cities, we will divide up the manpower and start heading out to the surrounding areas. That is where we will find them. As you have directed, we will have them return to duty or report to the nearest base for assignment, or if they refuse, have them taken there."

"See that you do it as soon as possible. That is just as important as the infrastructure. People are dying out there, and we need them back to work. I suggest you meet with the joint chiefs and make that a priority. You and the secretary of health and the secretary of labor get together and decide where they are needed most and help them make that happen. And, I want Agriculture, Commerce, Energy, Housing, and Transportation working on those areas. We need to find out where the food supplies are and, if necessary, to confiscate it. We need to get those supplies to the people. People are starving out there. They need food, they need shelter, they need medicine, and they need doctors. I want the secretary of homeland security and the director of the FBI to get a handle on the terrorist acts we have witnessed over the past two weeks and find out who is behind them, and I want them brought to justice. I don't care how high up that goes. Is that clear?" A chorus of nods and "Yes, Madam Vice President" were seen and heard around the room. "Any questions?"

Everyone remained quiet, except Senator Sage. He stood up at the table and looked around the room at everyone, and then he spoke. "I commend your efforts to stop the riots. And I appreciate the seriousness and gravity of the work our military is doing in trying to rebuild our cities. But I do not agree with using the military to force private citizens to work against their will. They have the right to be with and protect their families. They are our friends, relatives, and neighbors. They have worked hard their whole lives to support their families, while others ate at the trough paid for by them. Many have saved and prepared for times like this, knowing this government was spending itself into oblivion. What's next? Are you going to take their possessions so that you can feed the same people who caused all this? The people have to realize we cannot survive as a nation if we punish those who work and pay taxes to feed the lazy and then we buy votes with government checks. If that continues, I'm afraid you are going to encounter significant resistance. If that happens, are you going to turn our guns on those who paid for them? If you choose to do this, you need to answer that question first."

Vice President Whitman responded, "I appreciate your concerns, Senator. But what would you have us do? Let people die in the streets of starvation or lack of medical care? We do not have enough food stored up to feed them all. We are faced with a crisis of epic proportions that requires a major sacrifice by all. Those who have plenty must share with others. So, yes, we are going to conscript people into service for the good of the country, and if it comes to it, we will confiscate what we need to take care of those who are in need. It is only fair."

Senator Sage disagreed. "*Fair.* Liberals like to use that word, *fair.* Get your fair share. Pay your fair share. It's not fair for someone to have more than others, even if they worked for it and you didn't. But the problem is, it is always someone else's time and effort and money you want to share and be fair with. That is the trouble with socialism. Sooner or later you will run out of other people's money, and then the whole country will fall. History has taught us that time and time again. Don't you see? That is what the enemy has been waiting for, that is what they have been hoping for. Not to defeat us face-to-face or on the battlefield. They know they cannot defeat us there. They have been waiting patiently while we spend ourselves into oblivion for us to fall from within from the weight of our own entitlement system. The weight of our government supporting people who can but won't work, who talk on cell phones they did not pay for, who have children they cannot feed, who live in houses they cannot afford, who drive cars they cannot put gas in, and who eat themselves into obesity, while others work and pay the taxes that you use to buy their votes. They have become the majority. There is no way for the hardworking, taxpaying members of society to vote you out. That is what is wrong with this country. That is what has led to the problem we now face. If you continue to do that, one of two things will happen. Our economy will collapse further, until we cannot recover, and then we will no longer be the United States of America. A nation will arise that none of us will recognize, that most of us will not want to live in. Or the people who made this country great will rise up and take up arms against you and take their country back. The people will be pushed only so far, and then they will push back. If you try to take away their guns or what is theirs by force, they will fight back. Just remember, there may be three hundred million people in this country, but that hundred million with the food are also heavily armed. They believe in the right to bear arms, and they will. They not only have the guns, but also the bullets to go with them. They have been preparing for this day. The army may have bigger guns, but we only have a million or so armed soldiers in the entire military. So they outnumber the military a hundred to one. You have forgotten, right or wrong, these are the people who took this country from the Indians, fought the British, beat back the Nazis. They are not afraid to fight. They are not just the angry white males or Tea Party folks you like to denigrate. They are of all races: black, white, Hispanic, Oriental. Before their ancestors came to this country, they were the descendants of the Vikings, the Romans, the Greeks, Genghis Khan, the conquistadors, warrior tribes of Africa and Israel and the Ottoman Empire. Proud, hardworking, industrious, resourceful, and charitable, but ruthless if you harm their families, starve their children, or take what is theirs by force. You might have the upper hand at first, but they will hunt you down and find you. They will drag you out of your offices, they will find you at home, they will starve you out, they will cut off your communications, they will kill you in your sleep, shoot you in the streets, and hang you and anyone else who tries to stop them in the town squares. Unlike the Vietnam

War or the Middle East wars, there will not be any lawyers to tell them when to shoot or whom to shoot. No U.N. commissions on war crimes. No congressional hearings on objectives or goals to achieve. It would be all-out war. Kill the enemy by any means necessary, until they are all dead or surrender unconditionally. And you, my folks, will be the enemy. That is not a threat. I am not calling for war. But know this: If you continue on this path, it will happen someday."

When he finished speaking, there was dead silence in the room. Everyone swallowed hard. The words that every one of them feared were just spoken. What all the generals knew but were afraid to discuss. What the politicians all feared the most. The people, the descendants of those who built this country and made it great, would one day awaken and say "No more. That's it." They will rise up and take back their country and throw all of them out and start over and try not to make the same mistakes again. Just the Constitution and a new beginning. They all knew that if that were to happen, they could not stop it. No more playing the race card, or the blame game, or class envy, or persecuting the religious, or passing laws no one has read, or building bridges to nowhere. No more telling the citizens what they can or can't eat, or drink, or smoke in their own homes. How to raise their kids. How to run their businesses. How to spend their money. Now it was out there, on the table, in the open. Spoken out loud. A call to arms. We the people are the United States of America. Not the military, not Washington, DC, not the president, not the Congress. They all work for the people and by the grace of God. It is only by their will that the federal government exist at all, not the other way around. Senator Sage had called them out. The line in the sand had been drawn. The gauntlet had been thrown down.

Vice President Whitman was the first to break the silence in an attempt to relieve the tension in the room. "Gentlemen, I suggest we all take a deep breath and calm down. There is no need for threats. We are all just trying to do what is best for our country. There will be time for further discussions before we make those kinds of decisions. So I suggest we all get busy. There is a lot of work to do." She backed off her earlier statement in order to diffuse the situation, hoping the senator would let it go. But deep down inside, she had no intention of giving in to him or the Coalition. In the end, it was politics as usual. Put off anything unpleasant or controversial today until tomorrow. Let it cool off, then when everyone is distracted by another crisis, push your agenda under the radar.

But she didn't realize his speech was not just for show. The senator would not back down or let it go, now or ever. He was going to force them to choose sides. You were either going to be with them or against them. He felt that he alone among that crowd was the only one willing to stand up and speak for the silent minority who once were the silent majority. But they would be silent no more.

Everyone stood as the vice president left the room with her chief of staff and White House aides. It did not go unnoticed to her that the Senate majority leader, Senator Clark, and the speaker of the House, Representative Wheeler, were absent from the meeting. Whoever tried to kill the president miscalculated the resolve of the vice president. She may have been picked for the female vote, but now she was thrust into the role as commander in chief, and she was more than rising to the challenge.

No one in that room knew of their plan, which was to kill the president so that Vice President Whitman would then be in charge. Their hope was she would be weak and give in to the demands of The Coalition. The president had been sympathetic to their cause, as long as it got him reelected, but his usefulness to them had come to an end after they were fully imbedded and the economy collapsed. It was what they had been waiting for. He had looked the other way long enough to make it easier for them to get established in the country, under the false pretense of being just another Islamic organization looking out for the rights of its fellow brothers and sisters here and in the Middle East. He even held meetings with them at the White House, which gave them the appearance of legitimacy. But it had not gone unnoticed by the opposition party or some of the cable news networks.

But those in power appointed by President Williams and the mainstream media chose to ignore it, so the majority of the public was either uninformed, ignorant, or didn't care as long as the checks kept coming. But he was too power hungry himself to allow the final part of the plan to fall into place, and those behind the plan knew it, so at that point he had to go. But now they had shown their hand and had unleashed their final blow. If their plan failed, they knew they would all be rounded up and sent to military prison or shot, like bin Laden. It had to be all or none. There was no turning back. This was their final jihad.

Senator Clark and Representative Wheeler were in on the plan, and as far as they knew, they still were. What they didn't know was that they had been used by the Brotherhood, just like the president was. Their greed and power blinded them, which made it easier for the Brotherhood to manipulate them up to that point. But their usefulness to The Coalition was used up, as well. They also had underestimated the resolve of the vice president. She had broken a new glass ceiling and was paving new roads for women's rights. That was her agenda, and no man was going to push her out of the way. They now knew the writing was on the wall regarding their plan to get her to give in to their demands, so they were doing what they did best: damage control. Both were in their respective houses of Congress, trying to drum up support for impeachment proceedings against Vice President Whitman in order to stop her before she not only derailed their plan but also found out they were behind it. If they didn't get rid of her, the Feds would get them. And if the Feds didn't, the Brotherhood would.

CHAPTER 22
A WOMAN SCORNED

Monday April 21.
Millington Naval Air Station.

After the meeting, Secretary Hueling went directly to the chairman of the joint chiefs of staff and the secretary of the army. "I want you guys all over this, you understand? I don't want to hear her or the senator go off about this again. That kind of talk scares the crap out of me. Find those damn terrorists responsible for this, round them up, and if they resist, shoot them. And find all the damn doctors, nurses, policemen, and firefighters you can and have them get their asses back to work, or take them to wherever they can work. No exceptions. No excuses. Just get it done."

The secretary of the army in turn called the chief of staff of the army, General Young, and explained the urgency of following up on the directive of the vice president to catch the terrorists and to conscript the police, firefighters, and medical personnel right away, whether they go along with it voluntarily or not. No excuses. General Young in turn called all the combatant commanders, who in turn passed it along to all the base commanders. The base commanders called all the brigade generals, who passed it down to all the battalion commanders, who were ordered to pass it down to all the officers under their command.

None of them liked the directive, because they all knew what Senator Sage said was true. For the time being, they were just doing their jobs, following the orders of the commander in chief. It was an unspoken truth among them that, if it came down to it, they would not and could not turn their guns on and shoot their own people. If that day ever did come, it would truly be a decision point of no return. The precipice would have been crossed. What Senator Sage said would happen would in fact happen. They all hoped it wouldn't come to that. If it did, it would have to be another day. Not that day. Not yet. At that time, keeping the peace and trying to rebuild the country was their objective.

Colonel Henry sat in his office at the Naval Air Station in Millington, where his command center had been set up to oversee the Mid-South Stabilization, Rebuilding, and Relocation Project, the name of his new mission. He was in charge of one of the three battalions assigned to establishing order and infrastructure in the Memphis, north Mississippi, and west Tennessee area. The second battalion was in Nashville, Tennessee, and the third in Jackson, Mississippi. Colonel Henry's office was just down the hall from General Franks, his commanding officer in charge of the Mid-South Brigade, which was made up of all three of the Mid-South battalions. His boss was General Johnson, the commander of the Southern Division in Fort Hood, Texas.

The colonel's orders were specific. First, establish order in Memphis by inserting troops at strategic points around the perimeter to control the violence and movement in or out of the city. Find the terrorists responsible for the bombings and violence. They were to shoot only if shot at or to protect someone else from injury. Then once order was established, begin work on the repair of infrastructure: hospitals, electricity, water, and other utilities. Along with infrastructure, they were to simultaneously reestablish transportation and supply lines for food and medicine and to relocate critical personnel—police, firefighters, paramedics, EMTs, doctors, and nurses—where they were needed most. As those goals were achieved in Memphis, they were then to move out to the surrounding areas and towns and do the same.

The colonel was concerned for the safety and well-being of his wife at the farm but felt that she was in good hands for the moment. But he knew that as things calmed down in Memphis, things would heat up in the surrounding areas. They were tracking the reports of violence and the movement of people, which was occurring like concentric circles of a wave from the center of the initial splash of violence in the larger cities. As they moved farther and farther out, they used up the available food, water, and shelter in those areas, and so the wave of people had to keep moving. As the people left the cities, the rioters and terrorists followed. Batesville was on the direct path of the flood of refugees and the troublemakers who would not be far behind.

The colonel had to deal with this latest directive that reinforced the previous relocation component of his mission. It was very specific and left no wiggle room. If any officer came across or located any utility employees, policemen, firemen, EMTs, paramedics, doctors, or hospital-based nurses who had left their jobs, posts, or positions for any reason, they were to conscript and relocate them into service where they were needed most. This meant if they didn't agree to go voluntarily, they could be taken against their will. It was the one part of his mission that he had a personal objection too. Like his commanders, he too did not believe the government had the constitutional authority to do that to its citizens. But for now, orders were orders.

He had known all along that Mark was a doctor and Cindy and Mrs. Dickerson were nurses, but up to the present time, no one had officially reported it. He could play dumb and leave them where they were, but if any officer reported them, he would be forced to deal with it or face the consequences. He would no longer be able to ignore it or sweep it under the rug. If he did, and it was reported over his head, that would fall back on him. That would be a big problem for all of them.

The colonel had been able to talk to his wife by phone at the farm almost daily, and in fact had just hung up with her right before he got the word from General Franks. Mrs. Henry told him about the attack by the motorcycle gang on the day of arrival. She also told him about Cindy and Tammy going with the platoon back to Millington to work at the hospital. She described what Grandpa Brown had said about how bad things were in town, and that they were waiting on another group from Southcrest to increase their numbers for safety. They were doing well, otherwise. They had plenty to eat, and she enjoyed being with the other women and children. The colonel felt good knowing that she was happy and safe so far and that Mark was using his head by increasing the number of warm bodies on his side. There is nothing that says go away quite like a lot of gun barrels pointed your way.

The fact that Cindy turned herself in worried him, though. If she were to let it slip or intentionally tell on Mark and the others—or let on that he knew about it—it would mean trouble for all of them. Colonel Henry hoped she would keep it to herself. He felt an urgent need to get some of his troops to Batesville somehow, without it seeming as if he was jumping the gun just because his wife was there. She was there by her own choice, and if General Franks found out he played favorites to protect her rather than have her come to the base, where it was safe, that could be a problem. His intention was to speed up his work in Memphis so that he could move his timeline up and begin taking on the areas outside the metropolitan area, which would include Batesville, Oxford, Hernando, and many other medium-size towns that were county seats. He had to be careful about sending troops directly to Batesville, bypassing all the other places in the surrounding area without good reason, and not make it look too conspicuous. It was a lot to consider and a lot to juggle.

But things would get even more complicated. Later that day, when Lieutenant Stern got the word from above about the directive to place an emphasis on conscripting critical personnel, especially surgeons, he became extremely worried because of what Nurse Cindy had told him. He didn't know it at the time, but she told him with the hope that he would report it. Cindy didn't tell the lieutenant before they left the farm because she was mad that Mark chose his wife over her and just wanted to get away from them. But on the ride back, Cindy asked questions and found out that all surgeons were being called up for duty, and if they didn't have a hospital to work at, they would most likely be brought to Millington, where she was being taken. That's when Cindy came up with the idea to tell the lieutenant about Dr. Edwards, not for the greater good but in hopes that Mark would be brought to where she was. That way, she would have him to herself again and get another chance to win him over without his wife getting in the way.

Lieutenant Stern debated about telling anyone at the time, because he didn't know what kind of trouble it would cause for Colonel Henry. The lieutenant decided to report it, because he worried that if it got out that he knew about it, too, then he might be in trouble. After the directive was reissued, he had no further doubts about what needed to be done. He went straight to Captain Ellis, his company commander. "Sir, I need to tell you something. I'm not quite sure what to do with this information."

"Well, what is it, soldier? I don't have all day. What's bothering you?" It was obvious to the lieutenant that the captain was not in a good mood. He never was.

"Sir, you remember that nurse and that little girl we brought back from that farm, outside Batesville, where we took the colonel's wife?"

"Yes, I remember, what about her? You got the hots for her or something? Spit it out, mister."

"Well, that Mark Edwards fellow you met in the house with the colonel, he was a doctor, a surgeon. A general surgeon, to be exact. He and that Paul fellow singlehandedly held down that Southcrest Community Hospital for the last week before it burned. They took equipment from the surgery center, across the street, and did two surgeries in his garage. And he saved that little Tammy girl, too."

"Where the hell did you get all that info, mister?"

"From that nurse I was telling you about. She told me about it when we got back to the base hospital, while I was getting her situated. I didn't really make too much about it at the time, but since we got that call from the general, I thought I better tell someone. And she says they have a lot of food, animals, and well water, along with the guns and ammo that we saw. Things people need to survive. It's all in my report."

"That's just great. So you tell me, and now it's my problem. Thanks a lot, Lieutenant. Now I have to report it to the colonel, or it's my ass on the line. He already knows about it. So he either doesn't want to do anything about it, in which case he is going to be pissed at me, or he plans on doing something about it, and I'll just look like a shithead for bringing it up. Thanks a lot, soldier."

"Sorry, Captain."

"Sorry, my ass. Don't you have something you need to be doing, like rebuilding a city or something?"

"Yes, sir." He saluted and turned sharply and left in a hurry. Now the problem was Captain Ellis's. He was career army through and through. He did everything by the book. He left nothing to chance. He did not want this to fall back on him, so he did what any good officer would do in this situation. He typed up a formal report and sent it to his commanding officer, the colonel, and one to his boss, General Franks. It might piss off Colonel Henry, but that would be his problem.

When the colonel got the e-mail and report, it did piss him off. Cindy had opened a can of worms. He thought how Captain Ellis was and always had been a pain in the ass, and as usual he covered his ass. The lieutenant knew about it, and now Captain Ellis knows and his commanding officer, General Franks, knows. He will in turn pass that info up the line in his summary reports, and then everyone above him will know. It was in black and white and on paper. No denying it. If the top brass got any more heat about it from the Pentagon, it would fall back on him. He alone determined what happens with the personnel in his area of operation. All assignments, duty rosters, and manpower distribution were his responsibility. General Franks had much bigger fish to fry in trying to keep the brass happy and off their asses. He would get involved in such minor personnel details only if shit rolled down from above. And, everyone in the military knows shit always rolls downhill.

It became Colonel Henry's problem. What to do with Dr. Edwards and the farm? The directive was very clear: All hospital-based medical personnel, especially nurses and doctors, were a priority, and most of all, general surgeons were a top priority. Under the circumstances, they were the most sought-after human commodity. Trauma from automobile accidents had always been the major cause of death from trauma, but the riots and ongoing violence had catapulted gunshot wounds, stabbings, burns, and beatings to the top of the list. Hospitals were already short of surgeons before the shit hit the fan, but the situation had become critical. The military medical services were overwhelmed. People were literally dying in the streets due to a lack of paramedics and ambulances and the fractured EMS systems. And they were dying in the halls and ERs of hospitals from a lack of operating personnel, anesthesia, and, most of all, trauma surgeons. The military had ways of overcoming some of the problems and obstacles, but there was no one else to do the one thing that saved the most lives: surgery.

He knew when he sent his troops with them to the farm that day, the right thing to do in the eyes of the military would have been to have his wife go with him where it was safe. And he should have had his soldiers take Nurse Cindy, Dr. Edwards, Jack, and Paul to Millington and place them into service at the hospital, where the greater good could be done. The others at Southcrest and the farm would have had to fend for themselves like everyone else. But he cared for his wife and those people too much to do that to them. Doing so would have forced his wife to live on another military base, spending most of her time alone and surrounded by strangers, something he promised her she would never have to do again. She had come to know and love Lisa and the boys and the other neighbors in Southcrest. Forcing them go to Millington would have made them miserable and separated families and friends against their will. To him, they were what was good about America, the kind of people he and his troops were fighting to protect. The kind of people who would make his country good again. The decision was difficult then, but even now, if he had it to do over again, he would probably do the same thing.

He knew when he made that decision that if General Franks or the brass above him found out that he knowingly harbored a general surgeon while people in his district were literally dying in the streets, he would be in serious trouble. They would argue that he was motivated by his selfish desire to help get his friends and wife to a place of safety and comfort using government resources while others suffered. In their eyes and way of thinking, everything was black and white, and his concerns for the safety and well-being of his wife and the others should not have prevented him from doing the right thing. But what was done was done, and now he was faced with deciding whether to send a platoon to get them before it fell back on him or perhaps finding another option.

CHAPTER 23
THE MILITIA

April 21.

The farm, later that day.

The radio from the west guard bunker crackled. "Come in, come in base." It was Tim.

"Base here. What's up?" Mark was on base radio duty.

"I have motorcycles coming from the west. Looks like at least four. Two crotch rockets and two choppers. Moving slowly. They stopped at the gate, checked the place over. The bald dude pointed his finger at the house and acted like he was shooting a gun. They're leaving now. Heading east."

"East bunker, come in."

"East bunker here." It was Steve, on guard duty there.

"Did you get that? Motorcycles heading your way. Notify the Thompsons."

"Thompsons here, we heard you. Taking precautions."

"East bunker here, they're coming. Moving fast. Two shots fired at house. Two shots fired at house. Heading east fast. They're gone."

"Base to Thompsons. You okay?"

"Yes, we're okay, just a broken window and some glass. A little shook up. That was scary." It was Mrs. Thompson, in her kitchen with the kids and Mrs. Curtis. The others were out doing chores around the farm.

"Base to east and west bunkers. Better double up the guards. They may come back."

Mark found Paul and Grandpa and sat down at the table in the kitchen to discuss the situation. The other men were working in the garden and doing farm chores. Mark suggested, "I think we should double up the guards and have everyone on standby with their guns while they work in case they are needed. If they come back, there may be big trouble. I think they know we were in on the first go-round. They may be looking for revenge."

"I'll go to the east bunker," Paul volunteered. "If they come back by and try that again, they'll be sorry."

"Okay, just don't get yourself killed. And don't shoot unless they shoot first. We don't want any more trouble than we already have, and that will give away our bunker position and the element of surprise," Grandpa said.

"Well, that's true, but we can't have them doing drive-bys. Someone in the house will get shot. I would rather it be them than us," Paul argued.

"You're right. I guess if they pull out a gun and you think they are going to shoot, then let 'em have it. If you do shoot, make sure you get 'em all. We don't want them to come back," Grandpa amended after thinking about it for a moment.

"Okay." Paul grabbed a rifle and a few extra magazines, just in case.

Mark grabbed a rifle and was heading for the door. But Grandpa stopped him. "Where are you going?"

"To the east bunker, with Tim."

"You better stay up here. If someone gets shot, you're going to have to take care of him. I'll get one of the other guys to go down."

Mark started to argue with him but realized he was right. If things in town deteriorate and heat up, as they thought they would, he may be forced to do more garage surgery. "I guess you are right. Better go check my OR and get ready, just in case." Just as he said that, the lights went out at the farm. It had been a little over two weeks since the riots started in the cities. Mark and Grandpa looked at each other and stood quietly for a moment and waited. The lights did not flicker. They did not come back on. Mark picked up the house phone. "Dead." He picked up his cell phone. "No signal." He went back over to the table and sat down. "It can't be an accident that the power and phones went out at the same time. Someone planned that. Well, guess we better get ready. They'll be coming."

Grandpa answered back sarcastically, "Yep, things are going to get real interesting around here."

The east bunker radio crackled. Steve was on the radio again. "Come in, base. We have bikers heading our way. Looks like about four again. No crotch rockets. I hear a bunch of others coming in behind them. Can't see 'em, but I hear 'em. Sounds like a lot. Must be their buddies coming back for more. Paul has a bead on them. If they try anything, we are gonna take out as many as we can. Be ready."

Mark answered, "Okay, we'll get the men ready on our end. Heading for the west bunker and will send a few your way for backup." Grandpa headed out back to find some of the other men to send down front, half to the east and half to the west. Then he gathered up the women and sent them into the house and had them get armed and ready, in case they needed to defend the house. They grabbed their shotguns and stood by the windows and doors to keep an eye out for any intruders. The rest gathered up the children and took them to the inner rooms and got behind furniture for better cover.

Steve was back on the radio. "There's a bunch of 'em coming. Paul said get ready."

Grandpa was in the kitchen on the radio. "Help is on the way. Hang on." He was the last line of defense if they made it past the guards and the gate.

Steve shouted into the radio. "Wait!" There was a long pause. "Don't shoot." Another long pause. Grandpa held his breath. "They're here. They're here. It's the militia. It's the militia. Paul says it's the militia. They are passing us now. Four Harleys with American flags. A Jeep with a .50-caliber machine gun, six SUVs pulling campers, ten trucks pulling campers, two more Jeeps, four more motorcycles, more flags. Wow! They're coming your way." Paul left the others in the bunker and ran as fast as he could back toward the house, then across the yard and down the drive, all the way to the gate, yelling all the way.

Grandpa swallowed hard and held back tears. "West bunker, did you hear that? It's the militia. Hold your fire. Hold your fire."

Tim answered back. "I see 'em. I see 'em. Wow! There's a shitload of 'em. Sorry." Grandpa just smiled. They all climbed out of their bunker and walked toward the gate to see their new friends. Paul greeted them at the gate. His prepper buddies were obviously glad to see him, but the leader stopped Paul before he opened the gate.

"Wait! What are you doing, mister? Stop! All of you." Mark, Mr. Dickerson, and the rest all stopped dead in their tracks. "What in the Sam hell are you doing? Never drop your weapons and leave your cover until you know exactly whom you are dealing with and get the all-clear. The bad guys could be holding some of us hostage until they get through the gate, then you would all be dead." Then he started laughing and gave Paul a big hug.

Paul turned red and turned to Mark and the others. "Sorry about that, guys. Did I tell you guys Gunny is a smart ass?" Everybody on both sides started laughing. But Mark got the message and thought about what he said. He knew that Gunny was using humor to make a point. Mark got it. And he was right. They did need to be more careful. Things were about to get much more serious.

Paul introduced Mark, Grandpa, and the others to Gunny. Like Paul described him, Gunny was an impressive figure with a bald shiny head, arms the size of most men's legs, and a wit that was razor sharp. After all the hand shaking was over, Mark and Grandpa led them all up to the barnyard to get them all out of the driveway and out of sight of the road. No need to let the world know what was going on. After the dust settled, Mark sent the boys back to their guard posts, despite their objections. They were excited to see other people at the farm, not to mention a few new girls who were with them. Mark had Paul park them in the hill pasture behind the barn. In all, there were fifty-two of them. And altogether, there were now eighty people on the farm.

Someone was going to have to talk to these new people and get the family and the Southcrest folks and the militia to all work together, share resources, and get along, for only God knew how long. Someone was going to have to take charge and coordinate getting them settled in, figure out where they were going to set up camp, their water supply, sewer, work schedules, guard duties, and, last but not least, the food supplies, which would mean a much bigger garden. It would all fall on Mark to coordinate and oversee the entire enterprise, the farm, everyone getting along, utilization of supplies, allocation of food and fuel, and their health and safety.

Others would help. Grandpa would still have the final say on matters, Gunny would be in charge of his folks, and Mr. Dickerson would help with the guard schedules. The women would help with the farm chores and the food. Mark had a lot to think about and a lot to do. Then there was the newest problem: no electricity or phone services on the farm. But worst of all were all those folks in town with no water, no food, no gas, no phones, and no shelter. What they had at the farm was far from ideal. All of them were going to have to change the way they lived. No more daily baths or showers, no central air-conditioning or heat, meals cooked on woodstoves and lanterns for light. No telephones or cell phones or computers, no washing machines or dryers, no refrigerators or freezers. Rationing of gas and fuel for travel, no more propane deliveries, well water by windmill or bucket and pulley or hand pump. Food rationing and no more running to Walmart for toilet paper, toothpaste, deodorant, razors, or soap. Things truly were going to get more interesting.

The residents at the farm were not just faced with living in difficult conditions and living off the land like in the eighteen hundreds, but they were without the benefit of established trade routes that allowed even the settlers of this country to obtain supplies and staples that made life a little easier: sugar, coffee, tea, salt, nails, leather goods, metals, rifles, and ammunition. They would have to learn to make do with what they had on hand, at least until they could establish communications with neighbors. Hopefully, local farms in the same situation would be willing to cooperate and trade and barter with each other for things they needed and the others had.

How long the situation lasted across the country would determine how desperate their situation would become on the farm and any other place where people were gathered to survive, be it a farm, a ranch out west, a mountain retreat, or a small town. If they were unable to get any supplies for a year or so, they might be fine if they were well prepared. After two years or so, things would get tough. Longer than that, and things would get real serious. They might have the ability to grow food in the growing seasons, but the winters would be difficult. They would eventually run out of canning supplies, sugar, salt, coffee, tea, medicines, lamp oil, and soap. They would have to learn the ways of their great-great-grandparents. They would have to learn to hunt and fish again—not for weekend recreation, but for survival. They would have to learn how to make lye soap, dig root cellars, keep bees for honey, and use the wax to seal jars and make candles, smoke meat, spin wool, weave and knit clothing, use hand tools to make things needed for the home and farm, tan hide into leather, and so on. Dental diseases would become common. Eyeglasses would be hard to come by, to say the least. People would die of simple things that have not been seen in modern times: childbirth, infections, pneumonia, trauma, and appendicitis.

But the most immediate problem for the farm and anyplace like it would be keeping others from trying to take what they have. As difficult and different as things had been and would get on the farm, they at least had guns and ammunition, food, water, medical care and shelter, beans, bullets, and Band-Aids.

The things needed for survival that millions in the country didn't have, hundreds of thousands in the Memphis area didn't have, and thousands in the county didn't have. People of all walks of life, young and old, rich and poor, were displaced from their homes, businesses, and families. Caught off guard and unprepared for what happened. Some without food, water, shelter, no way to protect themselves, no place to go, refugees in their own land. All of them searching for the things that were at the farm.

People who are hungry and thirsty become desperate when they or their children are hungry and thirsty. They will do whatever is necessary to feed them. Even otherwise honest, law-abiding citizens will steal and become violent in order to provide or protect their children and themselves. They will take from those who have by whatever means necessary, even if it comes to fighting and killing. Those who didn't understand that would be in for a rude awakening in the weeks and months ahead. Mark understood that because he understood human nature, what humans are capable of when stressed, hungry, thirsty, threatened, and scared. They become the primates they are. Social convictions, good manners, charity all go out the window. Friends will turn on friends, and family will turn on family. Humans will do the unthinkable—even eat human flesh. History has proved that, over and over.

Mark had already thought about all of those things. That was why he wanted the Southcrest folks with him. That was why he wanted the militia on the farm. It wasn't enough to be prepared, to stockpile food and supplies, or hole up somewhere off the beaten path out in the countryside or hills. Solar panels and windmills can supply needed energy. Well water can keep away thirst, and a garden and canned goods can keep away hunger for a while. But only a lot of warm bodies with guns and ammo can keep the Takers away.

The Takers were not just the folks who had taken until the country could no longer afford to give any more. They weren't just those who always took from others and filled the jails and prisons. Not just those who felt as if everyone owed them something because of their race or position in life, be it by birth or hard knocks. It was anyone who wanted what they had at the farm and would come to try to take it. At first, it would be a few here and there, then more and more. Leaders would arise who would form roving bands of Takers, which would compete with and eventually take over other groups to form larger and larger groups that would try to take whatever they wanted from whomever they wanted. It wouldn't be just food or water or bullets that they would want. They would also want power, women, and to kill for blood sport.

Being able to defend yourself against them and defeat them would be the challenge that would determine who ultimately won out in the long run. Either the Takers would win, or people like those on the farm would win. Good people. Kind and gentle people who are not afraid to fight for what is right, hardworking, God-fearing people. People whose word is their bond, whose handshake seals a deal. People who do not double-cross or backstab anyone. People who do not need to take from others, because they plan ahead, save for a rainy day, take care of themselves. People who would rebuild the country back the way it used to be.

Young couples would court instead of live together and men would marry women and have children who would rebuild the churches and schools needed for a civilized society. People would actually sit and eat and talk together, instead of texting or surfing the web while ignoring the ones they're with. Lawbreakers would be tried by a jury of their peers, not the court of public opinion. Prayer would be allowed back in the schools. Bibles would be found on the teachers' desks again. Elected officials would serve their country and then return home, not just become career politicians. The government would be for the people and by the people and follow the Constitution again. Other like-minded people gathered together all across the country, hoping for the same things, would find each other and band together to stop the Takers and rebuild this country. That is why the eighty people on the farm were so important. It was a start. That is what Mark hoped for, for himself, for his family, and for his country. That is what he wanted the others to believe in, too.

CHAPTER 24
DIGGING IN

Tuesday, April 22.

The men met at the kitchen table early that morning to discuss the details of the arrangement for the new group at the farm. It was the blending of several groups of people for a common cause. Mark essentially gave the same talk as before, which everyone agreed to. The militia would follow the lead of Gunny and his two right-hand men, Hank and Skinny. Skinny was a retired police officer from Memphis, and Hank was their radioman. Everyone in the militia had a nickname, or handle, so Gunny nicknamed Mark Doc, because there were already two Marks in their group.

Then they got down to the details on supplies, food, guns, ammo, generators, and fuel. From the lists, they seemed to be in good shape in regards to lamp oil and fuel, at least for the time being, but any unnecessary use of the fuel would need to be discouraged. The main problems with housing were sewer and water. Several of the men offered to get the windmill up to speed so they could pump water without having to use fuel to keep a generator running. Latrines would have to be built at designated locations. Everyone would equally divide up the farm chores, cleaning, cooking, and laundry.

The food situation was another area of concern, not in the short run, because they had at least a full year's supply of canned goods and MREs among all of them, but they were depending on the garden and didn't know how long it would take before it was in full production. They planned to grow the full complement of vegetables, squash, melons, and herbs during the summer growing season, but also potatoes, turnip greens, and cabbages that could produce or be dug up into the fall and winter. They would have to hunt and fish as much as possible in the meanwhile to keep from using up their stored food supplies or having to kill and eat the farm animals, which they intended to save for the winter and when needed down the road.

The great unknown was when the country would be up and running normally again, when the riots would end, when the fighting would stop, when the terrorists would stop blowing things up. When farmers could get back into normal production was another concern. It would take the availability of fuel, parts, labor, electricity, seeds, fertilizer, herbicide, and pesticides to produce food. Besides the farms, it would take processing plants, trucking, and labor to process, package, and deliver food, and grocery stores that were not being looted to sell it. And then it would take a stable currency to buy it, and a working economy to afford it. It could be months or years, depending on several factors. No one knew. No one even ventured to guess. And as usual, the talking heads on the radio and TV and in Washington were busy blaming each other for the problems the country was suffering from.

But the most pressing business at hand was organizing and preparing the farm defensively for what lay ahead. That was turned over to Gunny. He pointed out the weaknesses in their defense and made several good suggestions that they all agreed to. The main one was a stronger show of force at the gate to prevent, or at least discourage, outsiders from trying to run through it. Second, a series of defensive bunkers would be placed at the top of the hill, in case larger groups tried to attack the house, barn, and surrounding area where the garden was located and RVs were parked. The bunkers would be dug into the ground at four points on the hill that could defend against attacks from any direction. One of the bunkers would overlook the drive and have a direct line of fire to the gate. It would be manned with several shooters armed with AR-10s fitted with scopes that could stop anyone coming up the drive. In a firefight, the bunkers would also serve to keep the direct line of fire away from the house and barns and RVs. The two existing bunkers down front would continue to be used to protect the gate and the Thompsons' house. Modified sandbags would be made out of the hundreds of used feed sacks Grandpa kept in one of the storage sheds by filling them with dirt and stacking them around the edges of all the bunkers on the hill and down front.

Third, rovers would patrol on foot along the front between the east and west bunkers and around the house and barnyard at night to prevent any sneak attacks. All of the men, as well as the teenage boys over fourteen and some of the women of the militia who volunteered, would share guard duty and carry weapons on them, or within arm's reach, at all times. Everyone on patrol and whoever was on duty at the base in the kitchen would carry a radio at all times. The big dinner bell behind the house would be rung only if there was an attack. It would signal that everyone needed to take their positions within minutes and be ready, with weapons in hand, day or night. Gunny had taught them well.

Last but not least, extra ammo would be strategically placed near the bunkers, dry and hidden from sight. The main bulk of the ammo and stored food would be kept in the basement. It would be accessed and used only if agreed to by the men of the roundtable who sat at the kitchen table and made the decisions. Those men were Grandpa, Mark, Mr. Dickerson, Mr. Thompson, Gunny, Paul, and Skinny. Glen was offered a seat, but he felt that their aggressive approach was leaving them open for future legal problems. Some of the women were asked to sit in, but they all felt that in matters of security and life-and-death situations, they would defer to their husbands. They knew they had their input, and if they objected to any major issues, the men listened to them. All agreed that if any significant disagreements that could not be settled were to arise, Grandpa had the final say.

Over the next several days, they finished digging in, and everyone settled into routines around the farm. Chores and work schedules were worked out, the latrines and outhouses were built and put to good use, and the garden was being expanded for the third time. The traffic on the road increased significantly and seemed to be getting worse by the day. Most were on foot, many traveling alone with backpacks or nothing but the clothes on their backs. There was an occasional car, truck, or motorcycle. One man even came by on horseback. Most were in pairs or small groups, looking tired and hungry. A family or two with small children came by and stopped. The guards felt sorry for them and offered them their lunches and water, which brought tears and words of thanks from the parents. Several others had stopped to check the gate, saw it was locked, cursed, and looked around, but no one tried to break through. A few tried to climb over, but as soon as armed men sprang up with rifles drawn on them from a bunker out of nowhere, they wisely decided to move on.

The most significant encounter was when a group of about twelve young men wearing hunting camo rode by in three jacked-up pickup trucks flying rebel flags and stopped at the gate. They appeared drunk and were obviously agitated by the locked gate. They brandished their weapons and threatened to break through the gate and to take whatever they wanted. But when the guards heard the threats, they popped up with rifles pointed directly at them. The group grumbled and cursed but moved on down the road. They did the same thing at the Thompsons' gate, and the guards responded in the same way. But the group was even more surprised when the guards popped up behind them from across the road. The apparent leader of the group growled curses at them and promised his group would return with others and make them pay. He said that whatever they had behind those gates must really be worth something for them to risk their lives.

After that encounter, Gunny decided that a second bunker needed to be dug in on the other side of the gate down front and the guards split up so that if someone did try to break through, they would be attacked from both sides, making it more difficult for them. The Jeep with the machine gun would also be parked where it could be used to protect the drive, as well as placed so that it could be seen from the road as a further deterrence to anyone who thought about trying to rush the gate. In essence, it would take a small army to take over the farm.

Hank's ham radio, CB radio, and police scanner were set up in the barn office and connected to a series of twelve-volt batteries and a converter to run it with an occasional charge from one of the generators. When the power went out, the sheriff's department went back to using CB radios instead of the FM band, so Skinny was able to contact them on the radio and actually had a conversation with the sheriff himself.

Things had already been bad over the past few weeks, with the mass influx of people and all the trouble they brought. But, after the power went out in town, the police chief, mayor, and county supervisors weren't seen or heard for a long time. Sheriff Taylor could do nothing to stop the looters and fighting that broke out. All the stores in and around town were ransacked, along with most of the homes. Someone had intentionally blown up the power substation that served town. And the telephone towers and lines had been torn down and cut, as well. The hospital was essentially shut down, and fires were burning out of control all over town and in the county. He and the few deputies who stayed with him were basically stranded at the jail in the middle of a sea of desperate people and doing all they could to keep them at bay and themselves and their families safe. They had actually turned the prisoners loose. They didn't have enough food and water for them and their own families, so it was either that or let them starve. The sheriff said he actually thought about letting them starve, but decided against it since some were in for only minor offenses. He contacted the state police, but they could not help. They had their hands full already. He did say that he had heard from a couple of other groups in the county that had a place and preparations similar to the farm. One was at the Clifton farm, with about thirty-five people, and the other at the Huffman farm, with about fifty people.

Pockets of people were holed up out in the county and getting by. But they were having to fend off attackers and were worried that if a large group were to attack, they would not be able to hold them off. They had food and water and guns but did not think far enough ahead that if things got really bad, it would take a small army to protect their belongings. The sheriff knew of several subdivisions in which the neighbors had banded together to protect each other, but when the power went out, the water went out also. So that meant they had to leave their homes in search of water. Very few people had enough water stored up to last more than a day or so, and even fewer had well water.

There had been reports of two large groups that were going around the county attacking people in their own homes, or when they tried to travel about, taking their food and weapons from them and sometimes raping the women. One was probably the motorcycle gang that Grandpa and Steve had the run-in with at the Thompsons' house. The other may have been a local group that the men in the jacked-up trucks were a part of. He knew of several people who had been murdered and was sure that many more homicides had not been reported. The sheriff asked and then begged for their help. He needed some good men to help make the county safe again.

After talking to Gunny and Mark and the others, Skinny talked to the sheriff again and offered their help. By their best estimate, they would have about sixty or so men and women who were armed and willing to help the sheriff. They advised the sheriff to tell the other small groups that, if possible, they should try to move in together to increase their numbers and to pool their resources. They also said he should try to get some of the isolated groups that had food and arms to also find a farm somewhere in the county that they could go to and set up a base.

Mark and Grandpa thought long and hard and decided that, if push came to shove, they could take a few more good families at the farm. So if the sheriff knew of any who had their own shelter, food, weapons, and ammo, he could point them in their direction. That was the price of admission. In their hearts they wanted to help as many as possible, but if they started trying to feed and defend everyone, they might not survive themselves. It was a heart-wrenching decision, but Grandpa, Mark, Mr. Dickerson, and the others agreed that was the way it had to be.

Within two hours of their conversation, the sheriff radioed in that he and three of his deputies would be rolling up to the gate with their families in their RVs. No one was as surprised as Grandpa. He knew Sheriff Taylor, but they had not always seen things eye to eye. With a head full of slicked back black dyed hair, the smooth talking hand shaking sheriff looked and acted more like a politician than an officer of the law to Grandpa. He campaigned on a platform that included some measures of gun control in the county and won out over the previous sheriff, who was a good friend of Grandpa. The previous sheriff had been in office for ages, but many new families had moved into the county from the city, and they didn't like hearing guns going off all the time.

There was some pressure being put on the county board of supervisors to ban shooting on any private property in the county, unless the owner obtained a conditional-use permit designating it as a shooting range or hunting club. Of course, the county would collect a fee every year and conduct inspections to make sure they were safe. The measure failed by one vote, but Sheriff Taylor, who had been the chief of police in Batesville, won his election by a narrow margin by promising to force another vote in the near future. Grandpa thought it was a stupid idea and told him so in person. Since then, Sheriff Taylor and Grandpa hadn't spoken to each other. Now, he was coming to the farm with his family and three of his deputies and their families. He must have changed his political views, or the situation changed it for him.

Suddenly, the radio crackled. "This is Sheriff Taylor. Come in, Hank."

"This is Hank. I read you loud and clear."

"We are coming in hot. From the west. Open the gate. Deputy shot. Repeat. Deputy is shot. They are right behind us. Still shooting at us. Trying to keep them off our backs. Tell Doc we need help."

Hank could hear shots being fired over the radio while the sheriff was talking. Hank called the base on the portable radio. "This is Hank. Just got off the radio with the sheriff. Deputy is shot. Still after 'em. Shots fired. Coming in hot. Open gate. Be ready."

Gunny was on base duty. He took the call. "Copy that. Coming in hot. Deputy shot. Will open gate. Will round up troops." Gunny then notified Doc and Jack that they had incoming wounded and to fire up the generator and ready the OR. Then he rang the big dinner bell behind the house. Everyone responded, armed and ready. Gunny knew they were coming in from the west, so he took six of his men, heavily armed with AR-10s and AR-15s, and, with weapons in hand, headed to the west end of the property, about one hundred yards from the gate, and waited. He knew they would bottleneck coming in the drive, even with the gate open, so that is when he would open fire on the trucks. The others were stationed at the two bunkers by the gate and the one at the top of the hill overlooking the drive. The machine gun on the Jeep was manned and ready.

After a few minutes, a caravan of vehicles came flying down the road. Gunshots could be heard before they could see them. Gunny radioed, "Here they come. Get ready!" As they approached, he could see the wives in front driving the trucks that were pulling the campers, and the deputies were driving their cars behind them. The sheriff was in his car bringing up the rear, with a deputy hanging out his passenger window, shooting a riot gun at the two jacked-up pickup trucks that were chasing them. Each of the trucks had several men hanging out of their windows, shooting back. And behind all of them were several motorcycles, the last one of which was a crotch rocket ridden by Ponytail. It looked as if Jacked-Up Trucks had teamed up with Motorcycles. The deputies' cars and trucks and campers had broken windows and holes in them from the flying bullets.

Just as the trucks pulling the campers slowed down to turn in the drive through the gate, the whole line of trucks, cars, and motorcycles had to slow down. That put the Jacked-Up Trucks crew at almost a dead stop, right in front of Gunny and his men. That's when all hell broke loose. It sounded like World War III for a few minutes, and then it was over. The men in the trucks and on the motorcycles didn't stand a chance, except for Ponytail, who had been there before and was leery, so he lay back from the others. When the bullets started flying at them, the trucks and motorcycles veered off into the ditches or stopped in the road as they were shot up, but Ponytail turned tail and sped away. All the other attackers lay dead of multiple gunshot wounds. In all, there were eight men, some just boys not much out of high school. It would be a big mess to clean up.

The sheriff and his crew managed to limp up the drive, into the barnyard, and behind the house. When everyone was accounted for, they found that one deputy had been shot in the thigh and was bleeding profusely from the wound. Another was shot in the chest by bullet fragments that came through his car door. Mark, Jack, Paul, and Nurse Dickerson went into action. Mark had them put the first deputy on the OR table, and then Mark cut his clothes off. They put the other on a cot in the corner of the garage. They took their vital signs and started large-bore IVs and ran in a bag of ringers lactate and two grams of Ancef into both of them. Then, Mark did a primary and secondary survey of the wounded deputies. He determined that the first deputy on the OR table had a wound to the right femoral artery and would bleed out or lose his leg unless he had surgery. The second had diminished-breath sounds and most likely had a collapsed lung with blood in his left chest. He needed a tube placed in his chest to drain the blood and reinflate the lung.

Mark put direct pressure on the thigh wound, which slowed the bleeding considerably, then he shouted to Mrs. Dickerson. "Hold pressure on his leg, right here, and don't let go until I say so. Paul, open up the general basic set and get out some 5-0 double-armed prolene. We need to operate on his leg right away. Jack, get ready to put him under. While you guys are getting him ready, I'm going to put a chest tube in the other deputy."

Mark opened a chest tube tray and set everything out that he would need: lidocaine, needles, syringe, gloves, Betadine, gauze sponges, 0 nylon suture, Kelly clamp, scissors, scalpel, sterile drape, and a thirty-two-French chest tube with a suction hose. Something was missing. He could not find a pleurevac suction canister. There was not one in the supplies they brought back from the surgery center. He checked again. He knew he had to place the chest tube to underwater suction in order to reinflate the lung and drain the blood to prevent air trapping in the chest cavity outside the lung. If he couldn't, the lung would continue to collapse, causing a tension pneumothorax, respiratory failure, cardiovascular collapse, and death. He would have to improvise. Mark knew that in the early days of surgery, surgeons used a series of glass jars with rubber stoppers to achieve the same result. So he had the women bring one-gallon pickle jars, along with lids and cork stoppers, from the kitchen. Using the jars, stoppers, duct tape, and the suction tubing, he made his own underwater suction canisters to connect to the suction machine. The sheriff was watching the whole thing from a corner in the garage.

Then Mark prepped the deputy's left chest with Betadine, draped it with a sterile drape, and anesthetized an area between the lower ribs in the midaxillary line with twenty cc's of lidocaine, using a twenty-seven-gauge needle and syringe. Then he made a one-centimeter incision between the ribs and spread the muscles with a Kelly clamp until he entered the chest cavity, which made a hissing sound when the air rushed out followed by a gush of blood that poured out onto the floor and his feet. Then he inserted the chest tube in the hole he made between the ribs, positioned it superiorly and anteriorly in the chest cavity, stitched it into place, and connected it to the suction canisters. The deputy felt a sharp stabbing pleuritic pain, as the reinflated lung rubbed against the inside of the chest wall, letting Mark know the lung was reinflated. The tube would have to stay in for two or three days, until the air leak in the injured lung stopped. Mark would know when the lung was healed and no longer leaking air when the bubbles in the water jars stopped. Then it would be time to take the tube out. Without the ability to obtain X-rays of the chest, he would have to rely on his eyes and ears only, the way it was done over one hundred years ago.

The next order of business was the thigh wound and the injured femoral artery. Jack placed the deputy under a general anesthesia, and Paul had the instruments and prep table ready. Mark did a quick scrub at the kitchen sink, then gowned and gloved. Then he quickly prepped and draped the entire leg and groin, while Nurse Dickerson continued holding pressure on the wound, which had slowed the bleeding and bought them time. Then Mark took over. "Great job, Mrs. Dickerson, you just saved his life. I've got it now. Thanks."

Mark put his hand where hers was and then inserted his left index finger into the wound to stop the bleeding while he finished prepping the area. Then he made an incision above and below the bullet wound with the other hand while still holding pressure on the bleeding artery. Using one hand to dissect the tissue away layer by layer, and with Paul retracting the tissue, they exposed the injured artery above and below the bullet wound. Then he clamped the ends off with vascular clamps, stopping the blood loss and allowing him to use both hands. He found the segment of the femoral artery that was transected by the bullet. After Mark cleaned up the jagged and damaged ends, it was obvious that there was not enough length to bring the ends back together. And he knew there were not any vascular grafts in their supplies to replace it with.

His best option was to replace the injured section of artery using a graft made from a reversed section of the greater saphenous vein from below the knee on the same injured leg. Mark had Jack give the patient five thousand units of IV heparin before he flushed the proximal and distal artery to help prevent clots from forming then closed the repair. When the blood from the final flush shot about two feet into the air, the sheriff turned pale and excused himself from the garage. When the repair was completed, Mark closed and dressed the wounds and then checked for pulses at the ankle of the injured leg. The foot was warm and had pulses present, indicating a successful repair. The next twenty-four hours would be critical. The leg would need to be checked frequently for graft failure, which would show up as pain in the leg and a cold, pulseless foot, which would mean another emergency operation to fix. Both patients would need round-the-clock care for the next day or so. It was going to be a long night for Mark and his team.

CHAPTER 25
JOINING FORCES

After all the dust had settled from the new families moving in, the mess was cleaned up down on the road, and the patients bedded down for the night, Mark, Grandpa, Mr. Dickerson, Mr. Thompson, Paul, Gunny, Skinny, and Sheriff Taylor sat at the kitchen table to discuss the events of the day and what they were going to do in the days and weeks to come. Lisa, Sarah, Grandma Brown, and the other women met in the living room to discuss plans for their newest guests. In the kitchen, Mark stood, formally greeted the sheriff and shook his hand, then spoke first. "Looks like your men are going to be all right, Sheriff, but we'll have to watch them closely for the next day or so. It will be a few days before we can get them up and walking on their own, and possibly a couple of weeks before they are back in commission."

"Well, Doc, I must say I've never seen anything quite like that. That was impressive, what you and your team did. I appreciate you saving my boys in there."

"You're welcome, Sheriff. Now, if you guys don't mind, I'm going to get back to my patients," Mark said as he turned and went back to the garage.

The sheriff continued. "Mr. Brown, I have to be the first to admit, I was wrong about you and your folks. You like your guns, and now I'm glad you do. If it hadn't been for you and your boys here, things would have turned out a lot worse for us. And I appreciate you letting us hole up here for now. I'm hoping things will settle down and we can get back to headquarters and out of your hair before long."

Grandpa thought for a minute before answering. "Mark usually does the introductions and all, but I know he has folks to take care of right now, so I'll speak for our group. We are glad we could help, Sheriff. I like a man who can admit he was wrong. So I'm willing to start over with you. It's not that we like our guns so much as we like our freedom, and we like to eat, and the guns ensure us of both. I can't say we knew this day was coming, but many of us saw it coming. The government kept spending more than it took in, year after year. More and more people were becoming dependent on the government for everything, while fewer hardworking folks footed the bill and paid more and more taxes. Sooner or later, it was bound to come to an end, and when it did, well, this is what we thought would happen. Let's just say some of us were prepared for it. We made sure we would be able to feed and protect our families. That's all we are doing here. We're not here to fight the government or start a second civil war. We just want to take care of our families, and for the government to leave us alone. We are willing to help those who we can and who are willing to help themselves, but we are not interested in helping people who expect someone else to take care of them, who aren't willing to work, who think the government or someone else should take care of them." Grandpa finished, leaned back in his chair, and sipped his coffee.

"Well, I don't have a problem with what you folks are doing here. In fact, I'm glad some people had the good sense to be ready for this. I guess the rest of us didn't see it coming. That's why we came running in here with our tails tucked. It's well and good to take care of our families, but in order to get things back to normal, we are going to have to straighten things out in the county. There are folks out there who are suffering, being robbed and killed in their own homes. Whether they were ready or able to take care of their own or not, they can't fight off all these folks. For them to have a chance, they need our help. I was elected to protect them, and without help, I can't do that."

Sheriff Taylor let what he just said sink in for a moment, and then he continued. "One of the reasons I came down here was not just for protection, but to ask for your help to do that. Together, we can bring law and order back to this county. We are under martial law, in case you haven't heard. This morning, I was contacted by an army colonel by the name of Henry who is in charge of this area. They are still working on Memphis but plan to send some men down here within a week or so. I told him how bad things were, and that I, I mean we, need help now. He suggested that we band together and form our own militia. He has given me his official okay to do that. As a matter of fact, he sort of told me to do that, but I have to deputize anyone who helps, and we will be under his charge."

By then, the women had come into the room to hear what Sheriff Taylor had to say, and he noticed a few smiles around the room. "I take it y'all know the colonel."

Several heads nodded around the room. "Some of us know him very well, and several of us have met him, and that lady there is his wife," Mr. Dickerson said as he pointed at Mrs. Henry. Lisa left the room to get Mark. She wanted him to hear what the sheriff was saying.

"Well, that explains a lot. Now I see why he told me to come here. He must have known you folks were able to take care of yourselves quite well. He recommended that we join forces with the other groups around the county and reestablish law and order in Batesville, then get the utilities and the hospital back up to speed. He also said I was to put Mark Edwards in charge of the hospital and the EMS system. And now I see why. Doc seems pretty capable."

Just then, Mark and Lisa walked back in the room. Everyone turned to Mark to see what his response would be. "Lisa said something about martial law and the colonel. Did I miss something?"

The sheriff continued. "That's right. I'm sure you knew that martial law has been declared, but now he has put you and me under his orders. We are essentially conscripted into the army. I am supposed to restore law and order, and he is putting you in charge of getting the hospital up to speed."

"What exactly does that mean?" Mark asked pointedly to see what he was getting into.

"It means he is not asking. He is telling us what we need to do and putting us in charge of this area. He said, because of the martial law, we could be taken off somewhere else and put into service against our will. He said something about a great need for surgeons and trauma care all over the country. He said that's why he is putting you in charge of the hospital down here," the sheriff explained hesitantly.

"Putting me in charge of the hospital. What does that mean? What about the administrator?"

"He said you were to have total control. They have to do what you say, everyone, from the administrator to the custodians.

We are to find any and all hospital employees, nurses, and doctors and put them back to work. Until then, you are to do what you can. He said you know how to improvise and get things done. I can see that is true."

"What do I do if they refuse and start threatening lawsuits, which they will—that's the way they operate?" Mark asked.

"According to him, under martial law, all present civil laws are suspended. The lawyers can't do anything, because the judges have no power without the force of the law, which is the military now, so that means you and me. They have to answer to you, you answer to me, and I answer to the colonel, and he answers to his general, and so on up to the president, who has the final say on everything, so we will be held accountable by military standards. So I guess if we don't do what's right in their eyes, we could be court-martialed. But by being under his command, we will have more leverage and less resistance to getting things done."

"How can they do that?" Mark asked.

"I asked the same thing. He read me the executive orders directly from the office of the president. It was quite lengthy, so I wrote some of it down. The original executive orders were signed into law in 1962 by President Kennedy. They were based on the Defense Production Act of 1950. Not many people know about it, even now. The last administration added to it through an executive order called the National Defense Preparedness Act of 2011. The way he explained it to me was, that by the president declaring martial law, which in this case is the vice president acting as president, she can and has invoked Executive Order 11000. In doing so, they can force any or all civilians deemed necessary to work under federal supervision, which is to be enforced by the military. By Order 10999, they can seize any mode of transportation. By Order 10998, they can seize any food supplies or equipment, even the farm if needed. By Order 10997, they can seize any sources of fuel or electrical power sources. And by Order 10995, they can seize any forms of communication, and so on. Essentially, by federal law, they can take whomever and whatever they deem necessary in a time of emergency and do whatever they want. They can even take over the businesses and assets of private citizens."

Grandpa became upset. "They can't do that. They can't just go around and take or do whatever they want."

Sheriff Taylor explained further. "I argued with him at first, but he was very convincing and told me I could check with General Franks. So I got in touch with him by radio. The general wasn't quite so nice about it, but he told me the same thing. So it appears that it is for real. I radioed the colonel back, and he said we had two choices. We could either do as he suggested and run things our way, or when the troops arrive, they would do it by the book. And he said something about some captain that is a pain in the ass, whatever that means. He strongly recommended I talk to you, Doc. He said you would agree with him."

Mark smiled after he thought about what the colonel said about the captain. "I'm afraid they can, Grandpa. I looked up that law long before all this happened and found out the federal government can do that. Martial law has been declared several times in the past, and it looks like now it's in effect again. It can be declared by the president for any type of national emergency, from natural disasters to wars and anything in between. Once martial law is declared, they can invoke all those executive orders, which are implemented by the National Security Council and Homeland Security and carried out by the different secretaries of labor, health, defense, transportation, commerce, agriculture, and so on. As a matter of fact, the president doesn't even have to declare martial law for that to occur. He or she can just declare that it is necessary for national security. So they can take over the hospital, power stations, and police powers, and they could even come take the farm if they wanted to in order to feed the masses of people who have come down here. As a matter of fact, they can round up all these refugees and put them in detainment camps, much like they did the Japanese back in World War II. That is a real possibility. I know the colonel well enough to trust him on this. We better do what he says. I'm sure he has his reasons. So I say we take his offer."

Grandpa was still mad. "How can they do that? What if we refuse?"

"They can because they have the US Army to back them up. No one in their right mind wants to fight them directly. It would be foolish. They have bigger guns. One tank rolling up the drive could take all of us out," Mark explained.

Grandpa wasn't ready to give up. "What if we all refuse, everyone, not just us? Would they fight all of us?"

"That is the million-dollar question. And I don't know the answer. It just depends on how many people feel the way we do—tired of the government taking away their rights and freedom, interfering in every aspect of their lives, and now forcing them to work against their will and taking their private property away from them. In order to enforce that, they would have to come and take away our guns. That is the big question—how many people would stand up to them and say no, refuse to give up their freedom and their right to bear arms? There are only about a million or so men in uniform who can carry weapons into battle. At first, they would win out because of their superior firepower. One platoon and a tank coming up the drive could wipe us out. But if there are tens of millions of Americans, or more, who think and feel the way we do and would be willing to fight, then in the long run we would probably win. We would be able to cut off their lines of supplies, food, fuel, communications, find them in their offices and at home and wear them down by attrition. This wouldn't be like the Civil War, when essentially the North fought the South. Even though it did divide some families, this would divide families, neighbors, and friends in every city in every state in the Union. It would be a revolution against the government that could turn into another civil war, especially if those on the other side wanted to fight to the end to see which way this country goes. It could come to that.

"But we wouldn't just be fighting the military. We would also be fighting against our fellow citizens, neighbors, friends, and, in some cases, even family members who took their side. It would be those who think like us, who want freedom and less government, against those who want more government and a continuation of how things were before all this started. Then, those serving in the military would have to choose sides and be willing to fight against their own neighbors, friends, and family. Their loyalty would also be divided between which side they believe is right. In the end, the generals who command the troops would have to decide which side they were on. I think most of them would refuse to fight and stand up to their commanders and even the president. History has taught us that the troops follow their generals, not the politicians. At least, I hope they would."

"Well, I would rather fight than let them take everything from me. I don't care if I have to stand alone, or if others are with me. I would rather die fighting than let them come take my guns, farm, or freedom. Some things are just worth fighting for," Grandpa said, slamming his fist onto the table.

Gunny and several of the men and some of the women stood and shouted out that they agreed with Grandpa. Mrs. Henry started crying loudly, and everyone turned to her. Lisa and Grandma Brown went to her and tried to console her. "You guys are talking about fighting against her husband, you know," Lisa said.

After a minute or two, Mrs. Henry gained her composure and wiped her eyes and spoke. "You don't understand. He would never do that. He told me if it came to that, he would be on your side, our side. He said all the generals would. They can't say it, they can't even talk about it in the open, but they talk about it behind closed doors. He said if the people took up arms, they would not turn their weapons on them. They would not be able to get their men to do that. He said they would lay down their weapons and walk away. They would not shoot their own people. They just wouldn't do that."

Mark went over and gently held her shoulders with both hands and said, "I'm sorry, Mrs. Henry. I know he wouldn't. That is why I think we need to do what he says. He is looking out for our best interests. We just have to trust him." Then she buried her face in his shoulder and cried again.

Gunny spoke up. "I agree. I'm in. I say we go along with his plan. What do we have to lose? At this point, we can at least have some control over what goes on down here. If we wait until they get here, things will get a lot worse in the meanwhile, and who knows what they will do? They might come down here and try to take the farm, or our food and guns, and then all hell will break loose. Better we do something now and hope Doc is right and that the colonel is trying to help us."

Mr. Dickerson stood up. "Me, too. I'm in. The sheriff is right, too. We need to do something to help take back the county. Your neighbors and friends and other good folks out there need our help. At least, we know who the good guys are. If the army comes in, they are not going to know us from Adam and will probably treat us all like criminals until all this calms down. Who knows how long that will be, and what might happen to us in the meanwhile? Better to be on their side from the start. Things will probably turn out better for us when they do get here, either way."

Then everyone else stood up and agreed and voted to help the sheriff. Mark looked at Sheriff Taylor and saluted. "Looks like you have your own militia, sir."

The sheriff answered, "And it looks like you'll have your own hospital, Dr. Edwards."

Mark wasn't sure that was a good thing, but at least he would be working near his family for the time being. He didn't know what the future held, but staying put at the farm and helping to straighten things out in the county and getting the hospital up and running was as good a plan as any. His mind started racing because he had a lot to think about. The sheriff was going to need a lot of help getting Batesville back in order. It was going to take other folks to help.

The first order of business would be to contact and meet with the Cliftons and Huffmans to see if they were willing to work with them. Then they would need to get with other groups in the county that had able-bodied and armed men willing to help. Then, working together, they would need to round up the riffraff and stop the stealing and killing and raping and let people know there was law and order in the county. Then they would need to restore order in town, get the power and water back on and phones working, and then get the hospital up and running as soon as possible in order to save lives. Then they would need to find farmers willing to grow and share food, for barter or trade, to keep folks from starving. Eventually, they would need to get the grocery stores and supply stores back up and running and schools reopened.

In the short run, most of the refugees would leave the area, due to a lack of food and water. Most likely, the ones who could would move on down the highway or Interstate 55. People were conditioned to move along major channels of travel. That's what they had become accustomed to. And, luckily for the farm, their little county road was off the beaten path and only a small percent of the refugees chose that path. But, even that small percent was enough to cause some trouble, which they had already seen.

So the fact that most would leave was a good thing, in a way, but some would remain. Sheltering them would be a problem, along with trying not to let them starve or kill each other or the locals. At some point in the near future, the army would show up and take over until things got back to normal, but when that might happen was not known. Hopefully, a civil war would not break out during all of it. If that happened, it would be anyone's guess.

Mark's thoughts went back to the first order of business, which was to get the militia numbers up and organized. They would need to get Hank to help them contact as many groups as possible by radio in order to minimize their exposure and not waste precious fuel driving around the county hoping to find them. Once they contacted any of the other groups that showed an interest in helping, a meeting could be set up. Hopefully, things would fall into place after that. But for now, until the hospital was up and running again, he would just have to help as many folks as he could where he was.

CHAPTER 26
COOPERATION

Mark was right. It was a long night. The next morning, the men met around the kitchen table to make plans. Mark was worn out from being up most of the night and had that rode-hard-and-put-up-wet look. He had been thinking things over in his head to keep himself alert, and he was slightly punch-drunk from sleep deprivation and a little talkative. "I've been thinking. We should get Hank and Skinny to contact as many groups, large and small, as we can on the radio to see who is out there and who might be willing to help. That way, we don't expose ourselves to trouble unnecessarily and don't waste fuel driving around on any wild goose chases. If we find others who can and are willing to help, I think we should tell them that Sheriff Taylor is in charge and wants to start a militia to help establish law and order in the county and Batesville. They need to know that the militia is legitimate and will be working under the orders of Colonel Henry of the US Army, whom we all know and trust. If they agree, then we can meet with them at their place or ours, whichever is deemed safer. Anyone else have any thoughts?"

Sheriff Taylor seconded that suggestion. "It's funny how great minds think alike. We may not be able to get through to all those out there willing to help, but by starting with the ones we can contact and agree to help on the front end, it would save a lot of time, trouble, and fuel. Unless anyone has any better ideas, I say we start there. I have gone over your defenses here with Gunny, and I think we are in pretty good shape."

Gunny then made a suggestion. "If we do decide to leave the farm to meet with anyone or to help someone else or go into town for any reason, until things settle down, I suggest we always leave some folks here to defend the farm against any surprise attacks."

"I agree. We don't need to lose what we have here while out trying to help others who may or may not need or want our help," Grandpa said. Everyone at the table nodded in agreement. "I'm going to say this again. I'm willing to help others, but they have to be willing to help themselves. If these other groups don't want to fight for their own lives, then I'm not for us risking ours. I'm not trying to be hard or difficult, but this country was built by those willing to take risks and fight for what they had. All these folks who just want someone else to do all the working and fighting for them while they sit around and complain ain't going to cut it anymore." Everyone at the table sat quietly after Grandpa's outburst, but no one disagreed. It was what most of them had been thinking to themselves but didn't want to say out loud.

Sheriff Taylor also sat quietly, not quite sure what to say to that. "We can't really just sit back and let people die, if there is something we can do to help them. We can't just let them starve or fall prey to thieves, if we have a way to give them food and protection."

Grandpa stared at him. "That's the politician coming out in you. I'm not talking about watching widows and orphans starve while I have plenty, or if they are able-bodied and have been working the garden beside me. I'm talking about people who are able to work but choose to sit on their fat asses in the shade and fan themselves while you work, and then expect you to feed them from your share and then complain that you didn't give them enough. Then some touchy, feely politician gets elected by taking some of your share and giving it to them so they will vote for him so they can keep sitting on their fat asses." Everyone at the table laughed. Grandpa was fired up and on a roll. Mark knew what was coming. He had heard it before.

"Now that you put it like that, I see what you mean. I really never thought of it that way. But what about those who don't like guns and have a dislike for violence or fighting of any kind? Shouldn't we protect them?" the sheriff asked.

"Well, you certainly should. You're the sheriff and that's your job." Everyone laughed again at Grandpa. "Seriously, we should protect those who can't protect themselves, those who are sick, weak, or unable to for whatever physical reason. But if an otherwise healthy man argues that he is against violence and sits idly by expecting others to risk their lives to protect him and his family, then no. People who sit in the comfort of their homes protected from enemies, both foreign and domestic, and complain about the way our military and police officers do their job only have that right because it was paid for by the blood of others who have risked their lives to protect this country. I will stand beside any man and defend this country, our freedom, and our families, but I will not defend the man who expects me to fight but will not fight with me. Those people from the city who chose not to own guns for whatever reason and cowered down, waiting for someone to come rescue them from the mob, are a cowardly bunch. If those folks would have banded together like real men, they could have stopped the rioters before they reached the city limits and their neighborhoods. America has become weak from within. That is why we are in this mess. I am not a racist or bigoted against any man because of his color or religion, but I cannot tolerate a man who is a coward and lazy, or who lies, cheats, steals, or takes advantage of the weak or slow minded. I believe in God and that every man will have to stand in judgment and be held accountable for his actions someday. I believe that every man has the right to life, liberty, and the pursuit of happiness. I will defend those rights, my family, my country, and the Constitution of the United States of America. And I will fight those who try to destroy this country and tear it down by buying votes with our money, those who defend the killing of unborn babies, those who think that we should have freedom from religion instead of religion, and those who want to take prayer out of our schools while they let guns and drugs in. We are tired of these things. People of my generation, who fought wars to keep us safe, cannot bear it any more. We are ready to take our country back. If those on the other side want a civil war, I say, bring it on."

Mark thought it was time to bring it down a notch, so he tried to shift the subject to something else, but Sheriff Taylor wanted to hear more. "You know, I haven't really thought about this stuff to the degree you guys have. What should the government do with all the displaced people who are hungry and could possibly starve? There is not enough stored food supplies to feed everyone for very long, and getting the food to everyone will be a huge problem, as well. What are our options?" Everyone looked at each other, but no one spoke up right away.

After a moment or so, Mark spoke up. "The total US land area is over two billion acres. The US government itself owns about six hundred million acres, or close to one-third of the total land mass. There are probably about fifty million people who have been displaced by the riots and probably about twice that who have been affected in one way or another. All of them need food now, or will need food in the near future. There is plenty of land to grow food on in this country. Enough to give each family forty acres and a mule, as they used to say. But getting people moved and seeds and supplies to them would be a logistical nightmare, and besides most people today have no desire or idea how to live off the land. They do not know how to grow food or work a garden, or how to hunt and fish. They could not build a cabin in the woods and live like pioneers did over one hundred and fifty years ago, even if they were given an ax and the needed supplies. People today no longer have the know-how and are soft and spoiled and used to getting everything from the grocery store and discount stores. They are used to air-conditioning and central heat, cars, and modern conveniences. We have become accustomed to and addicted to technology and electricity. Even if the government gave them the needed supplies and the land, most would not survive the winter. No, they will set them up in camps and feed them until the food runs out or things get back to normal. If that takes longer than a year, then millions are going to starve, or they are going to come take it from you and me. Either the hungry people will try, or the government will. That's just the way it is. So what we have to decide is, are we going to give it away, or let them come take our food and possibly the farm, or stand up and tell them no, if it comes down to it? I agree with Grandpa Brown. We should be charitable until it hurts, but if we give it all away or let them take it, then our families will suffer. All the hard work and preparing will have been in vain. If that happens, we will be in the same boat as those who didn't work, or save, or prepare for this. Another downside of allowing them to confiscate food from us and others like us who worked and saved is that in the end, no one will want to work. If you know that no matter what you do, or how hard you work, they are just going to take it from you and give it to someone else who hasn't worked or saved, then what's the use? Then we will all starve. At that point, the only thing left is for the government to force people to work against their will."

Mr. Dickerson was noticeably upset. "They can't do that. Force people to work against their will? That's enslavement."

Mark answered. "Yes, sort of like the conscription the sheriff and I are faced with. That sort of puts it in a different light, doesn't it?" Everyone around the table sat quietly for a moment and took in what was just said. It hit them that Mark and the sheriff were being forced by their own government to work for the government, whether they wanted to or not. It was like being drafted into the military. People objected to that for various reasons, but they had to enlist anyway and risk dying in a war no one wanted in Vietnam, or else leave the country. Something that was so unpopular at the time, that is was stopped decades ago. But now, people all over the country were being conscripted against their will: doctors, nurses, paramedics, firefighters, policemen, and utility workers. All forced to work, taken away from their families, enslaved by their own government. Very few had thought about it before the riots, and even fewer knew it was possible that an executive order and single signature by the commander in chief could do that to an entire country. But now, many would find out about it the hard way.

Just then, Hank came running into the kitchen, all out of breath, from the barn office where he was on the radio. "Just got off the radio with the Clifton Farm. They found me on the radio, said they just got attacked. Turned them away this time. Looks like the same group. Some guys on motorcycles and in big pickup trucks. They said they looked like bikers and skinheads. No one really got hurt, but they told them they would be back. They only have about twenty-five people at their farm. They want to know if we can work together and help them in case they do come back."

It didn't take but a moment for them to decide the answer to that question was yes. Everyone nodded in agreement.

Sheriff Taylor asked Gunny, "Do you think your folks can get ready by this afternoon to meet with them?

"Yes, sir, we can roll anytime. I'll have them ready." Then he said to Hank and Skinny, "See if you can set up a meeting this afternoon at the Clifton Farm, and keep trying to contact the Huffman Farm."

"Yes, sir, will do," Hank answered. Then they both left to get on the radio.

Sheriff Taylor and the other men planned the trip to the Clifton Farm, while Mark went back to check on his patients. Lisa, Sarah, Grandma Brown, and the other women went back to their chores. Some kept working in the kitchen, preparing meals on the woodstove. They had all decided to save the propane in the big tanks for hot water and later use, in case of a real cold snap in the winter or for some other emergency. Some went out to feed the animals and collect the eggs and to milk the cows. And some went to help in the garden.

The men finished up their discussions and then went to do their chores, as well. Some went to the fields and worked the garden, others continued pruning and fertilizing the fruit trees. Grandpa went to plant a field of corn to be used for food and some for fuel and was considering using some to make whiskey, which would be good for trade and for use as an antiseptic by Mark. Grandma laughed and kidded Grandpa about using it for his rheumatism.

The militia members had settled into a routine before the sheriff and his folks came down, and they were showing the newest farm members the ropes and assigning them duties, as well. Everyone with the sheriff's group agreed to work and pull their weight. They lived in their own RVs, like the militia folks, and used the new outhouses and the well water. A few of them still wanted to run their generators and lights, but after discussing the situation with Sheriff Taylor, he agreed with the other men that for the time being conserving fuel was more important than having electricity for lights and watching television. And the noise of the generators and the bright lights shining at night would be an open invitation for trouble from anyone looking for a place that appeared to be doing well.

For those who were hungry or looking for guns or other supplies, a place with electricity had a generator and therefore fuel, which meant they were prepared and most likely had food. Most of the masses of folks displaced into the area had been out of their homes and apartments and on the road for two or three weeks. Most were out of the basic necessities of food and water and medications. Many were living in their cars or trucks, or if they were lucky, their campers or RVs. Those on foot were living where they could in tents, under overpasses, in abandoned buildings, empty shacks—anywhere they could find shelter. Humans are creatures of habit and social by nature and feel more secure traveling in groups, so most were moving along the interstates and major highways.

But traveling with the masses was exactly the wrong thing to do. The sheer numbers of the refugees was too much for any town or small city to absorb. There just weren't enough shelters or food to take care of that many people swarming on a place all at once, like a swarm of locusts devouring everything in their path. And as the masses of people moved, so moved the trouble-makers and terrorists. For those intent on causing hysteria, what better way than to follow the hordes of people, where it was easy to be lost in the crowds and where the local law enforcement was overwhelmed and unable to respond. All of which made it easier for them to do their work, which included blowing up or disabling transmission towers, water systems, power substations, hospitals, dams, and bridges, and doing anything to disrupt power, communication, utilities, and medical care.

As the waves of people moved farther out, so did the trouble-makers who were hell-bent on stealing, robbing, murdering, and raping—the same thing they were doing on a daily basis in the cit-ies before the riots. But now it was magnified severalfold because of the lack of law and order. It was open season for them to prey on the weak, the old, the sick, or those left alone or unprepared. Even those with means of protection were outnumbered by the Takers who began to band together in larger and larger groups.

At first, the gangs and Takers took out the weak and unpre-pared, but soon they figured out that if those they attacked didn't have weapons or the ability to put up a fight, they usually didn't have other supplies or much food, either. The ones with food and supplies usually had weapons, so to be successful they had to take on those who were armed and ready for trouble. The natural leaders of the gangs, be it because of brains or brawn, took out the leaders of other groups and then took over their members, who either went along or were killed. It was either die fighting for someone else's food and supplies or starve or die alone.

They learned from their mistakes and found that by banding together in larger groups, they could take out smaller groups who were armed with fewer casualties. They learned that a group of ten or twelve well-armed men could easily outgun a group of two or three, and a group of twenty could take out a group of five or ten with an acceptable rate of casualties. So as the groups got larger and larger, they could take on bigger groups and other gangs with less resistance; and the bigger the group, the greater the rewards. The larger groups had more food, fuel, guns, ammo, vehicles, and women—everything needed by the Takers. But like killing, they didn't need the women—they were just for sport.

That is what Mark knew was coming. That was the reason he asked the Southcrest folks to the farm. That is why he invited the militia down to the farm. He knew a few would not do. He knew they needed the numbers on their side when the Takers come to take. It was not enough to prepare for hard times, to store up food, fuel, and other supplies. It was also necessary to defend it all, and that took numbers. That's why they needed to join forces with the other groups in the county that were armed and ready to fight. There was no way to know how big the groups and gangs of Takers were. Mark knew there were certainly several groups out there, but how big was the question. And that was what they needed to be ready for.

Skinny and Hank had made contact with the Huffman Farm as well, and they were going to send a group of men to the meeting at the Clifton Farm, which was halfway between them just south of town. Grandpa insisted on going, since he had known both families for a long time. Sheriff Taylor was going to head up the meeting and organize the county militia, as per the colonel's orders. The sheriff and a deputy were going to take their patrol cars, and Gunny and several of his men were going to take the Jeep with the machine gun and carry an American flag as a show of force and to provide protection. Gunny and the sheriff agreed and recommended that the Brown and Huffman farms keep enough men on hand in case of an attack while they were at the meeting.

The men headed out that afternoon for the meeting, while Mark and the others stayed behind to tend to the injured and the chores. After the men left for the meeting, the gate was closed behind them and guards were posted as usual. Things were quiet for about an hour, and then the radio from the east bunker went off first. "Base. Base. This is the east bunker. We have a group of motorcycles and pickup trucks full of men with guns coming up the road slowly. Looks like about five motorcycles and five trucks. Has to be at least twenty or thirty of them. What should we do?"

Mark was still in the kitchen and took the call. "If anyone is in the Thompsons' house, get them out of there now. All of you get out of there and get up here to the house. Stay off the main road and come up the pasture road. Try not to be seen. We will ring the bell and take positions."

Just then, the west bunker radio went off. "Base, this is the west bunker. We have a large group coming in from the west. Same thing, about thirty or so."

The hair on the back of Mark's neck stood up. He knew they were about to be attacked. "Everyone, get up here and take your places in the bunkers on the hill. Gate, all of you get up here now. Bring all the ammo with you." Mark ran out back and rang the bell. He had most of the women and all of the children go into the house, and then he had all the men and those women who were armed and ready to fight get the extra ammo out of the basement and get into position in the bunkers around the top of the hill. Then he had Hank get on the radio and notify Grandpa and Sheriff Taylor that they were about to be attacked from the east and the west by two groups of about twenty each. They were going to hold them off the best they could until help could arrive.

A thousand questions and thoughts ran through his mind in those few seconds. Should they stand and fight? Should they retreat and hide in the woods out back? Should they send the women and children to the woods, in case they got overrun? Would help come in time? Why did they attack now, when the others were gone to the meeting? How did they know? Were they watching and waiting for some to leave? How could they? There was nowhere for all of them to hide along the county road within sight of the farm, without being seen or heard. Maybe they had scouts watching the place. Or maybe the radio...That was it—they were listening in on the radio conversations. They had a scanner. That's how they knew the sheriff was coming to the farm and why they tried to cut him off. That's how they knew the others were gone.

Mark ran all the scenarios in his head. It would take at least twenty to thirty minutes for the others to get back with some help. They would have to hold them off until then. If the Takers took the farmhouse and the hill, it would take two or three times as many to take it back. That's why they had the bunkers dug in on the top of the hill and reinforced with the sandbags. It was a strong defensive position. There were about forty attackers and about forty defenders. The attackers had mostly handguns and TEC-9s and a few AKs and .223s. But the hill had several .308s and a Lapua .338, all fitted with high-power scopes capable of inflicting serious long-range damage before the attackers could even get into range to shoot back. With the narrow drive and the bridge across the ditch down front and all the fences to slow them down, they will be like ducks on a pond. All they had to do was get their best shooters into the bunkers with the heavy hitters to pick them off. By the time any of them reached the hill, they would be thinned way down, and with all the ammo in the bunker, the Takers would run out of ammo first.

"Get the big guns with the scopes out first and start picking them off before they even get through the gate, and keep laying it down hard," Mark shouted to Paul, Hank, and a couple of the militia members who were good marksmen. "When they get closer, everyone else lay it down hot and heavy. We have way more ammo than they do, so lay it on hard. It will stop enough of them and buy us time. They aren't used to that kind of heat. Get everyone in position, and let 'em have it." Everyone scattered to the bunkers and took their positions. Mark shouted to everyone again. "Watch our east side so they don't flank us. As soon as you get your scopes on them, let 'em have it. Everyone else, stay down so we don't take any stray shots. When they get to the fences and start climbing over, the rest of you hit 'em hard. Here they come to the gate. Let 'er rip."

Mark, Paul, Hank, and a few other militia members started shooting before they even hit the gate, dropping most of the motorcycle riders on the road, which slowed down the rest. At about three hundred yards, the .308s and the .338 were going right through the truck windows and doors and tearing holes in metal and men. Several trucks stopped dead in their tracks when the .338 tore through the engine blocks and locked them up. That just made it easier for the rest to zero in on their targets. Some return fire came back, but it was sporadic and falling short or wild. With the six heavy guns blazing in the first minute or two, several Takers were hit or killed before any could even get through the gate.

One truck did finally break through the gate, allowing some of the others to get onto the drive, but the big guns continued to take their toll. Then the attackers spread out into the fields and started for the hill. As they came closer, they had to cross two fences and the ditch, and when they did, the rest of the militia and farm defenders opened up with their AR-15s, which sounded like World War III just started. Takers began to fall, wounded and bleeding. When the rest of the Takers saw what was happening to their comrades in arms, they turned and ran back for the road. When they did, the snipers continued to put them in their crosshairs.

The Takers who attacked from the east side didn't fare much better. They had to cross an open field for over two hundred yards with very little cover, which gave the snipers plenty of time to cut them down. Most turned and ran back when they saw their own falling and couldn't see exactly where the shots were coming from. The ones who could all ran back to the road to regroup. Just then, a convoy of trucks and the Jeep with the machine gun leading the way came up behind them from the West and started cutting them in half. Besides the ten men from the farm, there were about ten from the Clifton Farm and about ten from the Huffman Farm. It was a bloodbath. The Takers on the east side who did escape took off down the county road as fast as they could with the Jeep in close pursuit, and they didn't look back or try to help their fallen comrades. But most didn't get very far.

Once the shooting was over, there were around thirty dead Takers, about five severely wounded, and about a half dozen with minor wounds who ran as far as they could as fast as they could. None of the militia or farm folks were seriously injured, and only a few had minor injuries. The sandbags and bunkers had done their job. After the smoke cleared and the dust settled, the sheriff was left with a difficult decision: What to do with the dead? And an even more difficult decision: What to do with the wounded? Sheriff Taylor discussed the situation quietly with Grandpa, Mark, and Gunny. Dealing with the dead was easy. They could be buried in a mass grave, and if anyone of authority questioned what was done later on, they could dig them up and do what they wanted with them.

The question was whether to treat the seriously wounded, let the walking wounded go, or shoot all of them. Most of the more seriously wounded would die or lose limbs sooner or later, with or without treatment. If they tried to patch the injured up, it would use up critical medical supplies, and if they let any of them get away, they would most likely go back and join the other Takers, and then they might have to face them again. It was a difficult decision without an easy answer. It was a moral dilemma of the first order: whether to finish them off in order to protect their families, or let them go and risk retaliation. No matter what they decided, others would criticize their decision and argue that they would have decided differently.

CHAPTER 27
CLEANING HOUSE

Big Al, the leader of the Takers, had made a fatal mistake in his decision to send his men to pillage the farm that was based on bad information. He was still under the impression that the farm folks and the Southcrest folks, along with the sheriff and his deputies and their families, were the only ones at the farm. He figured with the group heading off to meet with the other farmers, there would be about a dozen or so men left to guard the farm. He thought that sending thirty or forty of his men would easily get the job done. His orders were to kill the men and children and take whatever women they wanted. And to bring back all the food, guns, ammo, and fuel they could and to burn the place down.

What he didn't know was, even with the ten men gone to the meeting, there were still around thirty good men and women left to defend the farm. And, he didn't know they were dug in at the top of the hill with the modified sandbags around them for protection. And most of all, he miscalculated the firepower they had with all the ammo and long-range weapons with scopes. He had guessed wrong. His men paid the price.

It had been a difficult decision for them, but Grandpa and Gunny tried to convince the others that what the Takers had done was tantamount to attempted murder, and they were certain that the Takers would have killed all of them if things had turned out differently. And they were certain that the Takers had killed countless others around the county and would kill again. There was no court system to try them in, no jail to put them in, and essentially no police force or other government authority to place them into custody with.

Just as Grandpa, Gunny, and Mark figured, some of their own argued for leniency. Some argued that they should let them go. Some argued that they should help whom they could and then hold them as prisoners. But when Grandpa asked for any of them to raise their hands if they wanted to make that decision for the group, no hands went up. When he asked if anyone wanted to help them and care for them personally, no hands went up. When he asked if anyone wanted to guard and feed them for who knows how long, no hands went up. When he asked if any of them could guarantee that none of them would come back in the middle of the night and cut their throats, or kill their children, or rape the women, no one said a word.

It takes hard men to make hard decisions. The kind of decisions that change the course of events, nations, and the world. Weak-minded people who always make decisions based on emotion, what is popular, and what is politically correct place others in danger and put the burden of doing the dirty work, doing what has to be done, on someone else. Hard men make decisions to drop atomic bombs on entire cities of innocent citizens to end a world war. Hard men make decisions to wipe out whole towns because you cannot tell the good from the bad in order to save their own. Innocent people get killed in wars. Right or wrong, war is for killing. To do otherwise is not war but politics. And on the farm and the world around them, there was no room for politics. It was kill or be killed.

Right or wrong, hard men took this country from the Indians. They fought off the British and other foreign invaders. They won two world wars and fought a civil war to keep the country intact. Hard decisions and hard men with personal convictions, like those who built this country, were no longer popular. They had been supplanted by watered-down laws that protected the guilty, restrained by government oversight committees and lawyers who inhibited our soldiers from killing our enemies. They are labeled as bigots, homophobic, and racists by the media and vilified by a society that no longer revered strong-minded, rugged individualism. Instead, it pushed a culture of inclusiveness where hardly any conduct was immoral, that celebrated multiculturalism rather than patriotism, and that promoted other such catchphrases that were not just nonjudgmental toward but actually accepting of the perverse and criminal elements of society. Our society had become antagonistic and biased against the principled and moral members of society.

Right or wrong, if the social norms of the present modern society were in place long ago, the United States would still be a British colony, the west would still belong to the Comanche and the Navajo Indians, the South would have seceded from the Union without a fight, Hitler would have had his perfect society, and Japan would own Hawaii and the Philippines. The downside of society being run by hard men with harsh answers to life's problems can result in a world that accepts slavery, segregation, suppressed women's rights, and inequalities in the work place and society as a whole.

The harshness has to be tempered by fairness and softened by compassion for it to be controlled. That is why Mark stepped forward and stopped the shooting. "Wait! We can't do that. It may be the smart thing to do, but some of those men out there are just kids. Maybe they were forced into this, maybe not. Let's at least talk to them, give them a chance. Some are going to die no matter what we do, but let me patch up the ones I can. Before we let them go, we will make it clear to them what will happen if they show up again."

Gunny stopped Mark. "I know you mean well. You are a doctor first and foremost. You have compassion for your fellow man. It's in your nature to help. But we can't afford to do that. We can't risk it."

Mark turned to Grandpa and the sheriff. "I've got an idea. We know they have been listening in on our radio calls. We can patch up the ones who are walking wounded and intentionally let them get away and follow them back to their compound. Once we know where they are, we can scout them out to see how many there are. Then we can go in and get them or set a trap for them by staging an attack and luring them out using fake radio calls. It's your call, gentlemen."

Grandpa, Gunny, and the sheriff talked among themselves for a few minutes. Sheriff Taylor came back to Mark. "That's a great idea. Patch up whom you can, and then we'll leave them alone and let them escape. We'll have a team ready to follow them and report back to us. It just might work. We didn't have any trouble getting through town. Things have calmed down from the other day. I think since the lights and water have been out and all the stores looted, most folks have moved on down the road, looking for greener pastures. So once we get the power and water back on in town, we can plan how to rid ourselves of these gangs."

Mark thought for a moment. "I don't think we need to be in any hurry to get the power or water back on. That is actually in our favor right now. The longer that takes, the fewer people will stay around and the easier it will be to straighten things out. I suggest we finish taking these thugs out, then we can work on the power and water, and then we can work on the hospital."

Sheriff Taylor let that sink in for a minute. "You know what? That makes good sense. We're doing just fine here. The local folks can get by for a few more days. Maybe more of the refugees will move on."

"I don't think we need to tell the colonel about our plan. What he doesn't know won't get him, or us, in trouble," Mark said.

Mark and his team triaged the wounded. Two of the seriously wounded had already died before they could get to them. Three were mortally wounded and beyond anything Mark could do for them, but two had extremity wounds that could be patched up without big surgery. One of them was a boy of seventeen, and the other was only fourteen. The team worked on them and treated their wounds, gave them antibiotics to prevent infection, and then fed them a hot meal. Both thanked them over and over. Mark tried to question them, but neither would say much. So Mark and Paul arranged for everyone to intentionally be out of sight at the same time, leaving the door to the garage unlocked and them alone.

When he saw that they were alone, the older boy whispered, "Hey, Billy, you keep your mouth shut. Don't tell them nothin'. Look, the door ain't locked, and nobody's around. Let's get out of here." Billy kept his head down, pretended not to hear, and didn't answer back. "Hey, Billy, you listenin'? Come on, let's go. I said, let's go." When Billy didn't answer, the older boy got angry with him. "Forget you, man. I'm going to tell Big Al you turned on us. You hear me, man? I'm going to kick your little ass." The older boy went over and started hitting Billy in the face and head with his fists over and over. Mark and Paul were listening to their conversation just inside the kitchen door, and when they heard the commotion, they ran in and jumped on the older boy and took him to the ground. Paul landed a punch square on his jaw and knocked him out, then he handcuffed him to a stretcher until they could figure out what to do with him.

Mark went over and checked Billy for injuries and cleaned up his wounds. Billy seemed to be all right except for a bloody nose and some bruises. "Sorry about that. We didn't mean to let him hurt you. That won't happen again. Let me ask you something. Why did you join up with those guys? You're not like them. What happened?"

Billy started crying and sobbed into his hands. "They killed my parents and took my sister. They said they would kill her if I didn't do what they said. They gave me a gun and made me come over here with them. I didn't know we were going to do this. I'm sorry. I didn't mean to." Billy started crying again and couldn't finish what he was saying. Finally he composed himself. "They got my sister. I saw her the other day. I need to get my sister." He started crying again.

Mark looked at Paul and both understood what happened. But the truth was probably worse than Billy knew. They probably had already hurt his sister in ways Billy did not need to know about. In fact, she may have been better off dead. There were probably many others like her. They knew they had to do something to help. They had to find out where their compound was.

"Billy, can you tell me where they are? Mark asked.

"Yes, sir, I know exactly where they are. They're at my farm."

Mark and Paul looked at each other. "Can you tell us how to get there?"

"I can show you. It's on County Line Road. Route One, Box Eighty-seven. Down by the river."

"What about that other boy? Was he forced to fight like you?"

"No, sir. I think his dad is Big Al. He's the leader. I heard Little Al call him Dad. That's what the other guys call him. But Big Al slapped him and told him not to ever call him that in front of the other men. Little Al is the one who wanted my sister."

Mark and Paul both smiled. "Billy, we are going to help you get your sister back."

Billy smiled for the first time and went on to describe his farm down by the river at the south end of the county. His house sat on a seventy-five-acre horse farm with plenty of barns, a swimming pool, well water, and a generator that ran the whole farm when the power went out. Big Al came with about thirty men on motorcycles and killed his parents, his two uncles, and their wives. Big Al took his sister and forced Billy to fight for him and threatened to hurt his sister and kill them if they didn't do what he said. Billy told Mark and Paul that others had joined them since, and that there were about ninety men at his farm before this attack. He described how Big Al told them to kill everyone, take the food, guns, ammo, fuel, and everything of value, and the men could take any women they wanted for themselves.

Billy went on to describe that there were several other young women being held at his farm against their will. His house was way off the beaten path and down a long drive and hidden from the road, which is why they were able to hide out undetected. Billy told them that his dad was a banker and knew the economy was going bad. That's why his dad had the farm and the generator and why his dad and his uncles had guns. They tried to hold off Big Al's gang, but there were just too many of them. Billy said his dad told him and his sister just before he died that he was sorry that he didn't do more to protect them, that he never thought he would have to hold off so many bad people way down there where they lived.

Mark and Paul knew it was a common mistake made by many who think they are prepared for the worst. It takes more than food and water and a few guns to survive. It takes a small army to protect yourselves from the Takers when the shit hits the fan. That's why Mark and Paul wanted the Southcrest folks down at the farm, and why they were so excited for the militia folks to come down. There was safety in numbers.

They both did the math in their heads and figured that there would be about sixty of them left at Billy's farm. With the Brown family, the Southcrest folks, and the Militia members at the farm, along with those at the Clifton Farm and the Huffman Farm, there would be around seventy-five to eighty fighters to take on Big Al and the Takers. The odds were in their favor, but too close for comfort. They would need to increase the odds in their favor in order to decrease their casualties. To accomplish that, they needed to recruit some more good folks around the county to increase their own numbers and then make sure the fight was on their own terms so they would have the upper hand. That's what they needed to work on. With Billy's information, Mark and Paul spent the next hour working on a plan.

Mark and Paul went to the kitchen, and with Billy sitting beside them at the table, they called a meeting of the roundtable to discuss their plan. Everyone gathered to hear what Mark had learned. Grandpa, Sheriff Taylor, Gunny, Mr. Dickerson, and the other men sat at the table with them. Lisa, Grandma Brown, Mrs. Henry, and the other ladies also crowded into the room to hear what was going on.

Mark addressed the room. "Everyone, this is Billy Simpson. He was one of the men who attacked us today." The room erupted in grumbles and hisses and condemnation. "His dad, Mr. Simpson, was the president of the Batesville Community Bank." Everyone stopped, gasped, and then listened. "Mr. Simpson and his wife and his brothers and their families were killed by the gang that attacked us today." Everyone looked around and seemed confused. "They took his sister and forced Billy, here, to fight for them, and told him if he didn't, they would hurt his sister and kill him." Everyone looked at each other in astonishment. "Billy wants us to help him get his sister back." Eyes began to water and tears began to flow. "Big Al is their leader. That other boy in there is Little Al, his son. I told Billy we would help him get his sister back." By then, the women were sobbing and the men were rubbing tears from their faces.

Grandpa stopped Mark. "Billy, I'm sorry that happened. I knew your dad. He was a good man. I know you didn't mean to hurt us. We will help get your sister back." Billy buried his face and started crying. "You can stay here with us as long as you need to."

Lisa and Grandma went over and hugged Billy and told him it was okay. By then, everyone in the room was crying and feeling the pain of his loss. Grandpa and Gunny both realized they had been too quick to judge and punish the attackers without knowing all the facts or giving the men a chance to explain their actions. Billy's story touched them in a way none of them would have imagined. The Takers were not just thugs taking things from innocent citizens. They weren't just murderers. They were kidnappers, rapists, and child molesters, the worst of the worst.

They had forced an innocent child to attack innocent people. They had to be eliminated, whatever the cost, whatever had to be done.

Sheriff Taylor had heard enough. "What is your plan, gentlemen?"

Mark continued. "We figure there are about sixty or so of them left at the Simpsons' farm. With the Cliftons and the Huffmans, we have about seventy or so fighters. So we need to spend a day or maybe two, if time permits, recruiting some more folks for our militia to increase our odds. I'm sure there are other folks out there who have been hurt by these guys and are willing to help us get rid of them. Since we know they are listening in, we can use the radio to bait them, using Little Al as the bait. We can make it sound like the attack weakened us, but we still have some fight left and have Little Al as a prisoner. We can lure them over here and make them bring the fight to us, where our strong defenses can be used as an advantage. Hopefully, they don't know what we have set up. The others didn't. We need to send a group to scout out and watch Billy's farm. If Big Al leaves with a big group, they can give us a heads-up so we can be ready. If they leave some men there, we can go over and clean them out after we take care of the others here. If we have the numbers on our side and catch them off guard, we should be able to take them out without significant losses on our part." Mark and Paul sat in silence while the others took it all in.

Sheriff Taylor spoke first. "By God, with enough folks on our side, I think that just might work. If we can take care of these guys, then we can get this county back in order."

Grandpa agreed. "I know a lot of folks around here who will join us in a heartbeat. We can get out and start recruiting right away."

Mark finished his plan. "We need to keep an eye out for them to attack soon. Big Al will be wondering what happened to his son and his men, and he may come looking for them. So we need to go ahead and get our defenses in order. I think we need to get word to the Cliftons and the Huffmans right away and be ready for them. Gunny and some of his men need to go ahead and meet with them and get them on board, while Grandpa and the sheriff are out recruiting others. And we need to have some of our best men go over and scout out the Simpson place and gather what information they can about their layout and numbers and to watch for any significant movement."

Sheriff Taylor liked the plan. "I think this will work. Mr. Brown and I can divide up the recruiting and get right on it. Gunny, if you can, get our defenses ready and then send some of your best men over to scout out Big Al and his men. I think we can still use the radio, but we need to use a different channel when we communicate with each other and change the channel on a rotating basis, just in case they are still listening in."

Paul interjected. "As soon as Gunny visits the Cliftons and Huffmans and we are comfortable with our defenses, we probably need to go ahead and send out a false radio report. Big Al will be expecting us to communicate with the others, and if we don't, his curiosity will get the best of him and he might move on us right away."

Mark agreed. "He might anyway. As far as we know, none of his men contacted him after the fighting was over, and he has to be wondering what happened. So we need to at least send out our false message now and bait him into preparing for a full-out battle. That should keep him busy for a little while as we finish getting ready ourselves. If we can get the scouts over there now, we will know if he heads over here before we are fully prepared, and that would give us time to get the Huffmans and Cliftons on board."

Sheriff Taylor liked the plan. "Okay, gentlemen, let's do this. Time is a wasting. Y'all know what to do."

Gunny picked four of his best men to go scout out Big Al's group at the Simpsons' farm. Two of the men were former marine snipers and knew how to sneak up on the enemy unseen. The other two had been in the army and were proven fighters with battle experience. They took off in two trucks with enough gear and supplies to sustain them for up to a week, if needed. They went in by the back roads and parked their trucks off the road, well hidden from view two miles from the Simpson farm. They slowly and silently crept in through the woods, as they had done many times before in their training and in their combat experience. Each of the two teams of snipers set up their rifles with their high-powered scopes at different points far enough from the house where they could keep an eye on the comings and goings of Big Al's group but where they couldn't be seen themselves. Their companions acted as spotters and as radiomen to keep home base informed.

After the first few hours, they could tell that Big Al's group was not well disciplined. It appeared that most of the men had slept in late. They wandered outside to relieve themselves in the yard one by one as they came out of the house, the tents, and the stolen RVs, rubbing sleep out of their eyes. After watching them for several hours, they guessed that there were around fifty-five or sixty of them left.

While the snipers were doing their job, Grandpa and Sheriff Taylor visited about twelve farms between them. Most of them were doing well. They all had well water and food and a decent number of warm bodies for defense. None of them had been attacked directly, but several knew of neighbors and others around the county who had been. Some of the farms had recruited others to join them, and some already had family and close friends staying with them. The biggest group had around twenty-five, but some had only about ten or twelve. When they all heard about Big Al and his group of ninety that had been whittled down to about sixty, they all wanted to join in with the Browns and the Cliftons and the Huffmans and be part of the militia and help rid the county of the Takers. They all had the good sense to see that alone they could not defend against that many, but together they had a good chance to take them on. In all, there were about fifty who agreed to join and fight with the sheriff and his militia.

Before they could return to the farm, one of the snipers radioed to Hank and Skinny that they had spotted Big Al outside the house. They knew it was him because he fit the description that Billy had given them. He was about six foot four and three hundred pounds, bald headed with a beard, wearing a leather vest covered with patches and a .44 Magnum pistol on his hip. The sniper with the best view of Big Al described him yelling at the men and ranting and raving about something and waving his arms in the air. The men seemed scared of him and appeared to be getting loaded up to go somewhere. One of the spotters made the suggestion that they should take him out. If Big Al and his men were disorganized and following his orders only because they were afraid of him, that would send them into disarray and make it easier to divide and conquer them.

Hank and Skinny radioed Mark, Grandpa, Sheriff Taylor, and Gunny, who conferred with each other about the situation. They were slightly embarrassed that they hadn't thought of it themselves, so they gave the snipers the go-ahead. They advised them to take him and a few others out, if they thought they could do it and get away without being caught. The snipers were sure they could, so when they had a clear shot, they took it. Big Al went down with the first shot and then they plucked off four others as they were loading into the vehicles. After the shots rang out and the others saw Big Al fall, mass hysteria broke out. Men ran around in circles, like chickens with their heads cut off, in and out of the house and the buildings. But none of them knew where the shots came from, and no one appeared to be in charge. So the snipers picked off as many as they could as they tried to get in the vehicles to leave. They shot so many that they lost count. After several minutes, everyone had either been dropped by a .308 bullet or gone inside for cover. Then all was quiet. The snipers kept up their vigil and dropped anyone who tried to leave for the next few hours. Intermittent shots were fired aimlessly out windows and doors, but without a target, it was just wasted ammo.

Gunny and Sheriff Taylor rounded up about one hundred well-armed men and headed over to the Simpson Farm and surrounded the place, while the snipers kept what was left of Big Al's men inside and under cover. When the militia members were in place, Sheriff Taylor used the loudspeaker of his car to call out to the house. "This is Sheriff Taylor. We have you surrounded. We are the County Militia, under the orders of Colonel Henry of the US Army. Drop your weapons and come out with your hands up, or we'll open fire. If you leave empty-handed, we'll let you get in your vehicles and leave the county unharmed. We are not taking any prisoners. If you are found later, you will be shot on sight. You can leave either dead or alive."

After a minute or two, shouting and cursing could be heard coming from the house. Then a couple of shots rang out, and then it was quiet. After another minute or two, the first man came out with his hands up. Then he was joined by another, then another. When they got in a truck and left without being shot, the floodgates opened and others poured out of the house and buildings and RVs and loaded into vehicles and on motorcycles and hurried as fast as they could go down the drive and through the gate to freedom. The more who left, the more the others fought to get into the remaining vehicles and get out of there. Soon, no one else came out of the house or the other buildings. All was quiet.

Sheriff Taylor had the men wait another fifteen minutes before moving on the farm. Gunny and some of the militia members with the most experience in clearing buildings entered the house and other buildings and found them empty, except for several women prisoners who were left behind and a couple of dead Takers who had tried to convince the others at gunpoint to stay and fight. Billy's sister was found alive among the other women and was reunited with him in a tearful embrace. Physically, she was unharmed on the outside, but emotionally and psychologically she was a wreck. It would be a long time before she would be normal again. News of the victory was radioed to all the farms and was met with cheers and tears all around.

When the body count was finished, there were a total of forty dead Takers, between the battle at the farm and from the sniper kills at the Simpson place. No militia members we're killed or wounded in the process. A total of 130 weapons were recovered, along with several thousand rounds of ammo, a couple of hundred gallons of gasoline and diesel, and a large stash of stolen property: cash, jewelry, electronics, several generators, and a few appliances. The women were reunited with remaining family, if they had any left, and if not, they were allowed to stay at one of the farms. Little Al was ordered to leave the county and not to return, or be shot on sight if seen again. He quickly complied, leaving on one of the motorcycles left behind by one of the dead bikers.

With the defeat of Big Al and his band of Takers, the next order of business for Sheriff Taylor and the militia was to clean up Batesville and establish law and order in the county.

CHAPTER 28
TAKING
BACK THE TOWN

Sheriff Taylor and his militia moved into City Hall and the sheriff's office in town and began to reestablish order. Fortunately, most of the refugees had moved on due to the lack of power, water, and food. As per Mark's suggestion, the sheriff was in no hurry to do anything about that anytime soon. Although many local residents were being affected, turning the water back on before the rest of the refugees left would be even worse. It was a tough call but the right one. After just an extra three days, the majority of them moved on down the road. That left just a few extra thousand to deal with rather than tens of thousands.

From that point on, looters, rapists, terrorists, and murderers were shot on sight or run out of the county. The word got around quickly, and the Takers and the terrorists decided to move on to easier targets, so they followed the refugees on down the road. The refugees who did stay were allowed to camp at the fairgrounds but were told they would not be given food or water.

They were on their own. This was met with grumbles and shouts of racism, calls for fairness, and demands for help from the government, but when they were told help was weeks or months away, most packed up and left. Mark's plan seemed to have succeeded in markedly decreasing the number of refugees they would have to deal with. This made managing the needs of the local residents much easier. Those without the means to provide for their families were offered work for food programs with the local farms, but those who refused to work were not given food. Soon, they left, as well. This left a population about the same as before the riots, but those who remained were self-sufficient or willing to work. The sick and the shut in, along with widows and orphaned children, were taken care of through the local churches, which worked with the sheriff and the farmers.

A crew of utility workers was brought together and began reestablishing electricity to City Hall, the sheriff's office, the fire stations, the hospital, the water treatment plant, and the water towers in the area. After a couple of weeks, they had power and water to those areas. They continued to work to get power and water to the schools and churches and neighborhoods surrounding them. It would take months or longer to get power and water to the rest of the county.

Once the power and water were back on, Mark began working on recruiting help and supplies for the hospital. It took weeks to get a skeleton crew together, but with the help of his crew from Southcrest, they were able to start seeing patients and doing surgery again. Since communications were still down in most areas of the country, payment by insurance companies was very limited. On the other hand, most people had stopped paying their insurance premiums and light bills and no longer had large fuel or grocery bills, so they were actually better off without all those monthly payments to worry over.

Things that were the most basic to sustain life—food, water, health care, and shelter—were what people took care of. Bartering services for food, fuel, guns, and ammo became the local method of trade and commerce. Banking, paychecks, and paying taxes were no longer as important as putting food on the table. Money was no longer worth the paper it was printed on, and therefore it was not useful for currency. Gold, silver, bullets, fuel, whiskey, and such items became the favored method of payment.

Sheriff Taylor made a priority list for the utilization of fuel. Ambulance services, the hospital, police, utility companies, and farming were listed as top priority. Travel for the employees of those entities was next. Any surplus fuel after the priority needs were met was then divided evenly among the local filling stations that had working pumps for sale to the public.

Instead of putting prisoners in cells and feeding them three meals a day to do nothing but work out and listen to the radio until they could see a judge, Sheriff Taylor started a work-for-food program similar to the old penal farm system. Prisoners were housed at night in cells, but during the day the more dangerous ones were taken out in chain gangs to do hard labor on the city and county roads and on cleanup programs to get things back in working order. The less dangerous were put to work on local farms in exchange for food. Most of them complained bitterly about their civil rights being violated, but without anyone to complain to and most folks already doing without themselves, it fell on deaf ears. If they refused to work, they did not eat. It didn't take long for them to get with the program.

Around the county, corn, wheat, and other farm produce and foods were being grown and sold or traded locally, instead of being shipped across the country to be stored in grain elevators or refrigerated warehouses or traded by commodity brokers in the big cities. Anyone with land and the know-how took up their tools and started a garden and began raising chickens, rabbits, goats, pigs, cows, and other animals for food and for trade. People began to keep bees for honey and use the wax for candles. Some even started making whiskey and wine at home for use and for trade. Bullets, salt, sugar, coffee, and other commodities not locally produced or grown became worth their weight in silver and food. The local economy was based on local supply and demand. Food, guns and ammo, and medicines and health care were in greatest demand and brought the greatest return in trade or barter of goods and services.

Around the county and throughout the country in similar rural areas, people learned to get by with less, to travel less, to use less fuel, and to eat less processed—and therefore healthier—food. They began to travel by horse again, make fewer trips to town, ride bicycles, and work in their gardens and in the fields again. Horses and wagons became a common sight around town. Automobiles were still common, but since gas and diesel were so hard to come by and so precious, frivolous travel was cut down to a trickle.

Jobs became mostly agricultural- and farm-based again, as they were during the early part of the nineteen hundreds. People were leading a much healthier lifestyle, and the obesity epidemic that had overtaken the country over the past two decades began to reverse itself. People were forced to eat less and do physical labor and work with their hands. They began to make things at home, in their garages and shops. Handcrafted tools and furniture were once again finding their way back into the American culture. Homemade jams, jellies, pies, candles, baskets, and crafts were popular once again, as well.

Mark allowed the hospital services to be paid for by barter in goods or services as well as cash, but with the ever-changing inflation, it was difficult to tell what a dollar was really worth. But they needed some cash to pay the utility bills, supplies, and payroll for the nurses and techs. If someone needed surgery or care or medicines but did not have any money or gold or silver, the family could pay the bill in trade or services by working around the hospital doing upkeep, housekeeping, repairs, and so forth. It wasn't long before things were flowing smoothly around town and at the hospital.

And even though Mark did not demand payment up front for his services, many folks paid him in cash or trade, and soon he had more than he could ever use. Patients paid him directly, and those who couldn't pay weren't asked to, just like in the early part of the nineteen hundreds before the insurance companies and the government got involved in medical care. No precertifications were needed. There were no HMOs to deal with, no denials for care, no resubmissions for payment, no forms, no need for armies of social workers or nurses to review charts for length of stay or to satisfy insurance companies and peer-review panels. And best of all, there were no lawyers filing malpractice cases for every bad turn of event because, for the most part, there were no courthouse employees, no courts in session, and mostly because people were appreciative to get any medical care at all.

The hospital became very streamlined. Decisions were simple. If it was needed for patient care or to run the hospital, it was necessary. Everything else was not. There were no quality control issues to deal with, and no quality assurance issues, no state requirements, no federal requirements, and no OSHA or FDA worries. Like days of old, when hospitals first came into existence, they were run by doctors and nurses who took care of patients first, instead of administrators with PhDs and MBAs who never laid a hand on a sick patient their whole career. Decisions were made by a few, instead of by committees whose decisions had to be run up the ladder through the corporate hierarchy and back down by way of their lawyers and then back through more committees. Mark knew that would all change back over time. But while it lasted, it was much easier to get the right things done in a timely fashion, which made the hospital much more efficient than it had been in decades.

Back at the farm, those living in the RVs were making due with lamps for light at night and solar panels on the roofs of the ones that had them for charging their batteries. They also used what was left of their propane to run water heaters, for cooking, and to run their refrigerators. The house was getting by without a refrigerator and using propane for the hot water heaters only, and the woodstove for cooking, and lamps for light at night. Clothes were washed by hand in tubs with scrub boards, then hung on fences and clotheslines by everyone.

There was still diesel left in the big farm tank, so most of the plowing was still being done with the tractors, but soon Grandpa would have to get out the mules and the harness and plow the fields the way his grandpa did before him. The garden could be expanded as much as needed to accommodate the added mouths to feed. The fruit trees had been pruned and fertilized for higher production of apples, plums, and peaches, which would provide fresh fruit in the summer and fall and jams and jellies in the winter. The blackberries were pruned and being propagated so that more berries could grow and provide for fruit in the summer and be put up as jelly and jam.

There were momma cows with calves in the pasture that would grow and have calves of their own within a couple of years, thus increasing the herd quickly. As the calves were weaned, their mommas would continue to supply a steady supply of milk, from which the cream could be separated to be used for cooking or churned into butter. The bull calves would be cut and turned into steers to be slaughtered and used for meat as needed year-round. The chickens would provide a steady source of eggs and meat. And the pigs would also provide a steady supply of meat.

Even though no one knew how long it would take to get the electricity back on at the farm, Mark, Grandpa Brown, and some of the others knew it might be a long time—not weeks, but months, maybe even years. Some even hoped it would be a long time, because they were enjoying the simple life that came without the constant distraction of television, Internet social media such as Twitter and Facebook, cell phones, deadlines, and running here and there for takeout meals and every little thing. People were sitting together, talking and telling stories face-to-face again, instead of staring at a cell phone screens while texting or chatting with someone else hundreds of miles away while ignoring the ones they were with.

They were enjoying being together with extended families and helping each other with household and farm chores and the children. Others were around to give guidance to the young, so they felt loved and got a better sense of right and wrong. It's one thing for a mom or dad to tell and teach their children about God and the values of a life lived right, but another when they see it lived daily, for generations, in their grandparents and great-grandparents.

Families and close friends were once again helping each other with life's problems, which allowed different generations to learn from each other and to give advice about things they had experience with. They shared responsibilities, and there was a larger base of information to draw on to get things done. They enjoyed singing songs and playing music together and teaching the young the songs passed down from generation to generation. The elderly liked feeling useful again and being able to show the young how to make things by hand, how to cook, sew, knit, weave, and make clothes and quilts and all the things that make daily life more pleasant.

Not having discount stores and grocery stores to run to for everything meant it would be necessary for them to make most things on the farm, such as old-fashioned lye soap using the fat from the animals and the ash from the fireplace and woodstove. The beehives would not only provide honey but also wax that could be used to make candles. Wheat from the back pastures would be ground into flour to make bread, and the leftover field corn would be stored and ground into meal to make cornbread. The wheat stalks would make good bedding for the animals and provide bulk for the sheep and cows in the winter. Meat from the animals slaughtered in late fall would be smoked in the smokehouse, which would allow it to keep all winter, and the hides could be tanned to make leather.

Several of the militia members, along with Mark and Grandpa, knew how to hunt and fish. Deer, squirrels, turkeys, and rabbits were plentiful on the farm, as well as fish in the farm ponds and in the river. So with all that the farm supplied, and along with the stored and canned food in the basement and the MREs, all in all things were in good shape as far as food supplies were concerned. Besides food and water and roofs over their heads, they had at least some semblance of basic medical care and protection from all but the largest groups of marauders. So, no matter how long things took to get back to normal, the odds that the folks at the farm could eat and stay alive were better than those faced by most. It wasn't by accident or fate that it was so. It was by forethought and planning and preparation. Others would suffer greatly in the short run, and maybe even more in the long run if the fabric of society continued to unravel.

Some of the local radio stations continued to be on the air, although on a sporadic basis due to power outages and some of the towers being destroyed and disabled. The stations that remained on the air reported that the power was being restored in large sections of Memphis and soon the water would be back on in those areas. Camps were being established in and around Memphis where stranded and homeless folks could come for shelter, food, water, and basic medical care, all provided by the government.

Detailed reports described that the riots had all but ended within most of the major cities, due to a lack of power, water, and food. People were leaving those areas, mostly in search of food and water, not because of the presence of the US Army or a show of force by police. There were still many reports of violence, but they were mostly committed by isolated gangs and sporadic in nature. Most of the trouble had moved farther out into the surrounding towns and countryside. The small towns and cities immediately around the major metropolitan areas had suffered the most, but even towns as far out as one hundred to two hundred miles were being disrupted by all the city folks in their areas. No one at the farm or in Batesville needed anyone on the radio to tell them that.

Television news programs that were still on the air were following the violence out into the towns surrounding the major cities.

Most were focusing on the lack of food and water and services for the hordes of city dwellers who were refugees in their own country. They were claiming that the government wasn't doing enough for its own citizens, and very few were portraying the truth that they were the very ones who caused the problem in the first place by continuing to demand checks and help from a government that was broke and voting politicians into office who would continue the entitlements. Even after the country went broke, they continued to demand that someone else provide for them, and then they used violence to take from others what they wanted for themselves. But the farther they got from the cities, the more resistance they encountered. Their violence was being met head-on by armed citizens who were just standing their ground and protecting themselves.

The news media were portraying it in an entirely different light, however. They were making the case that the country folks were prejudiced, hateful, uncaring, and willing to let others starve while they had plenty. They did not mention the fact that the country folks had worked the fields, hunted, saved their food, and planned ahead. Many folks who lived in the country who did not have water or power and did not plan ahead were just as hungry and tired and stressed as the city folks, but they were not part of the stories being told on the radio and television stations.

Some isolated areas of the country were so far removed from the effects of the big-city riots that, so far, they had felt only small ripples of the shockwave that hit the rest of the country. But even those people living in the backwoods, mountains, distant prairies, swamps, and rugged backcountry were affected by the lack of power and the empty grocery store shelves, due to the effects on the trucking industry and the interruption of the supply chain of food from the farms to the grocery stores. People that far off the beaten path had always been more self-sufficient and more independent than most, but even they depended on the grocery stores and discount stores for most of their supplies, just like everyone else.

One thing was certain: If the violence continued much longer, everyone would find themselves drawn into the middle of it all sooner or later. They would have to choose either the side of the Takers, who wanted the government to take care of them all, or the side of those who just wanted the government to leave them alone. The country was almost evenly divided along those lines. The Takers were mostly city folks. Some were from rural small towns, but most were from the urban areas and suburbs. They were second and third generation welfare moms with multiple kids by many different men living on food stamps in government housing. Families without fathers in the house—and whose fathers were mostly drug dealers—with lots of cash but who did not pay any taxes into the system. Instead, they worked the system for all they could get out of it. Those who stole and took as much as they could from others and the government without any regrets, because they felt it was owed to them for some perceived past social injustices committed generations ago by people who were long dead and gone. Those so full of hate they would get satisfaction from shooting a man just to watch him bleed.

There were millions of illegal immigrants who were doing the same: living under the radar, not paying taxes, working the system, enjoying the American way of life, the jobs and lifestyle. Their women having children out of wedlock by different men, who in turn have babies by many women but don't take care of any of them, who are in gangs and rob, steal, and deal drugs. But all the while, their kids were getting an education and medical care paid for by someone else. Of course, not all of them were guilty, not even a majority, but there were enough to strain the system past the breaking point.

It was not a black thing, or a Hispanic thing, or even a white trash thing, because people of all races and ethnicity did the same. They took advantage of the system and continually voted down the party line in every election despite apparent corruption and obvious voter fraud where even the dead voted as often as they could. The same folks kept the same politicians in office in order to keep the checks coming, regardless of the consequences. They had the attitude that they were going to get what they could, while they could, as long as they could, even though the country couldn't afford it, and even if it meant the country would go bankrupt. And the same people continued to demand help, even after the government could no longer give them what they wanted, so they took from whom they could.

People had to choose which side to be on. To be a Taker, or to stop the Takers from taking, to stand up and say no more and make people be responsible for their own actions. To throw out of office the politicians who used and abused their power in order to feed their minions at the trough of entitlements paid for by someone else. To demand that if women want to have children out of wedlock, let them feed them, and clothe them, and pay for their education and health care. Let them work for their food and pay for the lifestyle they want to live, not expecting someone else to pay for it and getting a free cell phone to boot. To finally tell those who show up at a welfare office or health clinic in a new Cadillac, wearing hair weaves and designer clothes and with manicures and pedicures, to get an education and a job like everyone else who pays the taxes that have allowed them to live that way too long.

Which of the two directions the country would go was a decision that had to be made in the post-riots, bankrupt world America had become. It should have been made before, but the hard choices that needed to be made were unpopular. Any politicians who tried to cut entitlements were sure to be voted out of office. Even those who agreed that something needed to be done wanted cuts only in programs that did not affect them or their voters, which were few. Even though the country was already evenly divided over the budget crisis, too many people were getting some type of government benefits of one form or another, so that meant a slight majority always voted against entitlement cuts. Hard decisions were continually put off, year after year, even though several European countries had followed the same path and suffered the same fate.

But politicians would not necessarily be the ones to make the decision. Even though the same people were in charge in Washington, the public had a choice to make. The decision that had to be made all over the country was whether to follow the orders handed down by the federal government and the acting president by way of the military, to be told where to go and what to do and to allow them to take what they wanted when they wanted, or to stand up and so no, no more. To be willing to take up arms and to stand against them, and be willing to fight if needed to stop the Takers.

To know that even though the US Army has bigger guns and more sophisticated weapons, they have to climb out of their tanks to sleep and eat. They have to refuel and resupply their troops. With one hundred million armed citizens and only about one million troops, the odds would not be good for the troops.

Unlike the Civil War, where the nation was divided with the North against the South, it would be the entire country divided in half, with one side of the people against the Takers and the government. If the people who were for individual rights and freedom stood their ground, they would prevail. They had the resources, supplies, food, guns, and ammo on their side. If they became afraid and backed down, they would lose, and the county would lose. America would become a police state, a socialist society with the loss of personal property and the freedoms that made her prosperous and great in the past.

These were the things on the minds of Mark and Grandpa Brown and men like them all over the county and the entire country. The kind of men who built this country. Not like the men willing to fight for control of a street corner to sell drugs, but men with the pioneer spirit, not afraid of hard work, not afraid to fight and willing to sacrifice for the greater good. Those willing to make hard decisions and do the hard things necessary to protect their families and their country. The same kind of men who fought in the world wars, who fought the British, and wrote the Constitution. Whichever side prevailed would determine what kind of country America would become.

CHAPTER 29
TAKING BACK THE COUNTY

Several weeks after the riots ended in the cities, things were getting back to some semblance of normalcy in the cities, including Memphis and the surrounding counties. The rioters had moved on out farther into the countryside, looking for food and water and others to take from. As they used up the resources and met resistance, they moved on even farther out. As things began to settle down in Batesville, the situation in Memphis was improving, as well.

Back in Washington, Vice President Whitman had just learned the president had died of complications from a pulmonary embolism. A large blood clot developed in one of his injured legs, broke free, and lodged in his pulmonary artery, which blocked the blood flow from the heart and caused sudden death. Vice President Whitman was sworn in that same day as president by the chief justice of the Supreme Court. She was the first female president of the United States. She no longer had to second-guess what President Williams would do. She was the president, and it was all up to her.

Her first order of business was to call another Cabinet meeting. She was happy to hear from that many of the terrorists has been rounded up and the FBI was making progress on who was responsible for the death of the president. She continued to put off the Coalition knowing their days were numbered despite the objections of Senator Clark whose enthusiasm seemed to be fading as the FBI investigation progressed. With those issues moved to the back burner, she turned her attention to figuring out what to do about the riots and the situation with all the refugees, homeless, and starving people throughout the nation. After she was briefed on the current situation, it was clear to her that the most pressing matter at hand was finding a way to feed the hungry masses. It was her decision to invoke Executive Order 10998, in which she authorized the secretary of agriculture to order the army to confiscate all stored food supplies in warehouses and grain elevators and even food crops such as corn, wheat, and rice in the fields of farms throughout the country in order to feed the relocated people in the camps across the nation. Senator Sage raised his usual objections to that being a direct assault against the Constitution, but it all fell on deaf ears. President Whitman was now responsible for feeding the masses, and she wanted to make sure her constituents were fed. If the farmers got mad, that was okay with her. They didn't usually vote for her party, anyway.

So the order was handed down through the secretary of defense to all the joint chiefs and down to the generals and down to the men in the fields. Many of them, including Colonel Henry, didn't like it, but orders were orders. They would follow them as they were told, at least for a while. If there was no resistance, then the masses would get fed and they would all still have a job. They risked court-martial if they refused to pass the order on down to their men, which would not accomplish anything since they would just be replaced by another officer looking to make rank. If the farmers resisted, that would be another story. Chances were not all the soldiers would go along with that. Then the colonels could tell their generals that the soldiers were refusing to carry out the order, in which case they could not replace all of them. If they tried, the generals would not have an army to command. If the generals had no army, the politicians could no longer take from those who had to give to those who didn't to keep themselves in office, and things would have to change in Washington. The people would be in charge again. The politicians would have to do the will of the people, instead of the other way around, as it had been many years ago.

Colonel Henry's men had worked hard and restored partial power and water in several critical areas of Memphis, including the Trauma Center and University Hospital, and were recruiting nurses, doctors, and workers to staff them. Refugee camps and relocation centers were set up to provide shelter, food, and water and began accepting people. At first few came, but as the resources ran out outside the city and the word got around that there was food and water to be had, more and more showed up. Soon, the wave of people shifted direction and the inflow of people into Memphis increased dramatically. Those with homes still standing and transportation and fuel went home, but they had to travel back and forth to the camps for food and water. Those without homes, transportation, or fuel stayed at the camps.

Everyone who remained in Memphis who could be rounded up was questioned and screened for work duties, as well. All utility employees, hospital employees, nurses, police, firefighters, paramedics, doctors, and other essential personnel were put back to work. Those returning to the city were screened as they came back through the checkpoints and put to work if they had needed skills. Fathers and mothers with needed skills were taken from their families against their will and placed where they were needed most.

Colonel Henry sent a message to Mark by radio that Captain Ellis and two platoons of men were headed to Batesville to set up a headquarters and take over coordinating the cleanup and reconstruction. He warned them that Captain Ellis was a by-the-numbers kind of guy and would follow the orders handed down from the generals, which was to interview everyone, search the area for critical personnel, and put them to work where they were needed most. He knew Mark would be safe, since he was already under his orders to run the hospital, but that other doctors, nurses, policemen, firefighters, and so on might not be. He warned them that Captain Ellis was under orders to confiscate any supplies needed for his efforts, including food, fuel, supplies, weapons, and ammunition. He also told them Cindy was moved back to Memphis to work the OR at the Trauma Center, but Tammy was left behind against Cindy's wishes in the care of child services at the Naval Air Station in Millington. They had discovered that Tammy was orphaned, and so far no relatives had been found. But when she was asked who her family was, she told them Dr. Edwards.

Under the executive orders handed down to them from Vice President Whitman, Captain Ellis could take food supplies and confiscate farm equipment—even entire farms—and conscript the workers into forced labor if needed to feed the masses of hungry people taking up residence in the camps in Memphis and the surrounding counties. Feeding the hungry masses would be the biggest challenge they faced, after reconstruction, and the only way to achieve success with that would be to take food from the farmers. Colonel Henry did not suggest that they should resist the army, but he did say that his men were authorized to physically force individuals to go along. But he also said they were under strict orders not to open fire unless fired upon. So if anyone were to resist, they should do so nonviolently, and in such numbers that they could not be hauled off one by one. And he let them know if it came down to it, the troops would not likely fight their own people. He also said the generals more than likely would not have the stomach for that and many of the senators in Washington would not stand for it, either. Mark got the message loud and clear.

Mark met with the other members of the kitchen roundtable to discuss the situation. "What Colonel Henry said was that Captain Ellis and some of his men were on their way down here to set up headquarters and begin reconstruction and recruiting critical and skilled laborers to run the city and county police units, firefighters, utility personnel, and hospital workers. He also said they would most likely have to confiscate fuel and food supplies necessary to get the job done. He even said they could take farms and equipment, if needed, to feed the masses. So they are basically coming down here to get food and workers to run the cities."

Grandpa was visibly irritated by the suggestion that they could come and take their food supplies or his farm to feed all the folks who caused the problem in the first place. "If they try to come on my farm, they will be met with bullets at the gate." A few others at the table seconded that idea.

Sheriff Taylor interrupted their shouts for resistance. "Now, gentlemen, we can't fight the US Army. They are the law right now, like it or not."

Grandpa interjected. "They may think they are law, but many of us still consider the Constitution the law of the land. The laws passed by Congress should not infringe on our constitutional rights, and all these presidential executive orders that have been passed down do just that. We're not breaking any laws. We are minding our own business and taking care of our families. We have put up with all these tax increases and all these laws that take away our freedoms long enough. If they come down here to take our supplies, they are breaking the law. They have circumvented the Constitution, just so they can take from one group to appease another. We have the right to bear arms and resist our government, if needed. That is why the Founding Fathers added the Second Amendment, so that the government could not suppress its own people. That is why we fought the British. It is time for us to take a stand and say no more."

Mark tried to find a middle ground. "I agree, the people have the right to resist an oppressive government, but we don't want to start something that will get us all killed. Colonel Henry said they were under strict orders to shoot only if shot at first, so we have to find a way to resist without taking the first shot, but at the same time let them know we are willing to fight if it comes to it and that we will not back down. We need to have a show of force so they cannot roll in and start taking what they want and push us around. That will force them to make the first move. More than likely, they will not shoot their own people, even if ordered to. If enough people resist all over the county and the country, they will be forced to back down, and the politicians will know they cannot continue taking away our rights anymore. It will force them to do what they should have done long ago: stop taking from one group to buy the votes of another."

"How do we do that?" Sheriff Taylor asked.

"Armed passive resistance," Mark answered.

"What the hell does that mean?" Grandpa grumbled.

"It means we arm ourselves for a fight, but we use restraint and only shoot if they shoot first. We must have enough people to resist them and make it clear to them that we won't let them push us around without a fight. That will force them to either back down or use force. It must be a situation that is clear to everyone that they have to make a premeditated decision to make the first move that forces the first shot. We have to let them know we are the people's militia defending the Constitution of the United States, not just some angry farmers looking for a fight. The soldiers must be the ones to make that decision, so they are forced to declare whom they are loyal to: the politicians or the people and the Constitution. I am hopeful the soldiers will choose to defend the Constitution and not fire on their own people."

"And what if they don't? What if they decide to fight?" Sheriff Taylor asked.

"Then we fight! That is what we have to decide before we resist. We must be prepared to fight if it comes down to it. That is what we have to let them know. If they know we will fight if pushed any further, then it forces them to make that decision. The blood will be on their hands. That is the only way this works." Mark explained.

Grandpa was for it. "We need to have the numbers on our side. So I'll talk with the Huffmans and Cliftons and the other farmers around the county and get them on board. If the army shows up at any one of our farms, the others need to show up armed and ready to fight. I don't think I'll have any problem getting them to agree to that. They are as fed up with government as we are. If they come to take any one of our farms or food, they will have to deal with all of us."

"So how does this play out in your mind, Doc?" Sheriff Taylor asked.

"It's really quite simple. If they come down here and ask for our help and let us help make decisions, we cooperate and help solve the problems in our community, just like we have been doing. But if they come down here telling us what we are going to do and try to take what they want without our consent, we refuse. But we do so in numbers, so that they know it's not just us but the whole community of taxpaying, hardworking folks who are refusing to be told by our own government how we are going to live and what we are going to do with our own hard-earned resources. At the point, if they come to our farm or any of the farms in our militia to take our food or farms, they will know they have a fight on their hands. If enough people like us put up a fight, they will either back down or they will have a revolution on their hands. Using the excuse that the president ordered it will not suffice, in that we do not take orders from the president or any members of the government. We adhere to the Constitution and by the principles laid out in the Bill of Rights, and as free citizens of the United States of America, we rightfully defend our rights to own private property and the right to bear arms to defend ourselves from an oppressive government. If enough people stand up to them, it will stop this and turn the country around back to the way things should be. Back to a country where hardworking citizens are free to pursue their dreams, not burdened by too many laws or government regulations that interfere with that. That is what I see happening."

Mark paused for a moment to see if everyone was still with him. "Could this all backfire on us? Could they come down here by force and take it all away from us against our will? Yes, more than likely they could, at first. But, if the soldiers decide not to turn their guns against their own people, we could win quickly. If they decide to fight us, then it could turn into a long, drawn-out battle. But, if we and others like us are determined and willing to fight to the end, and there are enough of us, then the tide could turn in our favor. If we turn out to be a minority, then we will go down fighting for what we know is the right cause for this country. If we lose, this country will never be the same, and it will become a country we do not want to be a part of, anyway. That is how I see this going down."

"What are you talking about? Are you crazy? That is some pretty serious stuff," Sheriff Taylor shouted. "You guys are going to get all of us killed. Do you think the others will go along with that?"

"That is the great unknown. We don't really know how many will take our side and rally around us when the time comes. That is the big unknown that we have to gamble on. If a few or none show when it comes down to it, we will lose. If many show up, we will have a fighting chance. All of which makes me wonder if maybe we shouldn't get on the radio with some of the other counties in the area and see what they are going to do. If they resist, it would help our cause, because it would spread them out even more and make it harder for them to carry out the president's orders," Mark explained.

Sheriff Taylor looked concerned. "You guys aren't going to start an uprising, are you?"

Mark smiled. "Not an uprising—a revolution."

Sheriff Taylor thought about what was being said and planned, and knew he had to make a choice. There was no in-between. He was either with them or against them. But he knew that the majority of his constituents in the county felt the same, so for his own political reasons he agreed to go along with the plan.

If it worked, he would be a local hero. If it didn't, it wouldn't matter. The army would take over and he would be relegated to an errand boy or just another soldier, instead of the sheriff in charge. It wasn't something he was ready to give up. "I'll talk to some of the other folks in the county who were ready to fight with us against the gangs and see if they still have some fight left in them. I think we can round up at least a couple hundred of them to go along with the farmers. That would give us several hundred in our militia."

"I'm glad you see things our way, Sheriff," Mark said. "I'll talk to people in town and at the hospital to get the word out. If we can get a hundred or so from town, then we will have enough to make them think twice about forcing anything on us. At least they will know they will have a fight on their hands if they try."

Gunny stood up. "How soon do we need to get this done?"

"The sooner, the better. We don't know when Captain Ellis and his men will get here, and we don't know how quickly they will get around to confiscating food and farms," Mark said.

Gunny headed for the door. "If it's all right with you guys, I'm going to get on the radio with Skinny right now. Let you know what we find out."

With the help of Sheriff Taylor, Gunny was able to locate the sheriffs of the surrounding counties. They too had local militias of their own acting in a similar fashion. It seemed to be a universal response to the situation brought on by the riots in the big cities. They all seemed interested in forming a coalition and agreed to meet at the courthouse in Batesville in two days to discuss how they would handle the impending takeover of their farms and supplies.

Two of the sheriffs from the Delta counties who had been recipients of large amounts of government assistance over the years were reluctant to participate, but the militia members from those counties agreed to meet. The sheriffs of the other counties who were leading their militias were anxious to cooperate. One thing was clear: They were all worried about any further infringements on their rights. They all felt the same way: If anyone came to take their food, farms, or guns, they would not give up without a fight. So Gunny and the sheriff were able to make a verbal deal with them to reciprocate backup as needed if that were to happen. The unconfirmed number of militia members was several hundred, but how many would actually show up and how many would be willing to fight to protect the welfare and supplies of their members, families, and other law-abiding citizens was not yet known. Hopefully, they would find out at the meeting in two days.

Mark, Grandpa, Sheriff Taylor, and all the others carried on their daily duties at the farm, in town, and at the hospital for the next couple of days as they continued to coordinate with the other farmers and citizens in the area who also did not want any further intrusion of the federal government into their lives. As the word spread, the militia numbers grew. At first there were a few hundred, but within a few days, the estimated number grew to several hundred in their county alone.

The day of the meeting came quickly. Mark, Grandpa, and the others finished up their chores early so they could break for the meeting at noon at the Courthouse. Skinny came into the kitchen with a radio message that came through from the county to the north. A convoy of US Army vehicles was rolling down the interstate toward Batesville.

"Captain Ellis," Mark said. "Great timing. Should we call off the meeting or go ahead?" Mark asked Grandpa, Gunny, and Sheriff Taylor, who were all about to load up and leave for town.

Grandpa Brown was not going to back down. "I say we meet anyway, and if the sum-bitch gets in the way, we go ahead and have it out right there."

Gunny and Sheriff Taylor weren't quite so ready to have a showdown just yet. "The others are probably on their way already, so we ought to at least show up. If we can meet, fine, if not, we can at least talk to them and show them we are serious," Gunny offered.

Sheriff Taylor agreed. "We should at least show up and let them know whose side we are on."

Mark thought it over and agreed that it was best that they show up and just go from there. If they could meet and form a strong coalition, their chances of meeting the problem with greater numbers would be better in the long run. If they got interrupted or couldn't have an open discussion, they could at least let the others know what their intentions were and what the plan was. It was possible that their whole plan would be blown up and dismantled before they could actually form a coalition. It was a gamble, but it had to be done.

Gunny stopped everyone at the door before they left the house. "Should we take our rifles, just in case they try to stop us? They might take them from us in town if they feel like we are a threat."

Grandpa Brown was determined. "I'm taking mine, and if they try to take my gun, they will have to shoot me first."

Mark was worried that the whole plan would come unraveled before they even got a chance to finalize one. If Captain Ellis or his men saw all of them running around town with rifles slung over their shoulders, carrying pistols on their sides, and gathering for a meeting, it would be an obvious threat to his authority, and he would want to know what they were up to. Losing a few rifles and pistols would not matter much in the long run, but if Captain Ellis caught wind of what they were meeting about, it would show their hand too soon and would eliminate the element of surprise. Mark tried to convince Grandpa of that, but he would have none of it. So they went to town fully armed and uncertain of what they were getting into.

As they rolled into town, Captain Ellis and his men were already unloading in front of the courthouse and taking positions around the town square. He announced on his loudspeaker, "I am Captain Ellis with the United States Army. We are here under direct orders of the president of the United States. We are here to restore order and reestablish your utilities and to assist with feeding and housing those who need it. With your cooperation, we can achieve that here in your county and the surrounding counties, just as we did in Memphis. We will be setting up headquarters here in Batesville and begin going door-to-door to interview each of you to let you help assist us with this. Those with special skills will be asked to help out where they are needed most, and if we need certain supplies to accomplish this task, we are under authority to confiscate what we need. We will be in control over the acquisition and distribution of all the food, fuel, utilities, weapons, and ammunition supplies in a five-county area. All medical, utility, EMS, and city and county law enforcement personnel will also be under our jurisdiction. I am to remind you that my orders are to maintain peace and not to fire unless fired upon, or unless my men are in immediate threat of danger. I see several people with weapons right now. We will let you leave in peace this time, but let this be a warning. If we see any other weapons in public from this point forward, they will be confiscated. If you cooperate, all of this will be done in a peaceful and orderly fashion."

Mark turned and looked at Grandpa and the other militia members and interested townspeople who had gathered around them to see their reaction. Several of the men were angered by his words, and it looked as if some of them were about to say something to the captain. Mark stopped them. "Look, this is not the time and place. We need to do this on our terms. If we do this here and now in front of all these people where innocent people could get hurt, it will not turn out well for us. We will be the bad guys who started trouble in town. Let's see if we can catch the others before they all get out of their cars and ask them to meet us at the farm."

Grandpa and the other militia members thought about what Mark said and agreed to back down for the time being. Some of the other militia groups were just arriving to town and had missed the announcement. Mark, Gunny, Grandpa, Sheriff Taylor, and some of the militia members went around to their cars as they were parking and introduced themselves. They explained what Captain Ellis said and that the meeting was being moved to the farm. After they were reasonably sure they had talked to most of the other militia members and interested parties, they all headed out of town to the farm.

When it looked as if most of the interested parties were gathered at the farm in front of the barn and the introductions were out of the way, Grandpa and Mark had Sheriff Taylor speak first. "As most of you know, I am Sheriff Taylor. Captain Ellis and his men showed up right before we were supposed to have our meeting. If you missed what he said, I'll summarize it for you. They are in charge, they can take what they want and who they want, and do what they want, all by executive order of the president. They will take away your guns if they see you in public with them. I think that is the gist of it. So we thought it best to meet down here where we could talk in the open. To be honest with you, I was put in charge of establishing law and order in the county by Colonel Henry, who is Captain Ellis's commanding officer. Dr. Mark Edwards here, we call him Doc, is the surgeon in charge of the hospital. The colonel warned us this was coming, which is why we called all of you to have this meeting. We sort of got things back in order around here without their help, and after talking to most of you, I see that you have done the same. Doc has a plan that I am going to let him tell you about."

Mark stepped out front and faced the group. "Thanks, Sheriff. We wanted to see how you all felt about this and to see if there was another way to do this, besides letting the army take over our farms and our counties. I have to be somewhat careful here and not sound like we are instigating a riot or something. But from what I gather, most of you feel the same way we do about this or you wouldn't be here." Several shouts of acclamation came from the crowd.

"I'm sure most of you, like us, were prepared for times such as these. Knowing our government was headed the wrong way and spending itself into oblivion, we had the feeling this day was almost sure to come. We have worked hard to take care of ourselves, our families, and close friends. Now they want to come take that away from us, in order to feed those who didn't work, or save, or prepare. They want to come take some of us away from our families to work, for God knows whom, and for God knows how long, without any promises. Now they are telling us that they might even come and take our guns away from us. We don't know about you, but we do not think that should happen." Again, a round of rumbles and shouts came from the group.

"As for us, if they show up at our farm, we are prepared to make a stand and say no to them. No more. We have given enough. We have decided that we are willing to fight to protect the rights guaranteed to us by the Constitution. We are willing to fight for our freedom from an overly oppressive government, a government that no longer works for the people and is run by the people but instead feels that the people work for them. The people of this country have to decide which side they are on. As for us, we choose liberty and the right to bear arms." Shouts of hurrahs, amen, and acclamation again sprang up from the crowd as they waved their guns in the air.

"Right now, we are not proposing an open armed conflict. There is a better way to start. What I am proposing is forceful passive resistance. I know that doesn't sound right, so let me explain. They are under orders to take what they want and whom they want. If anyone resists, they are under orders to enforce this by physical force. Which means they can drag you kicking and screaming from your house, but they are not to shoot unless they are shot at first or are under the threat of attack. They are used to everyone giving in because of fear. Everyone who is in their right mind is afraid of our army, so they are used to getting their way. If someone starts a fight with them, they usually finish it. But things are different now. They might be willing to overpower and forcefully take from a few, because it usually ends there and everyone else becomes afraid and follows along. But if the soldiers themselves, who have brothers and neighbors and family and friends among us, were put in a situation where they were forced to make a decision to either leave peacefully or start a fight that might end with people getting killed—not against a few, but against many—I think most would ultimately choose not to do that.

"It is my contention that, if given that choice, they will lay down their arms and walk away rather than fight their own people, who they know are right. However, we don't know that for sure. And if I am wrong and they choose to fight, then we must be willing to fight. But, we must do so with the numbers on our side. If we face them together we can take them on, but divided we will fall. If we agree to do this, then when the time comes, if some of us back down, the others will pay the price. So it has to be all or none. There is no going back after it starts.

"How this works is, when they show up at our farm or your farm or your neighbor's farm, we all show up to tell them no. We don't start a fight, but we let them know, under no uncertain terms, that if they try to take from any of us, they will have to take on all of us. This only works if we stick together. If this works here and now and we win, then it could work all across this county. If we lose, then it may be the beginning of the end of our country as we know it. So what do you say? Do we stand together and say no more, or do we go back to our homes and wait for them to come for our food, our farms, our guns, and us?'

A loud round of shouting and hoorays went around the crowd. One of the militia leaders was the first to step forward. "We're in all the way. We have been ready to fight for some time now. But we see how this just might work in our favor without having to start the fight."

Each of the sheriffs and militia leaders stepped forward, one after another, and pledged their allegiance to the group. One of the leaders explained that he had already discussed working together with some of the other counties. He suggested that each of them contact some of their other surrounding counties, to see if they would be willing to do the same for each other. In essence, they would form a statewide network of militias that could possibly turn into a nationwide network. Mark and all the other leaders agreed that was a good idea and then went to the kitchen to sit down and work out the logistics and details of mobilization for any encounters that might come up. After they worked out the details, they all shook hands, and each left for home.

Sheriff Taylor looked at Mark. "Looks like we are we have chosen sides. I just hope it is the right one."

Mark answered, "No matter what happens, it's the right side. I just hope we are the winning side."

CHAPTER 30
THE RIGHT
TO BEAR ARMS

The very next day, Captain Ellis sent for Sheriff Taylor and had him report to him at the newly established headquarters at the courthouse. Sheriff Taylor did not want to go, but he knew if he did not show up it would send the wrong message to the captain, and then he would know where he stood. So he went reluctantly. He entered the courthouse, which had armed guards posted at all the entrances and exits. He was asked to check his weapon at the door and then escorted into a room next to the law library and kept waiting on purpose by Captain Ellis, just to let him know who was boss. After about fifteen minutes, a soldier entered the room and escorted him into Captain Ellis's office and stood guard in the room.

Without looking up, Captain Ellis spoke to Sheriff Taylor, more as if he was giving an order than an offer of hospitality, "Sit down, Sheriff."

His tone was not lost on Sheriff Taylor, who sat without saying a word.

"I know Colonel Henry put you and that Mark Edwards fellow in charge until we got here. But we are here now. I must say, though, you guys did a decent job of getting things back in order around here. The utilities are back up, the hospital is up and running. It has made my job easier. A few little loose ends to tie up and we'll be in good shape. But enough of that, though. Let me get to the reason I called you in. You and Dr. Edwards are under my command now. You take orders from me. You don't do anything without my approval. You check with me before you make any big decisions. All schedules, requisitions, and personnel issues are to be cleared by this office. I don't want you to leave the county without my permission. And that militia you guys put together, they are no longer needed. They are to stand down. Is that clear?"

Sheriff Taylor was expecting some changes, but he did not expect to be dressed down like a new recruit. He started to tell the captain off but figured that would not get him anywhere but in trouble. So he bit his lip. "Yes, sir."

The captain looked away and waved his hand in his direction, indicating he was to leave. "That's all."

Sheriff Taylor was escorted out of the office by the soldier and was met by Lieutenant Stern in the hallway. He introduced himself and halfway apologized for the rude reception, then informed the sheriff that he and another lieutenant had been assigned to him round the clock. Everything would be reported to the captain and he would send orders through them to him. The look on the sheriff's face spoke volumes, and the lieutenant could see the frustration. "Sorry, I know you have been in charge around here, but the captain wanted me to keep an eye on you.

So until further orders, we will be on your six. I'll have one of my men working with you for a while until you are familiar with how we do things. Oh yeah, that starts this afternoon. That soldier there will get you squared away and fill you in. And one more thing. They are moving your office across the hall. The captain is putting us in your office for now."

Sheriff Taylor took a deep breath and realized that Mark Edwards was right all along. He was being conscripted into the service without even being given the chance to ask questions, object, or even given a description of his benefits, if there were any. This was conscription without question. It violated his rights as a citizen in so many ways, he couldn't even begin to list them all. He wondered if the colonel knew what was going on. That would be the first thing he would ask Mark the next time he saw him.

But little did the sheriff know, Mark was about to have his own encounter with the captain. And, like his meeting, it would not go well, either. Mark was in the middle of a case in the OR when he received word that the captain wanted him to report to his office. The OR nurse coordinator had the misfortune of bringing him the message in the OR. "Dr. Edwards, I just got a message that a Captain Ellis wants you to come to his office right away."

Mark laughed to himself then said, "Well, tell him he is going to have to wait until I finish up here. I'm a little busy right now saving this little fellow's life."

"Dr. Edwards, there are soldiers at the desk, with rifles. They said they were here to take you to the captain. What do you want me to tell them?"

"You can tell them whatever you want, but unless they want to come in here and drag me out of this case while this patient's belly is open, then I don't really give a shit what they want."

The nurse mumbled something under her breath as she spun and left the room in a hurry. After a minute or so, she came back into the room in an even worse mood. "They said they would wait."

"Well, that's going to be fun," Mark said with a smile under his mask. Jack, who was giving anesthesia at the head of the table, and Paul, who was assisting on the case, both smiled back, because they knew Dr. Edwards enjoyed being a smart ass.

After the case, Mark wrote his orders and talked to the family before he presented himself to the soldiers. He did not like the fact that his busy schedule was being interrupted by the captain without any regards to the needs of his patients and the rest of the OR team. They would have to wait for him to return before starting the next case. So Mark figured he would be as big a pain in the ass as he could be for the captain. "Well, guys, glad you could come give me a ride. That was awful thoughtful of you." Neither soldier smiled. They just led the way to their Humvee. Mark was escorted into the courthouse and told to wait in the little room, just like Sheriff Taylor. But instead of staying seated, he went for a stroll around the building talking to folks, as if he was just a visitor, until the two exasperated soldiers found him wandering around. "Sir, the captain is waiting. He does not like to be kept waiting."

"Well, I don't like to be dragged away from my patients, either, so I guess we're both unhappy right now," Mark said loud enough for anyone in earshot to hear. He was led into Captain Ellis's office and was told by one of the soldiers to sit in one of the chairs in front of the desk. Captain Ellis sat with his head down, trying to look busy. Mark didn't wait for him to speak. "Well, what's up, Captain? Long time no see."

Captain Ellis snapped his head up and stared at Mark. "Mr. Edwards, I didn't tell you—"

Mark interrupted him. "That's Dr. Edwards, but since we're old friends, just call me Mark or Doc?"

The interruption irritated the captain. "This is the army, and you will be addressed as mister and you will address me as Captain Ellis or sir. Do you understand?"

Mark thought for a moment. "Well, I understand what you are saying. I know you are in the army, but I didn't know I was."

That infuriated Captain Ellis. "Look, smart ass. You have been in the army since the colonel put you in charge of the hospital and Sheriff Taylor in charge of the county. So you are expected to act like it."

Mark was quiet for a minute and then stood up to leave. Captain Ellis snapped at him. "Where in the hell do you think you are going, mister? I didn't dismiss you. Sit down." The soldiers in the room stepped over in front of Mark and blocked the door with their rifles held across their chests in front of him.

Mark looked at the soldiers and smiled. "Well, that's no way to treat a guest." And then he went back to his chair and sat down. He looked at Captain Ellis and waited for the captain to say something else, but he was still fuming, so Mark spoke up. "You know, I don't remember signing up, and I don't remember being sworn in, and I don't recall the colonel telling me what rank, if any, I have. If I am in your army, can you fill me in on the details, Captain?"

Captain Ellis was furious. "You can argue whether you are officially in the army or not, but like it or not, you are under my command. So you will do what you are told and act accordingly."

Mark questioned him further. "How do you figure that? I haven't agreed to that, or signed anything, or seen anything in writing."

"You have been conscripted into service by orders of the president of the United States."

"The president? By what authority?"

"Look, mister. I don't have time for this shit. It was a presidential executive order. That's all you need to know, so deal with it. You will do what you are told, or you will be placed under arrest and treated as a prisoner, or maybe even an enemy combatant. How would that suit you?"

"You can't do that unless you run that by Colonel Henry, and I don't think he would like that."

Now Captain Ellis was steaming mad. "I can, and I will. It might be a few days before he hears about it, so don't expect him to save your ass right away. Until then, I will be sure to make it as uncomfortable for you as I can. You got that?"

"So if you do, does it mean I don't have to work seventy to eighty hours a week at the hospital, taking care of all those sick folks and doing about four to five cases a day? That enemy combatant stuff is starting to sound better by the minute. Then you would have to find another surgeon to bring down here and someone else to run the hospital. That might take a while. People are going to die in the meantime. That will look good on your record."

Mark knew where the conversation would go before he started it, but he did it just to piss Captain Ellis off, and he succeeded. It left Captain Ellis speechless for a minute. He knew he couldn't replace Dr. Edwards easily, and the colonel would hear about it sooner or later, and that would present a big problem. So Captain Ellis wasn't about to do that, unless Dr. Edwards refused to work at all. He was forced to compromise for the time being, even though it really irritated him to no end. "Listen, you have been a big pain in my ass ever since I met you in Southcrest. Just because you know the Colonel doesn't mean you are going to be treated any different than anyone else around here. So don't give me a good reason to haul your ass off in chains, because I might really enjoy that. Just do your job and stay out of my way. You got that?"

Mark smiled to himself. Mission accomplished. "Well, I guess for now I will go along, but don't expect me to like it. Now, if you don't mind, Captain Kirk, ask those nice young men there to step out of the way and have them beam me back to the hospital before someone dies while we're sitting here wasting time." The young guards both gave a little smirk. They couldn't tell if the captain had just been insulted or not, but Captain Ellis knew he had been, and he waved them both away without looking up or saying anything.

Captain Ellis did not like Dr. Edwards, mainly because he was a smart ass and wasn't afraid or intimidated easily. There usually was friction between two alpha males from different walks of life, especially if there was no bonding event such as boot camp, officer training school, residency, or such. Having come from two different backgrounds, they clashed from the moment they met. Captain Ellis was used to people doing what he told them to do. He had to put up only with those above him in rank, but they had been where he was and had proved themselves. He felt that Dr. Edwards had an overinflated ego and self-worth and thought he was above it all just because he was a surgeon.

Some of it was envy, because Captain Ellis knew he would never have been able to make the grades to be a surgeon, while Dr. Edwards could have been an officer if he had chosen that route, and probably would outrank him if he were in the army. It all just grated on his nerves. Because Dr. Edwards was a surgeon, he was much more valuable and harder to replace than a junior officer in the army, and that irritated him, too.

Dr. Edwards disliked Captain Ellis because the captain didn't like him and let it show. Mark wasn't egotistical, but he wasn't intimidated by other men of power. His self-worth wasn't based on an inflated ego. It was based only on what he could do for others. Only people who tried to get in the way of that by erecting barriers of red tape, unnecessary rules, and bureaucratic nonsense irritated him enough to incur his disfavor. He judged men by their character, not the color of their skin or the size of their bank accounts or the stripes on their sleeves.

Mark gave the captain a hard time only because he enjoyed messing with people like him. He did it because he could, and people like the captain needed to be put in their place, because they did judge men by the stripes on their sleeves. The captain treated everyone below him in rank as if they were beneath him in worth as a human being. He let his rank affect his attitude, and after the riots and the expanded role the army was given by the president, he had let it all go to his head even more. He treated everyone around him, civilians and all, as if they were under his command. It was not lost on his men, and it was not lost on Mark.

The same soldiers who had picked him up drove Mark back to the hospital. He let them know he was not mad at them for the inconvenience. They smiled and left Mark on the steps of the hospital. He stood outside for a few minutes to think about how things might have turned out if it wasn't for the colonel. And how things might turn out if they were forced to resist the army and lost. Or how he might be imprisoned or sent off to work somewhere away from his family if he protested too much in the meantime. That would all have to wait for another day and time. For the time being, he had surgery to do and sick folks to take care of.

Things went on routinely for the next few days, but word came down from the generals that the president and the administration were putting more pressure on them to provide more food and supplies for the ever-increasing number of refugees returning to the cities. Their numbers had grown exponentially as people ran out of food and options and met more and more resistance in the rural counties. It was the path of least resistance, and as before, they had turned to the government for their sustenance, and, as usual, the government turned to those with to provide for those without. Those with had it because they worked and saved and planned ahead. Those without didn't, because they didn't work, save, or prepare.

Senator Sage and the other conservatives in Congress protested that the actions of the president and the party in power were the same thing that caused the breakdown of the economy and bankrupted the country; same song, second verse. The same problems were being dealt with in the same way, but just with a different angle. The politicians in power were keeping the half who were a slight majority suppressed and content by feeding them and taking care of them on the backs of the other half, who were a slight minority and paid all the taxes and voted for the opposition party. It had gone on too long. It would have to end, or everyone would end up taking until there was no one left to take from.

They argued, as they had before, that the problem with socialism is, was, and always will be that sooner or later the government runs out of other people's money to spend. If it continued to take from those who work and produce, before long they stop producing, and then there is no one left to get it from. It wasn't that those in power didn't get it. They just didn't care. It was where they derived their power. Taking from those who had to give to those who did not was an easy sell, especially when there was plenty to go around. But after decades of taking and giving, the gravy train ran out of tracks and diesel and conductors. They knew it would all come crashing down someday. They just hoped it would be later rather than sooner. But there was no plan B. All they had was plan A. After it failed, they just put a new saddle on that old nag and kept riding it as long as they could.

With the collapse of the economy, they could no longer collect enough tax money to buy food and supplies to feed the masses, so they turned to the only other option: take what they needed directly from those who had. Demanding higher and higher tax rates from the working classes, using the threat of jail and piling up penalties, was enough to keep most in line before the collapse. But, showing up on their property and hauling off the very food and private property they worked hard for and depended on to provide for their families was another thing. There was no way to sugarcoat it or dress it up as paying their fair share or helping the less fortunate. It was what it was. Taking from one group of people to give to another, by force, and it made a lot of people mad. Real mad. Fighting mad. And fight they did.

All across America, whenever the army came to confiscate property or food from private citizens and farms, it was met with resistance. Families, neighbors, friends, and militias, from a dozen to several hundred, put up a fight. Occasionally, it came to blows, and often it came to knocking down doors and gates. The reports on the news were mostly the same. When the US Army showed up, people who refused to cooperate were physically restrained and hauled away. Those who fought were overpowered, and those who shot first died. A few reports of small groups of army soldiers being ambushed or losing a firefight to larger groups and militias trickled in, but most of those stories were suppressed by the administration.

When the stories were reported by the major news outlets, those involved were depicted as homegrown terrorists, enemy combatants, unpatriotic right-wing wackos, white supremacists, skinheads, neo-Nazis, and the like. They were never called citizen militias or described as patriots resisting an oppressive government that was treading on the constitutional rights of its own citizens. And under the threat of their broadcasting license being revoked and their plug being pulled, they were told not to report the large-scale defections of soldiers all across the nation, soldiers who, when faced with the decision, threw down their weapons and refused to shoot at their own countrymen.

Those reports came only over the ham radios, because the sheer number of radio operators made it impossible for the government to find and stop all of them. Many were threatened, but most did not comply, for they felt an obligation to report the truth. It was in their nature. As in the past in times of war and natural disasters, the radio operators all across the nation were the last lifelines of communication. So the truth was told. Not only soldiers but also commissioned officers resigned rather than give orders for their men to kick in the doors of law-abiding citizens. Even a few high-ranking generals resigned after the presidential orders were handed down instructing them to take food and fuel without compensation from anyone who had significant supplies. The orders were specific: Ask first. If they refuse, then use force as needed, but shoot only if shot at.

That is what Mark and Grandpa and Gunny knew, because that is what the colonel told them. That was what they were depending on. But like many who resisted, they would draw the line in the sand. Their answer would be the same as the others who had resisted. You can tax us, you can red tape us, you can suppress us only so far, but when you come to take the food out of the mouths of our families or the guns out of our hands, there will be a fight. All the militia members were in agreement with that. They would not only stand up for themselves, but they would try to show up wherever they were needed to help others resist.

Mark and Gunny had a conversation with the colonel in which they discussed the fact that conscription had been used on several occasions in the history of the United States. It was first used in the Civil War by both the North and South, but it was highly unpopular and not used much. And again in World War I, with the Selective Service Act of 1917, which was also highly unpopular but upheld by the Supreme Court. It was also used in World War II and the Vietnam War. It was last used in 1972 and was ended by President Nixon and Congress in 1984. No one had been prosecuted for not signing up with Selective Service since 1986. But Congress would now have to pass it as a new law for it to be enforced as law again. Otherwise, it was another presidential executive order not passed by Congress and in violation of the Constitution. Therefore, it was also a point of contention with the militias.

So most of the militias across the country were unanimous on those issues. Those were the points on which they stood together in opposition to the government and the army, if it tried to enforce the policies. That was the line in the sand. If the loss of private property were to be forced on the people, then the country would by definition become a fascist state and no longer a democracy where the people elect representatives who pass the laws that they live by.

CHAPTER 31
THE LAST STAND

The very next morning, a platoon of soldiers rolled up to the gate at the farm in Humvees and an armored personnel carrier. The guards radioed up to the house that a Lieutenant Stern was demanding entry to the farm to take inventory of their supplies and equipment. In all, there were about thirty soldiers with Lieutenant Stern. The bell was rung and the farm folks and militia members all took their posts. There were over sixty armed men and women positioned and ready to defend the farm. Gunny decided to ride down to the gate in one of the Jeeps with Skinny and Hank.

"May I help you, Lieutenant?"

"Are you the owner, sir?"

"Well, not exactly. That would be Mr. Brown. He is still having his morning coffee. He asked me to see what you guys wanted."

"We are taking inventory of all the food and fuel supplies in the county. You're next on the list. So we need you to open this gate and let us do our job."

"Mr. Brown said he wasn't expecting any company this morning. Do you have an appointment?" A few giggles and snickers were heard from a few of the soldiers and the farm guards.

Lieutenant Stern turned and scowled at his men to quiet them down. "Sir, I don't need an appointment, we are here by order of the president to confiscate—" The lieutenant cut himself off. "To take an inventory of all the supplies of food and fuel in the county. All farms are on the list, and you are next."

"The president doesn't own this farm. Do you have a court order signed by a judge?"

"Look, mister, I don't know who you think you are, but the president is the commander in chief, and she ordered us to do this. So if you don't comply, we are authorized to use force if necessary."

"Sir, I am a retired marine gunnery sergeant, and if the president herself told me to go to someone's private farm and forcefully enter and take their personal property, I would personally tell her to kiss my ass right there on the spot. The government does not have the right to do that. That goes against the Constitution, and we have the right to defend ourselves against an oppressive government. So I guess I'm refusing to cooperate."

"Well then, I guess you leave me no choice but to use force. I'm going to give you one more chance to step aside and open the gate, or I'm going to order my men to break down the gate and enter anyway."

Gunny looked young Lieutenant Stern square in the eyes and spoke loud enough for the troops to hear. "Mister, I've served my country proudly for over thirty years. I fought for her and saw my friends die on the battlefield for her. And, I'm still willing to fight for her. If you and your men cross that gate, you will have a fight on your hands, that I can promise you."

"What, you three men and these boys here are going to stop us?"

"Yes, sir, and those folks up there on the hill, as well." Gunny turned and waved to the militia entrenched on the hill, and on his signal, they all stood and waved back.

The lieutenant looked the situation over and knew he was outnumbered, but he wasn't sure if he was outgunned. "Well, I can see you have a few men up there, but we are heavily armed and combat trained. Do you really think you could stop us?"

Gunny didn't even break a sweat. "I have been in more battles and firefights than you and all your men together, and defended weaker positions with fewer men against more firepower than you have. We aren't sitting up there with .22s and shotguns, mister. We have the same weapons and ammo as you, but more of it, and twice as many men. There are ex-military men up there, Navy SEALs, marines, army snipers with at least a half dozen scopes on you right now. They have been told not to shoot first, but if you start something, you'll be the first to go and your machine gunners next. So if you want to, come on in. We're ready and able."

Some of the soldiers looked around at each other, and then back at the hill with all the defenders dug into trenches with sandbags and at least one .50-caliber machine gun pointed at them, and they knew it would not go well for them if they tried. One of the more experienced sergeants with battle experience walked up to Lieutenant Stern and whispered something in his ear. Gunny could see the sweat beading up on the lieutenant's forehead and his breathing rate increase, letting him know the lieutenant was nervous.

Gunny spoke up again before the lieutenant said anything. "We are all Americans here. We all salute the same flag and have sworn to uphold the Constitution. All we are doing here is defending our rights as free citizens to protect our private property, and the right to bear arms as afforded to us by the Bill of

Rights. Even if the Congress of the United States passes a law that says you can enter and take our property without just cause or a warrant, we will still not step aside and give up our constitutional rights as free citizens. We will fight to defend those rights against any who would deny them, including you. If your men want to fight against their own people, those who fought beside them not long ago, then so be it. But you are the ones choosing to start the fight. We will not shoot first, but we will not be taken by force on our own private property by the army of our own government fighting against its own people."

The faces of the soldiers changed at that moment. They began to look down at the ground and shuffle their feet and lower the tips of their rifles. The lieutenant saw the mood of the troops change, and he took the advice of his sergeant and called off his men. "The captain will hear about this, and we will be back. I can promise you this. It won't go so well for you next time." The lieutenant ordered his men to mount up, and then they headed on down the road.

Gunny looked at his men and smiled. "Well, we may have won round one, but they will be back, and I bet Captain Ellis won't be too happy when he hears about this."

Hank added, "Yeah, and I'll bet they will come back with more than one platoon and a little more firepower."

Gunny answered, "Well, thank goodness they didn't bring more with them this time, or I'm sure they would have tried to take us. Sooner or later, they will bring the heat down with whatever it takes. Those guys don't like to lose. They can always bring in bigger guns than we have. We can only hold off here so long before they run us out."

Gunny told the guards, "Good job. Keep us posted." Then he loaded up and went back to the house to fill in Grandpa and the others.

Mark was already at the hospital in the middle of his first case when all that went down. He was not aware of what had occurred when the OR nurse coordinator came into the room and announced that Captain Ellis wanted him in his office again. When he finished and went to write orders in the recovery room, the soldiers were waiting for him. Mark knew whatever it was, it wasn't good. He walked up to them, ready to go. "Guys, we have to stop meeting like this. People are going to talk." He thought he saw the hint of a smile on one of the soldiers as they led him to their Humvee.

When they arrived to the courthouse, Captain Ellis was standing in the doorway of his office waiting on them, which led Mark to believe something big was going on. The look on his face let him know the captain wasn't happy about something. Mark started with his usual jabbing comments. "Well, getting sent to the principal's office twice in one week makes me feel like I'm back in school again."

Captain Ellis didn't say a word. The soldiers escorted Mark to one of the chairs and motioned for him to sit down and then took their places at the door. Then Captain Ellis did something that actually bothered Mark. He sent the soldiers out of the room. Mark knew that wasn't a good sign. "My men visited your farm this morning. They were turned away by some man they called Gunny and what looked like about fifty armed men. Lieutenant Stern made the mistake of falling back instead of calling for reinforcements. He won't ever do that again. I want you to know that we are coming back and will do whatever it takes to do our job. Your guys need to stand down, and I would further advise that you disarm and disband if you know what's good for you. We will not be intimidated, and we will do whatever it takes to carry out our orders. Consider this a warning. The next time, there will not be a warning."

Mark sat quietly for a moment and watched Captain Ellis take a deep breath and smile to himself, obviously enjoying having the upper hand. Mark couldn't decide whether to say something and possibly divulge too much, or to say nothing and act defeated. Mark decided to feel him out and see what other cards he had. "Well, I hope the colonel approves of your plan. You know his wife is staying at the farm with us. I'm not sure he would want something unfortunate to happen to her."

His probe did its job. "I knew you would try to hide behind the skirt of the colonel's wife," Captain Ellis fired off. "You civilians are all alike, hiding behind someone else for protection. You depend on us to protect you, and then when we show up in your county, you act like you don't want us here. Just because you guys ran off a bunch of amateur thugs, you think you are ready to take on us. We are the professionals here. You are out of your area of expertise, Doc."

That was not enough information. Mark could read his face and body language. The captain knew more but was holding back. Mark decided to throw one high and inside to loosen him up. "Well, if you get yourself shot up, guess who is going to be looking down at you on the gurney, Captain? Maybe you should be a little nicer to me." Mark smiled, knowing he one-upped him and inserted a veiled threat at the same time.

Captain Ellis's face turned red and the veins popped out on his forehead. Mark knew he had hit the right button. "If anyone is going to be laying on a gurney, it's going to be you."

Mark had him going but needed more. "Well, the colonel will not like that. Think I'll give him a call."

That did it. Captain Ellis exploded. "I knew you would pull that shit on me. You have enough food and fuel and supplies out there to feed half the people of this town, so I've already sent it up the chain to General Franks. The colonel won't stop us. If he does, it will get him in trouble with the brass. If he is worried about his wife, he has time to get her out of there by tomorrow, so go ahead and call him, see what good that will do you." Captain Ellis smiled widely, thinking he just shut Mark up once and for all.

Mark pretended to be on the ropes and at a loss for words, letting the captain think he had won the battle. Mark shook his head in pretend disgust, and cursed under his breath loud enough for him to hear. "Damn it! I'd kick your ass if I could." He remained quiet to allow the captain to soak in the moment.

"What did you say? You would kick my ass? Mister, I wish you would try. Right now! I'll let you take the first swing, no witnesses. If you win, I'll tell them I fell and hit my head on the desk. I hope you are there tomorrow and try to stop me. You'll be the first one I take down." Captain Ellis waited for Mark to respond, but he said nothing. "What? No smart-ass comment? I didn't think so. All talk. You are good at running your mouth, but when it comes to backing it up, you go all soft like the other civilians. That's why the country needs men like me. When the talking is done, we go in and get the job done. You doctors are all alike, hiding back behind the lines in the safety of the hospital, hanging out with the women waiting for the real men to bring you the wounded from the battlefields."

The captain waited a moment before finishing, just to watch Mark squirm a little longer. "We are coming in, whether you like it or not. We wouldn't want anything to happen to that pretty little wife or little boys of yours, now, would we? If you're smart, you'll tell your men to stand down and disarm. Now, get back to your comfy little job in the air-conditioning with the women, and don't get in my way again, or all of you will go down, and what's left of you will go to prison."

The captain didn't know it, but he had done exactly what Mark expected him to do. Now Mark knew his intentions. He was coming out looking for a fight. There would be no backing down on his part. Mark knew they had to be ready for them from the get-go. Mark rode back to the hospital without saying a word and tried to look as dejected as possible just to complete the whipped dog act, knowing the captain would ask the soldiers what he said and did on the way back.

As soon as Mark returned to the hospital, he sent Paul to the farm with a message for them to get on the radio and contact the other militia members from the surrounding counties and let them know what was going down at the farm in the morning. He wanted to let them know it was do or die, now or never. The captain would be there with all his men ready to charge up the hill. He asked for their help. It might be their last stand.

He finished up at the hospital around suppertime and hurried back to the farm to discuss things with the others. After supper, the members of the roundtable met. Everyone at the table didn't waver in his convictions. They would make a stand, whether the others showed up or not. They were not going to back down. They were not going to turn over their weapons, and they were not going to give up the farm. Hank and Skinny reported on their communication with the other militia members. The only ones they were sure about were the Huffmans, who said they would all be there at 0500. The Cliftons said they would try to be there but didn't know how many would come. Word was sent out to the other counties, but so far no word came back about whether they could help or not.

Even if others did show up, there would not be time for much planning or strategy. They would have to take the captain on with whom they had and what they had. Mark felt obligated to let the others know before it started that it was likely to end in a firefight, and they had to decide if they wanted to stay and fight or go home and accept that things would change forever. If they backed down, they would end up having to turn in their weapons, and then there would be no second chances. If they were going to make a stand, it would have to be at the farm.

Mark and the others didn't know who, if any, would show up, how many would come, or if they would be there in time. All they could do was be ready and wait. It was decided that all the women who were not going to carry a rifle into battle and the small children would leave the farm early in the morning and stay across the street at the Thompsons' house until it was over. It would make things easier for the militia to know they were not in the line of fire.

There were a lot of tears and prayers that night. Mark and Lisa talked, and he let her know how it might end. She was prepared for the worst. He confessed his love for her, and she for him, and they both cried in each other's arms. Mark went quietly to the boys' room to see them. It reminded him of the night not so long ago when this all first started. Mark kissed Daniel and Jeffrey on the forehead while they slept and fought back the tears as he looked at them for possibly the last time. Steve was awake as before and watched his dad fight back the tears. He had never seen his dad cry before. Mark came over and sat on his bed. "Son, I want you to go with your mother and your brothers tomorrow."

Steve would have none of that. "No, Dad. I want to fight beside you. I'm not a kid anymore. I can shoot as good as any of them."

Mark knew that but had his reasons. "I know, son. That's why I want you to go with them. If something happens to me, who is going to take care of them?" That caught Steve off guard. He couldn't argue with that. They would need him to help look after them. Mark looked at him and tried not to cry, but they both broke down and held each other for a long time. Mark went to the kitchen and sat at the table and bowed his head and prayed for answers, but none seemed to come. He went back to bed but couldn't sleep, so he stared at the ceiling for hours, trying to figure out the best way to handle the situation. But none of the scenarios he worked out in his mind seemed to provide a better way out.

Ideas came and went. They could run off, but they had nowhere to go, and they would become refugees themselves. Sooner or later, they would have to make a stand somewhere, sometime; better the farm than anywhere else. They could accept the demands of Captain Ellis and turn over whatever he wanted, but they would almost certainly have to turn in their weapons, which would leave them helpless against thugs and the Takers, once the army moved on down the road to the next county. Then there was the high probability that, before all was said and done, the government would need more food than it presently had. With the millions of mouths to feed, it might even take control of the farm from them and force them to work to help feed the masses in the cities. That would be unacceptable to all of them.

Before he knew it, the sun was slowly peeking over the horizon, and the rooster began to crow. Ready or not, it was time to get up and face the day. Mark intentionally left his surgery schedule open at the hospital. He had more pressing matters to deal with that morning. He would either be a little late, or in prison, or dead. The nurses and other doctors knew what was going down, and ultimately the whole hospital and every patient talked about it, and soon the whole town knew.

In the kitchen, Grandma and Grandpa Brown were already making some breakfast and drinking coffee. Gunny and the rest came in soon after. They made last-minute plans, and all agreed one last time it was do or die. They would not back down, no matter what. Before long, the Huffman clan showed up, as promised, with about thirty heavily armed men, and they were welcomed to the barnyard and offered coffee and toast. A few accepted, but most were too nervous to eat. After all the farm militia members were ready, they all took their places in the trenches and vantage points around the perimeter of the farm and waited with their radios and rifles in hand. No one knew when Captain Ellis and his soldiers would arrive, so they immediately sent the women and children to the Thompsons' for safety until it was over.

Gunny came up to Mark and suggested that they send a scouting party down the road to watch for the soldiers. At least an advanced warning might help. Mark agreed and Gunny sent a few of his best men down the road with a radio to hide and wait. An hour passed, but nothing happened. Another hour came and went and still no word. Mark and Gunny were getting anxious. The captain was so hell-bent on taking the farm, it didn't make sense that he would wait so long to get it done. Something was up. Another hour passed and then the radio crackled from the scouts down the road.

"They have a damn tank. An M1 Abrams. I repeat, they have a tank." Now it made sense why it took so long for them to come. They were waiting for the tank to arrive.

Marked looked at Gunny. "Gunny, do you still have the hand-held grenade launcher? We may need it."

Gunny shook his head. "I'll get it, but it may not stop a tank. We might get lucky and blow a track out and disable it, but it can still blow us out of the water from the end of the drive."

"We might need to do that, but first we are going to blow the bridge on the main road. That will at least slow them down and buy some time. Who knows, with any luck the tank might not get it across the ditch. It's pretty steep and narrow. Not good for a tank. We'll have to hurry. They'll be at the bridge in a few minutes."

"Damn, I wish I had thought of that." Gunny grabbed the launcher, a few grenades, and a few men and jumped in the Jeep with the .50-caliber machine gun in the back and tore down the drive as fast as he could go. The gate had already been opened for them, so he didn't have to slow down as he turned onto the road and headed for the bridge. After a few minutes, two loud explosions were heard about thirty seconds apart, and then all went silent again. A few minutes later, the Jeep was racing back up the drive, leaving a cloud of dust as it came up the hill. Gunny jumped out smiling. "That was fun. It's been a while since I got to do that. They won't be crossing that bridge. I left the launcher with the scouts, just in case. They are not far off. We will find out if the tank can make it soon enough."

Captain Ellis and his men heard the explosion but didn't really know how far off it was because of all the road noise from the Abrams tank, armored personnel carriers, and Humvees. When he came up on the blown bridge, which was still smoldering and had a section blown right out of the middle of it, he cursed loud and long. He knew who was responsible for that. He got the coordinates and determined that it was only two miles from the farm on foot, but to go around would take several hours. He was ready to get it done and knew if they had enough sense to blow one bridge they would probably blow the others from the east. For a minute, he thought that he might have underestimated Dr. Edwards and his militia. But he had a whole company with four platoons of soldiers—right at one hundred and fifty men in all—more than enough to take on the fifty or so at the farm. It just made him more determined to see Dr. Edwards dead or in prison. He ordered his lieutenants to leave the tank and other vehicles where they were and walk the rest of the way on foot. He ordered them to leave a squad to guard the vehicles so they could take them back to town when the job was finished. Lieutenant Stern started to ask if it was a good idea to try to take a fortified hill on foot without the tank, but he stopped himself and let it go. He could see Captain Ellis was not in the mood for suggestions.

It took about fifteen minutes for the company to dismount, gear up, and head down the road. The militia scouts radioed back to Gunny the position and numbers of the army company, which they accurately estimated to be about one hundred and forty soldiers marching toward the farm and about ten staying with the vehicles. Gunny told them to stay put and stand by and be ready to take out the squad and capture the tank, the APCs, and .50-cal machine gun. Two of the militia scouts were the same snipers who took out Big Al and his men. They knew how to operate the tank, and the rest could handle the .50 cal and APCs, which might come in handy. At least they would make a good bluff.

The odds were starting to look a little better, and Mark was starting to see other options open up to him. He turned to Gunny and Grandpa and the others. "When they get to the gate, let me go down alone and talk to the captain. We have some unfinished business, and I need to see if we can come to an understanding."

Mark smiled real big and winked at Grandpa and Gunny and hoped they would go along. "If this works, we might be able to turn this around without firing a shot. If not, do what you gotta do. Tell the snipers, if the shooting starts to take the tank and .50 cal, if they can, and drive them down the dirt road to the south of the main road, along the creek to the gap in the fence. That pasture road leads all the way up to the back of this farm. If they hurry, they can run the fences and come in from the southwest, hopefully in time to join the battle and maybe turn the tide in our favor. Even if we can't take all of them out, we can take out a lot of them."

Gunny was game. "Well, I certainly wouldn't want to get in the way of some male bonding. And if you two come to an understanding, what then?"

"I haven't got that far yet. I'm still working on our male bonding right now."

Gunny smiled. But Grandpa and the others weren't following what was going on. Grandpa had to ask. "What's he up to?"

Gunny grinned and said, "I think he is going to try and beat some sense into the captain."

"What makes him think the captain will fight him, one-on-one, when he has all those men with him?"

'I don't have a clue, but Doc seems to think he will. Maybe he is trying to buy some time. I don't know.

Grandpa couldn't figure out what Mark was thinking. "What makes Mark think he can beat the captain in a fight? He is a trained soldier, and Mark is just a doctor. That makes no sense."

Gunny had more faith in Mark than the others. He knew that Mark was the one in a hundred who was a warrior. "I'm not exactly sure, but either way, I think it's going to be a good story to tell the grandkids someday."

The radio crackled from down at the gate. "They're here. Captain Ellis is demanding we open the gate and let them in. What should we tell them?"

Mark answered. "Tell them I'll be right down."

Mark took off his pistol and rifle and gave them to Gunny. "Wait for me here. If I don't come back, do what you have to do."

"The hell you are. I'm going with you. I wouldn't miss this for the world." Gunny turned to Hank. "You know what needs to be done."

Hank shook his head. "Yes, sir."

Grandpa stepped up too. "You're not leaving me out of this."

The three of them walked down to the gate. Mark was unarmed. Everyone watched in anticipation, not knowing what was going on. When they got to the gate, Mark stepped up to the gate and faced the captain. "Captain," Mark said, staring him down just to get his blood pumping.

"Well, mister, what is it going to be?" the captain demanded.

"I thought about what you said yesterday, and I've decided not to take your advice. As a matter of fact, I never had any intention of taking your advice. I just want to know one thing. When you offered to let me take the first swing, was that just a bluff, or were you serious?"

That made Captain Ellis mad. "Bluffing? Are you serious? You were scared then, and I'm sure you're scared now. What are you going to do, call me out and let your whole family see you get your ass kicked? That would be quite embarrassing for you, don't you think?"

Mark had him going. "Yes, I was scared. Afraid I would kick your ass all over your office and get arrested for assaulting an officer."

"Why, you little spoiled-ass doctor, you think you can kick my ass? That's a joke. I don't have time to fool with you right now.

We are here to do a job, so open this gate before we open it for you."

He didn't take the bait as Mark hoped he would. He would have to push a few more buttons. "I wouldn't do that if I were you."

"What? Are you and your fifty men going to stop us? I have a whole company of men ready to take this place by force, if needed."

"Slow down, Captain. You have about one hundred and forty men with you. Ten are back at the tank and trucks. And we have over eighty heavily armed men dug in on that hill, with a .50-cal machine gun pointed at you. Now, the odds don't seem so bad to me at this point. Besides, I know that you are under orders not to fire until fired upon. We're not going to shoot first or budge. I guess we can stand here and stare at each other all day."

The captain was ready to climb the gate and choke the life out of Dr. Edwards. "You piece of shit. If you don't let us come in right now, we will just go back and get the tank and roll it up your drive and run over anyone who gets in the way. Is that the way you want it?"

"The tank and trucks won't be there when you get there. Some of our men are ready to take them right now. So we might as well settle this right here, right now."

That was all it took to get Captain Ellis fighting mad. "You think you are so smart. I ought to come across that fence and knock some sense into you before you get everyone on that farm killed."

Mark went over to the gate and opened it and stepped back. "I thought you would never ask. If you want to come in here so bad, why don't you be the first, Captain, and I'll personally knock you back out of the gate." Mark looked him straight in the eyes to let

440

him know he was serious. "Your men can wait outside the gate. Just you and me, Captain."

Captain Ellis was put on the spot with no honorable way out. He was being called out by a smart-mouthed civilian doctor right in front of his men. If he backed down, he would appear to be scared. He wasn't about to let Dr. Edwards get the best of him in front of his men. "You all heard him threaten me, didn't you?" Several nods and yes-sirs came from his men.

Mark stood and waited, hoping he would step through the gate. The reason for the confrontation was to draw Captain Ellis into a fight with him, one-on-one. He was hoping if he could defeat him, it would discredit him just enough in the eyes of his men so that they might stop and think about what they were doing and hopefully change their minds about following him. It was a long shot but worth the risk. If he didn't do something outrageous, chances were there would be a battle and many would die. He had to try to change the mood of the moment.

Captain Ellis saw the opportunity to kick Dr. Edward's ass in front of all his men and the militia. If he beat Dr. Edwards down, maybe the militia would finally understand they could not win against his army. He took off his gun belt and handed it to Lieutenant Stern. "When I finish kicking his ass, take the farm."

Like most combatants who start off face-to-face, they slowly circled each other looking for any weakness or fear, but both men were determined to beat the other. Captain Ellis was a trained officer with combat experience and practiced in combat fighting skills. Mark was a physician, trained in the art of healing, but he was a natural-born fighter. Captain Ellis was in good shape but not like he used to be, because for the past year or so he had spent more time behind a desk than out in the field. Mark was trained in Krav Maga and was in decent shape and had been working hard on the farm. He was leaner than usual, which made him quicker. They were both about the same age and size.

Captain Ellis made the first move with a right face punch, but Mark easily stepped away and brushed off his arm with a left block. Captain Ellis looked surprised, wondering where he had learned that. The captain and Mark both tested each other with a few punches, but neither connected. Then, Captain Ellis went at Mark with several punches and jabs, but Mark kept blocking and sidestepping most of them. Only one or two grazed him. Everyone on both sides of the fence was enthralled. It looked as if it was going to be a good fight after all.

The soldiers began to stand against the fence and cheer on the captain. He was their warrior in the fight, and they were sure he would win, so naturally they wanted to be for the winner. Captain Ellis was starting to sweat heavily and began worrying that he was looking bad for not finishing Mark off quicker, so he went for a combination left jab and a right cross, but again Mark stepped aside and blocked both punches. The captain was really curious how a soft civilian doctor knew how to fight like that. He was through playing. He went for the takedown by faking a punch to the face and going for Mark's left knee with a side kick, but Mark blocked it by stepping into it, and then landed a hard right fist to the captain's lower ribs which sent him back a few steps.

Captain Ellis was startled more than hurt, and he was thinking that maybe he misjudged his enemy. He decided to end it by taking him down, so he went for Mark's legs and wrestled him to the ground. But before he could get on top, Mark rolled hard to the side and threw him off with a hip thrust and rolled back onto his feet, leaving the captain lying on the ground. Mark let him get up, to the dismay of the soldiers. Most would have kicked him while he was down. At that point, the farm militia members were standing around watching, as well. After another minute or two, they began to walk down the hill to get a closer look. Curiosity and a good fight will draw a crowd every time.

Soon, both men were tired from the blows and kicks and wrestling on the ground for several minutes, and they were both out of breath, dirty, and sweating. Both landed a few good blows, and blood was coming from cuts on their lips and above their eyes. They continued to battle on for several minutes, like two bulls going at in a pasture. They tore up the ground and each other until they both could barely stand.

As they fought, many of the soldiers began to feel differently about Dr. Edwards. He was no spoiled civilian doctor. He was a warrior like them, ready, willing, and able to fight with the best of them. A few of them couldn't help but start cheering him on, careful not to be too outspoken, not wanting to suffer the wrath of Captain Ellis if he lost. But many of the men, especially Lieutenant Stern, didn't like Captain Ellis. He was a prick of the first order. Seeing him get his ass kicked was a joy to behold for many of them.

Captain Ellis made one last charge at Mark with what little energy he had left, and they both went down to the ground. They wrestled in the dirt with blood and sweat dripping from both. Finally, Mark got on top and face punched the captain until he gave up. But after Mark let him get up, Captain Ellis sucker punched him while his back was turned. That made almost everyone in the crowd turn on the captain. Boos and hisses came from both sides. No one likes a dirty fighter. Mark took a fist on the right side of his head and fell to the ground. Captain Ellis climbed on top and started hitting him with what little energy he had left. Grandpa started to jump in, but Gunny stopped him and shook his head. This was Mark's fight. Win or lose, it's what he wanted.

When the captain could barely raise his fists to hit again, Mark thrust both hips in the air and rolled the captain off him and fought his way on top again. He hit the captain square in the face a couple of times until he stopped fighting back. Mark got off, but this time he did not turn his back on him. Instead, he stood over him with his fists clenched and looked down at the captain until he waved his hands in surrender. The crowd cheered on both sides of the fence, to the captain's dismay. The fight was over.

CHAPTER 32
TAKING
BACK THE COUNTRY

Mark stood weary, bloody, and dirty from head to toe and looked around at the cheering crowd. He couldn't tell if the soldiers were cheering for him or just cheering because they just saw a good fight. He caught his breath and gained enough strength to stand before all of them and speak. "Sorry about that. The captain and I just needed to get a few things off our chest." The crowd roared with laughter. Mark waited a minute then continued. "Look, we are not here to start a fight with you. We are trying to take care of our families, just like you. We are not terrorists or enemy combatants. We are American citizens who believe in the Constitution of the United States of America. This does not have to do with party affiliation or politics. This isn't just over personal property rights. This is about the defense of the Second Amendment and the right to bear arms, the Fourth Amendment against unnecessary search and seizure, and the Tenth Amendment, which limits the power of the government to those delegated to do it by the Constitution. And the fact that the presidential executive orders violate Article 1, Section 1, in which all legislative powers are vested in the Congress, which are the senators and representatives, who did not pass these as laws. John Adams wrote, 'The moment the idea is admitted into a society that property is not as sacred as the laws of God, anarchy and tyranny commence. Property must be secured or liberty cannot exist.' So the presidential executive orders to take private property away from its citizens, which were not approved by Congress and therefore not the law of the land, are merely edicts passed down by one elected leader and enforceable only by the heavy hand of the military against its own people. That is the reason the Founding Fathers spoke of an armed citizenry that could prevent the government from oppressing its own people. It was the reason why James Madison proposed that the Second Amendment be added to Constitution, as part of the Bill of Rights. He said, 'A well regulated militia being necessary to the security of a free state, the right of the People to keep and bear arms shall not be infringed.' It wasn't an afterthought. It was for the direct purpose of preventing the federal government from using the military to take away the rights of its citizens. Having an armed populace that heavily outnumbered the standing army was the only deterrent to that. It was then, and remains now, the only and last recourse of the people. Those were the reasons the Founding Fathers added the Bill of Rights to the Constitution. Those were the reasons the militia back then stood up to its own government and army. That is why they were well armed. That is why they joined together in numbers sufficient to resist. That is why they fought to protect the rights of the people. If those rights were to fall, the United States of America would be no more, and the government of the people, by the people, and for the people would perish from this earth. That is why we believe in the right to bear arms—not against you but against an oppressive government, and would fight and die to defend that right, if needed."

The crowd was dead silent on both sides of the fence, with a few tears on the faces of many. Mark was unsure if they heard him, unsure if they understood him, unsure if they cared. After a moment, the soldiers began talking among themselves. A few arguments broke out here and there, but overall the mood changed significantly. Most of the soldiers met the militia across the fence all along the road, shook hands, and affirmed their allegiance to the same flag and the same Constitution. But the mood didn't last long before the captain gained his composure. "That was a good speech, Dr. Edwards. You need to run for office. But that doesn't change the fact that we have orders and a job to do. Now, you men get back in line and prepare to take this farm. That's an order."

Many of the soldiers were afraid of the captain and did what he said, but Lieutenant Stern stood up to him. "Sir, he's right. We don't have the right to take property away from them or anyone else. We don't have to do this. We can just move on and deal with this another way." Many of the men backed him up and agreed openly that they were against it.

Captain Ellis shouted Lieutenant Stern down and ordered his men to take the farm or face a court-martial. Most of the men slowly and reluctantly began to get back in line out of fear. Just then, a call came over their radio. "Echo One, Echo One, this is Red Dog. Come in."

The radioman answered. "This is Echo One, go ahead."

"Sir, you're not going to believe this, but there is a large group of citizens and soldiers stopped on the road behind us. They are getting out of their vehicles. They are armed and heading this way. Please advise."

Captain Ellis heard the report. "Tell them to find out what they want and report back." He turned back to his men and ordered them through the gate. Some of them complied, but others didn't, and several fights started breaking out among the ranks. Those who started through the gate were met face-to-face by militia members.

Gunny was up front with Mark and shouted, "Gentlemen, do you really want to do this? We will fight to protect our families and our rights."

The pushing and shoving was starting when the radio came on again. "Echo one, Echo one. This is Red Dog. They are crossing the creek and heading your way."

Captain Ellis shouted back at the radioman. "Tell those bunch of idiots to stop them."

The radioman stopped and shook his head. "Sir, you don't understand. There are several hundred of them, and they have taken over the tank and vehicles. They said they are the militia and are here to protect the citizens of Mississippi against any and all aggressors. And, sir, they said this is only half of them. The other half is coming from the East." Just then, a large convoy of Humvees, trucks, and Jeeps flying the American flag rolled up the road, and hundreds of soldiers began to unload. The pushing and shoving stopped as they all turned to see what was going on. What appeared to be an officer climbed out of his Humvee. He had on a uniform with silver clusters on his collar and was being followed by one of his majors and several of his captains and lieutenants. It was Colonel Henry.

The captain and all the others seemed confused. They didn't expect the colonel to show up, and they started to come to attention and salute. But he stopped them. "No need for that, gentlemen. I'm not in your army anymore. I'm with these gentlemen," he said as he pointed to the militia. "The general told me what was going on down here, but he said he couldn't stop it, that it was what the big brass wanted. I didn't like it, so I resigned my commission, and came down here to the farm and ran into these guys, so I joined up with them. So can we come to an understanding, or do we need to help these folks clear you off their land?"

Mark smiled and almost cried at the same time. Several of the militia members on the farm saluted and cheered. Captain Ellis was more surprised than ever. "Sir, I didn't mean to...I didn't know you would..."

Colonel Henry cut him off. "I know you didn't. That is your problem. You think everything has to be done by the book. But, son, sometimes the book is wrong and needs to be rewritten. Now, are you going to leave peacefully or not?"

Captain Ellis started to argue about following orders and getting the job done and so on, but before he could get it all out, several of his men fell out of line and stood with the colonel and the militia. After a few minutes, over half his men went over to the other side. That left Captain Ellis and a couple of lieutenants and about seventy or so of his men on his side, surrounded by several hundred militia and some of his own men who just defected. Just then, the Batesville Militia walked in from the west, led by Sheriff Taylor, Mark didn't know how they were able to pull it off, but after Sheriff Taylor met with Captain Ellis the other day, he rounded up the townspeople who were more than willing to join the militia to fight for their town and their sheriff and their county. They contacted the surrounding county militias, who joined with them to come help Mark and the others at the farm. They knew it would be a turning point for Mississippi if they let the farm and their militia fall.

Colonel Henry found out what was going on from General Franks, who didn't like it either, but he was afraid to go against the top brass, so he resigned, as well. When the colonel showed up, he agreed to lead them. They all came to help those at the farm. There had already been many deserters across the Mid-South, many of whom came along with the colonel. Those whose sentiments fell with Mark and the others at the farm and the militia felt what they were ordered to do went against the Constitution. And they were not willing to fight family and friends over the issue of taking from them to feed the Takers. After defecting, they worried about being arrested or court-martialed, so many of the soldiers followed their previous leaders into the militia, where they felt safe and protected.

Many who stayed with the army did so out of a philosophical belief that what they were doing was right. They sided with the president and believed in the cause and went along with carrying out the executive orders. The country was slowly dividing down the middle—those who followed the Constitution and believed in individual liberty and personal responsibility, versus those who believed in collectivism and the redistribution of the wealth of the country. The soldiers had to decide whether to stay with the captain and follow the orders handed down by the president, or defect and go at it alone, or join with the militia, where there was safety in numbers with like-minded people who wanted to change America back to how it used to be. Not an America with the segregation that was part of the past. Americans were all past that. Not an America with discrimination against minorities or women. America was past that, as well. But back to a country where a man's worth was determined by his character and his work ethic, where a man's word was his bond. Where people worked for a living, instead of trying to work the system. Where families lived and worked together on farms and in communities, instead of crowding into huge metropolises where every need was trucked in, piped in, and plugged in, and people were tuned in, turned on, online, and lined up for all their needs but did not speak to each other on the street or know their own neighbors or families.

That was the decision the soldiers faced. Just like in many other places across the country, it was coming down to choosing one of the two sides. Half went one way, half went the other. Families were divided, friends were divided, towns were divided—the entire country was divided. Only this time, it wasn't the North versus the South. This time every state, every town, and every city was divided, just as Mark and Grandpa predicted. The people were not divided on the issue of slavery or states' rights. They were divided on the issue of individual liberty versus the role and reach of the federal government against its own people. The government had become too big, too intrusive, and too self-destructive for the preservation of the Union as it was. It had collapsed under its own weight and was trying to keep growing by eating its own.

The differences between the two groups had grown so contentious in the political arena that a civil public discourse could no longer settle the issues that divided them. Captain Ellis was still willing to fight, but he had to choose sides, along with his remaining men. Colonel Henry gave them one last chance. If they chose the side of the militia, they would be welcomed in without prejudice and the past would be forgotten. But if they chose the other side, they would be allowed to leave unharmed but without their weapons, and no future passes would be given if they crossed paths again. Mark acknowledged that Captain Ellis may have been right about one thing: The time for talk had ended, and the time for men to fight was upon the nation.

The colonel looked over the men and spoke. "I resigned from the one thing I loved in life, other than my wife, because there are bigger things in life than my commission. The oath I took was not to carry out the orders of the president, but to uphold the Constitution against all enemies, both foreign and domestic. And I knew if those two were in conflict, I had to decide which was most important to uphold, the orders of a politician or the Constitution of the United States, on which the country was founded and flourished. The oath I swore was to God, not the president."

The militia, officers, and soldiers who sided with the colonel cheered. Captain Ellis and the other soldiers who sided with him gritted their teeth in defiance. They had chosen which side they were on. They were the half who believed that the politicians and the government had the answers to the problems in America. They believed in the redistribution of wealth, instead of hard work; multiculturalism, instead of individualism; a secular society, instead of a God-fearing society; freedom from religion, instead of freedom of religion; entitlements, instead of personal responsibility; and a nanny state, instead of family.

Colonel Henry ordered Captain Ellis and his men to drop their weapons and to leave on foot back to town. He also suggested that they leave the county in the next day or two, or they would be escorted out by the militia. He told everyone that the presidential executive orders would no longer be followed in their county or in northeast Mississippi. The militia was in charge now. They would defend their right to bear arms, uphold the Constitution, and defend the rights of the citizens against an oppressive, out-of-control government.

When the dust settled from the encounter, Colonel Henry had the militia members from the surrounding counties gather up some of the newly acquired weapons and ammo for their trouble. While they were busy with that, Mark sent a runner to the Thompsons' house to escort the women back to the main house and to let them know that it was over for the time being. Then the other militia leaders, along with Colonel Henry, Gunny, Grandpa, Sheriff Taylor, Mr. Dickerson, and Paul, helped and escorted Mark up the drive, congratulating him for beating Captain Ellis in the fight and diverting a potential battle.

While they were still talking at the top of the hill behind the house, the roaring and clacking of a tank and other Humvees came rolling over the back pasture hill and stopped just short of the barn. One of the snipers opened the hatch and shouted at the group, "Did we miss something?" He laughed, closed the hatch, and took the tank for victory lap around the front pasture while the rest cheered him on.

Mark, Grandpa, and all the others had a good laugh for a few minutes. All the militia leaders agreed to meet at the farm in the next few days to make further plans with the colonel and the men of the roundtable. The militia members from the surrounding counties gathered up their troops and newly acquired weapons and headed home. After they left, Colonel Henry and Gunny had the troops clean up the mess and begin making camp for the night. Then they all went into the kitchen to discuss plans for the coming days and weeks.

When the colonel entered the kitchen, Mrs. Henry ran to him and gave him a big hug and kiss. "I can't believe you're here," she said.

"You knew I couldn't stay away very long, dear," Colonel Henry said, as he gave her another big hug.

Mark entered the kitchen right behind the others. Lisa was waiting on him and ran to him and gave him a hug. She cried tears of joy. Mark hugged and kissed her back and said, "I was so afraid I wouldn't...I love you more than life itself."

Just then, Grandma Brown came through the door from the living room holding the hand of a little girl. "Look who I have here."

Mark recognized Tammy instantly. She screamed "Dr. Edwards" and ran to him. He grabbed her and lifted her in his arms, and they both hugged and kissed each other. "They told me the nice colonel said I could come live with you and Mrs. Lisa, if it was is okay with you."

Mark smiled at Lisa, who came over and gave both of them a big hug. Holding back tears, she said, "Of course you can. We would love to have a little girl around here."

Mark looked at Lisa as tears rolled down his face. "I guess we finally got our little girl."

Grandpa had left the room during the last of the commotion. He came back with several of his best bottles of whiskey and wine and started pouring everyone a drink. "I think this day ended well and we all deserve a drink, or two, or three," he said, laughing as everyone joined in.

Similar scenes occurred elsewhere around the country. The battles had begun and the war was far from over, but one thing was for certain: Neither side would give up without a fight. Some confrontations would end peacefully, but some would end with death and destruction. Washington and the politicians in power had many of the top brass and the firepower on their side, but the generals in the field were defecting quickly, and as was predicted at the kitchen table, where the generals go, so go the troops. As for Mark and his family, the militia, and those on the farm— none of them knew how all of it would end, but they did know that some day it would, and until then they had the resources and the know-how to survive, however long it took.

28715627R00252

Made in the USA
Lexington, KY
31 December 2013